THE SHRIEKING SHADOWS OF PENPORTH ISLAND

BY SERITA STEVENS

ZEBRA BOOKS
KENSINGTON PUBLISHING CORP.

ZEBRA BOOKS

are published by

KENSINGTON PUBLISHING CORP.
475 Park Avenue South
New York, N.Y. 10016

First printing: March, 1984

Printed in the United States of America

To Dr. Joyce Varney, Antioch University, London —
for her faith in me and dedication to writing.

Chapter One

It was definitely not ladylike — I knew that — and I could feel my straw bonnet push back on my head as the blue ribbons trailed down my neck, sticking to me in the heat. Nevertheless, I pressed my nose against the glass window of the first class coach. My heart was in my throat. Where was Tamara? Surely, the girl would not disappoint me — not at this late date; not after all the plans we had made.

Glancing down for a moment, I noticed a stain in my best pearl-grey foulard traveling gown.

"Blast!" I cursed, seeing that I was alone in the carriage. A slight ironic smile came to my lips then. It was just as well that Thomas was not here to hear me. He highly disapproved of my unlady-like utterances, but then, when did that matter? Thomas and I had already fallen out over this scheme of mine to take Tamara's place. Obviously, he did not understand what my sister, Jennifer, had meant to me—but how could he? He was only a man.

The noise of the engine made me start. Tamara still had to hand over the documents from her aunt and our schoolmistress; the documents that would introduce me to Lord Julian Hawley of Penporth Island as his new bride to be, Tamara Nilston. The fact that I was not Tamara did not matter, as long as he believed I was. I was thankful that I had given Tamara my own miniature to send; otherwise, it would have been disastrous.

I could still not fathom why his lordship had not sent Tamara a miniture of himself—or indeed, why nothing had come during the few letters that had courted Jenny. That is, if a singular offer to pay our mother's medical expenses could be called courting!

The idea of traveling so far from Edinburgh to the Scilly Isles off Cornwall seemed ghastly, especially when I realized that the trip would be of such a short duration—only the three weeks while banns were being read. But I was determined beyond all objections from Thomas or anyone else to find the whereabouts of my older sister. And my friend, Tamara Nilston, the bride newly chosen for this ogre by our former schoolmistress, was more than willing to go along with the part. So why not?

My heart pounded as I pressed my lips tighter together. I scanned King's Cross, the London station for trains to Penzance and the east. It was far bigger than our own Waverly and to think it was only one of many! Surely, Tamara hadn't gotten lost, or worse yet gone to Euston. No, she could not have. She knew which station we were to depart from.

I coughed as a nearby train belched black smoke about me. It seemed I could scarcely breathe for the smothering atmosphere but I had to see Tamara the moment she came into the station. I knew she would not disappoint me. It wasn't in her nature.

Still, my body trembled with anxiety as the time ticked slowly past on the huge clock in the center of the hall. I closed my eyes for a moment, vividly recalling the scene between Jennifer and my father on the day when our former schoolmistress, Miss Farrington, had come forth with the offer from this strange Lord Penporth. It seemed that he was desperate for a wife. Why?

Miss Farrington did not say. I doubted if the woman even knew, or bothered to ask. She was all flustered with the idea of providing a wife for a peer of the realm — even one so far off as Penporth Island. Knowing our financial straights, she had come to Papa with the honor of having his eldest daughter, and her favorite pupil, wed the lord. Of course, there would be a handsome settlement which would more than take care of Papa, myself, and our mother's bills — as yet unpaid.

How tearful that parting between us had been. Jenny had vowed on her honor to write every day. Only then did I agree she must accept and go.

9

There was, after all, no hope for it. Beautiful as she was, no one in town would offer for either of us — knowing that all monies would go to my father's pockets; knowing of the illness of our mother.

Jenny had been true to her word. At first, she had written constantly. The husband she described was a fearful ogre given to bearish temperaments. A hideous scar down his left cheek made him nearly unapproachable. It was obvious from her letters that she much preferred the cousin — a "puckish" fellow who amused her to no end. Often, she escaped from the pressures of her husband's demands by sitting at a pleasant pond. The island of Penporth, just to the north of St. Mary's and Tresco, had in fact been described in delightful detail. I couldn't help but wonder more about his lordship; I missed the confidences the two of us had shared. But my sister said little of Lord Julian.

It was only after Papa had contracted consumption, the same thing which had carried away our mother, and I became engrossed in the nursing of him, that I became aware that the letters had halted.

Frantically, I wrote not once but several times — begging for some response, searching the post daily. All to no avail. It was almost as if Jenny had died, but I couldn't and wouldn't accept that. We would surely have been notified by his lordship if something had happened to her, if something was wrong.

Looking back now on the letters, I feared that

she was dead. Her notes had hinted of her husband's dreadful temper. Had he perhaps murdered Jennifer in some jealous fit? I shuddered, feeling the fear run through me like a cold hand gripping my heart. I knew that even in the guise of Tamara Nilston, I was endangering myself by going to the island. If Lord Penporth had done in my sister, I could be facing my own death. Even so, this was something I needed to do.

I had to admit, I had been shocked to find out from the schoolmistress that Lord Penporth had accused my sister of running off, and that having filed for an annulment, he was now even more anxious to find a "suitable" wife. Once more, he was procuring the services of his aunt's friend to find him a passive and obedient wife—one trained in the bridal arts.

Just thinking of his accusations made me tremble with rage. I knew my sister would not run off. It just wasn't her nature. The taste was bitter in my mouth. It was just as well that Jen had been sent in the first place. His lordship would have had his hands full had I been the one to go. In Miss Farrington's words, he would have found me "quarrelsome, unbecoming, and far from having the proper respect that a wife must have for the master in her life." Ruefully, I smiled. How had I developed so differently from my sister? I did not know; I only knew that I could not stand the idea of having a man control the destiny that God had given me.

Closing my eyes again, I was thankful that the passive Tamara Nilston had given her heart to another, and had rebelled against her aunt's arrangement with the schoolmistress. I was thankful that Tamara had come to me to ask for help.

It was the leaf-brown straw bonnet with violet ribbons and pink roses that caught my eye. I saw the white muslin flounced skirt with the trellis of violet ribbons and stood abruptly in my carriage, nearly crushing my bonnet. It was not the proper thing to wear to a train station—even with the leaf-brown foulard overskirt, but then I was taking the journey, not Tamara.

As she neared within calling distance, I screamed out, "Tamara!" Unladylike, I leaned out through the open window, nearly losing my balance. She still didn't see me so I waved with my linen handkerchief to attract her attention.

"Tamara!" I called again, more frantic. "Over here!"

This time she saw me. Lifting her skirts, she broke into a dainty run leaving behind the young apprentice that she had only just wed.

Opening the carriage door, I stepped down.

In that brief moment, I became conscious of eyes upon me. I turned to notice a blond gentleman—impeccably dressed in gray striped trousers, a stark navy morning coat, and a top hat of gray silk. My heart hammered from the way he stared at me. He was handsome as . . . Apollo.

As he continued to stare at me, I felt my heart pounding furiously. My face flushed and goose pimples formed beneath my half flowing sleeves. Swallowing hard, I shivered as he continued to stare at me—quite unaccountably as he was assessing me for . . . for what I did not know. He seemed to be absorbing my every feature as if to memorize it. Whoever he was, despite his dress, he was no gentleman.

The worried thought came to my mind. Maybe he knew Lord Penporth. I prayed that, if he did, he would not be coming to the island during the three weeks I planned to be there. There would be problems enough for me in adopting the alias without worrying about meeting any of his lordship's friends.

The man turned aside then. A sigh of relief escaped me. I was worrying too much. My heart beat was still erratic but since he had now stopped paying attention to me, I could only assume that it was my unladylike shouting which had drawn his notice. Maybe he was wondering what type of lady I was just as I was wondering what type of gentleman he was.

I recalled then that Jennifer had stated the island had but few visitors. Chances were I would not see this man again.

Tamara reached me and we embraced just as the whistle screamed, nearly breaking my ear drums. The steam drastically increased, causing both of us to fall into a fit of coughing.

"You saved my life—utterly!" Tamara declared. "I am so in love with Peter, I. . ."

"Never mind that," I yelled against the noise of the train, "just give me your address where I might find you when I return three weeks from now."

"Oh, yes. Yes, of course," Tamara quickly produced a long envelope. Hastily, I took it and stepped back onto the train as the whistle broke the air again and the train jerked forward, starting me slowly on my journey to hell. Against the commotion, Tamara shouted, "Peter has already been making inquiries. We shall find a position for you before you return. A governess, perhaps. In any case, you will have a home with us."

The noise was too great. I could only nod. I did not want to think of my return to London, but I knew that even with Lord Penporth paying for the forward journey, all my funds would be consumed by the remainder of the trip. With Papa gone I had no choice but to look for work since, as Miss Farrington stated, "few men want a woman as argumentative and unstable as you."

There was barely time for me to put the papers in my reticule before the train lurched forward and began to move under me. Clutching at the side bar, I coughed violently as the steam swirled about me. Fear began to clutch at my heart as I watched Tamara growing smaller and smaller.

Once more, I glimpsed the fellow staring in my direction. Quickly, I closed the window to the car. I could no longer see Tamara, but I could no longer see him either. Pulling down the curtain, I sank into the cushioned seat. My heart was hammering with the rhythm of the train. There was no way out now.

I touched the documents and felt a shudder go through me. Well, what would be, would be. I was on my way to Penzance and within three weeks' time, I would, if the gods favored me, see the murderer hanged and my sister's name cleared.

If only I knew something more about Lord Penporth, but I was at a loss here since Jennifer had given me few descriptions. All facts pointed to him as her murderer for, surely, as her sister and only survivor, would I not be entitled to some word if something had actually happened to Jenny. The least should be the unpaid monies promised us by Lord Penporth after their first anniversary.

My head ached. I leaned against the faded cushion. I would have to think about things later.

Despite my excellent intentions and well thought-out preparations, the closer I came to the Scillies, the faster my heart began to beat, the more my throat began to hurt and my head to pound. Several times I read and reread my sister's letters, but try as I could, I gained no further clues other than what I already knew.

It was shortly after five when the monster train pulled into the Penzance station. With a few rushed words to the porter who grabbed my cases, I picked up my pearl-grey skirts, cursing as I nearly caught one of my lace flounces on the door. Taking along my hooded grey-blue cashmere mantle — a gift from his lordship for his new bride — I ran toward a waiting cab.

"I must get to the quay and quickly," I cried, pressing money into the man's hands as I jumped into the carriage.

"If it's to the Isles 'ee be goin', Miss, I b'lave 'ee be just a bit late." The driver waited impassively, reins still relaxed in his hands.

"That can't be."

The man just shrugged and glanced at me.

"Well, is there another way to get to Penporth Island?" I asked frantically, glancing about and seeing the porter coming with my luggage.

"None today, Miss. I b'lave they'll be none till Friday next. Sunday bein' the Lord's day and Monday . . . well t'morrow be the first day as ye kin hire one."

I pressed my lips together in frustration. I could feel my heart pounding in agitation. More so than ever I was beginning to doubt my wisdom in coming here. Had I known the ferry schedule, I would not have waited so long in London with Tamara.

I took a deep breath and tried to steady my nerves as I gazed toward the sea and the distant horizon where the islands lay, where my next three weeks would be spent. The hot afternoon sun was alleviated by a refreshing breeze from the Atlantic. It took the edge off the stifling feeling I had had during the train ride, but it did nothing for my anxiety. Why had Tamara not told me that she "the bride" had been expected earlier in the week?

The bile rose in my throat. I knew why. Tamara had wanted time to prepare for her new life. She had wanted to stay in Edinburgh since those were the last new clothes she would be able to afford for some time to come. Nevertheless, it had left me in a rather awkward situation now. Not all the haste this morning could have amended things and I did not like starting on the wrong foot. It boded ill for my plans. From all I knew of Lord Penporth, he might even have a temper at my tardy arrival and send me back the same day! Then I would have come all this way for naught and would have no opportunity to search for information about my sister.

Then I reasoned again. Whatever his reasons, Lord Penporth seemed desperate to have a wife — one that he did not have to take the trouble in choosing himself. Why else had he used Miss Farrington's services?

"Ma'am?" The porter drew my attention again to the problem of the immediate situation.

I glanced at the trunks all stamped with the feminine flourish — T. N. — and decided I might as well follow the recommendation in the letter which Penporth had directed to Tamara should she arrive early at the port.

"The Dolphin Hotel, is it near?" I asked the driver, blinking and shielding my eyes with the light of the dying sun.

"Near as yer two feet, Ma'am," he snorted. "Just down the road, there." He pointed in the direction of the quay where I had been headed. It was a mint-green building with a huge fish that swung in the breeze. "Could suggest a nicer one. M'sister. . ."

"The Dolphin Hotel will do fine." With the porter's assistance, I stepped up into the cab, my lace flounces trailing behind. As the driver said, it was near and I could have walked. In fact, after the day of sitting on that smoky train, I should have been grateful for the walk, but worry had nearly drained me of energy. Besides, it was not ladylike and Tamara would have ridden, so I supposed that I must, too.

Closing my eyes a moment, I leaned my head against the window and felt the sway of the vehicle as we travelled over the rough stones. My head ached with worry. I had had very little lunch and was feeling dizzy, besides. My mouth was dry and I craved a nice cup of tea to calm my nerves and quench my thirst. I knew the tea would not solve my problems but it might raise my spirits.

The Dolphin Hotel was not as modern nor as nice as Hyde Park, where Lord Penporth had arranged for his bride to stay the night before — but it was close to the sea. Again, I cursed silently with the irritation of having missed the ferry. It was impossible for me to wait a week here — I hadn't the funds, and I did not know if my heart could take it. The sooner I appeared at Penporth Island, the sooner I could find out the fate of my sister, and the sooner I could escape.

Exhausted as I was from my sleepless night before, I rang for tea to be brought to my room. I did not think I could stand staying in the general lounge that faced the quay. More especially, I could not stand the curious eyes upon me. I felt that everyone knew who I was and knew my real purposes here.

The hotel maid unpacked my night dress. With a critical eye, I gave her the mauve silk with the pink ribbons to have pressed. I would wear that, when I had passage. After all, I thought with a rueful smile, I wanted to look my best for the first meeting with my "affianced husband."

Changing to my lounging gown, I relaxed in the chair that faced the water and sipped the refreshing tea.

A sigh came forth from my lips as I closed my lids and tried to blank out the worry from my mind. I concentrated on the situation now before me. I suppose I should send a telegram to his lordship.

Proper form or not, the idea of any contact with the man before it was absolutely necessary weighed heavy on my mind. Lifting my legs off the stool, I drained what was left my liquid courage and slipped into a subtle brown dress — suitable for the moment.

Cooling my face with water from the basin, I took up my reticule and went down the old wooden steps to the front desk.

"Pardon, I . . ."

"If it be a telegram ye want t'send, Miss," the clerk pointed a long boney finger across the way to the small store near the pier.

My surprise must have shown. "How did you. . ."

The man gave me a slight smile. "Well, yer rooms were all reserved by his lordship, Miss. Tis to be assumed that ye'd be wantin' to let him know of yer late arrival."

"Why, uh, yes . . . I . . ." I turned toward the pier again. "Thank you."

The office for the telegrams was no more than a cubby hole and the grizzled old man did not

19

seem very friendly, but I wrote out my message as my heart pounded.

He grunted as I handed him the paper. "Don't ya want t'sign?"

"Oh. Oh, yes." I took the message back and began to sign my name with a flourish. Only as I was about to return it to him did I realize my nearly horrendous mistake. I had signed my own name! Cringing as my stomach churned, I took the paper back and hastily rewrote the message using Tamara's name, as was proper. My heart was in my throat as I handed the old man my missive.

He glanced it over and relief flooded me as I heard the clicking of his machine. I had nearly made a fatal mistake. I knew that from now on I had to think of myself as Tamara Nilston. Perhaps now, feeling the fear pounding through my blood, it was just as well that I had missed the ferry. Now I would have more time to prepare for the coming ordeal.

Leaving the small office, I decided, ladylike or not, I needed to walk. The hotel was only a few steps from the sea but the quay itself was noisy and dirty. A few boats dotted the landscape and bobbed up and down on the incoming tide. I scanned the water as I tried to see the ferry ship, but it was too far away.

Startled, I jumped slightly as a grey spotted gull swooped down low, spying refuse from a ship entering the harbor. Others, attracted by the cries of the first, appeared magically in the sky; all wanted the food. Their little eyes gleamed bright as they competed with each other. I watched for a moment, then turned away. Up the hill I walked, propelling my feet towards the High Street. Only a few shops were open but nevertheless, the browsing did take my mind momentarily from my problems.

Looking up, I was startled to see the name of the street. It was one that Jenny had walked on the day she had spent in town here. Was that an omen for me? I shuddered. Did that mean I would follow her same route. I prayed not.

Again, I thought of Lord Penporth. What manner of man was he to be so desperate for a wife and then to do away with her? Was he truly as mad as Emperor Nero and as brooding as Hamlet? That was how Jennifer had described him.

The queasiness rose in my stomach. If only I could gather my facts and present them to the magistrate without directly confronting the man—but in my heart, I knew that that was not possible.

I leaned against a wall to catch my breath as once more I recalled my sister's description of the man's violent temper. The goosebumps ran up my arms. I would not think of the danger to myself; I would think only of what I owed to my darling Jenny.

Walking up the hill, I felt the pull of my muscles—stiff and aching from the train ride. Even that pain could not take my mind off coming weeks. If only my mission would be fruitful. The lump stuck in my throat. Nothing could possibly bring my sister back to me. If only I had come sooner, if only Papa's illness had not distracted me so I might have realized sooner that the silence had been too long. However, then I would not have had the guise of coming to Penporth as a bride.

I stopped atop the street and glanced about me, trying to find my direction. No, I wasn't lost as I feared. The sea was just below and I could see that by following the snaking streets of Penzance, I would soon be back at the quay and thence the hotel.

For several moments I stood there, watching the sea foam and crest, wondering if I truly had the courage to press on.

Finally, I followed the street down to the boats.

It was not until I had made several inquiries that I found I would be able to pay for passage the following morning. It was only a fishing boat and headed for St. Mary's, but from there I knew it would only be another few miles to Penporth. I would have no trouble hiring another boat from there. Besides, I could not stay the week waiting for the ferry. I was determined to get this over with as soon as possible.

After haggling with man over the price, I agreed to be at the quay with my bags at nine the following morning.

Tomorrow, I realized, would be a real test for my "Scottish fibre."

Chapter Two

Tossing and turning, I heard the clicking of the minutes as they passed on the gold watch that Papa had once used. Sleep continued to elude me, yet I knew that were I to keep my mind clear for the morrow, I did have to sleep.

Despite my reluctance, I took some laudanum drops. They had been a farewell present from my schoolmistress who had thought that someone with my "high-strung temperament" might need when going into employment. I assume she hoped that the liquid would calm me down some. For this night, I hoped she was right.

I think the drops made things worse than ever. I had taken enough to numb my brain so that I wanted to sleep desperately but not enough to put me to rest. Dawn was breaking when I finally managed to doze but, even then, the nightmares came.

Several hours later, with a nasty taste in my mouth, and the sun streaming in on me, I woke with a start.

Hurriedly, I dressed, nearly tearing the seam of the mauve silk. I wanted to look demure, to look as a passive bride might, but as I coiled the curls at the nape of my neck, and fastened my straw bonnet with the pink ribbons, I frowned. I appeared to be more a governess seeking employment than a demure little bride. And neither expressed my true feelings. Well, it couldn't be helped. I would have to get to the boat.

It was difficult to keep my ladylike pose and still hurry down the steps of the hotel toward the quay, knowing that, behind me, the porter was following with my trunks.

I reached the wharf, my heart hammered and I felt the dryness of my mouth. There was no boat! The "Artie," which yesterday had promised to take me, was nowhere in sight.

"Blast!" I cried, cursing aloud, forgetting who and where I was. At that moment, I did not even care as I stamped my foot on the loose board of the wharf and felt the vibrations echo through me.

Tears came to my eyes. I felt my hastily done up curls tumbling down my back. My head pounded as the blood rushed through it at a nervous rate and my stomach tightened with pain. I could not believe that so much had gone wrong so soon. It was an omen, I was sure. If only I could get back to London, but no . . . I bit my lower lip, I could not. My own sense of fairness would not let me.

Putting my hand to my eyes, shielding them, I stared out, trying to see if the boat was about.

Water stretched like an endless sheet in front of me, sparkling in the sun. Somehow, I had to get to the island today.

" 'ee be looking fer Artis Polan? 'ee be right sorry, Miss, be 'ee couldna of waited. Twas the tide, 'ee see."

I glanced down and to my left where the speaker stood, bobbing in a small boat half the size of the "Artie." Fish, silvery dark with gaping mouths and wide eyes, lay everywhere about the boat, as well as in the man's large apron pockets. The stink was enough to make my stomach turn again.

"What . . . what time will he be returning?" I felt the words close in my throat.

"Can't rightly say, Miss. Artie's be one as to have vantage of the tide n' things."

"Yes," I said, feeling the bitterness well up. "I'm sure of that. The fact remains that I still have to get to Penporth."

"That so?" The man regarded me with a silent curiosity that gave me the shivers. "Why you be going there?"

I shrugged. It really was none of his business.

"If it be a holiday ye be wantin', Mary's far nicer."

My heart hammered in my chest. This was no holiday. I wet my lips. My mouth was still dry from the laundanum last night. Suddenly, I wondered if this man knew anything of my sister, if I dared ask . . . but no, I couldn't, not without revealing who I was. My voice faltered a moment. "Lord . . . Lord Penporth expects me. You see, I missed the ferry yesterday and . . ."

His eyes were like two slits of blue ice. "So. Ye be the one. We heard as 'ee were comin' but we didna expect 'ee."

My mouth was drier than before. I wanted to swallow but dared not. My pulses quickened as I spoke in an effort at being calm. "Oh? Why not?"

I tried to shield my eyes from the glare of the sun and focus directly on the speaker.

He shrugged in a closed Cornish fashion, meant to keep outsiders away. Before I could ask him again, he stated, "I be going to Mary 'bout twoish."

"Two? But that means I won't reach Hawley House until after five."

Again, he shrugged, staring at me, watching me as he evaluated me. "Can't be helped. I be waiting fer supplies n' the tide."

There seemed to be no other boats about which could take me and unless the Artie returned before . . . I sighed, and nodded. "Two, then."

Turning to go, I spun about once more, nearly catching my dress on a wooden piling. "How much will you charge me? I can not afford to pay a lot. I . . . paid your friend in advance and I . . ." The flush rose in my face. It was dreadfully embarrassing to be short of funds.

The man snorted. "Don't ye worry none of yer money. Artie'll return it. As t'me," he spat and then pointed a finger inward, scooping up another fish to rip apart. "I don't expect anything. When the Gov'nor be in a good mood, he be a right fine man t'deal with. I be pleased t'help 'is new woman. I be a Mary man, meself."

"The Governor?"

"Lor' Penporth." He stared at me as if to indicate that I was stupid for not knowing this simple fact. Shivering, I wondered what his lordship was like in a bad mood, but I already sensed that the man had told me all that he would tell. Penporth was obviously of island stock and Lord or not, these people protected their own. The Scots were the same way.

The thought occurred to me that if everyone on the island were distrustful of newcomers, my mission would be far more difficult than I first thought. Would I even be able to learn anything of my sister's disappearance? Was it worth the heartache and danger that I was going through to be there?

I focused my thoughts on the boatman again. "I will see you at two, then. You'll find me at the Dolphin, if you're ready earlier."

He nodded, slowly tipping his broken beamed hat.

Raising my skirts carefully, side-stepping the masses of dead fish on the pier, feeling their eyes accusing me of some unnamed crime, I hurried away. The awful smell of the dead fish continued to pervade the air. I felt sure that eyes, other than the fish's, and the boatman's, were upon me — but no one else was near. It was almost as if I was some freak in a circus show. Was it merely because people knew I was to marry Lord Penporth or did they know something of Jennifer?

Nervously, I brushed the loose curls from the nape of my neck. I longed to ask some of the people about the first wife, but fear kept me silent. Too many questions on my part would undoubtedly lead to questions on theirs. Perhaps later, after I had settled at the house, I would return via the ferry and talk to some of them here. Perhaps by then, they would come to trust me.

The rest of the morning I spent walking about the town. There was little that I needed to add to my luggage since I would be on the island only for a few weeks. However, I did purchase some headache powders at the chemist.

Toward noon, I paused by the pier again, wanting to check on my transportation.

I was astonished to see the "Artie" being towed in by another. Low in the water, she seemed nearly ready to sink. It was obvious even to me that something was wrong.

As I stepped into the shadows of the shop nearby, I was glad that I was out of sight.

"Matter, Artie," my new boatman called out, as he continued to pull the fish apart.

"A hole. A damn blasted 'ole! Nearly sunk me. Right in the side of the water line. If it hadn't been for Jimmy nearby . . ."

"Now, Artie, I know ya check yer stuff. What happened?"

Artie Polan glared at his friend. "I checked it last night. They ought t'know not to tangle with

Artie Polan. That hole weren't there last night. Someone did that. Someone monkeyed with me boat." He snorted angrily and accepted the rope as he pulled the low boat into the pier.

From my place in the shadows, I shivered. I could no longer hear the men talking now but I had heard enough to cause fear to run through my veins. To think: if I had not overslept, I would have been on that boat. With my added weight, with my trunks — well, I did not want to think what might have happened.

There was a gripping in my stomach as I mumbled a silent prayer for having been allowed to miss those final moments. It was only when I finally went back to the hotel and forced myself to drink a soothing cup of tea, that I realized that I had made no secret of who I was (or rather who I was supposed to be). Would someone have tried to kill Tamara before her wedding?

I was confused. I knew that Tamara stood to gain a modest sum on her twenty-first year, and that all of it would go to her husband but, with his known wealth, I did not think that would be a reason for his lordship to wish the new bride dead. Besides, she wasn't even his bride yet — not for another three weeks.

Had he perhaps had spies on us? Did he know of Tamara and learn that her heart was already engaged? Did he know who I was and what I planned? My heart fluttered pitifully like a bird trapped in a cage.

I swallowed the dryness in my throat. Should I just return to London? My appetite was gone. I pushed away the uneaten plate of biscuits.

No, I would not be a coward. Papa had named me Victoria for our courageous queen and I was determined. I would do what had to be done.

With trembling hands, I pulled forth some parchment and wrote a letter to Tamara.

Exactly at two p.m., a young boy of thirteen ran up to the hotel. As the only woman sitting in the hotel lounge, I thought myself rather obvious. Putting down the copy of Mr. Dickens' latest novel, which I had not yet been able to concentrate on, I waited for him to approach me.

"Miss Nilston?"

Pausing a moment, I nodded. It was odd having people call me by another name and yet I was expected to respond. I would have to adjust to that. I stood, suddenly feeling a chill run deep through me. I recalled my grandmother talking of people walking over your grave as I shivered once more. Even my deep breaths, constricted as they were by the corset that I put on, seemed shallow and painful.

"Ye be all right, Miss?"

Pressing my lips together tightly, I tried to regain my composure as silently I prayed, "Jenny, help me."

"Miss?"

The boy's concern brought my attention back to the present. At thirteen, he was nearly my height, even with my flowered straw bonnet.

"Yes. Yes," I replied, hearing the hoarseness of my voice, "I'm fine. You're from the boat,

I take it."

"Aye, Mr. Trewyan says t'tell ya t'come. That yer cases?"

I nodded, not trusting myself to speak more than necessary. Even as I walked to the door, I was conscious of the stares I was receiving. Was anyone here responsible for that boat being sunk? If so, they gave no indication.

The boy took my trunks up as easily as if they were cotton sacks. Following him, I marveled at his ability.

At the quay, I paused. I was relieved that the fish had been cleared away from the boat—at least from the front part where I would be standing. Silvery scales still shimmered in the onwood, but seeing me, Mr. Trewyan laid down a canvas cloth. I supposed that being the new Lady Penporth gave me some rights. Nevertheless, I was relieved that my skirts would not touch those tainted boards.

Taking the gnarled hand, I allowed the old man to help me into the boat. The smell still pervaded the air but perhaps, with the sea essence, I would not notice it so much.

My stomach tightened and threatened revolt as the anchor was hoisted and the aging boat, groaning like a dying man, started on its way to my new home. I watched as the wind gently puffed the sail and wheeled us about the little islets that jutted off the Cornish coast. We rode into the spectacular sea which lay between Cornwall and the Scillies.

As the front of the boat rose to meet the blue

sky, the boy at the tiller called out in delight, "Ain't this wonderful?"

I couldn't help but nod and relish the feeling of freedom that the boat and the wind caressing my cheeks gave me.

Passing Land's End, I felt a twinge of regret. It looked so beautiful with the shimmering of the sun haloing it. "I will return soon," I vowed, "Very soon." In any event, I could not possibly stay on Penporth Island past the three weeks of the banns.

Wrapping the cashmere mantle tighter about me, I felt the wind continually tugging its playful fingers at my hair; it pulled first one strand free and then another. Finally, I succumbed to temptation and removed my straw hat. True, it was unladylike, but there was only the boy and the sailor to see me.

Without my bonnet on, without the fear that it would blow off, I felt more freedom to move forward and, smelling the salty freedom of the open waters before me, feeling the sun warm on my face, I knew that I was doing the right thing. Whatever would come of this, it was far better than being a companion to someone.

With a twinge, I thought of my school mistress. She would no doubt have scolded me for not having my parasol out, for exposing my fair skin to so much sun in the first place. However, I knew that my moment of joy would be short-lived and I intended to make the most of these few moments of freedom.

The boat quivered at a high peak, like a pawing

horse, and then fell forward into the sea valley, the stern rearing high. The boy shouted wildly with excitement. I had to admit that I had never experienced such a thrilling ride. In the face of that, my complexion seemed of little importance.

The roughness was beginning to make me suspect that a storm was coming, but there wasn't even a tail of one in sight. The sky was dazzlingly bright with a splendid afternoon sun and a great static heaven. No, the only storm that raged was the one within me.

As the bow dipped forward to greet the Atlantic swells that were coming toward us, I could swear that to the far Northwest I could see part of the island, but it was too early to tell.

The progressive rolling of the sea beneath the boat now produced a rolling of my stomach. I strained for a further look at the distant rocks, wondering just how much more there was of this bumpy sea, and glad that I had not eaten much this day.

There were no other boats about and it seemed as if we three were the last in the world, alone on the vast Atlantic.

Even as the thought came, a bank of fog engulfed us. Shivering, I was beginning to wonder if we would ever reach the island, if maybe nature was also against me.

"Don't ya worry, Ma'am," Mr. Trewyan called out, sensing my anxiety, "we get these here often."

I made no reply, but his words soothed me a bit.

It was only moments later that we broke through the mist and I became keenly aware of the rocks just ahead. Though one could scarcely call those humps, Eastern Islands, islands. Nevertheless, they were land and I was thankful to see them.

Even as I strained close to the boat edge, I heard Mr. Trewyan comment, "Ye'll make a good island wife, Ma'am. Sea's in yer blood. I kin tell."

I turned to him, unsure of how I should respond. Forcing a slight smile, I took his compliment. Maybe I would make a good island wife — but not at this time.

The land became grey-green as the boat approached. The sea, too, seemed bluer. Gulls gyrated about our heads now, waiting for the garbage to be thrown. As it was, they swooped low, attacking the food. Their shrieks unnerved me but I supposed I would have to get used to them — at least for the duration of my stay on the island.

St. Mary's mooring, just ahead, seemed a magical haven. I wished I could stay there and not go on as I took in the sun's slanted rays shining on the wet and slippery jetty.

Surprised that he was not stopping, I turned toward the seaman. It seemed that he planned to take me directly to Penporth. That was too bad. I had wished a moment on St. Mary's to explore, refresh and compose myself, but I supposed the sooner I got this ordeal over with, the better it would be.

As we neared Penporth, I hastily tried to repin

the coils of my dark hair which had escaped. It was not an easy task to reattach the straw bonnet in the winds but when I finally did, I could see the pink ribbons fluttering behind me like shadows.

We passed the lighthouse, skirting about several fledging islands, before going into Crow's Sound. Papa's gold watch told me that it was half past five now. My stomach and throat were once more tight and tense. This was not an ordinary meeting of a husband and his bride to be. Would he believe that I was Tamara Nilston? Each movement of the waves seemed to jar my stomach more.

The eastern parts of the island seemed to continue their greenness to the water's edge but I could see, at least from St. Mary's, that the fact was not true for the western side. Not all the islands were treeless. Tresco, to the left of us, had a lush multitude of trees.

" 'Tis a pretty garden there, Miss," the boy told me. "I 'elped Gov'nor Smith with the plantin' meself."

"Does he own his island like Lord Penporth?"

"Oh, Miss, 'gustus Smith be dead. 'Twas when I were about ten. 'Is nephew owns it now. They be owners of the whole islands . . . except of course," he shrugged toward Penporth. "Strange that Gov'nor Smith shoulda given 'em the island like that."

Hope surged through me. It was obvious the boy had stories to tell. I didn't want to hear about the island's ownerships. I wanted to hear about my sister.

Clearing my throat, I prayed I did not betray my feelings. "What do you know of Lord Penporth's first wife?"

"The first 'un? Why nothin'. He be right good to her — as I reckon she just upped and went away. Leastwise, that's what folks hear."

I took a deep breath, trying to steady myself as the boat continued to bump along. "You sound as if you don't believe it." I knew that I didn't.

"Can't say if I do or don't." The boy was watching me with some study. "Ya know, ya look a bit like 'er."

That caught me by surprise. Few people had ever told us that we looked alike. Most were, in fact, surprised to find out that I was "Sweet Jenny's" sister.

I tried to stay as casual as I could. "Perhaps it's just the way the light is hitting, or the dress. I imagine she dressed like this."

The boy nodded, obviously not totally convinced.

"Of course, I did go to school with her." My heart hammered. If I could not fool this boy, how could I fool her husband who supposedly knew her intimately. I wondered how many others would notice the similarity that he did.

After a pause, the boy smiled. "Guess I was wrong. Ye do 'ave dark hair and green eyes where 'ers were blue and 'er curls were blonde, but there is a sort of tilt to the head that seemed the same."

"Tilt to the head?" I flushed, "Oh, that is probably from our posture classes," I said, trying to explain it, and feeling fear gnaw like a little mouse eating away my stomach. "I swear to you. We are not related."

The boy shrugged. "It don't matter to me if ya are. I was just sayin'." "He pointed up towards the mansion on Tresco and relieved, I turned my attention to the famous abbey.

Islets and rocks edged the sound here like stepping stones to an enchanted kingdom. I wondered if I would have a chance to explore here but, considering my mission and my desire to leave Penporth, as soon as possible, I rather doubted it.

Glancing at the timepiece once more, I saw it was nearly six. We were at the northern end of Tresco now and, as the boat lurched by the wild western side, I had my first glimpse of Hawley Hall.

The breath caught in my throat. This place would be my home for the next few weeks. My pulse seemed the only sound as I stared ahead— seeing the grey Cornish granite building that lorded over the island. It was a three story structure with numerous windows that all seemed to glint maliciously at me. As if in omen, a large gull shrieked and flew low, circling over the house.

Shivering, I felt the earlier dread return to me—tenfold. My instincts told me to return to London and I was probably being foolish not to, but how could I leave Jennifer's fate unknown. Besides, if I fled, then the exchange of places would come out and Tamara's marriage could still be annulled by her aunt. I would not be the cause of my friend's unhappiness, especially when I could bring a murderer to justice.

I would go on as planned. Surely, it would only take me a few days to make the discoveries I needed and then I could be gone.

From the desolation of the island, I fancied that it would be difficult for me to hire a boat from Penporth, especially if I were to leave without permission of the island's lord and master. With that in mind, I turned to Mr. Trewyan.

"Would it be possible for you to come to Penporth on Tuesday next? I've forgotten . . . some items and I wish them from the mainland."

Chewing on his long—stemmed pipe, the sailor hesitated. "There be a boat on Friday, Miss. Y'need only t'tell Mrs. Stewart. She'll see ye done up right."

Mrs. Stewart, I knew from my sister's letters, was the housekeeper, but I needed to convince the man that I wanted him to come for me.

"I am sure she will, only with all the worry over my coming, I am afraid that I might forget to tell her or I might forget to talk to the boatman." I handed him a half crown. Did my explanation sound inane?

Even if this cost me a major portion of the funds I had, I had to be sure that help would be available when I needed it. My hand continued to hold out the coin as he stared at me.

Then, grunting, he pushed my hand away. "Vera well, I'll come, but I can't stay long."

"No. Of course not. You won't need to wait. I quite understand." Hesitatingly, I returned the coin to my pouch.

We were circling the house now. The scenery of the land was becoming more desolate. Loneliness brooked over the island. Where did the people of the town live? Surely, the Hawley family were not the only inhabitants of the island. I glanced over at Mr. Trewyan, then at the water, and the islands behind us. I was tempted to have him take me back to St. Mary's. I dug my nails into my palm and told myself that I had made my choice and I would see it through.

A stiff breeze came up behind us, blowing the boat further toward the island. It was too late to turn back. The words echoed in my mind. IT IS TOO LATE.

A commotion beneath the bow drew my attention away from my own morbid thoughts. The boy pointed out the brown fledgling bird—fat and frightened, trying to get out of the way, flopping over the waves like a stage funnyman falling over his large shoes. I couldn't help but identify with this poor bird. Our fears were the same: his was of being rammed by a huge boat and mine was of a man with a volcanic temper. The difference being that one knew the bird would soon become a grave, graceful white bird like those now curving, dancing in the sky above the boat. My own fate was less certain. Was my imitation of Tamara as awkward as this gannet's?

The landing place was tucked into an elbow of rock, a motherly arm to keep out the worst of the waves. "If the sea bain't right," Mr. Trewyan told me, "it can't be done." I took a deep breath. I knew he was referring to Tuesday. Nodding that I understood, I turned to watch his skill as we maneuvered into the rocks. A white, low and uneven sand greeted us.

Was I not to be met?

I glanced up, seeing the house looming above me, its back toward me. No, I felt no welcome here.

Chapter Three

Quelling my nervousness, I allowed the boy to assist me out and watched as the men placed my trunks on the high rocks. "It will be safe fer a bit. Just 'ave them get it afore the tide comes in."

I nodded. Water was already swirling about my feet, dampening my shoes and making me quite uncomfortable. I held my skirts as the boatman gave me directions to the path that would lead to the house.

Taking out my reticule once more, I saw him shake his head. "I told 'ee. Keep yer money. Ye might be needin' it. Sides, Artie will give me what he had from you."

"You will be here on Tuesday next?"

"Aye. Said I would and I will, if I can."

The spray of the sea leaped up, fully drenching me as the boat pulled away. Cursing, I turned toward the path. How was I ever to meet Lord Pen-porth looking like a wretched urchin?

Frustrated, feeling that this did not bode well for my plans, I began to pick my way up the foot path. It irked me that there was no one to meet me. I had, after all, sent the telegram.

The white sand clung to the hem of my skirt, forcing me to move slower than I wanted. Tears stung my eyes. My dress was utterly ruined, but that was not what was making me cry. Had Jenny experienced the same welcome as I? 'Twas no wonder she hated this place so.

Reaching solid land was not much better. Brambles spread out about the path, like drowning souls, all waiting to grab at me, scratching me, tearing at my dress. I thought about Tamara as I pushed forward. It was just as well that I had come in her place. She would never have survived in a place like this.

The sun going behind the clouds made me glance up. The island had darkened momentarily, giving it a menacing feeling. I wondered if this tiny trail would ever end. Did people really live here? With each passing moment, I was beginning to feel more and more like a prisoner bound by the sea.

I forced myself to continue on and then, like magic, found the trees appearing. With the sand still clinging to my legs, I hurried on. Even as I entered the tunnel of shaded groves, I knew that Jennifer had been here, for she had told me that Lord Penporth's uncle had planted them espe-cially for the island. They were reminders for me that life did indeed exist on the island and that Jennifer had been here.

Turning for a moment, I glanced at the waves below me as they tore apart the rocks with a fury unsurpassed and then came back for more. The white froth spread over the humps and ridges of the rocks only to die away like strips of white muslin being unravelled out in the heavy blue farther away.

I took a deep breath and felt my heart pounding in my chest. Lifting my shoulders, throwing them back as our schoolmistress had taught us, I prepared myself for the moment. My dress was a mess and my hat askew, my curls sagged and my throat was parched and no, I did not feel prepared to meet my sister's murderer but perhaps looking as I did would make him regard me as harmless.

Glancing up at the window of the house, I saw the curtain fall back. Someone, at least, had noted my presence but no one appeared at the door and so I continued forward.

The three porticos made a lovely, cool porch — away from the glare of the sun. Feeling my stomach tighten, I was aware of my hand trembling as I raised it to the door, knocking once.

The silence which surrounded me was unnerving. Only the cry of the gulls seemed to acknowledge my presence. Someone had to be here! I had seen the curtain move.

I raised my hand to knock once more as the door was silently swung open on well-oiled hinges. The interior of the house was dim.

Blocked as it was by the man who stood before me, it gave me little impression of what lay beyond.

"Yes?" He asked with an impertinence that Papa would not have allowed in his servants.

I studied his coal black hair, parted to one side, and his penetrating black eyes, which gave me the shivers. How could Lord Penporth, indeed, how could anyone employ someone as frightening as he. Across the swarthy skin, there was a scar that ran from his left eyelid across his cheek and to his mouth making it seem to curl into a sneer. His body was thick, but not fat. Rather it was well-muscled and strong in a bullish fashion. It was his scowl, the meeting brows, and those eyes that most unnerved me and made my heart beat faster. I thought of the villain in the Italian opera I had once seen in London—the poisoner for Caesar Borgia.

"Did you want someone?" he repeated, studying me with that insolent eye of his.

I took a deep breath and tried to recall from Jenny's letters just who this might be but my mind had gone blank. From his dark clothes, I could only assume that he was a butler but butlers did not stare so. Did he, like the boy, notice the resemblance? I prayed not and felt fear flood me.

Cooler than I felt, I met his eyes. "Yes, I wish to speak with your master."

The dark eyes seemed to travel up and down me settling on my throat as if he were undecided as to bite or slash. I tried to keep my shivering to a minimum but I did not think I was succeeding very well.

"And who might you be?"

His attitude was surly, even for a member of the household. Even if I stayed only a few days, I would be sure that Lord Penporth knew of his man's inhospitable way of welcoming guests and making them feel like intruders.

"I am . . ." I paused for a moment, frantically trying to recall my new name. "I am Tamara Nilston. I am, soon, I believe, to be your new mistress, and I do not like your way of speaking to me."

"My new mistress? Tamara Nilston, you say?" A flicker of a smile shadowed the dark face and disappeared.

Was the man reading my mind or just finding my dress, sandy and torn as it now was, inappropriate. The curls seemed heavier on my neck now. I wished that I had put them up better and that I had not taken my bonnet off on the boat. I supposed I deserved his stare for that and for not doing what was ladylike and remaining in the cabin of the boat.

He continued to stand there, staring at me.

"I do not think your master would be pleased at your surliness. I would like you to announce me and then show me to a room where I might freshen up. Since no one met me, my luggage is on your rocky landing below. I suggest you have one of your understaff fetch it." There, Papa would have been pleased at the way I had taken my stand against a servant. He always said

I was too soft.

Rushing past him into the sunlit part of the hall, I felt a fearful revulsion as my skirt accidently touched him. I could feel him staring at my back. Was it torn—or had I somehow given myself away? I was beginning to regret my outburst of a moment ago. I could not afford to alienate anyone in the house who might give me information of Jenny.

Trying to regain my control, I turned and felt my face flush due to his continued examination of me. The blood rushed through me—both from anger and from fear. I was not quite sure yet which held the upper hand.

Once again that fleeting smile crossed the man's face and he shrugged. Without another word, he directed me toward a study.

I was about to protest that I wanted to freshen up first but he was gone.

"Blast! I muttered to myself. "Well, I will just have to make the best of things," I said as I attempted to tuck the stray hairs under my hat.

The room was luxurious; the floor was thickly carpeted and soft but the rest of the room seemed hard and cold. The heavy oak wainscotting matched the furniture. Only the multicolored book jackets, which lined the room in rows upon rows of titles, relieved the monotony. In a corner, there stood a single table and lamp, as well as several leather wing back chairs.

Still damp from the splashing, I shivered. It would be dreadful to become ill here, I thought.

I glanced about the room once more and located the bell cord. Would his lordship think badly of me if I rang the bell and asked to be shown to a room first. I wondered if that surly butler was actually looking for his lordship. Somehow, he did not strike me as one to follow commands. I wondered why Lord Penporth kept him on.

My fertile imagination told me that the man must know some secret of the lord's. Maybe he had seen Lord Penporth kill my sister; maybe he had seen other things and his lordship kept him on the island to silence him?

Shivering again, I advanced toward the drawn curtains. The heavy blue velvet put me in mind of the Hyde Park Hotel and I thought of Tamara. I dearly hoped that she was well and settled into her new life.

Sensing that I would be more at home with the light, I pulled the draperies apart. The shock sent chills running down my spine as I spied on the path before the house the same blonde gentleman who stared at me in King's Cross. Had it been he? Was he Lord Penporth? Did he realize the switch?

My head pounded with the dread hammer of fear. Ought I confess the switch now and get it over with, ought I leave now before Lord Penporth could be found—but how would I get off the island I need not, of course, tell him my true name—only that I had come in place of Tamara.

I allowed the drapery to fall back into place with the whisper of fabric. Numbly, I stood there, staring at the dark walls, and shivered again. Maybe I should return to the landing. Maybe some passing boat would see me and have mercy. If I could get back to St. Mary's.

In a daze, I turned toward the door, not realizing that it was not the door through which I had entered.

The cool breeze from the sea blew in from the open French windows as I stepped into the adjoining room. Unlike the other room, this was light, bright and large. Decorated in Chinese style it had Oriental vases, Persian rugs, and a large picture window which gave an expansive view of the water beyond. Lulled into a false moment of security by the immediate beauty about me, I forgot my fears.

I stepped forward to admire a painting, then quickly realized my mistake. There, turning the pages of a gentleman's magazine, his back toward me, was the blonde man I had seen moments earlier. My paralyzed feet would not move. Should I attempt to leave the room now—with him already in it?

I took a step backward. The floor boards creaked, startling me.

"Laura, do we know what happened to that girl yet?"

"She's here," I said, assuming that he meant me.

"What?" He glanced up and spun about. His blue eyes were wide with surprise as he stared at me.

"Oh, so you are here." A smile crossed his face. His blue eyes twinkled in the sunlight.

"By God, girl, it looks as if you've had a time

of it." His dimples widened charmingly, capturing my heart. How could Jenny have called him an ogre? Immediately recalling my sister, however, I felt myself on guard.

"When did you arrive?" He asked as he continued to study me.

"I . . . just a few moments ago. Your butler . . ." I began as the dark haired fellow entered the room without knocking. He had changed from his black afternoon frock coat to one of blue and grey check. It relieved his sombre appearance but only mildly.

The dark eyes took me in briefly before he addressed the other man. "I see you have already found her, Percival. Did you know that she was coming? I did not."

My mouth nearly dropped open as he stared at the man called Percival. "I . . . I sent a telegram when I reached Penzance," I said to neither and to both — not knowing who was who now.

"Percy, did we receive any telegram?"

The blonde gent smiled. His eyes were still on me. "Matter of fact we did, Julian. Alfie rowed it over from Mary's last night but you were too busy . . . " he gave a casual shrug. "Sorry, I forgot to mention it."

There was a thunderous vibration as the man, who I now belatedly realized was Julian Hawley, Lord Penporth, crossed the room to where I stood. Without acknowledging me, he disappeared into the study whence I had come. Moments later, he re-emerged holding a yellow piece of paper in his hand. My telegram.

Chapter Four

Now more than ever, I wished I had not been so bold with this man. Had he not stipulated from Miss Farrington that he wished her to send him a passive bride? I was, I knew, anything but passive but I had vowed that during these few weeks I would hide my spirit . . . and I had already broken that vow.

Lord Julian Hawley turned toward me now — surveying me as cooly as one would a horse at an auction.

The blood rose to my face. "Sire, you'll excuse my manners before, but I thought. . . ."

"No, Miss Nilston," he said, smiling, changing his features entirely, " 'tis I who beg your excuse. My cousin did not tell me of your intended arrival . . ." He glanced at the sheepishly grinning fair-haired chap, who now indeed looked as my sister had described him — a "Puck." "I would have sent a boat to meet you, or at least met you at the landing with a gig. We are not so uncivilized here as you might think."

My mind went blank as I searched for words. "Oh, I did not mind. I. . ."

"Tell me. Was it you or your companion who was ill in London?"

I swallowed hard and then recalled an illness was the reason that Tamara had given for the delay. "My companion, Sire." I lowered my eyes, trying not to stare into those black depths.

"And where is she now? I was given to understand that the companion would be accompanying you. At least," he paused as he studied me, "that is what your aunt told me."

I blanched. Tamara had told me nothing of what had transpired between her aunt and his lordship . . . and I had not even thought to ask.

"The woman came with me to London but I came the rest of the way on my own."

"On your own!" He thundered. "On your own! By Jove! If I had known that. . ." He seemed to get control of himself then. "I do not like the idea of my bride traveling alone — like some common harlot." He glared at Percy, accusing him of what I knew not. Inside, I felt myself trembling. Now I knew what Jenny had meant by his volcanic temper. If he became this enraged merely because I had come on my own, what would he do if he found out who I truly was? Would I be able to stand up to him for the three weeks while banns were being said.

I kept my eyes cast down. I knew I would have to find out what I needed as quickly as possible and be at the landing Tuesday next to return to St. Mary's.

The calm after the storm was amazing. He quieted as quickly as he had exploded. As he smiled at me, he seemed almost pleased that I had not shown fear of him then.

"I will have Laura and some of the island women keep you company, on occasion, but I fear, my dear, you will often have to provide your own entertainment — at least until the child arrives. Then, perhaps, we can have a woman from Penzance to assist you."

I stared at him. I longed to tell this arrogant fellow that I would have no child by him, and that, if my plans fell right, I would soon be away from here and he would be facing a judge.

Glancing at Percy, I wondered how much he suspected. If he but breathed a word of seeing me in London with Tamara, I would be at an end.

My eyes once more turned toward the swarthy man as he pulled the bell cord.

The girl who appeared was short and stocky, wearing a blue serving gown. Her reddish brown hair was tucked under an untidy cap. As she entered the room, I again thought of my sister's letters and tried to recall who this might be. It was obvious from her sureness that she was not just an ordinary servant.

I turned toward the servant girl and felt a hand upon me. It was his lordship's. There was another moment as he seemed to search my face. Did he see some resemblance to Jenny? I prayed not.

"Where did you say your luggage was, Tamara?" His voice was now kind and rather gentle.

"I. . . ."

"They've been brought up, Julian," the girl, Laura, addressed him.

"Fine," he nodded.

"Cousin," Percy's lackadaisical drawl broke the air, "I do believe that our guest is rather hungry and in sore need of a bath." He grinned at me and stepped forward to wipe a smudge off my nose. I recoiled for just a moment and felt the tension from Penporth behind me.

He grinned at Julian. "Surely, you can't mind this, can you, Cuz?"

Behind me Penporth continued his angry silence.

After a moment, he responded and talked to me. "You'll forgive me for not seeing to your needs earlier, my dear, but I was making sure that the room was cleared for you." He paused, "You don't mind if I address you as Tamara, do you?" There was a pleading in his eyes that I was not accustomed to in one of his authority.

"I . . . no . . . of course not, Sire." I took a deep breath, trying to remain as passive as I could and not feeling the strain of my heart as it pounded against my chest.

He nodded and turned to Laura. "You will prepare a bath in my room for Miss Nilston and have your mother bring up dinner for her."

"Your . . . room?" My voice gave way like cracked wood. "Sire, that is highly. . ."

"My name is Julian, Tamara." He reached out again to touch me and I felt the warmth of his hand on my shoulder. "Even my servants call me that." He glanced at Laura. "We do not stand on ceremony here, my dear. As to the impropriety of your being in my room, I admit that it does you credit; however, since we will be wed the day after next, I hardly thought it necessary to completely install you in another room. For the next night or two, I shall sleep in the guest chamber."

"But I . . . but the banns." My head was spinning as my voice tightened. "There are three weeks of banns to be read."

"My dear Tamara," he seemed astonished at my surprise, and once more he seemed to stare at me before addressing me, "Did your aunt tell you nothing of our letter?"

Wide-eyed and weak-kneed, I cursed Tamara's forgetfulness. The aunt may have told Tamara, but Tamara had not told me. "No, I . . ."

"I have a special license. In fact, had you come last week as your aunt originally informed me, we would now be wed."

"Imagine being so impatient for a mere child," Percy interrupted. "Damned expensive that special license was."

Lord Julian ignored his cousin. "Banns have been said in St. Mary's. As it is, 'twill take a day or so to get the vicar from there."

Her throat was dry. Had Tamara purposely not told me for fear that I would back down?

"But. . ."

He cut me short, still measuring me with those

eyes of his. "Truly, Tamara, I am surprised. You are sure that your aunt made no mention of this. I shall have to write her."

"No, don't!" I cried out. "I mean, it is possible that she did—only I was in such a state about coming that I . . . I do not recall." It seemed as if there were a thousand ants biting my neck. I forced myself to glance up into those dark pools. "Would it not be better for us to know one another before . . . I mean, what if we are not suited."

Percy smiled, and swung his legs over the chair. "Good idea that. After all, Cousin, marriage is for life . . . that is, unless they run away."

I shivered. He was talking about my sister but I still did not believe that my sister would have run from her duties—even with this man. I might, but she would not. She was too good.

Penporth gave his cousin a cold stare that made my stomach tighten with apprehension. His hand was still on my shoulder in a possessive manner; his black eyes seemed to possess and pierce my very soul.

"There will be time enough, Tamara, for us to know each other after the ceremony."

Spinning about, he left the room then.

"Well, come on, then," Laura told me, "I haven't all day, ye know."

I nodded, dully. What in heaven's name was I going to do?

At the foot of the stairs, Lord Penporth again emerged. He motioned for the servant girl to move ahead.

As his hand touched me, I felt a shiver going up my spine. I would have to do for at least another few days and not let this man know how much his touch upset me.

"Tamara," he said my name softly, almost tenderly, "I do realize that this is a shock for your delicate system but as you probably know, it is important to me that you conceive as quickly as possible."

I stared at him. What was this? What had Tamara left out now. Certainly Jenny had said nothing of the man's obviously desperate wish to have a child.

"Did your aunt spare you that, too?" His hand caressing my cheek gently caused a strange sensation to flood my body. "I am sorry for that, then. This is a shock to you, but there is no help for it. I had one delay already and there must be no more," he paused. "You see now how hideous I am; how I could not very well go seeking a wife myself."

"I. . ." Taking a deep breath, I turned to meet his gaze. I wished I could tell him that, indeed, I had witnessed worse men than he. He had, of course, first put me off with his scowling manner but when he smiled, I could almost forget my fear of him. It was not something I could say then, though.

"Do not worry, my dear. I shall bother you as little as possible — once you have conceived." He leaned over then and kissed my smudged brow, causing my heartbeat to quicken. "We will speak again of this tomorrow — after you have refreshed and rested. You will then give me the letters your aunt has promised."

"Yes, of course. I. . ." I glanced up the stairs toward Laura, who had her hands on her hips, eyeing the scene before her with obvious distaste. Letters? What letters? Again, I cursed Tamara for not telling me everything.

Julian Hawley smiled at me once more, making his features ruggedly handsome. "I do believe that my aunt's friend made the right choice this time."

I could say nothing more except, "Perhaps."

Without further words, I hurried up the steps toward the girl waiting for me at the top.

The room—his room, my room, it really did not matter anymore, I thought in my daze—had plenty of windows and a wonderful view of the island with the sea surrounding it. Below me, I could see the path that led to the town and a group of buildings there below. Turning back toward the room, I quickly passed the double bed and paused at my trunk which had already been set at the foot.

Again, my eyes traveled toward the head of the bed and I swallowed hard in nervous anticipation. Somehow, I would have to avoid that . . . because, unless I succeeded in getting what I wanted and leaving the island in 48 hours, there would be little comfort in thinking that the marriage was a farce. Just because I was not using my own Christian name did not mean that he would not demand his marriage rights.

I began to pace the room. Sweat was on my

brow. I had been so certain that the wedding would be postponed the usual three weeks.

Like the study below, this room was pannelled in dark oak. A lounge lay at an angle to the fireplace and a writing desk stood near the window but, other than that, the room was spartan. Had this, too, been Jennifer's room? Had my sister also been imprisoned here and suffered? How ironic. As children we had shared the same room. Now, it seemed we would do so again.

Two of the village men, Morgan and Connor (I learned their names from Laura) brought in a large wooden tub filled with hot, scented water.

"We're glad t'make yer acquaintance, yer ladyship."

I wanted to protest that I wasn't yet wed to Penporth but the whole island seemed to accept that as foregone. I nodded.

"I would like to get to know the island as soon as possible," I said, forcing a smile. "Do you think your wives. . ."

The men glanced at each other. "Lizabeth might be a bit of help. In fact, she'll be glad of seein' ye, but Morgan, here, he ain't wed yet."

"Oh, I see." I turned again toward the window as suddenly I did not feel like hearing stories or of questioning them about the island.

The men left as Laura re-entered. "Can I help you undress?"

I shook my head. "No, thank you. I can take care of myself but perhaps you could see about repairing and cleaning my gown."

The maid stared at me—as if resenting my

order.

"I will do my best, Tamara."

I took a deep breath. While I did not mind the use of "my name" from Julian Hawley—rather I could not mind since he had so insisted—I did not like being addressed so by the servants. "I would appreciate it, Laura, if you would address me as Miss Nilston. . .or. . ." the words seemed to stick in my throat, "Lady Penporth, when I am wed."

Laura glanced at me. "Right, Miss."

I winced as the door shut firmly behind her. Well, I had obviously alienated her. I had not meant to but it had happened. My mouth was dry. I would have to make friends with Laura and see what she knew of Jenny.

Slipping into the hot sudsy water, I wished I had learned the art of holding my tongue. Words always seemed to come to me before I thought about them.

It wasn't long before Mrs. Stewart came knocking. The sliced meats and soup looked lovely but I found that despite having eaten little that day, I was not hungry.

"Master says that you'll be by yerself this night but don't you worry none, my sweet, there'll be plenty of time fer ye t'know him later."

"Yes," I responded, tying the robe about me. I rose and went to the window. "Yes, I am sure of that. I could see several people moving about in the village now that twilight was approaching. Smoke rose from the chimneys of two huts and another person was drawing water from the well.

The sea danced as the rising tide hid those little turtle-like humps I had seen before. The light playing on the rocks was like a rhapsody.

An unconscious sigh escaped my lips. I wished I could truly appreciate this serene beauty.

"Mrs. Stewart, what happened to his first wife?" My back was turned to the older woman, purposely.

"Why d'ye ask, Miss?"

"I . . . was just curious." I forced myself to stay calm as I could. "I mean, she was my school mate."

"Well, Ma'am, I can't rightly say. I do know tain't were none of the master's doing. Julian treated her right proper. Though he did get on his high horse a bit. I'd say he be right kind t'her. Pretty girl, she were. Just took a notion t'er head. I guess she wanted out."

"Just like that?" I turned now. The curiosity was too much for me.

"Right, Miss. Just like that. One day she were here and the next not. But that won't affect you none. The marriage's been annulled. Yours will be right and legal. Don't you worry none. Cost his lordship plenty to have it so."

Frustration made me sigh. My marriage being legal was the least of my worries.

"Ain't ya gonna eat none?"

"Maybe later," I glanced at the food, feeling the fluttering in my stomach.

Mrs. Stewart gave me a motherly smile. "I'll leave it then. You sleep tight now." She shut the door, leaving me alone with my thoughts.

Sinking onto the lounge, I felt my mind spinning. My reputation, my virtue would be nothing — if I did not leave here soon. I closed my eyes. Yes, he even looked like a murderer, and a ravisher of women. But how was I to get proof in such a short time.

I picked up the knife from my tray and eyed it for a moment. Then, without another thought, I slipped it under the mattress. One never knew when it might come in handy.

Sitting at the writing desk then, I decided that if I noted down my thoughts and impressions, I could perhaps make some sense of things, think of some solution.

With pen and ink in front of me, I stared at the paper. No words came to my mind. I could not think of anything to say. The silence about me was intense and though the window was open, I could not even hear the murmur of the sea. I listened now. The house hardly betrayed a sound. I drew a deep breath. The extraordinary silence about me seemed to deepen and with it came a sense of cold. I seemed to be in a space apart, removed to where no human touch, no human voice could reach me. Indeed, I felt such utter despair that it seemed as if my spirits would never lift. I was totally alone here.

The stillness deepened. It seemed rather that I could hear every quick beat, every pulse of my body. A vague terror began to possess me . . . and I fought against its insidious influence. Bending my head down over the paper, which I had set out only a moment before, I tried to force myself to write but my hand would not move.

It took several moments for me to gain control of my nerves as I started to put down in sequence all that had passed this day—though I was sure there was little chance of my ever forgetting it.

Swallowing hard, I had a sensation of being observed but no one was about. With one more glance, I quickly finished the writing and hid my notes and Jenny's letters in the base of my trunk. I knew I would sleep that night, worried as I was but exhausted. Still, I felt my skin crawl as I slipped between the sheets of the double bed and sank into the soft feathers.

I was alone, tonight, but for how much longer.

Chapter Five

The mattress was soft and feathery. My fatigue propelled me into sleep but I woke suddenly in the middle of the night, my heart pounding, thinking that I heard voices outside my door. Now I wished that I had locked it.

A vague sense of fear that my doom was near made me shiver violently. Listening, my body stiff, unable to move, I waited. . . and waited. Finally I heard the footsteps receed as simultaneously the white muslin curtains blew inward, billowing like sails of a ship that I wished I was in.

I did not recall having left the window open and now the chill forced me to slip from my bed to close it. Beyond the protection of the glass, the sea was brilliant with the silver moon playing its music upon the waves. They seemed to orchestrate themselves with a hushed rhythm all their own. I breathed in the salty air before pulling the casement shut. Only then did I spy the figure beneath the window.

Alarmed, I withdrew a bit. It was impossible to identify the person and I could only wonder if he had been stationed there to prevent my departure. Upset, I forced myself to ignore him and glanced further out to the calm horizon, to the night sea. A small white sailboat appeared at the very edge.

As I stood there watching, the sail enlarged and came closer. It seemed to have some sinister connotation but, after all, this was an island community and I was probably making too much of it. The figure beneath my window remained motionless rather like the Queen's Beefeaters and I was sure now that he was here to watch me.

Rather than alert the person to my presence and risk danger to myself, I went to the bed again without latching the window as I should have done. Immediately, despite my troubled thoughts, I fell back to sleep.

The sun and the chirping of the birds woke me. Daylight should have brought some relief to my fears yet my position seemed more terrifying than it had last night. The house was utterly quiet and I saw that Laura had not yet been to my room with the hot water. Sitting upright in bed, I felt my heart in my throat.

No, Laura had not been with hot water but someone had come in. At the foot of my bed lay a wreath of black flowers such as one might find in a funeral. I stared at it for a good few moments, almost afraid that the thing would come alive and bite me. When it did not, I tentatively reached out to it. The flowers were apparently quite old for one crumbled in my hand.

Taking a deep breath to steady my taut nerves, I picked up the wreath and, opening the window, threw the present out. Even as I did so my stomach tightened and I shivered. Not even washing with the water that was left in the pitcher nor with all the water in the sea would have eliminated the feeling of dread that I had.

However much I might want to leave though, I would not be scared off by such a trick as this. I was here to find out about Jenny or . . . I shuddered at the prospect of tomorrow . . . it seemed I would be doomed to spend a good deal more time on this island than I had planned.

Removing my thoughts from their morbid track, I donned a blue muslin with a slight bustle. It was one of the things which Tamara had fixed for me and even though I might consider myself in mourning for my sister, Tamara was not.

My first job was to search Tamara's trunks to locate the letter which Lord Penporth had referred to the night before. Tamara's wedding dress had not yet been unpacked and I took it out now. Such a lovely and delicate feel. The material was so soft and pliant, so smooth that it slipped through my hands. It was much, much too beautiful to be worn in a sham ceremony yet unless I could locate the facts that I needed and leave the island quickly, wear it I would.

Patiently I laid out the other clothes — an olive green cloth dress with brown silk frills and the evening dress of silver grey silk with the rose trimmings. I laid out, too, the silver-handled brush set, half hoops, as well as the bonnets to match the dresses. But there was no sign of any letter from Tamara's aunt to Lord Penporth. I was sure she would have had nothing of importance to say and wondered why he was making such a fuss about it. Unless there was no letter, unless he suspected that I was not Tamara and was doing this just to unnerve me.

I thought again of seeing Percy at the station and wondered how much he knew even as I continued to search the trunk for sides and angles. What would Penporth's reply be when I told him that I had lost his precious letter. I shook my head. It was a mystery to me what Tamara's aunt would have written to him that he should find so important. I crossed my fingers and prayed that I would be off the island before the time came for a confrontation.

Donning shoes of the same blue color, I decided I would do some investigating of the house before the others rose. The utter stillness made me feel as if this were a tomb; perhaps for my sister it had been. My stomach cringed as the bile rose. Perhaps for me it might be.

I decided to start my search in his lordship's study where I had been the night previous but the odor of freshly brewed tea that wafted from the breakfast room drew me there instead. My growling stomach made me realize that I was ravenous.

The breakfast room, itself, was empty but an urn of steaming water, biscuits, butter and other pastries as well as bacon, eggs and porridge were arranged on the side table. I glanced about and decided that there was no harm in eating something. If I had to make plans to leave today, who knew when my next meal would be.

Before I had done, my plate contained a sample of everything. Jennifer had written what a superb cook they had here but I never expected such ordinary food would taste so well. My mouth watered even as I reached for second helpings. Finishing my tea, I knew that it was growing late. My watch had stopped the night before and I had seen no clock here yet though I had heard the chimes. I suspected it was about half past eight. It surprised me, therefore, that I was the only one to breakfast. In our household, Jenny had been the only late riser.

Gulping down the last of my tea, I left the room and this time my steps were redirected back to Penporth's study. My hand trembled as I touched the crystal knob and my heart palpitated as, steadying my breath, I turned the handle ever so gently. The corridor and rest of house were still, as empty and silent as they had been when I had first awakened. It therefore shocked me as I tiptoed into the room to see Penporth seated at his desk. He looked up as the door swung open and I wanted to die on the spot as he smiled at me. I could not even swallow my fear.

"May I assist you with something . . . Tamara?"

My heart hammered. Why did he pause when saying Tamara's name? Was that meaningful to me?

The lump in my throat was hurting. I swallowed again. "I . . . believe that I am lost. Where is the breakfast room?"

"From the direction you've come," he grinned. It's the second door on the left. I do not believe you should have trouble finding it." He stood now and crossed the room to me, taking my arm. "Come. Let me escort you."

"I. . ." His grasp was firm as a strange sensation seemed to flood me. I fought down my fear. "I am sure you have more important things to do, my lord."

His dark brooding eyes met mine. I wished I knew what he was thinking.

"There is nothing so important to me as seeing that you are well and truly taken care of, my bride. I trust that you slept well last night?"

I nodded. "Yes, your lordship."

A frown creased his brow. "I thought you were going to call me Julian."

"Yes . . . Lord Julian." The name came to my lips easier than I thought it would. I wondered then if he was the man who had been under my window the previous night. No, surely not. His lordship would have one of his servants do such work.

"No," his eyes searched my face for what clue I did not know. "Not Lord Julian, just Julian. I find it difficult to hear myself being called Lord anything especially from one," he paused as he brushed away one of my stray curls, his fingers touched my skin causing me to flush, "from one who is to share my life. My first wife had great difficulty with that. I hope you will not." His eyes were again staring into mine and I could only stare back, drawn as I was into those unfathomable depths of his. I recalled that Jennifer had indeed referred to him as his lordship or Penporth in all her letters to me.

"So you will agree to this small whim of mine?"

I swallowed hard and felt not fear but a warm flush as I now spoke. "I . . . will try . . . Julian."

"Good. Good." He smiled and for the moment one could almost call him handsome. "Now, I shall take you to breakfast. I have already eaten but you must be famished."

He started back along the hall with me and still in a daze I started with him until it dawned on me what an awkward scene it would be for him to still find my dirty dishes there. I stopped after two paces.

"Actually, I would much prefer to walk in the morning air before eating. I do not feel very. . .hungry at this moment."

He dropped his hand from me and stared. Those piercing eyes seemed to cut my heart and fret out my secrets. His lips—one thick and the other thin—pressed together in a disapproving line. "You would go out like that? Without a bonnet? Without proper walking shoes?"

"Yes. Yes," I replied, rapidly. "Just a bit of a

walk. I do not need to go too far." As long as it was far from him, I continued the thought.

He laughed. "You can do only a bit of a walk on this island. We've only 15 miles round and six across. Nevertheless, try not to get lost. There is an abundance of hills and some caves with rocky parts as well as some very low muddy areas."

"I shall be careful," I promised, and hurriedly left him before he could say more.

Only when I was outside did I gingerly touch my arm where he had held me and wondered why it burned so. The only conclusion to which I could come was that he was the devil incarnate.

Having failed in my attempt to investigate the house, I concluded that questioning the town people would be the next best thing. I would, of course, have to be careful about the phrasing of my questions for I did not know how their sympathies lay in regards to their master. Perhaps fear would prevent them from telling me anything of importance. Indeed, it would be easy to fear Penporth. I knew that I did.

From the path where I stood, I could see the hedge rows of the village and sparkling April flowers. The sun was gloriously bright and I wished I could feel as cheerful as the weather would have me do.

I did not take the same path as before and therein lay my nearly fatal mistake. It did not seem possible on an island so small that one could get lost and yet that is exactly what I did.

Like the other path, this one trailed down the hill of the house in the same direction. Foolishly deep in my thoughts, I did not notice the difference until I had reached a decayed and hollowed hut built of stones and crumbling with time. The sea rose and fell, crashing upon the naked rocks below me. The sun had gone behind the protection of the clouds making the land about me seem dull, grey and lifeless. It was not the sparkling, happy place of moments ago. I cringed as the "eyes" of the "dead" house stared at me. This was not the path to town. The ledges looked cold and bare. Somehow, it seemed I had reached the western part of the island for, looking across the channel to the south, I could see the island of Bryher. Its hills were reflected as smudges and birds of various families stood independent and one-legged, groping in the mud at the shore.

Turning around to try again to have some sense of direction, I could see nothing about me but the sea surging with stormy excitement. It was making me nervous, making me feel as if I should return to the "safety" of the sheltering house whose outline I could no longer see. I continued to stand there and stare at the sea realizing all the more with the distance to the other islands just how much of a prisoner I was here. Frustration welled up in me. How would I escape this cursed place before tomorrow? How would I elude Penporth's desires?

He must have been thinking of me for a shiver went up my spine and I felt as if someone was watching me but when I turned there was

71

no one about.

Forcing myself to continue, I began to climb in the direction in which I was sure the town lay. The early heather and gorse on the piles of the minor hills were wet and matted. It was stupid of me not to have guessed the proper direction but being on this island had totally confused my senses.

When I finally reached the top of the hill that I had chosen, I realized my mistake. Looking out over the many pointed summits and towards the fields flowering like oriental carpets, and then to the busy sea channels alive with boats, I could see the town in the distance but it would take me much longer than I had anticipated.

A boat edged between the main island and islets off our shore. I thought to call out to him for some assistance in reaching the town but then I realized that he would never hear me. In fact, apart from the interruption of the sea birds, there was nothing else moving about me — no other live sounds that I could hear. Two tears stained my cheeks. I was becoming upset with this whole situation and now wished I had listened to Tom.

Well, there was no hope now but to continue on the course which I had started. Turning, I headed in the direction of the stream that I could hear babbling over the stones but could not see. In the distance a donkey brayed. He had to be near the town. Perhaps it was not as far as I had thought. Perhaps after all I was on the right trail.

The donkey's honk had reminded me of Papa when he had had his last cold; it also reminded me of Edinburgh. How very far that seemed.

Would I ever escape this place? Well, perhaps I was being a bit melodramatic. That was a fault which Papa and Miss Farrington had often accused me of.

Continuing on, I told myself it would not be much farther. Penporth, himself, had told me that it would not be a long walk. But then he knew the island. I did not.

Irritated at myself for giving into my momentary weakness, I trudged on and reached a lighthouse that seemed deserted. Out of breath but determined to find my way on my own, I walked to the top. Part of the wall beneath was crumbling but on the whole, the building and land were safe enough. For a few moments, the sun emerged again. The view was a heady one. I could see not only Bryher and Tresco but also St. Mary's, St. Martin's, and Agnes to the Southwest. The wind here was crisp, blowing up the water like a man with a small axe chopping it to pieces. Spray jumped high and I fancied that once or twice I could feel the droplets of water hit my hot skin. Angry waves blew up upon the rocks below my feet and the rays of the sun colored them into tiny rainbows.

Yes, I could see the town and was surprised at how close it now seemed. I had overstepped it by only a bit. Hawley House, from here, also looked close but then I was sure the distance was deceiving for the time felt to be nearly ten or later.

Once more my attention was called by the compelling sea below me. It was like a moody child craving attention. I knew now why this temperamental expanse was called a cruel and jealous mistress. Even as the sea thrashed about the island, scooping up its vast arms to engulf whatever was in its path, it leaped over islets that were too shallow to withstand or hide from its might. How fitting that Lord Penporth obviously a cruel and inhuman master, had an island estate ruled by one more terrible in fury than he.

The sun departed once more and I hurried down the rickety steps. Time was passing. I had yet to obtain the needed information and to find passage off the island as well.

Climbing another narrow path that seemed to wind up and into the waist of the island, I noted that this was the only clear path I could take. Well, it would lead me to the town for I had seen the town from the top of the tower and knew that it was in this very direction.

As I passed the trees towering over me, I now realized what a tremendous thing they were compared to the rocky barrenness of the other islands. Penporth's father must have had foresight to plant these when he did. At least, I assumed that was who had done it.

Despite my huge breakfast, I found myself now getting hungry. I picked up a handful of red berries which the birds were also eating. If they were safe for them, then they should be safe for me as well. The tart taste was much like goose berries but rather than relieve my hunger, they only made me desire more.

When I came upon the second lone cottage, I decided to swallow my pride and ask for directions. Curtains breezed from the windows as I approached but again, I could see no sign of life about. Someone must live here!

I pressed my face against the pane of glass. In the window, there was another face staring back at me! I jumped clear off the ground and stumbled back, falling into an overgrown garden. The desolate whisper of loneliness pervaded the place as the sea breeze whistled through the trees. My hair lifted at the nape of my neck.

Shaken, I stood and found that my left ankle hurt me but I was still able to hobble about. The reflection I had seen in the dusty pane had been merely myself. It seemed that Penporth Island, outside of the manor and the few that lived about the well, was a ghost island. What, I wondered, had happened to chase all those people away from their homes? Had Lord Penporth anything to do with it? I would not put it past him—that much I was sure.

Frustrated and aching, it seemed that fate was fighting me at every turn. I had to get off the island and as soon as possible. Could I merely settle for telling my suspicions to the police constable at St. Mary's? Would any benefit come of that?

At the side of the cottage was a muddy path going into a group of small hills. It was not anything like the road that I had previously trod but it had hoof marks going up and I concluded that the village must be in that direction. It had to be. I had made too many wrong turns already this morning and did not want to delay much longer.

From the start, I had had my suspicions but if I did not retrace my steps, this was the only other path to follow. Still, you would think that a village would have a slightly better road than this — no matter how primitive the town.

Pressing my lips together in frustration, I continued on, moving to one side and then the other to avoid the branches that would surely have scraped me even through the cloth of my gown. Sweat was now on my brow and I wished I had indeed taken that bonnet.

The markings of the road were now like parallel streams of slate colored water and between them was a morass — a pudding of mud and squelchy pools. Outside the bounds of the path, the ground seemed soggy and yielding. My blue slippers and white stockings were no longer their original color. They, plus the hem of my gown, had been quite soaked. My face now hurt and I suspected that I was horribly sun burnt. Grimacing, I felt the dry pain on my face. Penporth had been right in that aspect at least. I supposed he would gloat at seeing his opinion justified but there was nothing I could do about it now.

Pausing to catch my breath, I could see a few thin sheep grazing but they were well away from where I stood.

It was becoming painfully evident that I would never make any progress where I was and so I began to veer off the path, scrambling up the steeper side of the hill.

Bending at one point to catch a root so that I would not fall, I heard a distant but distinct sound of a rip and immediately felt a breeze at my side as my dress gaped open.

I blushed hotly but I had no choice but to keep on this course for there was no way I could get down the way I had come. Not, at least, without tumbling headlong into the sea. Continuing as I had come, I now cursed his lordship for not giving me an escort to town. He should have known that, not knowing the island, I would get lost. Had he meant this to happen?

The sheep, I am sure, thought me crazed, speaking as I was, and it was only through sheer effort and a promise that over the next hill I would see the town and Hawley House that kept me going. Mud now squeezed out over the tips of my shoes and water seeped from their seams. My feet were wet and cold. My ankle throbbed with pain but tolerate it, I would.

Finally, I gained the top and wiped the sweat off my brow feeling the mud streak me. I was joyfully surprised to see that I was only a short distance from town and that I was also nearly above it. It should be only a simple matter now to get down there, should it not?

I assured myself that it was simple—even though the path down seemed even more dangerous than the one I had come up. Well, my only other choice at this point was to jump and risk death on the rocks if I could not stop my fall.

My heart hammered as the sun beat down upon me. Once more I glanced about. No. There was no other way. How had I ever gotten myself in this mess?

"Oh, Jennifer," I said out loud, "why did you not just come home or write me?"

Sinking down on a muddy rock, ruining my already spoiled dress, I put my hands to my face. Would Jennifer have come out after me had I been the one to disappear? I wondered.

Having gotten my courage back, I stood once more and chose the former way, finding it necessary almost immediately to crawl under some wires. I then found myself within a hollow. There was nothing but swamp around me! Up until this moment, there had been islets of scattered firm ground to which I could leap. Now there was nothing but muck oozing out of the ground.

I used all the curses I had ever heard from my father. Thank goodness only the crows were about to hear them. Every attempt to turn about was wetter and deeper than the last. At one point, I stepped out of the morass, praying that I would locate firm ground, only to find that the slipper from my left foot had been sucked in!

I now placed my foot firmly into a thick cold mess. The tears which had only started before now began to fall in abundance. The suction of the mud had wrenched my foot again. From their peaceful place atop the hill, the sheep stared at me.

I pulled my other foot from the mud. A gurgling sound preceded it as, with effort, I released it. How that hurt! A miserable hot wind blew in and made me feel more awful, more achy, more lonely than I had ever felt in my life.

Sobbing, I tried to balance on the one foot and release my slippers from the mud but all the activity was only causing me to sink deeper. I could not find them.

My knees now gave way and I tumbled backwards into the ugly mess. Mud clung to me, oozing like puss from the tears and openings in my clothes. (I had torn my dress several times since that first moment it seemed). With a more desperate effort, I righted myself and grabbed hold of the branch that reached out over me. Thank the Lord for those trees!

Once again I found myself free and climbed up a bit. The land was only slightly more solid here. Twice more I fell. Mud and water streamed through my hair, into my eyes, down my neck, and into my petticoats. How could I ever meet anyone like this? How could I ever convince someone to get me off their cursed and wretched island looking as I now did?

My tears mingled again with caked on my reddened, achin on. I don't know how I did at a clearing not far from self, had once more e that that was just as was to get to my roo my worst nightmares wer and Penporth strolled out of the stant.

I knew that I looked a sight but I don't believe deserved the treatment meted out to me. Both of them stopped and stared. Percival began to laugh hysterically while Lord Hawley just grinned — an obnoxious grin.

"What . . . what happened to . . . you?" Percival managed to coax out between spasms of laughter.

I was not given an opportunity to answer for Penporth responded. "It seems as if she did exactly what I told her not to do. She became lost and fell into the quagmire."

Percival could not contain himself and began laughing violently so that he was almost doubled over.

Inside, I was trembling but I held my head high and tried to ignore the men as I walked forward. At that dreadful moment, my ankle that I had so far managed on, gave way and I collapsed — sprawling in front of them. I did not know who I hated more at that moment — Percy for his laugh-ing, Lord Penporth for his cold assessing stare; or myself for having been so foolish and clumsy.

Penporth bent down beside me and assisted as I struggled to a sitting position. It was obvious that he was disgusted with me for I could see his nose turned up at the unpleasant smell.

"Are you hurt?"

I did not answer. My throat clogged with tears. Instead, I shook my head and prepared to stand on my own. Percival finally stopped his laughing.

"I say, I am sorry, dearest girl, but you do look utterly ridiculous."

"If you have finished with your merriment, Percival, you might instruct Obediah to fetch the bath and have Mrs. Stewart heat up the water."

"But of course, Cousin!" He made a sweeping bow and then disappeared into the house.

"You can go, too." I told him, standing. "I am fine."

The pain that racked my whole body now belied my words. I began to move forward, gingerly, conscious of the horrid black eyes upon me. If only I could have gotten to the door, I could have managed but once again my ankle collapsed and I screamed out! His lordship's arms were about me before I hit the ground.

"Let go of me!" I writhed, not knowing which was more painful—his touch or my ankle. "I can manage," I said, teeth clenched.

"The devil you can!"

I was given leave to say no more for I was hoisted over his shoulder like a sack of potatoes. I could not kick for he held my legs, though I did pummel his back a few times.

"Be still!" He demanded as he carried me up the stairs. I cried out with surprise and agony as he smacked my behind like a mule. "If you act like a child, I shall treat you like one."

"You are a beast!" I said, my teeth again clenched.

I don't know if he heard or not but there was a grim smile on his uneven lips as he unceremoniously dumped me—clothes and all into the tub of water. He departed the room without saying another word and left Laura and Mrs. Stewart to cope with me.

I am not by nature a modest person but I objected to the way Laura practically tore my clothes off. "They are ruined anyway. Once that muck gets in them, it never comes out."

I resigned myself and allowed her to remove the rest of my clothes. The water had already taken on a Stygian color and smelled offensively. I was obliged to get out, dry myself, and wait for them to empty the tub and refill it.

This time, the work began.

"Be careful!" I cried out as Laura seemed to tear at my hair. "It's all stuck to your head," she explained. And so I had to face the torture in stoic silence. It was my punishment for not following the path as I ought.

Once that had been done and I had been assisted into a night dress and dressing gown, Lord Penporth returned.

"Sir!" I cried, as I attempted to pull the bedcovers over me. "I think you might have the courtesy to send your words through a messenger."

He smiled—but it was more of a sneer. Clearly, he enjoyed my discomfort. "My dear Tamara, whether you wish it or not, you'll be my wife within twenty-four hours. I see no reason why I should observe a propriety now that I shan't observe twenty-four hours hence."

I blushed deeply but with my burnt skin I doubted it showed. I prayed not. My stomach churned with fear knowing that I was now trapped. With my ankle as it was, there was no way that I could leave the island.

"Well, what is it that you want?" I asked, lowering my eyes as demurely as I could.

His eyes met mine for a moment but he said

nothing. Then, leaning over, he threw off my bed-clothes and touched my sore ankle. I winced and withdrew with the pain, gritting my teeth as he looked up questioningly.

"I can not tell how badly you are injured if I cannot examine it."

I took a deep breath and steeled myself for his touch.

"As I thought. Well, the Granny should help."

"The Granny? Granny? Who? If there is something wrong with me, I think it should be seen by a doctor."

"Perhaps in Edinburgh it would have been but here we have no choice." He turned toward Laura who, having faded into the background of the room, now came forward. "Send MacKenzie for the Granny."

"Julian, I really don't think . . ." she began.

"Must I always repeat myself, Laura?" The thunder in his voice threatened a storm. Laura backed down and with a sympathetic look toward me, disappeared to deliver the message. At least, I had one friend here.

"I will not . . ." I started, but I could not finish.

"You are in my home and you shall do as I say. I do not know what Miss Farrington teaches you girls but it certainly is not the wifely obedience she claims."

"May I remind you that I am not yet your wife."

"May I remind YOU that you will be shortly. Perhaps I had best write to your schoolmistress and find out how it was that she kept you girls in line. Neither you nor my first wife seemed properly trained in respect."

I stared at him — open-mouthed. I could understand his words applying to myself but not to Jennifer. Jennifer had been the paragon of virtue and respect. She had never even whispered a word of discontent to Papa or to Miss Farrington.

Puzzled, I became flustered and unsure. "Very well, I will see the Granny, if you wish it, My Lord."

"Do not mock me, Tamara. You will not like the results." He turned then, leaving the room. All I felt was relief. I had not been mocking him — my mouth was a thin line — only showing him the respect that he asked for. I could taste the bile in my throat and wondered why Julian Hawley, Lord Penporth, was so unsure of his status. Did that hold some key to Jennifer's disappearance?

Sighing, I leaned back on the pillows. I only knew that I could not have him writing to our schoolmistress. All he would need do is tell her that I lacked proper respect and my game would be over. Like Jennifer, Tamara Nilston had also been respectful and quiet. She would know immediately that it was not Tamara who had come. Would she betray me, I wondered?

Laura re-entered the room as I opened my eyes. "He is gone?"

I nodded.

"Truly, I am sorry about your fall." She sank down on the bed. "It's a shame that you will not be given the necessary time to let the ankle heal on it's own. May I call you Tamara?" She smiled. "I was on intimate terms with his first wife and often called her Jennifer. I hope you do not mind."

I shook my head, afraid to speak, afraid I would interrupt her train of thought and miss some vital information. Besides, I realized that if she called Julian Hawley by his Christian name then she was no ordinary servant. I saw her smile again at her small victory and thought that Jenny had been right. She did smile like a Cheshire cat.

When it appeared that Laura was not about to speak, I found my voice. "What . . . what was she like? His first wife, I mean?"

Laura shrugged. "She did not like the Granny. That much I can tell you. That woman is a witch."

I tried to gather my thoughts, to direct my questions. "I do not believe in witches," I said. "Why did Jennifer not like her?"

"The same reason the town folk do not. They believe her a witch. That's why she lives at the edge of the road. They all respect her . . . and fear her. So far, they've had no trouble with her but. . ."

I shivered. "That is stuff and nonsense."

"Jennifer did not think so. I believe the witch cast a spell over her."

"What?" My eyes widened. "What type of spell?"

Laura played with the crocheted bedspread that covered me. She shrugged. "All I know is that she has the power and you should be careful of her."

We could talk no more for a soft tap on the door told me that the Granny had come. Had she heard us?

The tiny, pale woman who entered looked as if she had been dead ten years past. Flesh was taut over her nearly bald head and face. She stared at me with knowing eyes that made my skin crawl. I also knew that she could give me away, if she wished it.

The woman glanced toward Laura who quickly left the room but not before crossing herself.

The servant was quickly replaced by his lordship. My eyes rested on him briefly and met his look. Recalling our earlier conversation, I held my tongue and tried not to acknowledge him or the agony I was in. I would have loved to talk to the old woman regarding Jennifer but now was not the time.

A hot poultice was placed over my swollen ankle. Death would have been less painful, I think. It was almost too bad I had not chosen to try and jump. Then, at least, I might actually have made it to the town! However, not even that was assured.

"Will she be well enough for our wedding on the morrow?"

"She will," the Granny nodded, "if she rests this night and does as I tell her."

"She will do that," Penporth assured. "She will do that."

I closed my eyes and tried not to think of the

moments ahead. There seemed no way out for me but to go ahead with this masquerade. I wondered now how Tamara and her new husband fared.

In the early evening, Percy came to visit and cheer me. In spite of his Puckish ways, he really seemed kind. Jennifer was right. He was a charming talker and how he listened. I came quite close to actually confiding in him. Just his way made me want to talk of myself but neither of us mentioned the train journey and I prayed that I did not say anything which would lead him to suspect me but somehow I had the feeling that he would protect me.

Alone again, I decided to re-read Jennifer's letters. Wincing with the pain, I hobbled about to the chest where I had hidden my package. I especially wanted to read what she had written about Percy.

I had only returned to the bed and readjusted the covers when the heavy steps outside my door made my heart stop. Quickly, I shoved the letters under the mattress as Penporth entered the room without so much as a knock.

"What is it now?" I asked, indignant at his lack of respect for me, and hoping that he would not notice the flurry of activity.

His dark eyes took the scene in and then he adjusted my covers. "I thought Granny said you were not to be up."

Blast that man! Could I not hide anything from him?

"I wanted to get a book."

He gave a slight nod. "Well, you will not need to read now. You will need to rest. I have a potion for you which the Granny has just now mixed and brought over." He came toward me holding a vial. I could only stare at it as Laura entered the room and stared at me—almost it seemed in warning.

I glanced again at the vial and then at his face. Did he know? Was he about to poison me, murder me as he had murdered Jennifer?

I attempted to move away from him, to lean over to the other side of the bed, but my foot now swathed in bandages and ointment was so huge that I could not maneuver out of his way. "I do not want anything. I will not drink anything."

"You will, Tamara! Do not make me argue with you."

"Is this what happened to your first wife?" I asked in fear before my mind could stop my tongue. "Did you kill her, too?"

He dropped my hand and glanced at me. "What gave you the idea that Jennifer is dead?"

I blinked, not knowing what to say.

"I will forgive your indiscretion just now, Tamara. I suggest you drink this vial. It will not hurt you. I promise you. In the future, I do not expect to hear the name of my first wife mentioned again. She has left this household and what has become of her, I do not know."

There was a pregnant pause. I did not know what to do or what to say. If he told the truth, that Jennifer had indeed fled the house on her own, I was sure he must have had something to do with it and therefore, he was still at fault. But no, I could not agree with him. Surely, if she had gone she would have contacted me. She would have. . .

"Do you take the medication?" His glare brought me back to the present.

I stretched out a trembling hand.

"Now drink it."

With his intense dark eyes boring through me, I lifted the vial to my lips.

Laura was there, watching me.

"Drink it," he ordered again.

I sighed. Avoiding his eyes, I tasted the bitter fluid. It took a moment before I could swallow but I knew he was watching me and so I did.

Silently, my heart pounding with fear, I handed him back the vial. Well, what would be, would be.

Did I see a glint of humor in his eyes? He was obviously pleased with himself and with his action. Adjusting the covers over my injured leg, he then turned and lowered the gas lamp.

"Goodnight, my young bride. I trust you will be better on the morrow."

I stared after him, after the closed door. He had not locked it, but how was I to escape now?

Chapter Six

Today was my wedding day! Or should I say—Tamara's wedding day? No, it was my own doom that I was sealing. In fairness, I must admit that the Granny's ointment and that miserable potion helped me. The swelling in my ankle receded—enough, at least, for me to put on the white stockings and white satin slippers without flinching. My face, too, did not sting as it had yesterday.

Laura helped me into the lovely ivory silk and pearl wedding dress which had been prepared for Tamara. It was lucky that we were both the same size. The Spanish lace veil, which was placed over my head even made me feel beautiful. There was also a sumptuous train of white roses which had been donated by the island people, all of whom seemed anxious to meet me.

With Laura's assistance, I did my hair up in

ringlets and placed some of the flowers in them. It would have been nice if I had felt the happy anticipation that I should have felt on this day but all I had now were jittery nerves. Oh, why had I come? Why hadn't I just stayed in my lovely Edinburgh and married Thomas.

True, I did not love him but then I did not hate him as I did this brute of a man. The only consolation I had was that I would soon be a widow when Penporth's guilt was found out. As a widow, I would have more freedom than I had as a single woman. My mind turned to Jennifer. Where was she? Well, wherever, she was at least safe from this man's clutches. I only hoped that my own sacrifice would prove to have some purpose.

Shortly before the ceremony, Penporth came to my room. Laura was fixing the last of my curls.

She slammed the door upon him as he tried to enter. I smiled. It was something that I longed to do but could not. "It's bad luck to see the bride before the wedding, Julian!"

"Nonsense!" He forced open the door. "I did not see Jennifer and that did nothing to help me!" He strolled into the room. She stopped her activity to stand in front of me—shielding me from that malicious gaze. It was an act of friendship, I was sure. If ever I had the means, I would reward her.

"Leave this room, Laura."

"What and leave you with the bride? Not for a pound note I won't."

"You'll get more than that in your final packet if you do not. It seems you often forget your status here."

"You, too, forget my status," she glared at him. "I am here for as long as I wish to remain."

There was an awful silence as her back stiffened. "Indeed, my lord, that is something that I never forget."

"Then," he eyed me so that my heart quivered, "you would do well to leave us. I wish to talk alone with my bride."

I could sense her reluctance as much as she must have sensed my fear but it seemed we were both puppets to this creature who was determined above all else to have his way.

As she left the room, I glanced toward the bed. The knife was still there but it was too far and too awkward with my feet propped up as they were now, for me to stand.

The door shut with a finality behind her. Shivers rippled my skin. I started to stand.

"No," his voice was hoarse. "Stay where you are."

There was an ungodly quiet as he walked about the chair, seemingly to examine me. I sweated those few moments. What was it he had to tell me? Had he learned who I was? The blood seemed to rush through me as I waited and felt my heart pounding. If he planned to kill me, I prayed he would be quick about it.

"Tamara?"

"Y . . . yes?" My eyes fluttered open to face him only inches from me. I was surprised that I could even speak. Why was it he hesitated in using the name?

"You are better, I take it?"

I think I nodded. I am not quite sure. My lips were dry and so was my throat.

"You recall our conversation on the first night? When I mentioned the letters from your aunt?"

The letters from Tamara's aunt? In all that had happened these past twenty-four hours, they had slipped my mind.

"Ye . . . yes." I squeaked. It seemed that not only had I taken on Tamara's name but her personality as well.

"Well, where are they?" His eyes seemed to glint with a humor that I did not understand. "I should like to have them now."

I . . ." I shifted in my chair. Every nerve was taut. What did I tell him?

"No, don't get up. Just tell me where they are, Tamara. I shall fetch them. 'Tis no use you standing any more than you must."

It was considerate of him to be concerned of my standing yet that was not uppermost in my mind. I stared up at him, my mind blank.

"Tell me where they are, Tamara."

My tongue, dry as it was, managed to wet my even drier lips. I do not know how I spoke but I did. As my eyes met his, I said quite honestly, "I do not know. I . . . don't recall seeing any letters from . . . from my aunt. If she gave me them, then they are lost." I took a deep breath trying to steady myself, knowing that I was probably put-

93

ting myself in deep jeopardy. "If they are that important, you shall have to write to her. It's possible she forgot to send them."

"Is that a fact?" He raised a brow. "You are sure you did not lose them in London?"

"Well, I . . .I do suppose it is possible that they fell out of my trunk when I unpacked at the hotel there."

There was another pause. His next question totally surprised me. "Tell me more of this companion of yours. The one that left you in London."

My eyes widened and my heart pounded. "She . . . she was very nice." I swallowed hard. "I do not believe that she was capable of thieving, if that is what you are asking. Besides, what good would the letters do her?" The lump in my throat was nearly impassable.

"Your aunt felt otherwise. I do not think she approved of your friend."

A chill went through me. I prayed that Tamara's aunt had not given my name as the companion. "What . . . what did she say to lead you to think so?"

He gave a shrug and eyed me with his critical manner. "Why did she leave you in London rather than come out here with you as I was led to believe she would?"

She . . . she was offered a better position in London and I . . . told her that I did not mind coming on my own."

"So you dismissed her?"

I took a deep breath. "You could say that, I suppose."

His chair was so close to mine now that I could feel the tension coming from him. He took one of my hands which lay motionless in my lap. His thumb began to stroke my palm in a thoughtful manner—almost as if he was studying it to read it!! It was creating a sensation in me that was . . . well, it was quite strange.

"Perhaps an investigation of this woman should be started. What is her name and where did you last have contact with her?"

I stared at him. An investigation? I pulled my hand from him. It was he who should be investigated, not I. What in the world was I going to do? Any name that I gave him would surely cause me grief—especially if Tamara's aunt gave my real name.

My blood rushed through my brain as I fought desperately for some answer.

"You know my dear, I believe you are very innocent. You appear to be quite trusting as far as people go. Offtimes those that you think you trust most will cause you the most harm."

"Then I suppose that you trust no one." I sat upright in the chair now. "If all you wanted were my aunt's letters then perhaps I should return now to Edinburgh and fetch them for you. I tell you my companion did not touch them. It would not bother me if you wished to call off this farce of a wedding. I do not love you. I do not even know you. I . . ."

His hand on my shoulder forced me back into my seat and I was aware of having again spoken too quickly for my own sake. My heart continued to pound wildly as I avoided his eyes.

"That is true. You do not know me and most probably you do not love me. I doubt that Jennifer loved me or she would not have run away but I can tell you this, should you provide me with the heir I desire, you will be most comfortable. And no, I do not wish to call off the wedding. It shall go on as planned. As to the letters," he stood now to his full height, "we will talk about that and about your companion at a later time. I have paid too much for this special license to let it drop now." He paused. "My cousin will be here shortly to escort you to the church."

He turned then and left the room. My heart continued to pound as I stared at the door. I was alone with my sense of dread again.

Percy came within the hour and assisted me down the stairs to the garden path, and towards the small open carriage which would take me to the church. I probably could have walked on my own now that the wrappings were off my foot but it was just as well, I thought, for Penporth to believe that his bride was still injured.

As Percy helped me into the vehicle, I had a very nervous moment. He stared at me just for a second and then he took my hand in his. "You are so very beautiful, Cousin Tamara. You remind me of Julian's first wife. But then, all brides look fetching. I wonder if your beauty is merely skin deep or if you truly have a heart. I have a favor to ask of you."

"A favor of me?" I was puzzled. "What could you possibly want from me, Percy?"

He lowered his eyes a bit, his hand clung to mine like a man hanging on to a lifeboat. "I must ask you . . . ask you not to mention seeing me on the train. You have not yet said anything to Julian, have you?" He looked up again with those little boy eyes. I shook my head.

"No. I have not." My whole body seemed to tremble, wondering what this was coming to.

"Oh, that is marvelous." Percy's eyes lit up and he clapped his hands. The relief in his face was a joy to see. "Promise me truly that you will not breathe a word of this to him. He does not like my being in London. He does not think I travel in the proper society."

"But Percy what were you doing on that train then, if it was not on business for your cousin?"

He glanced away then. "Saying goodbye to a friend." He turned and grasped my hand more feverishly than before. "If you speak one word of this to Julian, it will doom me. He. . .he will cut me off utterly."

Not knowing what to do, I pressed my lips together and nodded. "Of course I will not say anything." My own heart thumping with relief that I would not have to worry about Percy exposing me completely overwhelmed my earlier fears. Only as he again took my hand and leaned over to kiss my cheek did I wonder what it was that Percy had involved himself in. I should not have allowed such a liberty and vowed it would not happen again.

All the way to the church as we bumped along the road, I could not help staring at him. Thank goodness that he was concentrating on the road before us and therefore did not, I think, notice my concern.

Only as we reached a smoother portion of the road did I recall what exactly was to happen shortly. It was Percy, himself, who forced me to think of the matter when he again mentioned Jennifer and how she, too, had been silent on the trip to the church.

I wondered then if he really did see a resemblance between the two of us. I hoped he did not. I hoped more earnestly that Lord Penporth did not.

Julian Hawley was already waiting at the town kirk. As Jennifer had related, it was a stone Norman church in the center of the town. The green itself was surrounded by crude homes — smaller than I was used to. Flowers and bees were in profusion this lovely morning. It would have been a perfect day — were it not "my wedding."

The whole of the island population had turned out for this occasion but instead of being with his people as I would have expected, Penporth stood apart in kirkyard. He was dressed in grey trousers, vest and with a frock coat of the same color. He did not look much like a happy bridegroom but then I was not a happy bride. Indeed, Percival at my side — in his slim morning coat with the long velvet collar and square pockets, and with his striped trousers — seemed to be much more the groom. It was like seeing beauty and the beast.

As we drove nearer, I saw that his lordship was standing in front of a headstone that in comparison to the others looked new. He bent over and arranged some flowers in a reverent fashion. The action touched me and seeded a doubt. Was Julian Hawley really as evil as he looked?

"Whose grave is that?" I asked Percy. "His mother's?"

Percy gave me a swift look and I felt immediately that he wanted to protect me from hurt. My good Percy. "No. That is the grave of his first wife."

"She . . . she died recently, then?" The shock on my face must have been plain. "But I thought you told me she ran away?"

"Then you know the story of his previous marriage." His hands were so close to mine and though we did not touch I could feel the warmth from him to me.

"Only . . . only that he was wed before and that there is confusion about . . . about Jennifer's last days."

My companion nodded. "That is exactly what it is. Confusion. No one knows actually when or if she is dead. She simply disappeared and left the island one day. A boat was found drifting and Julian assumed that she had fallen into the sea during a storm that night. To be fair, I do think that he mourned her a bit and that is the reason he had the special grave done up. 'Tis but a mock, you know. That's really why the special license was necessary—to have Jennifer declared dead."

"But. . .but what if she is not dead. He can't marry me then."

"Oh, she is dead." Percy assured me with a chill that went down my spine. "There is no way she could have survived going out on that night."

"But surely . . . why would she take a boat across if she could not handle it?"

He shrugged. "Desperation? You must ask Julian for that answer. All I know is that they had a dreadful quarrel just hours before the storm broke. She probably did not even realize that the storm was coming."

I was silent now. I did not dare ask but I did see that Penporth was so consumed with guilt at having murdered her that he felt it necessary to pay homage as a bereaved widower. He could not be so sure of her demise unless he, himself, had a hand in it, I told myself.

My own hands tightened on the side of the cart. How cold I felt—even with the bright shining sun and the birds merrily chirping. The feel of doom seemed to be closing in on me here.

I recalled now the dream I had had the night before coming here. It had been a dream about Jennifer and me and a shadow that hung over both of us. It was the same shadow that now threatened to engulf me.

I had come here sensing that my sister had been murdered, yet, somehow I had hoped to find that that was not the case. I had hoped and prayed that she was yet alive but what further proof did I need. Here on this island was her grave. Even though she did not repose beneath that stone — though perhaps she did and Percy did not know — it was enough for me to know that Lord Penporth had murdered her. If only I had been able to locate this yesterday then I would not now be in this predicament.

All the hatred I felt for Penporth now culminated in an ache worse than I had ever experienced. My temples throbbed with the intensity of my thoughts. Even as he walked forward to greet us all I could see was red. If only I had that knife here I would have plunged it directly into his heart.

Tears prickled my eyelids and I wiped them away with the handkerchief that Percy handed me. I was aware that he was watching me closely, perhaps too closely. Well, as long as he did not call upon me to explain, it did not matter to me what he thought.

Penporth was almost upon us. I took a deep breath to steady my nerves and looked into his dark eyes. It was for Jennifer's sake that I had begun this masque and for her sake, I was determined I would continue — until I could see justice done. I steeled myself as he took my arm to help me down. My knees seemed to buckle as I slid off the vehicle.

As before, he caught me and supported me with his strong hands. I could not help but wonder now if these strong hands had also perhaps strangled the life out of Jenny?

"You are all right?" He peered down at me and I felt like one of Mr. Trewyan's fish, caught at the end of the hook and about to be torn apart. I swallowed hard and nodded.

"I am fine."

"Good. Then let us get this done with." He gave a nod of his head and those still standing outside — presumably to get a first glimpse of me, the bride — filed in.

From the recess of the church, I could hear a violin playing. It moved me so that fresh tears came to my eyes, veiling my vision.

Confident of his own power, he took my elbow and guided me along the short gravel path into the kirk. Laura thrust a bouquet of red and yellow flowers into my hands. They were too beautiful to be used this way, I thought, but I held them all the same.

The kirk was cool and dimly lit by the two windows on either side of the altar. I swallowed and the saliva that had built up in my throat managed to get past the lump and the dryness but I could not stop the churning in my stomach. My heart beat seemed to echo loudly in the tall cavern about me. I prayed that I was doing the right thing; that Jennifer, wherever she was, was watching over me. As we began to walk up the shabbily carpeted aisle, my heartbeat quickened and seemed to echo loudly in the cavern about me. I noticed the Granny off to one side. Were people truly afraid of her abilities? There were, including Laura, Percival, and Mrs. Stewart, an audience of about twenty-three. I was sure that Jennifer had told me there were more on the island but that was not a concern now.

With Penporth holding me tightly to his side, I was forced to keep my focus on the short service. Numbly, I listened to the words, nodding when the minister did but only after Penporth nudged me.

When it was finally required for me to respond I did so but my voice sounded hollow and far away (as I wished I were). My thoughts turned to the grave outside. Would my being here do any good at all? If only I had listened to Thomas and stayed at home!

After the service, I was carried by my "husband" back to the pony trap. It was just as well for I do not think I could have stood much longer.

Silently, he arranged my dress and slipped onto the seat beside me as the people issued out of the kirk. It was that instant when a ragamuffin child of not more than seven or eight — the kind you might find in Cannongate or the East End — ran up to us. She threw something at us and yelled, "May you rue the day you re-married."

Before I could say anything or before Penporth could catch her she scampered off, headed for the woods. No one moved. No one did anything but whisper.

"Who was that child?" Penporth thundered as he stood now in front of the trap.

Not a one knew. Then the Granny came forth. "She be one of the wee folk, Master. The signs 'r there. 'ee shouldna 'ave married so soon."

"Stuff and nonsense!" Lord Julian cried, his face an angry contortion. "That child is as alive as I am and she was hired by someone to do this. Percival?"

Percy rolled his eyes heavenward. "Oh, come now, Cuz. You know that I could never do anything like that, Julian." He leaned against the well, his blue eyes wide with the accusation but he kept his hands in his pockets . . . "Besides, as you say, it is all stuff and nonsense. Why not forget it all and have the wedding feast." He licked his lips in anticipation of the food.

The others murmured their agreement though I did notice some distance now among the group. Penporth grunted and climbed back into the trap with me. Nodding, he picked up the reins.

"I hope you do not believe in all that rubbish," he said turning to me.

I shook my head but nevertheless I was more upset than I cared to admit.

A generous buffet had been set up in the main hall of the house. Mrs. Stewart had outdone herself in preparing pickled vegetables, meats, fowls, fruits, cakes, and pastries. It all looked luscious but my appetite had left me. Others came from the surrounding islands now to offer congratulations. For the first time I met Mr. Dorrien-Smith, the Lord Proprietor and heir of the Augustus Smith family. Now owner of Tresco Abbey, he was also the closest thing to law on the islands. I learned then, too, just how it was that Penporth Island had been lost to the group. The first Lord Penporth had apparently won it in a gambling debt with the original island owner, the Duke of Cornwall, who in the 30's had given up his lease on the lands here. I tried to talk to the Lord Proprietor alone but alas each time I saw him, he and Penporth were deep in conversation or laughing together as old school chums might. I knew then that my mission to get information and blacken Penporth's name would not succeed here. He would probably no sooner believe my tale than would the constable of St. Mary's. No, I needed to get more information before I could leave. Then, I could go to Scotland Yard.

I smiled up at Percy who brought me a plate of food. With the lively dancing of the reels, it was almost a shame that I could not partake. I would have loved to have joined in. It was dear Percy who kept my glass of wine filled and my thoughts occupied so that I would not think of later, or of the painful things that were coming to me now. I could only pause to wonder what Jennifer had thought of her wedding day and if it was anything at all like this. Did she dread the moment to come as I did?

If so, I knew she would not have said anything for it was not in her sweet nature.

At Percy's insistence, I hobbled about to welcome several of the guests. I wondered that they did not comment that I was not a very happy bride. How could others be so joyous at this occasion. Ah, if only I had walked forward eagerly; if only I had joined hands with a man that I truly and dearly loved to spend my life with.

The festivities seemed to continue on well into the evening. About tea time, I went up to my room to change. My face was flushed from heat and drink. Rinsing in the warm water, I cooled myself and allowed Laura to assist me with the tea gown of pale mint green. I did not look at the bed, so prominent with its bedcovers pulled back, but I could feel the tension within me growing.

The first guests did not leave until half past nine. Others seemed to remain for whatever food they could still obtain. All during the afternoon, Penporth had paid no attention to me. Could I — dared I hope? Even though it was early, I took the opportunity to return to my — to our — room.

Changing to my night dress, I brushed out my hair with a nervous vigor that almost tore it from the roots. The immediate problem now surfaced. How would I avoid contact with that odious man. I knew it would do no good to lock the door. That would only infuriate him but there had to be a way.

Idly, my hand played with my toilet articles and touched the bottle of medicine which the Granny had left behind. I then recalled the laudanum which the schoolmistress had given me before I had left. To calm my nerves, she had said. Well, if I needed calming, it was now but in truth I had no intention of taking anything. Still, if Penporth were to think. . . .

Now ready for bed, I poured part of the medicine into a cup at the bedstand and then, giving it a moment to dirty the glass, I spilled the contents out the window. Yes, I thought, as I examined the glass, it looked as if I had drunk some.

Once in bed, with the lights out, I lay back and tried to think. It was early yet but with luck, he would notice my disappearance and come up soon.

I was right. He did not wait long for soon I heard his heavy step on the stair. Rolling on my side, I feigned sleep. The door opened with a loud creak and the light flared brightly as he adjusted the gas. Having lain there in the darkness for so long, it was difficult not to blink and open my eyes . . . not at least to peek at his reactions, but I resisted.

The floor boards groaned with his weight as he moved over towards me. "Tamara?" He spoke softly, touching my shoulder.

I did not respond but forced myself to continue breathing steadily.

There was a silence. I do believe it was then he saw the glass. I wished I could have seen his face but that was impossible. He murmured something that sounded vaguely like a curse and then more clearly, as if he was not quite sure I was asleep or not, he said, "There will be other nights, my dear girl. You shan't avoid your husband for long."

With that, he adjusted the covers over me and turning down the gas, left the room.

I waited then, outwardly motionless for some time but inwardly quaking with more fear than the previous night.

Finally, I dared stir and turned on my other side. The bottle of medicine and the glass were gone. He was going to see that I did not use that trick again. Well, I would not need it, if my plans worked out.

Except for the chiming of the grandfather clock, the house had the same doomed silence as it had that first night. Escape, I realized now, was my only hope. I had not the courage to see this "wedding night" through—even for the three weeks or so that might be necessary to gain the information about Jennifer. I would have to admit that I was wrong in coming here and mourn my sister in my own way. I was sure, if I could reach London, Tamara could find a place for me. She had said that she would.

Still in darkness, I slipped from the bed and dressed hastily. I hated having to put on my lovely mint green but it was what I had left out from earlier and I could not now be bothered to find another outfit.

As I began to do up the buttons, there was a sound in the hall. Footsteps! My heart raced and rushed the blood to my brain as frantically I looked for a place to hide, praying that it was not Penporth come again to check on me.

Petrified, I remained where I was, scarcely breathing.

The steps passed the door and with a relief, I recognized the low whistle of my friend, Percy. He would, I believed, sympathize with my plight. Even if he saw me, I did not believe that Percy would turn me in. Nevertheless, it was not a chance that I wished to take.

When finally I had dressed, I took my shawl from the chest and went towards the door. The rest of the luggage could stay here. Perhaps once he saw that I was not returning, he would be good enough to send the clothes on. The only things I had taken were my reticule and my sister's letters. Those I would not give up on any account since it seemed they were the last things of hers that I possessed. Besides, it would be necessary to show these to the constable. Why had I not just gone to Scotland Yard in the beginning? It would have, I believe now, been far easier.

The hall was silent. I listened there for a good few moments before I opened the door and peered out. The gas burners were on the very lowest of flames. There seemed no one about.

Taking a deep breath to steady myself, I gathered my courage as I gathered my shawl. Quickly and quietly I hobbled down the hall and to the stairs. Which room had Penporth chosen to use this night? Had I already passed it? I was sure that he could hear the beating of my heart as it raced in fear, echoing loudly in the empty corridor. I knew that that was the only sound I was hearing!

No one was in the lower rooms, either as I crept steathily past them. I was able to reach the front doors without trouble and gave a silent prayer. No one, thank goodness, had bothered to lock the door.

Once out in the moonless night with the stars glittering their greeting, I turned toward the path we had taken this morning. It was necessary for me to cut through the town to get to the quay where the fishing boats would be. I did not like the danger of the townsfolk seeing me, yet I had to risk it rather than be lost as I had been before.

My ankle was again throbbing. Well, when I reached the mainland, I would have a real doctor look at it.

It was difficult to follow the path in the darkness. I stumbled more than once and very nearly lost my way in the brush. Twice I had to retrace my steps, praying that I would not again fall into the quagmire.

The moon had come up now and gave me some light but it was not enough. For moments there, it seemed as if my quest was hopeless. Had I not been so afraid, I think I might have stopped there and just cried, but fear of what lay behind me if I were found out, forced me on.

Just when it seemed as if I would truly have to give up, the town came into view. There were still lights on in many of the huts. I hoped that none of them would see me. The thought had only occurred to me when a woman came to the door to shake out a rug. I do not think she noticed me for her lights went out almost immediately afterwards. As fast as my sore foot would carry me, I walked through the town. At the other end, beyond the church, was the Granny's cottage. I recognized it by the fact that, like her, it stood alone. Like her, it seemed old and in need of vast repairs, yet it stood against the weather that bombarded it from the sea just like the old woman herself.

Only as I approached, did I see her sitting on the front steps. My heart stopped as she called out, "Nice night, M'Lady."

How, I wondered, had she known that it was I?

Certainly, I was too far away for her to see my features, for her to see anything but my shadow and my shawl covered my face. There was nothing, it seemed, that I could do except to nod back.

"Yes, it is," I responded. "I just thought I would take a stroll."

"Yes. Nice night," she said again. "Only do be careful of that foot of yours."

I nodded, watching to see that she stayed where she was. Unless Penporth, too, had the power to read her thoughts, she at least did not leave to inform him. I breathed easier as she went inside.

Quickly, I walked past her and behind her hut to where the quay was. There were no windows on this side of her hut and none of the other windows from here seemed lit.

I hurried toward the boats. They bobbed up and down on the incoming tide, beckoning me. Most of them would have been too large for me to handle on my own—besides, I knew nothing really about boating. Only once had I rowed and that was on a calm lagoon with Tom and Jenny.

At last I saw a boat which seemed perfect for me. Even the name was perfect. It was called, "MY GOOD JENNIE". It seemed to be an omen. Less cautious now, I hurried forward. Jenny had brought me to this island and *The Jennie* would take me out. I would row as far as St. Mary's and then take the steamer packet from there. Someone would surely return the boat from there to its rightful owner here. If I could have trusted anyone, I would have hired him to row me across but as it was I could not be certain how the tenants felt about his lordship. Somehow, I doubted that they would take my side against him.

Having made my decision, I stepped onto the rough little pier and was about to get into the boat when from behind me I heard, "Tamara, my dear, I'm so glad that your foot is better and that you are awake enough to take a stroll."

I turned to face "my husband," Lord Julian Hawley, scowling at me. His scar was outlined in the moonlight. The smile on his lips now seemed to cut through my heart like a vampire's fangs at my throat. I shivered.

"Uh, yes. I . . . woke suddenly . . . and felt that I needed . . . some air."

"There are plenty of places nearer to the house that you could have walked, my dear. There is, in fact, a lovely little garden."

"I'm sure of that but you forget that I am new to the island. This . . . this is the only path I knew."

"Except the one which you got lost on." He smiled again. He did not accept my excuse but then I had not expected that he would. He extended his hand. "It is nearly two in the morning, my dear. I know that I am now very tired. If you have had enough air, we should go back to the house *now*."

He said those words to brook no fight from me and as he came forth, I gingerly gave him my hand. There seemed little else for me to do and I cursed my luck for having run into the Granny. Maybe in addition to his other evil ways, he also practiced witchcraft. How else could she have communicated to him?

She stood in the doorway, nodding to us both as we passed. It was as if she had expected to see us — a loving couple on an evening stroll. Only we were not a loving couple and this was not just an evening stroll.

I was thankful, at least, that Penporth had brought the pony trap. Having come this far on my own, I did not think I could have walked the distance back to the manor — no matter how short.

After helping me into the trap, he returned to the house of the first woman I had passed. Only then did I realize that it had been she who had informed on me. I watched, anger welling up in me, as he handed her the coins. I supposed I should have expected as much.

Restless, I shifted my position in the carriage. The horse neighed impatiently and Julian Hawley turned about almost immediately aware of my movements. He was again by my side almost instantly — though he should have had nothing to fear. On this island, on his island, I could go no where without his knowledge.

Nothing further was said about my attempted escape or about the potion that I had supposedly drunk. We drew up outside the house and I was glad that no one was about. He swooped me up into his strong arms, giving me no time to get off myself, and carried me into the hall, up the stairs and into our room. I did not fight as I had before. It seemed this time there was no use.

Silently, he placed me on the bed and then

turned to lock the door. I heard the fatal click and my heart thumped with fear. I glanced about the room. There was no place I could go to. No place I could escape to. Only the smallest glow remained in the gas lamp. It was his shadow that I had seen in the dream hanging over my sister; his shadow which now tormented me.

He began to remove his clothes.

"What . . . what are you doing?" I asked, petrified as I tried to leave the bed, yet unable to keep my eyes off him.

"Get back into bed."

"No. I am not yet tired. I slept earlier," I lied, swinging my feet over the edge rebelliously.

"Do you intend to deny me my rights, Tamara? I am, as of this afternoon, your husband."

I stared at him not knowing what to say, feeling the pounding of my pulses. It was not enough that he had prevented my escape. It seemed that he was now going to humiliate me, as well.

"Please . . . do not. . ."

"Pray, why not?" He moved closer to the bed now. My stomach tightened.

Why not? Why not? There were trillions of reasons why not but most important was that I was not truly his wife. However, I could not tell him that, could I?

He put his arms about my shoulders and pulled me forward as I remained stiff and motionless. I felt his lips graze my brow and create a strange sensation there. My lips were dry. I licked them slightly as I tried to speak but the words failed me.

His thumb stroked my cheek as I tried to think and could not.

"If you can think of a reason why I should not become your husband this night, then tell me. I will listen."

I stared at him mutely.

"My dear young bride," his voice was husky in my ear, "I know you are scared. Indeed, your lack of education there does you credit. Be assured, child, I shall be gentle with you. I am not the ogre you seem to think me."

"But I . . ." My voice cracked as tears came to my eyes and he stroked them away with his fingers.

"In truth, it is a shame that your aunt did not speak with you of your duties before she sent you on your way."

I swallowed hard. "Please . . . I am . . . exhausted."

A patient smile touched his lips. "You said only now that you were not tired. You'll need to make up your mind better than that, Tamara, my bride." His thumb traced the bone of my cheek. I shivered once and then again as his lips brushed mine creating butterflies in my stomach.

"You will sleep better for it later. I guarantee that." He paused. "Come. Kiss me." His trousers were off now. My eyes focused momentarily on the bulge that was forming. It looked like a huge snake. Never before, not even when I had bathed Papa during his illness, had I seen a man. I felt my eyes widen in horror.

His hand touched my neck. "Come, sweetings.

Let me assist you to take off that dress."

I shook my head and freed myself of him. Going to the window, I glanced down at the surging sea with the white waves crashing in the darkness against the rocks. "Please, I beg of you," my voice was scarcely my own, "do not touch me. I . . . I pray you understand. This is not proper." I did not turn to him but continued looking at the sea. My eyes were closed. I wished he would disappear.

There was a horrid silence between us. For just that moment, it seemed as if he had, indeed gone.

I was about to utter a prayer of thankfulness, to open my eyes and turn again when I felt his presence behind me. There was no place I could move . . . not, that is, without falling.

Reaching behind me, he shut the window. Then, taking my hand, he drew me back with him to the bed but did not force me down. Instead, he engulfed me in his arms, holding me just like that.

Suddenly, I began to sob. Tears fell like the rain. This was not—none of it was—as I had expected my wedding night to be. How many times had Jennifer and I talked and dreamed of the men we would wed, of what this moment would be like. Neither of us knew anything except what we heard from the servants—but it had been enough to scare us both. I wondered then if my sister had been as frightened of him as I now was. Perhaps, innocent as she was then, she had not been. She had no reason to be then. She did not know, as I did now, what type of man he was. I recalled again our whispered secrets of the "naughty things" people did when they were in love — but I was not in love with this man nor did I ever expect to be.

His arms stayed about me. He was warm and strong. I did not even think as I laid my head against his hairy chest — crying still. His lips touched my eyelids. I knew then that there was nothing I could do but submit.

I was only vaguely aware of his hands as he removed the rest of my petticoats. I felt the breeze from the cracks in the window and realized now that we were both naked, that no matter what I did or said, he would have me — penetrate me with that painful stiff rod of his.

As once more I tried to pull back in fear, I found myself tumbling onto the bed. Tears once more came to me as he lifted the satin sheets to cover me and adjusted the pillows behind my head. For the life of me, I do not think I could have moved then — even though he disappeared to blow out the gas lamp.

I closed my eyes, feeling only the darkness about me. Could he have left?

The silence told me nothing.

Then, I heard the creak of the floor boards as he moved closer to me. The fear increased my panic as I felt his hand on my shoulder. I knew I was trembling like a newly caught fish and was grateful when he again took me into his arms and held me as the bed — where I had slept alone for the past two nights — now groaned with his weight.

I will not cry out! I told myself. *I will not cry out.*

I believe I must have repeated this at least a dozen times with my eyes still closed, unaware of his movements until I felt his hands stroking me, moving his calloused palms up and down the length of my body creating strange chills in me. Despite myself, I found my body moving closer to him.

"That is better," he whispered as his tongue touched my ear and his fingers touched my breasts, trailing down my waist. Inwardly, I wanted to scream but I would not. I could not. It would not do Jennifer's memory justice. I was sure that she had suffered in silence and so, I vowed, would I.

His breath was heavy on my neck as his tongue pricked my skin. He put his huge mouth over mine, forcing my lips apart. I do not know what it was I was doing but for the briefest moment, I put my arms about him, and allowed my tongue to touch his. It was a strange, yet pleasurable feeling. It almost felt natural to be in his arms — yet how could it, I told myself. How could I allow this to happen?

My hands seemed to have a life of their own as they stroked his thick dark hair. I did not want to do it and yet I did not want to just lie there.

I gasped as he lowered his mouth to my exposed nipples and I jerked toward him, feeling the marvelous sensation as his tongue sent waves of delight washing over my body. I gasped again at the wonderment his hands were creating touching me, stroking my lower body. The pulsating force he was causing made me want to cling to him, made me want to press closer to him — strange as it was. There was both pleasure and pain as I realized and tried to keep conscious of the fact that I should hate this man, that I should not like what he was doing to me — and yet I did.

The flush of shame covered me as I closed my eyes. I would not look at his face. I would not . . . "Oh. . . ."

The moan came from me. There was no other place it could have come from and yet I was not conscious of emitting it.

I clung tighter to him as if hanging onto a life raft in a storm but kept my eyes closed.

For one brief moment, I felt his body atop me. Opening my eyes, I looked up into his face.

"I will be gentle, my dear," he whispered huskily in my ear.

I could only stare at him, having only the vaguest idea of what he meant.

His mouth met and covered mine as I felt my legs being nudged further apart. I felt my eyes widen as . . . as there now came a sharp, searing pain. I wanted to gasp but could not as his mouth still covered mine, stilling my voice.

He plunged deeper into me as I clung to him — wishing, hoping, praying that that would be soon over and yet in only a moment I felt myself being carried away on a wave of pleasure as his thrusting now incited me to moan again. His mouth worked against mine as I realized that I was digging my fingers into his scalp, into his back and pressing myself against him for all I was worth like a shameless hussy.

As I felt the wave of pleasure rush over me, my eyes grew wet with tears. I had enjoyed it — and I was disgusted with myself for it, for him humiliating me. How I hated this man! I knew that I could never return to Tom soiled as I was. I knew that I could never marry anyone now. I was ruined and it was his fault.

I shut my eyes and tried to control the tears as I realized that it was not only his fault. For he did nothing but what could be expected of a new husband. The fault was mine for coming to this island under false pretenses. I knew at that moment that, like it or not, I was truly married to the man.

He had rolled off me. His hand trailed along my now cooled skin. I blinked the tears away and opened my eyes.

"I trust I did not hurt you too badly, Tamara."

I could scarcely believe it. His voice was almost gentle. His hand brushed against my nipples. I swallowed hard, embarrassed to see that they again hardened with his touch. How could my body respond to his touch as it did, knowing what I suspected of the man?

I did not answer him. Instead, I turned my head away.

"Never mind, my dear," he said, like a tutor instructing a pupil, "it will become better as time passes. I assure you that." He paused as his hand closed over mine. "Besides, it will only be until you can tell me that you carry my heir. At that time, I shall leave you alone if you still desire."

I still could not speak. My throat had closed off and ached with the cries in me, with the tears that welled up. I closed my eyes again and pretended to be asleep, praying that he would now leave me in peace. It seemed as though he intended to spend the night here with me in the bed — in his bed.

Stiffly, I lay, waiting for the rhythmic sound of his breathing and then with care not to wake him, I eased myself off the bed. Between my legs, there was a wet achy sensation. Was it this awful, this strange for every female? Had it been so for my poor sister?

Unable to remain in the bed, I rose and put on my robe that had fallen upon the floor in my hasty attempt to dress earlier. From under the mattress, I pulled forth the knife I had hidden yesterday.

The sharp steel gleamed in the moonlight. I glanced to the sleeping form on the bed. Relaxed, he almost looked innocent. I had again to remind myself that he had murdered my sister . . . that he had just now defiled me. The monster deserved to die.

I raised the knife and then realized that I could do nothing. Others might have the ability to take lives but I . . . I . . . could not. I would only bear my grief and find out, without a doubt, how he had lured my sister to her doom. Then, I would, without hesitation, joyously watch him hang. Ashamed of my own cowardice, I slipped the knife back into the mattress but I refused to sleep next to him.

Wearing only my dressing gown, I curled up on the lounge and fell asleep.

When I woke again it was nearly noon. I knew that because my stomach growled and the sun was high in the sky. I had been covered during the night — probably by Penporth, I assumed. Wincing, I recalled what happened.

I was just about to order a bath when one of the undermaids came in with a tray of food.

"I don't want anything," I said, eyeing the platters. In truth I was rather hungry but I felt in a perverse mood and did not want to satisfy his pleasure by knowing I had eaten.

"But M'Lady, his lordship says. . ."

"And I said, 'I do not want to eat.' Take it away."

The poor girl was utterly confused. Silently, she put the tray down and moved to change the sheet where my blood had stained it. I blushed hotly knowing what she must be thinking and lowered my eyes to the book which I pretended to be reading. It did not matter what she thought, I told myself. Soon the blood of her precious master would run and drench the earth as it seemed my sister's now did.

She disappeared. Still in my dressing gown, I sat down at the desk and began to brush my hair in front of the mirror.

It was not very long before I heard the heavy tread of steps in the hall. My brush paused in mid-air and I felt fear prickle my spine. As the door opened, I stiffened. He, himself, carried in the tray which I had just refused. I wondered then if he was going to try and poison me. It was probably an irrational thought but then I did not seem able to think properly in his presence.

"You slept well, I trust," he said, putting down the tray and coming to stand behind me.

I forced myself to continue with the brushing. The silver handle glinted in the mirror with the sunlight hitting it.

He stared at me — demanding a response, and so I gave a slight nod.

"Good." His hand touched my shoulder, making me stiffen. "I have brought up your breakfast — again, Tamara. Personally, I do not care if you do not wish to eat but as the mother of my child, you must keep in proper condition until then."

I pressed my lips together in frustration. Was that all he was concerned about? I wondered if he had killed my sister because she could not or would not bear him a child.

"I . . . I do not want anything. I am not hungry."

"I said, as the mother of my child, I insist you eat. Tomorrow, you will come down and join the rest of us."

"I said I will not eat." The brush was still in my hand. I threw it towards him — as if to make my point but all it did was infuriate him. He bent to pick up the brush. As he examined the handle, studying it in detail, I began to fear. I should not have thrown it. It had been a childish thing to do.

I was now petrified of his temper.

He glanced at me. The silence between us was terrifying.

"Beautiful workmanship," he commented finally. "Did they belong to your mother?"

I nodded, still not knowing what to expect. The brushes were the only items of my own that I had brought with me and I suddenly realized that Jennifer had also had a similar pair. Had I now given myself away?

I inhaled sharply as he came forward, brush still in hand. What did he intend to do? The boards creaked with his measured step. Holding myself stiffly I met his gaze.

"May I . . . may I have it back?" I swallowed hard.

He shrugged and raised it. I pulled back.

"Hold still. I should like to brush your hair." Swallowing hard, I felt my body go weak. That was not what I had expected. I nodded and allowed him to have his will.

Grudgingly, I had to admit that it felt good to have his powerful and yet somehow gentle fingers stroking my head. After a few moments, I had sufficiently recovered my courage to say, "Thank you. That is enough. I will put my hair up now."

"No, don't." He touched me again sending a shiver through me — a shiver that was not unlike the shameful feeling I had experienced last night.

I blushed hotly. "You have lovely hair — especially when it is loose and free. It reminds me . . . of someone else."

I pressed my lips in fear but said nothing. He

did not continue his thought. From his pocket, he withdrew a necklace of huge emeralds. They were lovely — and they matched my eyes — but I could not take them.

"This is your wedding gift, my dear," he said.

"From whom?" I was puzzled.

His hand touched my cheek. "From your devoted husband. Who else?" He placed the strand about my neck. For an instant, I had a brief sensation of choking. That was it! He had choked Jennifer with these!

I wanted to tear them off but could not. He was too strong.

He fastened them quickly and the heavy weight hung loosely about my neck giving off their sparkle in the light. Yes, my eyes did seem greener now.

"Please. I . . . I do not want them. I should much prefer the money . . . the thousand pounds which you promised my aunt."

"Don't be a fool, Tamara. Of course you will have them . . . and the money as well. Your aunt has already been sent her portion. I will give you a draft to deposit any way you wish before the end of the week."

I stared at him. If I had my way, I would be off this island before the end of the week. My mind told me yes but my instinct told me that that would not yet be.

"Please. I don't want them." I quickly undid the clasp and tossed them on the bed, next to the tray of food.

"You are being obstinate today, aren't you?"

"All I wish," I glared at him, "is to be left alone. I did not want to come here and . . ."

"But you have come and you are my wife. You shall also accept what I choose to give you."

I glanced at him through the mirror image and did not like his scowl. It made my heart patter with fear. I waited. Then, he reached out. His hand against my cheek. He stroked my neck causing a pleasant chill over and down my spine.

"I will brook no disobedience from you, my wife. I was far too tolerant of Jennifer. I shall not have you leaving me as she did." I could not move for fear that my actions would somehow betray me. I could not even meet his eyes in the mirror. My heartbeat quickened. I feared the consequences of being too bold in my rebellion. No, I did not want to leave him as I suspected Jennifer had—dead, or gone from this universe.

I did not move even when his lips grazed my cheek and my neck.

He took the jewels then and set them back in their case. My back was still stiffly upright and I was conscious of his eyes totally on me. Once more he bent his head, touching, caressing me. I shivered both from fear and . . . I am very much ashamed to say . . from the feeling that his kisses as he nibbled at my ear lobes were creating.

His voice was soft but held more meaning than I had yet heard from him. "I will brook no disobedience from you," he repeated once more as his hand rested on my exposed nipple, tugging, stroking and demanding its ready response. "You are my wife, Tamara. I will have you when I want you."

I did not speak. I could not. The strange sensations which had come over me last night were beginning to overwhelm me—fight them as I might.

"Turn and kiss me, Tamara," he commanded. "Be my obedient wife."

My heart pounded frantically. My mind spun. I did not want to obey him and yet I wanted very much to. Confusion tore at me.

"Turn and kiss me," he said again.

Like a statue, I did as he asked and saw that slight smile on his face as he bent his head and his lips brushed mine.

I do not recall the exact actions of those next few moments for I was lost in a haze of my own choosing. Once again, his mouth claimed me and I put my arms up to his neck, and felt myself being lifted from the chair. He must have removed my night dress but I did not realize the fact until I noticed that I was again on the bed.

For just that moment, the fear returned to me. It must have shown in my eyes. He stroked my brow. "Do not worry, my little bride. It will not be as painful this time."

That was all he said as his hands caressed me and drew me into the sinful, swirling pleasures. I closed my eyes so that I would not see the man before me, so that I would not think of what was being done to me. I felt . . . well, it was indescribable. There was no pain this time only . . . a sensation of swimming higher and higher on the cresting wave as we had done with the boat. The waves were rhythmic and the sense more powerful as he touched, tugged, caressed and tormented me. Still, I would not open my eyes.

My hands touched the hard muscle of his shoulders as I clung to him and felt myself being thrust forward into the tidal of pleasure.

In the distance I heard several low moans. Was that me? No, surely, it could not be. It would not do for me to even think of something so unladylike. Though I might have been a "tom boy" in my other gestures, I had always thought myself to be well trained here.

Again, I heard the moans as he nibbled my ear and brought me to the very top of the mountain. With eyes still closed, I pressed deeper towards him, feeling the distinct pressure of his entry and hearing myself gasp as the slight pain once again became pleasure and I fell with him into the eddies of whirling sensations and delights. The dark corridors seemed to claim me as I felt his breath warm and heavy on my neck.

Had he spent himself? Was he done?

This time I opened my eyes to see Hawley beside me.

He smiled at me, touching my lips with his fingertips gently. "You are learning, my little bride. Soon you will feel the passion, too. Soon you will be able to tell me that you carry my heir."

I stared mutely at him, not wanting to admit to either him or myself that indeed there had been pleasure in the past few moments. I wondered that he was not angry with me for the noises I had made so . . . hideously. Coupling was supposed to be a wife's duty. It was not, as our schoolmistress had taught us, anything for pleasure — and yet, rebellious as I was, it seemed that I had indeed found pleasure in it. Tears came to my eyes. It seemed that once more I was a failure here as in other things. I felt deeply ashamed of myself that I had not been able to prevent myself from crying out; that I had allowed my body to betray me with a man that I did not love.

Saying nothing more to me, he rose from the bed and kissed my brow. Only after the door closed did I allow myself the luxury of crying myself back to sleep.

I woke once more to find the food had gone and the emeralds neatly on the dressing table. I placed them in the drawer and dully rang for Laura's assistance so that I could dress for dinner.

"You'll excuse my saying so, Tamara, but you had best be careful about making Julian angry. He can be quite violent when his temper flares."

"Yes," I grimaced, "I am sure that is so." I closed my eyes still feeling the pressure of his body on mine — both hating it and yes, wishing again for it.

"His first wife did not take my suggestions to heart. I don't believe that she learned her lesson until it was too late."

I glanced sharply at the maid. "What do you mean?"

"Only that she often upset him."

I frowned.

Laura left the room before I could ask more. I glanced again toward the bed. Had Jennifer's body betrayed her as mine had? I stared at my image in the mirror. Forty-eight hours ago I had been a different woman. I was still the same Victoria Damien but now I was Victoria Damien Hawley and while I looked the same, I knew that I was not. Tears pricked my eyes as I again experienced disappointment in myself.

Going to the bed, I searched for the knife but it was gone. Who had taken it? Had Julian Hawley known it was there? The fright made me stiffen.

At dinner I ate very little. Even playing with the food as I did, I could feel Penporth's eyes upon me. Once I looked up and once our gaze met. That was enough for me to blush hotly and look away.

Percy had already gone into the lounge for coffee. I stood as my husband came to stand near me.

"Please," I said without glancing up, "I should rather return to my . . . to our . . . room." The words choked. "My head aches."

"I am sorry about that." His hand touched my cheek. "Shall I send for the Granny to give a powder?"

I shook my head violently. "No. I believe a good night's sleep will do it."

His lips were a tight line. "As you wish, Tamara." Then he thrust an envelope into my hand.

"What is this?" I looked up for the first time to see those unreadable black eyes.

"The money I have promised you, It is your draft for 1,000 pounds. I believe that is what was agreed upon."

I sucked in my breath. I did not want to accept the money but I knew that I would desperately need it when I left the island. Nodding, I took the envelope from him and hurried up the stairs.

Once in the safety of the room, I opened the letter. He had scribbled a note to the effect that there would be more once the baby had come. But there would be no baby. There could not be.

Pausing only a moment, I sat down to write Tamara. It would, I hoped, go off in tomorrow's post. I enclosed the check for her and told her to be careful with it. It was unnecessary for me to give her the sordid details of my life here for I knew that would only trouble her so I said nothing, only that it seemed as if I would be here longer than we first had planned.

Now my problem was to get the letter off the island without Julian Hawley or Percy seeing it.

Chapter Seven

He did not come up to the bedroom that night. I told myself that I was grateful for that and fell into a light sleep, unable to become comfortable.

During the night, I woke and thinking that I heard flute music went to the window. The sounds were soft and sad as my sister had written they would be. She had not told me who played such a haunting tune and I could not guess.

The robe was by my bed. I pulled it on and opened the window further so that I might guess the identity of the player. For that moment I was mesmerized not only by the brilliant white moon playing but also by the crashing of the waves as they hit the rocky shore below me. Despite all I had heard about night air, I took a deep breath and felt more relaxed than I had since coming to this place.

Sounds of the flute again wafted about me bringing tears to my eyes. Who was it? Percy? One of the men? Perhaps it was one of the woodland nymphs that the Granny had spoken about. No, I did not believe in those.

The branches of the trees moved gently with the breeze and the tones continued to soothe me as I sank into the window seat. It must have been a good hour before I realized how long I had been listening. My eyes were again heavy with sleep but all I could think of was who that mysterious player was.

The music continued for another half an hour. I was still listening to the sounds of the sea when I realized that it had stopped. In a melancholy mood, I moved back to the bed and dreamed of colors surrounding me.

Despite my restless night, I woke early. It was, I believe, about half past six.

No one else appeared to be up.

Dressing in a simple cotton gown, I went down stairs but of course the table was not yet laid.

On my own, I located the kitchens in the cellar of the house. I could have fixed the fire and made tea but I did not want to stay about in case Penporth should come down. I had already learned that like me he was an early riser. In the end, I settled for two large slices of coarse bread spread thick with butter and fresh strawberry jam.

Then, determined to be out of this house, I left by the back entrance. This time, I chose a path that from the description in Jennifer's letters would lead me to the pond.

Even for the early hour, it was warm and yet invigorating. As I stepped along, I began to feel more vital than I had since coming here. I even began to hum. It was, I soon realized, the song that the flutist had been playing. I told myself that the lightness of my spirit grew, being away from that man but in truth I could not say if that were so.

Watching the light playing off the thick leaves of the trees and the dew sparkling like the emeralds now in my dresser drawer, I could not help but think of him. Well, being away from him for several hours should help, I told myself as I continued through the magical tunnel formed by the grove of trees.

As Jennifer had described, I heard the twitter and chirp of the birds and the murmur of the water. But even though I knew of the pond's existence, I was not prepared for the serene beauty of the spot. My breath caught in my throat and I sank onto a nearby rock from whence I could absorb the pure blueness of the sky reflected in the calm ripples of the water. Even the fish were perfection in shape and form. Like the music last night, the silence that enveloped me was healing my hurts. I no longer felt harassed by this island. I knew that when I felt unable to deal with Lord Penporth, I could come here. This had been Jennifer's spot as it was now mine. My heart was here on this very rock with her.

Closing my eyes, I prayed, "Oh, Jenny, Jenny. Give me some clue as to what happened to you — and help me to deal with this situation as best I can."

I waited a moment and heard nothing but the calmness remained.

It was strange how loneliness was the one thing in life that I feared and yet even in Edinburgh it was the lonely walks on the Crags that used to draw me, summon me to go to them and share their isolation. I had here a feeling of separateness, of being suspended in time from the pavements of Edinburgh and London. Even Penzance seemed millions of miles away. I was filled with a stupid aching—a longing to be held and loved like a normal girl. What would happen to me? Would Tom take me back and marry me—once this charade was over? No, I had already acknowledged that I did not love him but there was no one else I could think to turn to.

With a suddenness I remembered the nightmares that had plagued me the past year. The dreams had been of Jenny walking by this pond and the shadows that hung over her had frightened me.

It had been those dreams which had propelled me to risk my life and come here. Anxiously, I glanced about but could see nothing evil in this place . . . nothing that would cause the terror I had felt. Was it, as Thomas had told me, just my own version of Jennifer's letters. Momentarily, the place had lost its peaceful touch for me. I decided to move on. Later, when the unease had left I would return and see if I could find some clue of my sister that I now missed.

The path on the other side of the pond led towards the western shore. I looked across the rocks and St. Agnes. The grass above on the short cliffs was coarse. Gulls worked in and out among the moving seas. Far out, toward Bishop Rock where the main lighthouse stood, where the ships could see the last fragment of England as they were washed over by the cold ocean, I could now see a lone vessel.

With the wind blowing my hair free, I glanced about at the brilliant gorse and rocks and boulders in various shapes. My imagination being what it was, I instilled the lives of past centuries into these forms. There was so much here to dwell on without thinking a morbid thought. No, I would not remain here now. I wanted to sit and think but also I wanted to explore as much of this island as I could. Somehow, somewhere, I would find information that would lead me to Jennifer.

Continuing on the path, I discovered yet another lone cottage. Its thatched roof was solid and the garden seemed well tended, yet it was quite a walk from the village. It seemed improbable that anyone would actually live on this lovely finger of the island yet as I watched, the curtains of the top floor seemed to sway. No wind had blown just them. I could only assume that someone was there.

I walked up the neat gravel path and knocked at the door. No one answered but determination to seek out everyone I possibly could, propelled me on. The door squeaked as I opened it and I came face to face with a grandfather clock—its cherry wood cabinet and gilded pendulum bearing a clipper ship under full sail. This wasn't an ordinary tenant's cottage.

"Hello? Is anyone at home?" I called out.

There was no reply. I saw a table near the window with a lace cloth upon it and candlesticks. The place setting was for two. Cozy little corner, I thought, as I edged forward. Over the mantelpiece in the darkest part of the room was a daguerreotype of a couple on their wedding day. I stepped over to look at it and could not help but think of my own wedding so recently.

The girl wore a full tulle veil held by rosettes on either side of her head. She was big busted but her hips were slender. There was an eager inquisitive look upon her face, directed fully at the camera. Her man was dark with a full moustache and very solidly built. A few inches shorter than his bride, he had black eyes which seemed to look away into the distance of sunlit waters.

He wore the uniform of a ship's captain. I was struck by the amazing resemblance between him and Lord Julian.

From above me, there was a creak of wood. Someone was up there! Was it Jennifer? Was she perhaps being held a prisoner? Or was it something else that I should fear?

I felt eyes upon me, watching me, and an uneasy sensation crept up my spine; my stomach knotted. Should I leave? I was trespassing and yet no one had answered. As Lord Penporth's wife, I was Lady of the Island and therefore had a right to know "my people." How odd that sounded? Besides, I was intrigued by the obviously higher standard of this cottage. If the person up above wanted me gone, then he should say so. I put my hand on the rail and felt fear. Perhaps . . . no, it couldn't be a trap. Yet as I crept up the worn stairs, I felt like a child of nine, scared of her own shadow. The house seemed to groan as I walked up. I could hear things scuttling about me away from the opposite side of the wall. I kept thinking that I heard footsteps behind me but I was too frightened to turn about.

At the top of the stairs, I paused. There was only one door. Its knob was well tarnished as if many hands had gripped it. Quite suddenly, there was a tiny voice. "Who's there?"

At first I thought I had imagined it but the high falsetto came again. "Jonathan, dear, is that you? Have you come home?"

Like a woman in pain, the door gave a scream as it opened. I wanted to run but I had come this far. I would not leave. Before me by the wide window seat was a white-haired woman with brilliant blue eyes and skin that was remarkably clear. The rest of the room was simply yet elegantly furnished with a huge fourposter bed, an occasional table, and two chairs by the fireplace.

"No. You aren't my Jonathan, are you? Who are you?"

I began to answer.

"Never mind. I know who you are. You're the new one. He did not say you were coming today. I would have had tea."

She looked at my hair. Pehaps I had a leaf or two caught in it for she continued, "You've been by the trees, haven't you. Lovely trees. She liked them, too. They killed her in the end."

"Who killed her?"

The woman ignored my questions and went on. I felt suddenly as if I was not standing there in that bright sunlit room but back home with Papa as he hallucinated in his fevers.

"She was prettier than you. She was beautiful." I should have objected to the comparison between Jennifer and myself but I did not.

The woman came forward with a tottering step and I ran to catch her, lest she fall. She clung to me with a strength that outshone my own. It was a tough, wiry strength of the type that one would need on such an island as this. The old woman, I was realizing, was harmless. Her hands, bony fingers, reached out and journeyed over my face as if seeing through her fingers like the blind.

"You'll do," she grimaced. "No one, mind you, expected you to be beautiful. Do you want some tea now? Be careful when you go home through the woods. It was the trees which killed her."

"Please," I said, taking the narrow hand in mine, "tell me what you know of the other Lady Hawley?"

"Ah!" She laughed—it was like a witch's cackle. "There were plenty of Lady Hawleys. Which one shall I tell you about?"

Before I could speak I was startled to hear footsteps below. This time I did not have to imagine them.

"Jonathan? Jonathan, is that you?"

"No, Aunt," came the response. It was the

voice I had grown to hate. His heavy steps trod the stair. I tried to press back into the corner but her hand held me like a claw now, grabbing hold of me so that I could not run free.

"Oh, hello." He eyed me quickly. "You've met my great aunt Margaret, then, Tamara?"

I could only nod.

"She is extraordinarily small for her age and she is plainer but . . ." the aunt began.

"Oh, but will she do?" he asked her.

Margaret rubbed the tip of her nose with an ivory fan that had lain in her lap. "She should do. She has a charming expression. Rightly considered, if she had more fashionable clothes and ate a bit more, I do believe . . . are her hips wide enough? Her eyes are like the other's. Are you careful of the woods, Julian? Did you bring my fruit?"

"Yes, Aunt, quite careful." He bent to kiss her and I took the opportunity to leave the room. I was not going to be poked and prodded like a horse at an auction.

Halfway down the stairs, I heard him coming after me. I did not want to speak with him but he caught up with me all the same.

"You must excuse my aunt, Tamara. She sometimes forgets and rambles on but she means no harm."

I was silent a moment. Perhaps I could forgive her but not him. "She told me that your first wife had been murdered."

"I have told you. Aunt sometimes talks without thinking." His voice was cold. "Wait here. I shall walk you back." He turned on me and began to go up the stairs. Having no intention of waiting for him, I continued down. I did not think he would come after me again but he did. His hand grasped the upper part of my arm.

"You are hurting me."

"I said you were to wait for me and you will do as I say. The island may be small but you have already become lost once." Those cool black eyes seemed to search me—as if he, too, now noticed the similarity between me and my sister. "I have no wish to wait dinner a second time."

"Dinner? Is it that time already?"

"It is," he replied gruffly, gently pushing me down into a chair by the fireplace just opposite the picture. "Now will you stay or must I tie you down?"

I did not know if he would carry out his threat or not. "I . . . I will stay." How meek I sounded then, but he was quite frightening in his persuasion.

It took only a few minutes for him to run back up the stairs. I heard him say goodbye to his aunt and promise to see her the next day. Then he returned to me.

"Come, my dearest," he said with only the slightest hint of irony.

I glared at him, hating the mocking tone of his voice. I was determined that I would return and talk with the old aunt for I was sure she knew something of value to me.

He took my arm and led me out the door. As we walked along the strip of land that led back toward the path, I asked, "Why is it that she lives so far from the others? If she is your aunt, why does she not live at Hawley House?"

"Because," he said patiently, like a teacher explaining to a backward child, "she wishes to be by her husband's grave. He died at sea. She's convinced that he will come back for her one day soon and it will be from the sea."

"But surely . . ."

"Not all wives are so distasteful of their husband's affections. I see her every day. She lacks for nothing."

"What a dutiful nephew," I responded dully and pulled away. We were near the pond now. I had no wish to trespass upon my secret spot — upon Jennifer's enchanted place — with this defiler of young women beside me. Besides which, the aunt did have moments of lucidity and therefore what she had said about the murder having taken place by the trees might have some meaning. Surely, my dreams coincided with the fact.

Regardless, I had no wish to be with him and so ran ahead — pretending that he had gone. If I did not see him pass my rock . . . if I knew nothing of his presence there, then I could still have it be a sacred place for me.

He called after me but the way here was narrow and I ignored him. My fear of his evil influence over this lovely pond was stronger than my own worries of any physical violence.

Without mishap, I reached the path that led to the house. He caught up with me as I entered the door but said nary a word. Only his eyes, burning fiercely, told me of his anger.

I went up to my room to wash and change for the meal. I was famished but it was another hour yet before the food would be served. His footsteps echoed in the hall and for one horrifying moment, I thought he would again enter and claim "his rights."

He did not.

Laura came to call me and I went down as ordered. At least if they all ate, then it would be safe for me as well. My stomach now growled with unabashed hunger.

Not counting last night when I had eaten very little, this would be the first meal which I had shared with the family. Percy and Julian were already seated as I entered and I had to take the only available place, at the other end of the table, opposite him. His eyes were like ice picks boring their way through my skin. I looked away and turned my attention to the tomato soup which Laura was serving. I kept my eyes down, concentrating on the soup as if it were the most delicious food I'd ever tasted. They were both, I felt, staring at me. The one time I did look up, I caught his eyes upon me and then Percy's. I don't know which I minded more. Both of the men made me feel uncomfortable. I blushed and wondered how to alter this unnatural situation of one woman with two men.

When Laura entered the room carrying a tray of breads, I stopped her. "Put that down, please, and take a seat there." I pointed to the place across from Percy.

All three of them stared at me.

"Have I done something wrong, Lady Penporth?" She glanced over to Julian and then to Percy. He shrugged, slightly.

My resolution faltered a moment. "Indeed not, Laura, but I would feel more at ease with another woman at the table. Besides which, I gathered that you are more than just a servant. I should in the future wish you to take all your meals with us."

She again looked to Penporth but I dared not.

There was a deathly quiet. I wondered if I had gone too far. I was sure from the looks I had seen that she loved him. As to his feelings for her, I had not yet guessed . . . but then nothing about Julian Hawley seemed easy to guess at. The gas lights from the chandelier glimmered on the silver reflected our own features. It even seemed to bounce off the old wood — polished to a shine — taken from ships broken and sunk off the coast.

Percy broke the stillness. "Yes, that's a jolly good idea, Tammy. After all, it cannot do to have an uneven number."

A supporter! He understood, at least, how I felt. Still, I dared not look at my husband. My hand clenched the soup spoon. I began to feel as if I should never have said anything. She remained standing with the bread plate in her hands.

Then I heard a chuckle that startled me. He was playing with us!

"Well, Laura," he said, "Your mistress has given orders. I see no reason why they should not be obeyed."

For one who usually balked at taking commands, Laura seemed to move toward the empty place with an amazing speed. Smiling at me, she placed the bread platter on the table, rang for one of the under maids to do the serving, and then sat down. My sigh must have been audible.

We began to eat again and my thoughts were calmed that I, at least had been supported against Penporth now.

"I hear that you have been out to see the old lady," Percy said, as we were between courses. "A bit senile sometimes, Tammy. I should not take notice of her words."

Julian glanced at me. "That is exactly what I told her," he said.

"Nevertheless," I braved his black stare counting that he would not do anything with two witnesses present. "I still wish to know what happened to your first wife. Your aunt says that she was murdered and it was very possible that she saw something. Was she questioned by the authorities?"

It was Percy now who laughed. "Grandmama always used to read those pulp novels and now she believes herself to be in one. She saw nothing."

Penporth towered over the table now. The air about him seemed to vibrate and a thunderous look was in his eyes. "Whatever she did or did not see is not for discussion here. I do not wish to hear or talk about Jennifer's disappearance. I do not want it discussed."

He threw down his serviette on the table and left the room. The food was still on his platter.

We all waited until the noise of him died in the study. I was shaken by his reaction and for me it confirmed exactly what I had feared.

"Stupid, isn't it, for a man to be so infatuated with one woman. There's plenty about." Percy smiled at me and Laura now. "You realize, of course, that is why he chose to marry without courting you. That . . . and his looks."

I was not surprised that Penporth should have been somewhat hesitant about his physical appearance. He was not the type of man one would necessarily dream of having a romance with and yet, Percy's comment shocked me. "Are you telling me that he loved her? But he did not court her, either."

Percy's look made me realize that I had overstepped my bounds. "How would you know that?" He paused and tapped his fork against his plate. "Oh, yes, you went to school with her, did you not?"

I swallowed hard and nodded. "Yes, I did." I waited a moment forcing my heart to calm. "Did he love her, Percy?"

My new cousin shrugged and reached over to take another slab of the cold beef. "Julian is a hard person to understand. He was definitely infatuated with her. From the first moment that she arrived on the island. He could not believe that Grandmama's friend had sent him such a delightful creature. In fact, he rather reminded me of Othello. Probably that is why she ran away—

from his possessiveness, I mean. He would not let her out of his sight."

"But I thought . . ." I paused and realized that I could not reveal what her letters had told me without exposing myself. "I mean, do you think she would leave like that?"

He chewed thoughtfully but it was Laura who answered me. "She was a flighty, spendthrift beauty that accepted homage from men as tributes overdue. A girl like Jennifer needed the adoration of many admirers — more than even Julian or Percy could provide." She shrugged. "She was suffocating here."

I stared into my plate. I had never thought of my dear sister in those terms. I had never considered her to be flighty or indulged and yet it had been four long years since I had seen her. Could she have changed?

The food no longer appealed to me. I pushed my plate away. Perhaps Jennifer had run away but then where was she and what then was I doing as Tamara Nilston Hawley?

Chapter Eight

The tension continued for several more moments before Percy broke the silence by his laughter. Jollying Mrs. Stewart into bringing out her famous apple pie, he lightened everyone's spirits.

I was able to excuse myself and not wanting to return upstairs, I went into the music room. The wainscotted room reminded me of home, of when Jenny and I had played walnuts and oranges, trying to guess the initials of our true loves. Who would ever have thought that our lives would end up thus?

The room was empty and I had the urge to play the piano. It had been quite some time since I had done so — mainly because of Papa's illness. Before Jenny had left, I had played infrequently. She was so much more talented than I that I had not wanted to show off my ignorance. Still, knowing that here I faced the comparisons of first wife/second wife, I sat down on the stool.

My fingers stretched for the keys and were guided by an instinct all their own. It was a Chopin piece I played. I knew that much — though I had forgotten the title. The melody was halting, at first, but as my memory returned, the music danced out.

Suddenly, there were white slender hands about my shoulders. "Oh, that is lovely!" Percy exclaimed and before I could protest, his arms had gone about my waist and had whirled me out of the chair. He was humming the tune I had just played as he caught me up and to my amazement, we were dancing. I laughed — just for the joy of it. It was the first time I had done so in this house.

"Per . . . Percy, let me down."

"No. I shan't." He gave a mischievous smile and continued to spin me about. "I am happy and it is the 30th of April. Tonight is enchanted. Did you not know that, Tammy, love?" He smiled broadly and hummed another tune. I could only laugh more then as he twirled me again. I had the feeling of this all having happened before. No, not to me, but to Jenny. She had described such a scene in her letters. It was all completely the same — except for Penporth.

True to history, Hawley entered the room just at that moment. Percy refused to acknowledge his cousin's frown and continued to dance me about — smiling and humming to himself. For me, however, the sight of my husband had forced the gaiety out of the present. He seemed to have ruined everything.

Percy halted in front of him. "You really should take dance, Coz."

He glanced at me, his eyes seemed to sear me. "Perhaps one day, I shall." Turning on his heel, he left the room. I could see from the stiffness of his posture that he was upset — even if the slamming of the door had not told me. I stood for a moment regarding the door, puzzled. What was wrong with having a bit of fun?

Percy broke my concentration as he bowed before me in an exaggerated sweeping manner. "Another dance, my dear?" He moved closer. In fact, a bit too close for my comfort. "Perhaps, instead, you would like a walk in the moonlight?"

I turned toward him and forced myself to smile. Suddenly I was feeling very tired. "No, Percy, thank you. I believe I shall go up now."

"What? At only half past nine. The night is young yet. Surely, you jest. Let's not allow old Julian to spoil our pleasures."

I shook my head. No. I was not joking. I truly was tired. Giving him my best smile, I pulled my hand away from him. "Goodnight, Percy. I shall see you in the morning, I suppose." I started for the door, feeling his eyes upon me.

The bedroom was empty. I do not know what I expected but I guess I had hoped that he would be there — so I could talk to him. Yes, that was all I wanted to do. Talk to him.

I crawled into the empty bed and felt the coolness of the sheets. I thought of Percy and my sister. What had their relationship been? Had she walked with him in the moonlight?

I did sleep that night but I slept poorly and I slept alone.

The sky was dull and dreary when I woke. Just seeing the greyness made me feel gloomy. Coming down stairs to break my fast, I thought I would do some further explorations but Laura, who found me in the breakfast room, made it clear that she was determined to stay with me and sew.

Not until much later in the afternoon, with the gloom still heavy in the air, did I have the opportunity to escape her and tour the house. If anyone found me, my excuse was merely that I was trying to find my way about. After all, as lady of the house, I should know what the house held.

My heart pounded as I went into the library. I was doing nothing wrong, I told myself. Why then was I so nervous?

As a pretext, I chose a book and sat out in the gardens until I saw that Percy, Penporth, and Laura were all engaged in other tasks. Quickly and quietly then, I left the room and slipped upstairs.

No one had ever told me how to find the attic but I felt that that would be the best place to start my search. If anything of Jennifer's were left, it would be here, would it not?

I swallowed hard as I reached the third floor

and could find no obvious door. I knew an attic existed for I had heard the servants speak of it. My blood pounded as I moved forward.

It seemed that the floor boards, noisy as they were, would not keep my presence up here a secret for very long. Each groan of the wood was like a scream of warning. I was keenly aware of the fear that raced through me, tying my stomach in knots. Perhaps this was what Julian had heard the other night when I had tried to escape. After all, he had not seemed much surprised at seeing me out.

I reached the gas light in the hall. Heart still pounding, I turned it up. The sky was darker now and there was very little illumination here. I could see now that there were some narrow doors at the end of the hall.

My stomach was in knots as I tried the first one. Locked. Then the second. It, too, was locked. Where else could the stair be? The only other choice was at the opposite end of the hall. If there were two doors here then they had to have some there.

The guess proved correct. Hidden against the wall was another door. It screamed when I opened it and made my heart quiver but these were at least the steps that I searched for.

In the dim light from the hall, I could see cobwebs on the narrow rungs, decorating the corners. Only the first few steps were visible to me but just seeing all that dust made my nose twitch into a sneeze. I waited a breathless moment, wondering if I had been heard. Again, I tried to calm myself. There was nothing wrong with my exploring the house.

Seeing how dark it was, I decided to return to my room for a candle. I could see that when the door was shut behind me there would be absolutely no light coming in at all. It was not that I was afraid of the darkness but only of what it might conceal. My nerves were taut now as I glanced about. I had the feeling that someone was watching me but no one seemed to be around.

Down the steps back to the first floor landing. My spine prickled with each whisper of my gown, with each moan of the floor boards. My hair rose at the back of my neck. I found myself counting my paces and stopping to listen. Still, I heard nothing—but it was not enough to ease me. My senses were alert with fear and my nerves raw as if they had just been cut. I *was* being spied upon and I was sure that it could only be Lord Julian or one of Julian's assistants.

Once in the safety of my room, I grasped the door handle and then leaned my weary head in exhaustion against the thick wood. Only then did I hear the footsteps—Percy's long legged stride as he walked past and then Laura's bold step—as they disappeared down the corridor. Neither of them had reason to watch me . . . unless, I wondered just how much Laura did love Julian. What was she willing to do to gain his love? The way she looked at him when she thought no one was about left no doubt in my mind.

I chided myself again for thinking about that.

Laura was not the type of girl to hide in corners. If she had wanted to follow me, she would have stayed with me the whole afternoon. No, it *had* to be Lord Julian. Determined not to be stopped by him, I picked up the candle from the bedstand and then, listening against the door once more, I cautiously opened it.

The corridor was clear now. I left the room without turning back — though I dearly wanted to see if anyone was behind me. Carefully I climbed back up to the third level and paused at the top, hearing the quickening of my heart as I tried to listen for any other unnatural noises.

Upon reaching the upper door, I found that the attic stairway seemed locked. That was impossible unless it had been done purposely by the person behind me. Whatever the reason, I was more determined to get in. Taking the handle tightly, I began to twist and jerk it. Just when it seemed as if it would not move, I felt it give. Pulling again, I nearly flew backwards with the force. It had not been locked, only stuck.

The blood rushing through me, I grasped the rail as I tried to get my breath and realized that my force had very nearly flung me head first down the three flights of stairs.

Calming myself, I relit the candle which had gone out and began to climb the gloomy stairs.

To my amazement, there was no handle grip here. The staircase was free floating and it made me hurry all the more, not knowing who might be lurking in the shadows below.

Within this tunnel, the sounds of the storm

outside were muffled but the sounds of the storm within me were not. My heart pounded so loudly that I feared by its noise alone, I would be found out. I had left the door open to gain whatever light I could, yet now it closed behind me with a bang. Had it been the wind? I grabbed the top of the stair nearest me, leaning forward dangerously so and seeing the narrow space to my right where I had almost fallen. It took me a moment to recover myself and when I did, I paused, still longer, to listen. I heard nothing and saw only the swaying of the spiderwebs. Cautiously, I tred forward and once more nearly screamed as tiny insect feet crawled up my skin.

Relief filled me when I finally reached the top and saw that the large room was well lit from enormous but dusty windows. The storm outside was still blowing. I shivered with each gust of wind sending pellets of rain against the glass and moaning through the cracks in the wood and brick. But I was here now and would not return to my own room until I had at least looked about.

I set the candle on a dusty end table that looked to be of Queen Anne style. One of its claws had come off and the table was supported there by a thick book. Nevertheless, it was steady enough to hold my light. Behind me was an ornate gold-plated mirror with streaked glass. There was a thin crack radiating out from one side of it. I wondered who it was that would have the seven years bad luck. It could only have been Penporth. There were other odds and ends here. A dress-making dummy, a child's play horse, boxes of books unread and doomed to mildew, trunks of old clothes and much more. Nothing seemed to be of real importance . . . nothing that would tell me anything about my sister.

My own curiosity was attracted by a large silk screen done in Chinese style. It was a beautiful and delicate piece of workmanship and I thought it a shame to have to spend the remainder of its days hidden here among the refuse. I advanced forward to examine it further and wondered if I could convince his lordship to let me bring it downstairs when I saw that it already served a purpose up here.

Behind the Chinese wall was an area of room about half the size of the present room. It was neater and cleaner than the section through which I had just come and it was sparsely furnished with a platform and chair, a high stool, a table and easel. Against the wall there were several canvases leaning against one another but covered from view.

Slipping in back of the screen, I felt as if I were entering a different world. Obviously, it was a workroom of someone. I recalled now that Jenny had written about Percy's divine watercolors. Was this his studio? I doubted that anything here would give me a clue to her fate but now that I was here I wanted to see what Percy had painted. I did not think he would object since I was already up here.

Pushing off the dust cover, I began to examine what was here. Most of the paintings were not very good. They were of island scenery, boats, and the like. Atop one of them were the painter's palate with scrapers and knives of various sizes.

Bored with Percy's talent, I glanced at the canvas on the easel. Covered with a black drop cloth, I wondered if it was even worth looking at but my own curious nature got the best of me. Lifting the material, I dropped it almost immediately and felt my heart pound as the muscle tightened in my throat.

With a trembling hand, I again raised the cloth. Yes, it was a half finished picture of Jennifer . . . her green eyes glinted in her cat-like way with their long lashes sweeping the expanse of her high, fair cheekbones . . . her red-gold hair tumbled down about her bare shoulders seductively, beckoningly. It was a Jennifer I had never seen before and yet I knew it was my Jennifer, my sister, that had been depicted here. The artist had given her a secret smile. It was a smile that I knew well when she had been in one of her teasing moods. I continued to stare wide-eyed at the painting. It had not been done in water colors but in oils and it was good — far better than the other paintings here. It could only have been Percy who had done this but did that then mean that Percy was in love with her? I could not understand my sister posing so. Percy must have done it from memory. Or had she, too, been in love with Percy? If so, why had he not stopped her torment? Why had he not left the island with her and saved her life . . . why? why? Did Julian Hawley hold some sway over his cousin? Had he threatened Percy as well?

Disturbed, I placed the material as it had been over the portrait. The rain was still hitting the windows with a fury and I felt uneasy being up here alone as the wavering light flickered off the walls.

Puzzled, I returned to the first floor and my room. No one had seen me, I thought. Whoever had followed me had gone.

Relieved, I closed my door, and, seated at the window seat, stared out into the violent storm as I tried to understand what I had just seen.

The rain continued all that day and for the better part of the next. On Sunday, I was surprised that no one went for services.

No one came down for tea and as nothing had been set out, I went toward the kitchen.

It was only as I neared the door that I heard the quarrel between Mrs. Stewart and her daughter.

"Don't 'ee go takin' advantage o' things. 'ee getting above yerself, Laura, m'pet."

"On the contrary, Mummy, dear. You were never treated as you should have been. I am not going to be *their* servant all my life — not especially when I am equal to them."

" 'ee be a fool. Nothing 'ee could do or say would make 'ee equal."

"That is only because you lowered yourself," Laura hissed.

I heard the sound of flesh hitting flesh and I recoiled instinctively. There was a silence. I was sorely tempted to look in, but I did not.

"No, Mummy, you are right. I am not their equal. I am their better. I have the patience that neither of them has."

She stormed out of the room and did not see me for I had stepped behind the door. I wondered now if I had done right in asking her to join us at the meals, bowing to her desire to address me by my Christian name. It was obvious that Penporth had not thought so or her would have ordered it done before. Well, it was done and things would just have to proceed from there.

I waited for a moment and then, on the pretext of being hungry, entered the kitchens. Mrs. Stewart was at the stove with her back to me. There was an awkwardness that I did not know how to broach. Finally, in halting words, I asked, "Mrs. Stewart, do you object to my having your daughter join our meals? After all, it is an awkward situation—having such an odd number."

She came round then still holding the huge wooden spoon in her hand. Tear drops sparkled in her eyes. "Onions," she said, pointing to the kettle as she wiped her eyes with her sleeve.

There was another awkward silence. I helped myself to a piece of cake from the bin.

"It not be 'er fault, M'Lady. Laura be headstrong—like I were at her age. She has to but learn her place. That be all. She be a good girl, though."

"Forgive my asking," I said, nibbling on the cake, trying to act as unconcerned as possible, "but what is her place. I am a bit confused." It wasn't done, I knew, to sit and gossip with the servants but how else would I find out anything.

Mrs. Stewart sank down into the chair, her face had reddened more and tears began to fall. "It's not such for one as 'ee t'know, M'Lady. I were a wicked creature."

"Oh?" I stopped and the cake fell from my hands. Embarrassed, I began to pick it up. "You mean Laura was born out of wedlock, then?"

Sobbing, Mrs. Stewart nodded.

"But who . . . " I gasped. "Surely not his lordship!"

She shook her heard. "Nay. Julian be a good man — just but stern. 'Twas his father, Richard. We be young, then. We meant na harm. Laura were the result. 'is will stated that she were t'ave a position 'ere fer as long as she wished and fer 'er to be comfort'bly provided fer but she ain't satisfied with that. She be thinkin' that she should've been like 'is lordship's sister."

I was silent now. So Laura was my half sister-in-law. How strange. Absentmindedly, I patted Mrs. Stewart's hand. It was too bad that the situation was not more normal. I would have loved to have had someone close to my own age that I could have confided in.

"Does his lordship know her feelilngs?"

She nodded. "Please, M'Lady, don't mention it or he be cross with me. He be fearful when he be cross. He think it best as she would go to London and find a new place but my Laura don't want to leave. She talks about goin', 'bout travelin', only she don't go but once."

"Oh? Where did she go?"

Mrs. Stewart shrugged. "Mr. Percival, 'e took her to some friends, she says."

"Well, perhaps if she were to marry and settle down . . . " I echoed the same hollow sentiments that had been told to me. "Perhaps then it would work out."

Mrs. Stewart shook her head. "It be a sad business, it be." She turned away from me and again picked up the wooden spoon. There seemed nothing for me to do but leave. I wondered if Jennifer had known of Laura's status and if so, why she had not mentioned it in her letters. Obviously I had been wrong about the girl's feeling towards my husband. Was there then something between Laura and Percival . . . or was I reading wrong again. I chose to believe the latter. I did not think that Percy would become involved with his half-cousin.

Just as I was leaving the kitchen, I turned. "Mrs. Stewart, does anyone on the island play the flute?"

"The flute?" She was puzzled. "Why his lordship did when 'ee were a young one. Don't know if he still does."

"Julian?" The name squeaked from my throat. I felt the surprise shock me. "Surely . . . surely, he is not the only one. Does Percy or one of the men?"

She shrugged. "Tis a fact that I do not know, M'Lady."

Scooping up another piece of cake, I nodded my thanks and headed out the back door. With the sun now out, I had to leave the house and the pond seemed the perfect place. I had thus far learned very little about Jennifer's stay on the island and I hoped that by going there, I'd get some hint of things.

The calm waters and musical birds soothed me as before. It was so lovely here that, believing myself to be alone, I removed my shoes and stockings to dangle my feet and let the mild waves lap my toes. Perched on my rock, at the water's edge, I tried to concentrate on Jennifer.

It was nearly a half hour before I was aware of any other sounds. I had closed my eyes, trying to understand all that was happening about me and to me, when I heard the music again.

At first, I thought I was dreaming—but no, it was flute music. The haunting melody suited my mood perfectly. I recognized the song to be one of unrequited love. Could *that* be Julian? No, it could not. I had seen him leave the island this morning on business. I wondered then if he had been in love with my sister—if like Othello he now suffered the pangs of his deed.

I found it hard to believe that a man as cold and hard as he could be in love or even consider it and yet . . . Percy had said he had been infatuated with my sister.

I shut my eyes again to savor the tones as they floated through the air about me. I was saddened when they drifted away and stopped and for the first time I realized that I was now thinking of the man by his Christian name. It startled me to come to that understanding because I knew that it would make my work here even more difficult when it came to reporting what I was certain I would eventually find. Determined to steel my heart against any affection for the fellow, I opened my eyes.

Immediately, the air seemed to change. The birds were no longer humming so happily and the water now bit rather than licked at my feet. The sun had gone behind a cloud and in back of me, a twig snapped. Startled, I turned but my sudden movement caused me to slip from my seat and I plunked into the water. I could not yet see who it was, for the water was in my eyes, but strong arms went about me.

"Oh, my poor darling Tammy!" Percy cried as he withdrew me from the pond. "I am so sorry. I did not mean to frighten you, my pet. It was only that you were so lost in thought. It seemed a shame to bother you.

"Tell me, do you swim?" he asked, after a moment.

I did but I recalled that Tamara did not. "No. I am afraid that I never learned."

"Oh, what a shame. What a shame. We shall have to teach you." He placed his frock coat gently about my wet shoulders.

My curiosity could not be contained any longer. "Percy, were you playing the flute just now?"

"Flute? Me? No, my precious. I prefer the piano or the harp. The flute is too . . . " he made a face, "too common."

I did not agree with that but said nothing in response. "Who was it then? It sounded so . .

sad."

"Must have been Julian. He always plays sad things. Never yet heard him do a cheerful song."

Despite what I knew from Jennifer and what I had just heard, I could not marry the facts. That sensitive, soul stirring music, that sad, haunting melody did not seem as if it could have come from my cold, masterful husband . . . unless he was not as cold as he pretended to be. Flushed, I realized that there had been times when he had indeed been gentle with me. Far gentler than I had expected.

"Does no one else play?" I shivered with the knowledge.

Percy shrugged and put his arms about me again. "We must get you to the house or you shall be ill." How tender and loving his gestures were towards me. I almost believed that he actually cared for me. I glanced up to him, about to thank him but another twig snapping alerted us to a third person.

Before I could pull away from Percy, Julian chose to pass the pond obviously on his way to visit his aunt. His glowering looks told me what he thought of the two of us standing here—me wearing Percy's coat.

"Charming scene," he quipped, staring at me.

"Cousin, I can explain. Your wife took a tumble and . . . "

"I do not care to hear your explanations, Percival. It seems that the pattern is repeating itself. I am warning you now. Tread lightly." He glared once more at me before strolling off in the direction of the little cottage.

"Julian . . . Julian . . ." I started to call after him, to run to him. Whatever my feelings for him were, he must not blame Percy for what was an innocent gesture.

But Percy had taken my hand. "Let him go, Tammy, my pet. He'll be in a foul mood for the rest of the day but then he will forget it. The important thing to remember is that neither of us has done anything wrong. Though I am afraid . . ."

"What are you afraid of?" I glanced back at the trees where Julian Hawley had disappeared. My heart felt heavy.

"'Tis nothing. Come. Let us get you back to the house and get you into dry clothes." He linked his arm through mine. "I will accompany you."

My skin seemed to shiver at his touch. I was sure it was the wet clothes and nothing else that caused my discomfort. A wind blew up from the ocean, chilling me. "What did he mean about the pattern repeating itself?"

Percy blushed. "Nothing, my dear cousin. I have told you, Julian was quite possessive of your predecessor. He suspected everyone of being involved with her, including myself."

"But you weren't, were you, Percy? I mean, she was your cousin's wife." My eyes must have betrayed the hope that he had not been and yet there was the painting that I had seen only that morning.

He shrugged. "To know Jennifer was to love her. I, like many on the neighboring islands, were captivated with her beauty and her charm but no, I was not involved with her."

We had reached the house again. He ushered me up to my room and took off his now damp coat. "I will have Mrs. Stewart bring you up some warm tea." He smiled at me now. "We have to take proper care of you."

I was touched by his concern. Julian had not felt any concern for me and it hurt me. I had to admit that. "You are sweet, Percy. That's all right, though. I shall go down to the kitchens once I've dressed."

"As you wish, Cousin." He gave me another of his charming smiles and left the room.

Removing my wet clothes, I put on a fresh chemise and lay down on the soft bed. My head was aching and I was exceedingly tired. I wished again to think but all that came to my thoughts was the scene at the pond.

It did look compromising. I knew that—myself standing there with my legs bare, next to his cousin. I trembled, feeling his daggers of hate as they had come to me. Surely, if he were as sensitive as the music suggested . . . no, another had to be playing. Julian was far too cold a man to have such stirring feelings. The question was—would he punish me? Would he force me to flee?

Flushing, I told myself that I had already suffered worse than I could have imagined at his hands. It would be useless for me to leave now after the sacrifice I had made. I had to find out what had happened to my sister.

He was at dinner that evening but he said nothing—to any of us. The meal was the most silent and uncomfortable that I had ever been at. How homesick I was to hear Thomas' angry brogue. Him I could have laughed at and told him how foolish he was being. Julian, I could not.

As soon as it was possible, I took shelter in the library but found myself unable to read. Jennifer was on my mind—as always.

Back in the bedroom, I locked the door and with trembling hands removed Jennifer's letters from my secret drawer in my desk. I was more curious now as to her relationship with our mutual cousin but the references which I found were totally innocent. Had Penporth killed her in a jealous rage? Was that now to be my end?

A pounding on the door startled me.

"Open up, Tamara!"

It was *him*.

"I . . . I have a headache."

"There is no reason for this door to be locked! Open the door now before I smash it down!"

Petrified, I replied, "I am coming!" Hastily, I jammed the letters back into their place and hurried to do his command. He was in before I had even flung the bolt back.

"Julian . . . I . . . "

He snarled. "I do not wish to talk. I am tired and intend to sleep in my own room tonight. If you are ready for sleep early, fine. If not, kindly occupy yourself elsewhere and do not make any noise when you come in."

Relieved — and yet a bit disappointed, I admit — I glanced toward the bed. "I will be ready shortly." So saying, I began to prepare for sleep.

His breathing was already rhythmic as I crawled in beside him. His muscular body was like a warm mountain ready to spew forth a volcano explosion or perhaps more like a lion — dangerous at one moment, calm at the next. In spite of it all, I felt comforted at his being here, asleep, next to me.

Once or twice, I glanced at his face. In sleep, his scar seemed less harsh and he more handsome. Yes, his nose was sensitive. Funny that I had not noticed it before. For the first time, I wondered how he had received his scar. Was it a war wound? Or was it from some foul deed? He sighed in his sleep and shifted positions. I had to move hurriedly to avoid being struck by his swinging arm. Finally, he settled down and I, too, adjusted myself by putting my head against his firm, hirsute shoulders.

I lay awake on my own for a bit longer, my nostrils filled with his male scent, as I listened to the night sounds and wondered again about the day's occurrences. It was, I believe, quite late when sleep finally came to claim me.

I had hoped for oblivion but instead I was immediately transported back to the pond. It was strange to notice that I wore my night dress and then I saw that it was not I but Jennifer who stood there in the waters of the pond, with the ripples blowing over her and her long red-golden hair flowing; her gown getting damp. Though there seemed to be no storm, the water was no longer calm and soothing but rough and angry. The earth seemed to tremble as if from a volcano; the tide was increasing. Jennifer's body was paralyzed with fear. Her eyes were wide in horror. My own heart pounded and my stomach tightened painfully. I felt her fear as if it had been myself. Only I did not know what it was she feared. As she turned, I saw there was blood on her head and neck. Her hands were outstretched. She cried out for help. I came nearer, wanting to assist her, calling for her to take my hand. I, as much as she, was now in danger of drowning from the high waves that splashed us both — but there was more. Why couldn't I see? Why could I not reach her, or save her, or help her. My own heart bled with the desire as I stretched out, desperate to be of service. I was aware of the shadows that were increasing about us both. The terror within me was increasing. I heard the pounding of my heart as my blood rushed to my brain. I had to help my sister. I could not leave her in the pond, bleeding as she was.

Again, I stretched out my hand, crying out, begging to her as my tears fell down my face as the darkness of the storm shadowed us both.

"Jennifer! Jennifer! Please. Get out of the water! Please!" I stretched again toward her and could see her, too, stretching towards me but not quite meeting my fingers. The torment in me was insufferable. "Jennifer! Jennifer!" I screamed out once more.

Something, not Jennifer, touched me.

The terror made me scream again as I woke to find myself in Julian's strong arms. He held me against him, stroking my hair. Relieved that I was no longer in the dream, I allowed my tears to fall.

"Hush, dear girl. Hush. It was just a bad dream." He held me, rocking me, as I cried into his arms, dampening his shoulder. He was so warm . . . so comforting . . . I could almost forget the agony of terror that I had just been through . . . or who had caused it.

Through the veil of my tears, I managed to look up into his eyes and stammer. "I . . . I was so frightened."

"What frightened you, Tamara?" His hand was still on my hair comforting me. It was his deep voice but it was considerate, concerned and so unlike what I knew of him that it brought me to my senses. I was with him . . . with Jennifer's husband . . . Jennifer's murderer. I pulled back abruptly.

"No . . . nothing." I sniffled and stifled my sobs, now hiccupping a bit.

"Come." He undid the buttons of my night-dress with his thick fingers. "You are drenched in sweat. Let us dry you and get some fresh clothes on you."

He was treating me like an imbecile. Yet I did not mind. I was still too frightened from that nightmare. I allowed him to remove my gown.

There was a silence. I did not want to speak but he did. "You called out the name of my first wife. Did you dream of her?"

My tongue would not move. I only nodded.

The blanket was about me now but other than that I was naked.

"What did you dream?"

There was no choice now but to tell him of my nightmare and pray that he would believe that it had been caused by the talk of the past few days. I was amazed at his sympathetic look and when I was done, he again took me into his arms. He was the lion protecting his cubs now . . . for certainly I was no lioness.

"Do you feel better now, my dear?"

"Yes, thank you." How odd that I should feel so secure resting next to the very man who committed the foul deed which caused my nightmare.

"I mean your headache. Is that well?"

I glanced up at him. His eyes, deep and unfathomable, told me nothing. For a moment, I was about to say no and then unaccountably, I looked up at him. "Yes, Julian. I do feel well enough — if that . . . is what you mean."

He said nothing but his lips grazed my brow. Once more I shivered but it was not an unpleasant shiver. Grateful that he had calmed my nightmarish agony, I put my arms about him and returned his kiss. How exceedingly strange it felt . . . but strange in a nice way. My lips tingled with his touch as the sensation spread throughout my body. I was aware of my breasts brushing against the roughness of his body; of his hands roaming my most sensitive areas. There was a sense yet of safety as he held me and I pressed my body against him in a horrid, wanton manner.

He kissed me again, deeper this time, as I forgot who he was, who I was, and why I was there. I allowed myself to hunger for his passion and felt my body and my mind slipping from me into a whirling vortex of pleasure. I still did not understand how I could enjoy his actions, knowing as I did that he must be Jennifer's killer.

His fingers played their magic on my willing body as our tongues met in desperate longing. I was not prepared for his initial thrust yet there was none of the pain that had come before. Within moments, I was again hearing that strange moan that I knew now could only be coming from me. I wanted to control myself, to control my emotions, my body, but I could not. I was but clay to his touch. He had cast a masterful spell upon me and I knew fearfully that when he played with me as he did now, I would forever be at his mercy.

No matter how I tried to fight him, my body would not obey and I felt my hips rising to meet his as I pressed toward him and we rode together on the high wave of pleasure, cresting when he collapsed atop me.

Almost immediately, he left the bed. I could not see his actions but a moment later I felt a cloth being thrown down on me. "It's a clean night dress. Put it on. I do not want you to catch a chill," he said gruffly.

I did as I was told and felt his body again beside me. Then, as we again lay back on the feather bed, I felt the tears come to me. I, who had always prided myself on my strength and independence, I who had always stood up to

Papa, was a weak creature when it came to . . . to this man. I turned away from him as my tears wet the pillow . . . and I felt his arm warm as he encompassed me.

Chapter Nine

I was alone at breakfast the next morning. When the maid entered bringing my toast, I asked, "Is Mr. Percival still asleep?" Julian, I knew, was already awake and working in his study.

"Oh, Ma'am, Mr. Percy's left for a bit. Took off right after tea yesterday, he did. Such a rush, I never did see 'im in afore 'Is you all right', says I?"

I interrupted her tale. "Where did he go?"

"Oh, I couldn't say. I do believe . . ."

"Where is Laura then?"

The maid was miffed that she could not continue her story. "In the sewing room, I believe. She says . . ."

I took the toast from her. "I will speak with her later, if you don't mind. Thank you."

"Yes'm." The girl curtseyed, leaving me on my

own in the huge wainscotted dining room. It was hard to believe that this all came from ship wrecks, everything including the collection of Chinese plates in the rough oak cabinet against the wall.

I had just taken a bite of the toast when I spied Morgan through the window. Seeing him made me recall that I had never yet been to the town. All I had really seen of it was on my wedding day and that had mainly been the kirk, the graveyard, and the village green . . . and of course, the Granny's that night. But I knew none of the people. No one whom I could truly count on as an ally, should it be needed.

Mrs. Stewart came into the room to serve the eggs. I shook my head and stood. "Which is the quickest path to town. I would like to go this morning."

"Oh, Miss, I'm going t'town meself. What did ye be wantin', M'Lady?"

"Nothing really. I . . . I just wanted to see it at closer quarters and perhaps meet some of the people."

"Glory be. There not be much to see. Just some houses, the church and the Granny's. Old Mrs. Pelan, 'er be the manageress of the general store like and takes orders fer boats goin' t'Mary's or the mainland. Were there anything you wanted in special?"

I shook my head. "But I'd like to accompany you, if you don't mind."

"As 'ee wish." She smiled at me and then patted my hand, ignoring our class difference. "I can see

175

as 'ee have a good heart. Not like the other. She be so concerned 'bout her beauty and the likes . . ." Then she reddened and pulled away. "Pardon me, M'Lady. I do be too familiar. 'ee be lookin' like such a good girl. I didn't mean t'talk like that."

I stared at her, not understanding her remark. Jennifer had never been overly concerned about her beauty. Though it was true, she was prettier than me.

At first her apology made me think that she knew Jennifer was my sister. Then it was obvious by her comment that it was only our status which she spoke of. I realized too, that she was trying to cheer me. Were my worries so evident then? I wished my motives were as pure as she assumed them to be.

"It's all right, Mrs. Stewart." It told her. "I know what it's like below the stairs." I sipped my cooling tea and nibbled a last piece of the toast.

" 'ee do?" Her eyes widened.

"I mean, I've heard that the servant's gossip. It's quite natural, I think, for you to have opinions of your own." I gulped down the rest of my beverage. I had not eaten much but I felt odd eating here alone without the others.

Like a dutiful servant, she went to fetch my shawl and then from the corner of the room, she took a wicker basket. "Mrs. O'Dea's been feelin' poorly. I've made her a mite of soup and some cakes. Thought as I'd take her a bit."

"Oh! I mean that should be my job, shouldn't it?"

Mrs. Stewart shrugged. Her smile told me that

she appreciated it. " 'ee can bring 'em in if 'ee're a mind to. 'Twould be nice t'let the others know that their Lady is a thinkin' of 'em." I nodded and taking the basket, we set off.

The saddest sight for me to see was the houses without their inhabitants—windowless and doorless, their roofs caved in. We saw many of those as we descended to the town. They were not on the same path I had taken but another that led us around. "Used t'be lots more folks here but . . ." Mrs. Stewart jerked her hand toward one of the cottages. "Children go off. Livin's hard here. No money. Not many of us old ones left and only some young ones."

I thought then about the child who had come to the wedding. "She didn't belong to the island, then?"

Mrs. Stewart's eyes rolled in alarm. She crossed herself. "Not that I know of. She be one of the little people."

I laughed. "Mrs. Stewart, surely you don't believe in that."

"I do. I do. That's what 'appened to the other."

"What do you mean?" I stopped in the path and taking her elbow made her stop. My own heart seemed to hurry on. "What do you mean?"

Seeing my agitation. Mrs. Stewart just shrugged again. "Nuthin' Lady. Just that *she* didn't believe either and look what happened to 'er."

"But what did happen to her?"

Mrs. Stewart shrugged. I had the feeling that she knew more than she was telling me. "'Tis not a subject for ye to dwell your pretty thoughts on," she said, moving ahead of me to clear the path.

Both of us walked on in silence. I allowed Mrs. Stewart to lead the way to a group of three cottages at the east of the green. These huts were well kept up with neat gardens and mended thatch. Flowers blossomed all over in a profusion of color. It would even be nicer later in the year — but I had no intention of waiting to see that. Like the Hall, these were built of grey granite. White curtains blew from the open windows. As we went into the third of the three cottages, I could not help noticing that the inhabitants of the other two were standing at their doors, observing me and whispering among themselves as to my presence here.

Inside the hut, it was much the same as the other ones I had seen. One basic room, neatly kept. A fire had been started but it wasn't going very well. Unconsciously, I took up the poker and pushed the logs a bit. From the look Mrs. Stewart gave me, I knew she did not approve but the fire was going better now. That was all that mattered. I replaced the poker and noticed the three blackened kettles that hung, empty above the fireplace.

There was only one small crude table and two chairs. The sick bed was separated from the rest of the room by a thin curtain of worn rags. I slid them over. They bunched in the center. A woman pale and sickly in the dim light lay propped up by a large wooden slab. As I stepped closer, I saw that her skin was covered with red spots.

Immediately, I thought of the disease which

Dr. Jenner had cured. I tried to keep from coming too close to her and yet my curiosity was burning. I said nothing but stared at the thin blanket which covered her.

"Hello, Mrs. O'Dea. How are you feeling? Have you been seen by a doctor at all?"

"Oh, M'Lady. I be right poorly. Tis kind of 'ee to come and visit me."

I merely smiled and handed her the basket that Mrs. Stewart had prepared. "But have you seen a doctor?"

"No, M'Lady, the Granny'll take care of it." She looked in the basket. "Oh, M'Lady. I be taken ye kindly. It's right nice o'ee to think o' a poor soul as me be."

"Well, let's hope you get better soon." I took her hand. Skeletal and lifeless, it was a fragile thing. "It's too bad that there's no one here who can take care of you."

She gave me a smile that wrinkled her already lined face. "Me man need to be out or we'll not be eat'n at all. Course M'Lord, he be ever so nice, sendin' out things and the like when we be poorly but we ain't ones t'cept charity."

I wanted to tell her that this was no charity but I could see that the argument would not hold here. "Will you send word when you are better?" I picked up an embroidered piece that contrasted sharply with the rags about it. Obviously, she had done that herself. "Perhaps I'll have some work for you later."

She nodded and managed to smile. I returned her smile. It gave me a good feeling to be able to

179

help. I was also determined that someone of medical capability would come to see this woman. I knew I had no business quickening her hopes when I would soon be gone but it seemed to come naturally to me as if I had a responsibility. She must have sensed my thoughts for she asked, "Yer stayin' longer, then?"

My insides trembled at that remark. I wouldn't, of course, admit the truth. "By all means." The lie pulled at my heart and tore at my taut stomach.

"That be good then. 'Twas a shame the other left as she did."

Here was my opening. Even with Mrs. Stewart here, able to report back to Julian, I forced myself to ask. "Do you know for sure that she left then? I mean, I've heard she was murdered."

I held my breath and waited.

"Murdered? Nah, that's not what I do know. Course 'er left. My Dixon rowed 'er cross t'Hugh Town. Bad night it were but 'er were insistent. Actually, 'e didn't row 'er the whole way. Jist took 'er to Tresco. Made 'im go back, she did. Said, she'd go on 'er own so as 'e wouldn't be troubled."

"And he let her?"

" 'ad to."

The shock must have been clear upon my face and I tried to cover it up the best I could. Now I was grateful for the poor light of the cottage. "Mrs. O'Dea, when does your husband come home? He really should be here with you."

"Dixon won't be back till dark, M'Lady. I said as 'e's gotta fish."

"I see. All the men fish then?"

"Just 'bout. Those that don't, well, some work the land but that be harder by far. Most things come over from Mary's or beyond."

It seemed that there was not much I could do at the present. Disturbed and praying that she would soon get well, I patted her hand again now seeing the blue veins standing out. "You'll be better soon, Mrs. O'Dea. Perhaps I will come to call tomorrow."

"I'll be thanken ye kindly, M'Lady. 'is Lordship be right lucky t'have found likes of you."

I merely nodded and wondered how lucky he'd feel if he found out who I really was. Taking the basket, I left with Mrs. Stewart.

As we strolled through the town, it appeared that Mrs. O'Dea was right. Now, as it had been on the afternoon I had come—was it only a week ago—the town was empty of men. Only a few women gathered at the well. Mrs. Stewart nodded to them and they dispersed—to talk about me, I assumed.

"Well, I've done me bit. I'll be leavin' a list for the mainland. Sure there weren't anything 'ee be wantin'?"

What I needed was not something I could obtain so easily. "No thank you. I believe I shall go back now. My head is aching a bit and I'm very tired."

She smiled at me as if she knew a secret. "Yes, a rest would do 'ee good."

I left her then and walked slowly back through the town to the pond. It was all so confusing. So very confusing.

Tuesday morning promised to be a glorious day. The weather was sunny, bright and I felt full of good spirits. Julian had again slept in the room with me last night — but even that had not disturbed me, I told myself. In fact, I had slept later than I had intended to.

Unfortunately, the day did not keep its promise.

Julian had already breakfasted when I came down. He was, in fact, just leaving the room. We exchanged civil greetings but from the tone of them one would never have known that I had just shared the man's bed. A coldness swept over me, bursting the carefree feeling I had had a moment ago. It seemed that despite what had passed between us, I was no closer to knowing this man whom both myself and my sister had married than I had from her letters. Well, perhaps it was better this way. Perhaps, I told myself, if I felt nothing for him now, I would not be so sad when I had to turn him in, when I would see him hanged.

My hand trembled ever so slightly as I poured my tea and buttered my toast.

He returned to the room just then. I glanced up, a piece of bread in my mouth. I had been about to smile at him but received a cold stare instead. Then, I saw that in his hands were several letters.

"You have some post, Tamara."

"Post?" My heart jumped as the blood rushed

182

through me. Who would write me here? I put down my tea cup suddenly, feeling some slosh over the side and onto my hand. Julian stood next to me and I could feel the angry vibrations coming from him. My nerves coiled as my whole body tensed.

Silently, he handed me two letters. One had the post mark of Penzance. The envelope proclaimed it to be from the Dolphin Inn. That outer one had been opened. Within it was the letter that I had addressed to Tamara "Victoria Damien" (my own name which she was using. It had been our code in the case I was forced to write her.) Puzzled, I saw that her name had been slashed across with a huge red mark. The second letter was from Edinburgh. It was in Thomas' writing. I cursed the man for contacting me here. I had expressly told him not to do so. Well, at least, he had addressed it to Tamara.

"Are you not going to open your post?" he asked, taking his seat.

The blood pounded in my head. I did not want to open these with him here. Yet, he was calmly pouring another cup of tea as if he had all the day. I watched as he began to open his own letters. He pretended to be unconcerned but I knew too well from the tension that I was feeling that that was not the case. I swallowed my fear.

"It seems that I do not have to do that. One, at least, has already been opened. You had no right to do that. The letter was addressed to me."

With that same cold glare that I had come to dread, he responded. "That letter, my dear Tamara, had already been opened enroute. But I should like to know, who is your friend?"

"My . . . friend?" I stuttered now, feeling my tongue trip over my words. I wished now I had kept my thoughts to myself.

"Yes, your friend. The girl to whom you have addressed your letter—Victoria Damien, I believe. How well do you know her, Tamara? Why did you write her from Penzance?" The dark eyes assessed me with the power of the devil within. At that moment, I prayed for someone—anyone—to walk into the room, to break the spell.

No one came to my rescue.

"I . . . she . . . I knew her at school. Only . . . slightly. I . . . really do not know her well at all." That, of itself, was true. With the confusion and thoughts that had attacked me of late, I did not know who I was or where I was at times. I wished I could think of something more but no words would come to my paralyzed mind.

His mouth was a thin line of anger. "Was she the one who accompanied you to London?"

"No! I . . . I mean. Yes. She was on the same train." I could feel my stomach jumping and my face redden with every thought. This inquisition was worse than I could have imagined. I wanted only to get out of this room, to stop these questions before I gave myself away. I had never been good at lies and now I was sure that I was making a fool of myself.

His black eyes continued to devour me like the panther's sharp teeth. "Is your friend related to the family of my ex-wife? Did she ever tell you

184

that she was?"

"I . . . no . . . she never mentioned the fact."
My mouth was dry. I wanted to sip the tea but
under his critical gaze, I could not even seem to
manage that. He did not move a muscle but continued to watch me.

"I shall ask you once more. Did Victoria Damien accompany you to London?"

My fear was like a snake eating at my insides.
Did he know or not? In that second, I decided
that he did.

"Well, what of it! She has done you no harm."
I stood then — for just that instant breaking the
paralyzing force which had held me to him. "I am
leaving this room." My voice was high with false
bravado.

His eyes did not leave my face. I wished I could
have died right there. I was sure I must have
shown something but he remained silent. My
heart continued to thump wildly but I could not
move again.

"No, you are right," his voice was low and more
dangerous, I thought, than before, "she has never
done me harm."

As if to vent his own anger, he tore open another envelope of his own and appeared to read
the contents. I continued to stand there quaking
in my shoes, wanting to leave and yet not wanting
to.

Finally, he looked up. "I am sorry if I have upset you, my dear. It seems that like her sister, your
friend has a wayward nature. She has obviously
left London with no address." He glanced at my

letter from Thomas. "Why not open your other post?"

"I tell you . . . she is merely an acquaintance. I barely knew her at school."

He ignored my comment and seemed to be waiting for my other answer.

"If you do not mind, your lordship," I said, seeing him glance at me with a raised brow, "I will read my other note later." I tucked it into the pocket of my dress. "If you are worried that it is from Victoria Damien, you need not be. I know it is from another friend."

I was at the door now. "Are you going to forbid me receiving letters from my friends? Have I not given up enough for you?"

From his look, I knew that was something I should not have said yet, once it was, I was glad that it was out.

I left the room then, not wanting to hear his further remarks.

It seemed that the bedchamber was the only place I could escape to and so I went there.

Despite his former protest, I bolted the door of the room before sitting down to read. Within the letter to Tamara, Thomas had written to me.

"My dearest Victoria:
It has been ages since I've had word of you. Was your journey pleasant? I assume that Miss Nilston forwarded you this or perhaps she has no need to do that. I suspect that you are still on that wretched island and that you have learned nothing. Well, I have de-

cided to take advantage of some business which I have in London. You are but a day's journey from there. I shall see you on or about May 15th. If you own that you are sorry, perhaps I shall take you back. Please give my regards to Miss Nilston or is it now Lady Hawley?

> Fondly,
> Thomas McAuley, esq."

I twisted the plain gold band that bound me to Julian Hawley, Lord Penporth. How heavy it felt. How well Thomas knew me. I realized that I missed him—missed teasing him—and that I missed Edinburgh. I also realized that Thomas could not come here. If he appeared on the island and identified me, than all I had suffered would be lost. There would be no chance of my finding out the story of my sister's final days. Hastily, I crumpled the note.

Then, on second thought, I took it to the fireplace and watched as the vellum became brown, curled, and turned to ash. I did not blow out the flames until the very last bit of paper had disappeared and my fingers, themselves, were nearly consumed. Carefully, then, I brushed the ash about the hearth. No one could find anything now.

The 15th of May was only a little over two weeks away. Somehow, I had to prevent Thomas from coming.

With a few minutes thought, I had penned a note to him.

"Lady Hawley is quite ill," I wrote. "We are all under quarantine. No visitors are allowed on the island at the moment. Dearest Thomas, I thank you for your concern and will write again when it is convenient for you to come.   Yours, Victoria."

I also wrote a short note to the landlady of the lodgings that Tamara and her new husband had taken. I asked what had happened to my friend. I was only a bit perturbed. It was possible that they had not liked the rooms and had found others. Though I would have thought she would have contacted me with her new address. Using the wax in the desk, I melted some and sealed both letters.

The downstairs hall was empty except for Mrs. Stewart. I caught her as she was carrying the remainder of the breakfast dishes into the kitchens. "Mrs. Stewart, I must post some letters. Is it possible to get them out today?"

"Gracious no, M'Lady. We only get post out 'ere once a week—unless some of the fishermen take mail across from Penzance for us and the return be going out the same day. Next pick-up won't be fer another day or so."

"You can, if you wish, bring it over to Hugh Town, dearest cousin," Percy said, entering the room. "It would have more of a chance of being posted quicker were it there. In fact, I was thinking of rowing there myself this morning."

I was so relieved to have the letters on their way that I gave him an impulsive hug and then pulled back as I saw the look of surprise on his face and on Mrs. Stewart's. Wordlessly, she disappeared into the kitchens, leaving Percy and myself alone.

"When did you return? I'm glad to see you. I hope you forgive me but I must get these letters off."

He gave me one of his most charming smiles. The dimples widened. "I quite understand. I came back only a half-hour hence. My business did not take long."

"But do you mind going out again so soon? Do you not want to rest?"

He adjusted the silken cravat in the mirror. "That I can do later." Then, still looking in the mirror, he said, "Perhaps you would like an outing yourself. The air would do you good. I fancy you've not seen our 'big town' yet."

"As a matter of fact, I have not." The idea appealed to me. It would be lovely to leave the island, even for a little while and see other people. Then the impropriety of it struck me. "But . . what . . . of . . . "

"My cousin? He has just left for Tresco. It shan't take us more than an hour or so. We shall be back long before him. Do you feel up to it?" He had now adjusted his coat and run his fingers several times through those golden curls of his. It felt odd having a conversation with a mirror image, but *that* was Percy.

"Yes, of course, I am up to it. Why should I not be?" I am afraid that my relief was all too evident but all I really cared for was seeing the letters put on the boat for the mainland. If I did not get them out of here, myself, chances were that Penporth would find out about them. And that would never do.

"It really should not matter, anyway," Percy said, finally turning to face me. "I mean, even if my cousin did find out about it . . . " he gave me one of his lazy smiles, "after all, there is nothing between you and me. We are merely innocent friends."

His remark was more of a question than a statement. I nodded. The clips with which he had done up his cravat were made up of several brilliant diamonds. I found myself fascinated by them, looking at them rather than at the twinkle in his eyes.

He pulled a packet from his left pocket. "Oh. I almost forgot. This is for you."

"For me?"

"Yes, I found it in a small shop in Penzance."

I tore open the wrapping with an eagerness. It had been donkey's years since I had received any presents. It was a beautiful white lace jabot for my blouse. "Oh, Percy! It must have cost you the earth!"

I held it up to the mirror image of my neck. The work was like a delicate spider web weave. Even in Edinburgh I had never owned anything like it.

"It's nothing, Tamara. Your smile is worth more than the money."

"Thank you, Percy." I was aware of the tears in my eyes, wishing that I felt toward him as he apparently felt toward me. "There really is nothing wrong with our going to St. Mary's, is there?"

He grinned again, showing his dimples and his full set of white teeth. "Of course there is nothing wrong with a simple outing. Get your bonnet and perhaps a parasol. I will meet you by the east jetty."

Again, I nodded and he spun about on his heel like a young girl showing off a new gown. He disappeared down the corridor and I ran up the stairs to put away my gift and get what I wanted.

The row to Hugh Town was pleasant — more so than I had imagined it would be. The sun was shining brightly and I was glad that Percy had told me to bring my parasol for I had it up most of the trip. The sea was calm, almost like the water of the pond, and we floated along with the breeze kissing my face and rippling the frills of my yellow muslin.

Percy's rowing seemed effortless as he maneuvered the oars. How graceful his slim blonde body was and what a contrast there was between the two cousins. I found myself wondering that they were related at all — one so versatile, pleasant, and handsome and the other so stern, silent and fearsome. (I could not say ugly for even to my own heart I had to admit that Julian was not as ugly as I first had thought. His features though did lack the smooth classical features of his cousin's.)

It took a little over an hour for us to reach the pier at St. Mary's and there were hundreds, it seems, of other small boats like ours as well as the large ones which would make the passage to the

191

mainland.

"It certainly is busy," I commented, trying to get my thoughts off my own worry.

Percy nodded. "You shall have no trouble posting your letters from here, Tamara, dear. If you give them to me, I will see to them."

I hesitated. "I think I would rather take them myself." I saw his chagrin. "It is not that I do not trust you, Percy. I do. Only they are rather important to me. Besides, I should like to see where the post office is for myself. I mean, there might be a time when I can come over on my own and . . . "

He smiled indulgently. "Do you really think you could manage to row on your own?"

Now it was my turn to be miffed. "If I wanted to . . . perhaps . . ."

"Tamara, dearest, you would not get farther than the end of our island. I assure you. It is not as easy as it seems."

I had had enough arguments for the day. "Perhaps you are right, Percy."

"Well then," he scooped his arm through my elbow. "I shall escort you to the post office then and . . . "

"And . . . ?" I glanced up at my companion.

He shrugged. "And then I think we shall take some well deserved refreshment before the journey back."

I suddenly felt ashamed of my momentary mistrust. After all, he already knew part of the secret — did he not? My heart pounded as I forced myself to be pleasant and calm.

"Whatever you say, Percy."

As he led me off, I found that I had to stretch to keep up with his long stride.

The post office was a corner room of a smallish house just off the high street. The old woman who came to the window assured me that my letters would go out that day. "Believe as Mr. Tynder's here. He may be goin' this very afternoon."

"Oh, that is good news," I replied. Paying the postal fee of several pence, I took the letters from Percy who had stood benignly at my side. I was sure he was going to say something about not letting a woman pay and so I hurriedly took the money from my reticule and placed it on the counter.

The woman nodded, then slid the window down. Upon it hung a sign, NEXT SAILING AT THREE P.M. NO MAIL SORTED YET.

"She sorts, as well?"

"My darling Tammy," he said with laconic amusement, "On an island the size of St. Mary's, everyone does more than one thing. Come," he took my arm, "I shall die of thirst if we do not get some drink soon."

I smiled at his exaggeration and allowed him to again lead me back to the high street.

The place he had chosen was a pleasant little garden overlooking the harbor. From here, it was possible to see all the activity of the multitude of boats and people as they moved back and forth along the water and the land.

The outdoor tables were cozy little iron wrought benches with fluttery green umbrellas above them. Several other people were already in the garden and more followed us. My eyes took in every movement with the eagerness of a child long deprived of sweets. Though they seemed few after London, they were more than I had seen in the time upon this island. Percy ordered a lemonade for me which was cooling and tangy sweet. I don't recall what he had but it was a stronger drink, I am sure.

Time passed swiftly as we sat there. Before we realized it, it was well into the afternoon.

"Perhaps we should go back now," I said, slightly uneasy as I drained the rest of my drink. It had become warm sitting in the sun and now was no longer as refreshing. Still, I had enjoyed the outing enough to make me forget the anxiety of this morning's confrontation with Julian.

"Yes, perhaps we had." He also finished off his refreshment. "I'm glad I was able to be of service to you. Those letters must have been important to you."

Nervousness gripped my stomach as I again remembered what had happened. "Yes. They were." He, of course, wanted me to say more but I had no intention of betraying myself anymore than I already had.

Together, we stood and walked silently back toward the boat. I was beginning to worry. It had been a mistake to come, but how else was I to have gotten my letters posted so quickly.

As I stepped into the boat, Percy said, "I heard what happened this morning."

"You did? How?"

"The servants." He smiled. "Poor Tamara. I

can see it beginning already."

"What is beginning?"

"Why Julian's . . . uh . . . illness. His possessiveness. Already he has opened your post. He is questioning you on your friends. Pretty soon, he shall forbid you to leave the island."

"How can he prevent me?"

"He gives orders to his people and to us. Julian is not one to be disobeyed when he commands something — even if you, yourself, doubt the wisdom of it. Then he insists he must accompany you everywhere. And then . . . " he shrugged. He was in the boat now and had begun to row out toward the island again. "Either you will succumb and be his prisoner . . or he will force you to leave the island as Jenny did."

Despite what Percy said about my sister, I felt the need to defend Julian suddenly. "He told me the letter had been previously opened."

"Tamara," he had taken on a paternal tone, "it's an excuse, of course. I'm surprised you swallowed it."

"Well, I did not exactly but . . . " there seemed nothing more I could say. The remainder of our voyage was awkwardly silent. I was thinking of what he had said about Julian. I was still wondering what I could do to hasten matters and get away . . . when the island came into view. My heartbeat quickened. On the shore was Julian! My stomach contracted with a fear worse than I had felt this morning — if that was even possible.

I focused on his strong arms — folded as they were across his chest, and his eyes which were glaring at us both while he waited for us to land. There was no doubt now as to the meaning of his looks.

"I'm afraid, dearest Tammy, that your husband is rather displeased at the moment." He whistled a tune.

"There is no reason for him to be upset," I tried to calm my trembling nerves. "Our ride was a perfectly guiltless one."

"Ah, but you know that he's an extremely jealous man. He . . . "

"He, what?" I demanded. Was Percy trying to tell me the truth which I already suspected?

My companion merely shrugged. "You know he frightened his first wife away, but then I told you that."

I said nothing but in my heart I felt that was not what he had been about to say.

Talk was stifled as we now maneuvered into the little sheltered cove where Mr. Trewyan's boat had first let me off.

Looking every bit the lord of the island, Julian came down the few steps to the jetty to meet us. "I trust you have had a pleasant time." His own voice was anything but pleasant. I shivered.

"It was," I said, forcing myself to respond as I turned my back on him to step out of the boat.

"Now, Cousin," Percy put an arm about Julian's wide shoulders. I realized with a jolt that Percy only wore his shirt and trousers. He had taken off his jacket during the rowing. It had not bothered me then . . only now. To anyone who saw it, it would seem compromising. "It was all quite harmless, Julian." Percy was explaining in his casual manner. "We just had an innocent jaunt over to St. Mary's. Tammy wanted to post some letters."

"I see." His arms were still folded.

"Do you?" I asked, searching his face.

He did not trouble to answer me. Instead, he turned and walked away from us—stiffly—as if he had been hurt. He should not have been angry. We had done nothing wrong, yet I was deeply troubled by his reaction. Would he, I feared, play Othello to my Desdemona? Was that what had happened to Jennifer?

I'm innocent. That's all that should matter, but I am afraid that Percy may be right. Unfortunately, I had forgotten that Mr. Trewyan was to call yesterday. I should have waited here for him or at the cove. Then, I might have escaped for good. Who knows? It probably would have been my best choice considering all that is now happening. The question is—would I have done it? Would I have left without what I came for? I still knew nothing about my sister's disappearance. I was still getting confused messages about her and about my own heart.

In the evening, I approached Julian about having a doctor come to the island. He paused for just a moment before he glanced up at me from the papers he had been reading.

I noticed a flicker of a pulse in his brow. His scar seemed to tighten as he stared at me. "Is there something I should know, my dear?" The way his eyes roamed my body, I knew what he was thinking then. I knew only too well. My heart beat quickened as I flushed with remembered sensations. I could not give him the answer he wanted. I realized that if I gave him the answer that he so desperately sought, my future here would be far different — or would it?

"Of course there is something you should know. I suspect one of your tenants might have the pox."

"What?" He slammed the desk drawer shut and stood. "That is impossible! Who?"

"Well," I backed down a bit from his sudden emotion. "Mrs. O'Dea. She is covered with blotches. I should think . . . I promised her that I would have a doctor sent to her."

Relief seemed to spread over his face. "Oh, it's only Sara, is it? That is not the pox, Tamara. It is merely a skin rash. Yes, the doctor has been to see her, as has the Granny. She gets it at least once or twice a year. It is nothing to worry about."

"Oh." I felt foolish again for I knew that I had erred.

"I think you should have a care before you jump to conclusions, before you promise things . . . like visits from a doctor."

He returned to his seat. I felt myself dismissed as the coldness again came between us. My heart withdrew. I had so hoped that I would be able to talk to him. But I realized at that moment, he would not listen to me about his false suspicions any more than he probably listened to Jennifer.

Turning, I made to leave the study.

"Tamara . . . "

He said my name with an almost hopeful sound. I again looked toward him. I was too far now to see his eyes, but that made no difference. I could still sense their penetrating stare. There was a moment of utter silence before he spoke. "Tamara, I would greatly appreciate if you would not be seen so many places with my cousin. It . . . it gives rise to talk."

Again I moved closer.

"That is ridiculous and well you know it. There is nothing between me and your cousin. If there were . . . I certainly would not flaunt it. Besides, if you are not around and I wish to go someplace, I see no reason why Percy cannot accompany me." Not waiting for his response, I hurriedly left the room and felt the speeding of my heart.

He did not come to my bed that night as had been his custom of late—and while I told myself that I did not mind it, it could only be that he still blamed me for the journey today. Well, if he wished to think ill of me, there seemed nothing I could do. Oh for the true information about my sister and the chance to leave this island.

Chapter Ten

On Wednesday afternoon, I was again on my way to Mrs. O'Dea's, but this time I was alone. I had brought with me another basket of food as my excuse and I hoped that I could get her to speak of Jennifer.

Two days had passed since my excursion to St. Mary's. I prayed that Thomas now had my letter and would heed it, for, being that this was the fifth of May, I had very little time remaining to get the information I sought.

My efforts in this instance were rewarded. As I approached the small hut, I saw a burly man with a worn jerkin repairing a fishing net. His cap was an odd-shaped piece of canvas.

"Mr. O'Dea?"

Blinking, the man seemed startled at my approach. He stood suddenly allowing the fishing net to fall along with the mending materials. He swept the remnant hat off his head.

"How d'ya do, M'Lady? Can I be of assistance?"

I nodded but knew that I would have to choose my words carefully. I was certain that my inquiries would reach the ears of his lordship and it would not do for him to suspect my motives.

Smiling at the man, I extended my basket, my excuse, and I felt the tightness in my chest. "I have come to pay a call on your wife and bring her these," I handed him the food. "She is better, I trust."

He nodded. "Thak'en ye kindly, M'Lady."

I flushed then, feeling my heart hammering as I broached the question. "Your wife tells me that you rowed Lady Jennifer across to Tresco that night."

"Aye. That I did. 'Twas a miserable night but she paid well. She be in a frightful hurry t'leave. Shame 'bout later, I say. I tol' her as the seas be too rough for her to row but she 'sisted that she could do it."

"What do you mean about later?"

"Well, her boat were sunk as I predicted."

I pressed my lips together in frustration. This was the same story I had heard before yet I still could not believe it. "Did she say nothing else when she left? Did she mention why she was in such a hurry? And were you not worried that his lordship would be angered?"

"Aye, I was worried, but she were right distressed and had reason I would guess from what

Master Percival did say. Seems she knew she were barren when she did come." I blanched because I knew that Jennifer would not known anything of the sort. "Mr. Percival," he continued, "did say as she feared being pushed aside, so to speak. She wanted to go to Lun'dun and hoped a solic'tor would help her divorce him."

I stared at the man not realizing I was doing so. I could see Penporth's motive. His desperate desire for a child had produced a rage when he learned she could not have a child. Who else would have such a motive?

Still, a divorce? A solicitor? My sister had known no one in London—unless perhaps Percy had given her some names. Still, I could not fathom my sweet sister being involved in such a scandal as that.

"Was she . . . actually scared for her life?"

The man flushed and look away. "That I canna say, M'Lady."

"You are sure that is what she said and that she had a boat of her own on Tresco?" I found that curious since Jennifer was no better an oarsman than myself. I realized then by the way he was looking at me that my questions were probing too deeply for the moment.

"Aye," he said, slowly. "That is what she said. I be right sorry that she be unhappy but it were fer the best or you'd have not come."

I took a deep breath to steady my nerves. He was right about that. Had it not been for Jennifer's disappearance, I would most probably have stayed in Edinburgh and wed Thomas. But was that for the best? My body flushed beneath my gown as I momentarily thought of what I had been through this past month, of what I had experienced at Julian's hands, in Julian's bed. I did not know if that was for the best.

Meeting his eyes directly I asked, "If I were unhappy . . . and proved to be barren . . . would you . . . uh . . . assist me to leave, too?"

He stared at me, as if assessing my question. His face had become stone. I could not read it. "Could be? Would hate to see 'is lordship 'urt again, but we all do know as how he does want this child."

A sense of relief swept over me. I knew now that should I need it I would have an ally.

"D'ya say ye wanted to see m'wife?"

"Yes, certainly," I responded, nearly forgetting why I had said I had come.

He nodded. Turning toward the cottage, he led the way inside. I paused at the door as a flash of light made me question. "Mr. O'Dea, can you, do you recall perhaps what Lady Jennifer was wearing that night?"

I could still not believe that Jenny had been so foolhardy as to take a boat across that expanse herself. It was not like her. I wondered then if Mr. O'Dea was one of his lordship's favorites. Had they perhaps prepared an excuse in case someone did come to investigate?

He regarding me curiously. "Twas powerful dark but I do believe as it was a blue cloak . . . and a blue dress. Some fancy material. But 'twas her, M'Lady, if that what you be thinkin'. I swear it be. Told the constable just that."

So there had been an investigation of sorts? My heart sank. If they had already checked up then chances were that I would not find anything that would give any more insight. I knew, too, that Jenny had a blue cloak for I recalled packing it for her. In a daze, I withdrew some coins from my pocket and handed it to the man.

"I would greatly appreciate if my husband did not know of my questions. He . . . does not want me talking about his first wife."

The man grunted and nodded. Accepting what I gave him, he turned again toward the cottage. I followed him.

His wife reclined as before behind the ragged curtain. I noticed now, as Julian had said, that the spots were nearly gone. That would teach me to make quick judgements — or would it? My husband had been right here. Was he also right about Jennifer? Was I here now without reason? The thought chilled me.

After spending only a few minutes in the hut, I left them with the food.

Disturbed, I walked along the rocky path of the western coast and again mulled over the strange story. Would Jennifer, herself have suggested a divorce so . . . so outright as that? I could not think so, though I did recall that the "contract" which my father had signed had agreed that Jennifer could leave the island at any time after she had produced the heir. But even if she knew that he had the funds to push through such a bill, Jenny would surely not talk in that manner to a servant. It was just not in her nature. Why she seldom spoke to our housekeeper. Always she had left me — the brash, younger sister — to communicate her wants and to handle the servants and Papa.

If she did leave of her own accord, I still held Penporth responsible for, as the man said, he must have chased her away with his possessive jealousy. I wondered then how long he would give me to tell him I carried an heir before my own life was in danger.

I realized then, that as quickly as it had come, Penporth must have paid a goodly sum for the House of Lords to grant the divorce as swiftly as they must have. What would he do — what would I do — if Jennifer were not dead . . . if she now showed up!

Upon my arrival here, finding Jennifer alive had been my most desperate desire but God help me, my heart was not at all sure that that was now the best thing.

Confused, I wiped the tears away as they brimmed out of my eyes and veiled my vision. Could it be that I was beginning to care about Julian?

A chill of loneliness swept over me and a deep desire to be held by . . . yes, by my husband. I had to admit that he was, even if I did not approve of the situation. I also had to admit that murderer or not, I did enjoy his embraces, his attentions. What, oh what was I going to do. Even worse, what was going to happen when he learned the truth about me. He was the only one with power and money enough to hush up Jennifer's death . . . and mine, too, if he chose.

No, I told myself firmly, nothing would happen. By the time he learned my true identity, I was sure I would be off the island. Besides, my emotions were only playing tricks on me. What I felt for Lord Penporth was not love. It could not be. I was . . . merely adapting, since I was at his mercy. It was only that. Another shudder passed down my spine.

True or not, I would think of him no more now. With a determined effort, I pushed him from my mind and continued my walk.

Even before the churning sea came into view, I heard the screech of the sea birds as they dipped and flew over the land. There were more now than I had ever seen before. In fact, they seemed more vicious than ordinarily. I hurried along curious as to their focus.

It did not take me long to reach the shore. What mattered now was finding a safe path down to the sandy beach. The water looked black and cold. The sun having gone behind a bank of clouds made the land look bleak. I shivered. The cries of the birds seemed louder now, more deliberate, as if calling to their mates: "Come join the feast."

I don't know why I thought what I did but my conversation with Mr. O'Dea had made me think of death . . . of Jennifer's death . . . and of the possibility of her being drowned and washed up on shore — bloated and unrecognizable.

While still in that frame of mind, I spied the

body. It was on the beach — a white, helpless form stretched out across the solitary sand. My heart leaped. "Jennifer!" I cried out, not even thinking that anyone might be about. It had to be Jennifer. Her presence here would be proof that Penporth had murdered her. Did not the dead come back to haunt those who had done them cruelly? I wanted to run forth, down to the rocks, down to the shore — but I did not. Maybe it was the shadow in the rocks that caused me to stop. Whatever it was, I was glad that I paused for, as I watched, Penporth emerged from the path and went over to the form. My eyes widened. I was scarcely aware of my own breathing as I felt my pulses pound. Was he now considering what he would do with the evidence? Was he going to toss it again into the sea?

He bent as if to pick up the body. I was sure now that my last chance was disappearing. Forgetting all caution, I shouted, "Don't you touch her!"

Picking up my skirts, I ran unaided down that perilous path. Had I been wiser, I would have chosen a surer more deliberate course. As it was, the loose rocks pelted me and fell about my feet, causing me to skid and slide unevenly. My only concern, however, was to get to the beach where Penporth stood hovering over the body like a vulture deciding which part to first digest.

The pebbles fell on the rocks with an erratic rhythm like sleet hitting glass. Despite the noise, despite my cry, I do not think Penporth even heard me. At least he did not look up from the body which still held his concentration. Running toward him, I paused close enough to see his scar tauten in a frown.

"Don't touch her!" I said again as my flying skirts settled down behind me. I was prepared now to confront him. Even the fear which had so long held my tongue could not keep me in check.

Only as he looked up with a quizzical glance to me did I realize that the body was not my sister's. It was not even human. "Oh." I caught my breath and felt embarrassment flood me.

I began to examine the animal that lay there on the sand. It's fur was a shiny white, it's large brown eyes were wide and it had a helpless look of desperate need. My heart went out to it as I felt the tears come to my own eyes. Yet, it was not my sister and I was nowhere near gaining my end. I was glad that I had not yet said anything to Penporth which would have further endangered me.

"What is it?" I left my skirts out of the sand and wallked about the animal.

"A baby seal," he said, without looking up at me. Bending down again, he stroked the animal's neck. The pup responded by blinking and barking softly—a bark that was a plaintive cry for help like a baby cast out of the womb before time. Totally taken in, I, too, bent down beside it.

"Can I touch it?"

"That's up to you."

Like Julian, I stroked the animal's head. It regarded me for a moment and then with a shudder that shook her whole body, she barked again. "What's wrong with her? Where's her mother?"

ı don't know. Apparently, the baby's become separated from her. I'm afraid that without it's mother to care for it, it will die soon."

"Oh no!" I reached out to touch it again.

He held my hand back. I was acutely aware of the strength of his grip. "Perhaps we had better not do that. The mother will probably be scared away if she sniffs human scent on the baby."

Forgetting now about my other worries, I concentrated solely on the unfortunate animal. "We can't let it die," I said, restraining my hand so as not to endanger her. I looked to Penporth now but could not read his face. Did he guess what I had been thinking before I came down here? I stared again at the seal. It was an effort for me to avoid cuddling the innocent animal in my arms. Behind me, Penporth stood; I could feel him watching me. For that moment, we two, with the animal, were the only ones in the world.

The seal broke the spell by it's plaintive bleating.

Despite what Julian had said, I reached out to stroke the head and felt the soft, warm fur. "I don't care what you say," I turned to him now. "Her mother's deserted her. I shall go to the house and fetch some milk for her."

I expected a rebuke but received none.

"You may do as you wish, Tamara, for I've no desire to frustrate your maternal instincts."

I blushed. Afraid that he would suspect I was with child, I said, "Surely, you have paternal feelilngs as well. It's such a helpless creature. Anyone with a heart would care!"

He laughed — as though I had said something funny — and moved closer towards me. I felt myself trembling with his nearness and hoped he did not guess the baseness of my thoughts.

"You leave me no choice but to agree with you. For whatever I am, Tamara, I am not heartless."

He put his arms about my waist and drew me up. I felt the sharpness of my breath. His touch burned me in a way I did not care to admit. He seemed to sense my feelings.

"You need not fear me, Tamara," he said, his breath close to my ear, "despite what you may think, I do have principles."

I reddened again, not because I was sorry but because of the horror of my thoughts. I had actually wished him to touch me . . . him . . this man whom I suspected of murdering my sister. I had wanted him to take me into his arms.

"I . . . I'm sorry," I stammered. I lowered my eyes and saw the sand and seal hairs over my skirts. With an effort, I brushed myself off and felt him help me as well. Again, I blushed. I should not be reacting this way. I should not. It was not correct. Not that being correct had often worried me — but in this instance it most certainly did.

Forcing my attention back to the seal, I asked, "Will she be safe, left here?"

"For the moment." His voice was gruff as he left me. I watched astonished as he took off his frock coat and laid it down over the infant animal.

"Your jacket . . . it will get ruined."

"It's old," he said, and took my elbow.

Surprised, I turned for one last look at the seal and allowed my husband to lead me up a path different from the one I had impulsively slid down. Even here, it was difficult climbing. Once, my feet lost their hold. I felt myself falling back. A panic clutched me, but my fall was halted by Julian's strong arms catching me from behind, his body prevented any injury to mine. I found unaccountably that I shivered with his touch. More and more, I found myself unable to control my emotions as I tried to understand this man who was causing this unnatural feeling in me.

Were my suspicions wrong? But how could they be when all the facts that I now possessed pointed to him. Even my sister in her letters had made it clear that she wondered of his sanity and feared him. I told myself that it would not do to fall in love with him. I had to remain objective. It was the only way for me to learn what really transpired. I knew he had been the murderer. It could be no one else. Perhaps I was being stubborn and bullheaded but all indications were of his guilt alone.

I separated from him when we reached the top of the path. Being near him was making my pulses race and making it difficult for me to think. Though my heart was racing, I quickly moved ahead toward the house.

Mrs. Stewart was in the kitchen supervising the cook at dinner. "M'Lady!" She cried as I appeared in a bedraggled state. "Are 'ee injured? Have 'ee fallen again?"

I shook my head, glancing at my gown and realizing it was in a state. "No, I am fine but please. I should like a cup of milk and a spoon."

"What?"

Julian had stepped up behind me then. I was aware of his presence before I heard his voice. "Yes, that's exactly what she wants, Mrs. Stewart. Put a little honey in the milk, too, if we have it. We've found a baby seal on the beach."

"Oh, the poor mite." Mrs. Stewart muttered and moved to ready the things we had requested.

Both of us remained standing there. I did not look towards him but I knew from the way my skin tingled, from the way my heart raced, from the way my pulses pounded, that he was studying me intently now. His deliberate coolness was definitely upsetting to me.

Shame at my own bodily reactions flushed through me. I told myself again that it was not natural. Was he perhaps seeing some familiarity between Jennifer and myself — was that why he stared so? Were my reckless ways bringing me to the disasterous end that both Papa and my schoolmistress predicted?

The unnatural silence about us was broken as Mrs. Stewart returned. In her hands were a large bowl filled with milk and a wooden spoon. "Put two tablespoons of honey in. That be right, I reckon."

"I'm sure that will be fine, Mrs. Stewart," Julian said. Stepping forward with a smile on his uneven lips, he took the bowl.

"Are you returning with me?" I felt my eyes

widen in surprise. I had not expected him to come, to want to continue assisting me and I found the armour which had just begun to form cracking once more.

His eyes seemed to search my face and then my heart. I was forced to glance down as my face reddened. I swallowed hard as he touched my hand and spoke. "I would not be a very considerate husband if I let you go down there alone, would I? Besides, you would never make that path without some assistance, Tamara. And," he paused, smiling so that his scar stretched, "I certainly cannot have my coat left down there." His eyes seemed to twinkle with delight at my discomfort. Going to the linen closet, he removed a patched cloth. "This should do nicely."

I forced myself to nod. "Yes. I believe it should." I was still amazed at his consideration. He handed me the material and, turning with the milk bowl in his hand, started back toward the beach. Picking up my skirts, I followed him quickly until I had reached him. We then walked in silence toward the cove.

As we neared the sandy spot, I could see that the birds were once more flying low. They knew — or perhaps just hoped — that the seal was going to die. I pressed my lips together in determination. That would not happen if I could help it.

We reached the path down. Julian took my hand. "I shall go first, my dear, and then I shall lift you down."

I nodded, holding the milk and the linen as he stumbled partway down toward the steadier rock.

When he reached up for me, I first gave him what we had brought and watched as he set it down.

He lifted his arms once more. "Come, Tamara."

I hesitated, seeing the breach between us.

"Do not worry. I shan't let you fall. Come now. You were certainly brave when you came down the first time."

"That was before I knew." I made a face. "Very well." I took a step forward and felt the moment of terror before his strong arms grasped my waist and pulled me to him, placing me safely on the ledge. For just a moment, with his hands still on me, we silently stared at one another. There was a moment of discovery that jarred my very bones.

Unnerved, I spoke quickly. "I . . . I think we should . . . continue on."

"Yes, you are right." His scar quirked up into a smile; his voice was gruff. "We should." But he did not move. Instead, he leaned forward and kissed my brow.

"I . . . what is that for?" The flush consumed me as I felt that damnable stirring in me.

His fingers touched my cheek. "For caring about the seal; for caring about Mrs. O'Dea."

The heat pounded in me. It would be awkward if he were ever to learn that my interest in Mrs. O'Dea had been purely to learn what she and her husband could tell me of Jennifer.

Julian turned then before I could respond. Taking my hand, he led me down the rest of the way, past the rocks, warning me to dig my heels in so I would not slip.

As we reached the level ground, Julian went ahead. Flaying his arms, he drove the birds away. They became angered and squawking loudly, one dove down as if to attack. I could not watch. Hands over my eyes, I peeked through my fingers as Julian deflected the bird, stunning it. He continued to wave his arms wildly until they disappeared into the sky. Relieved that he was not hurt, amused at his actions, I burst out loud laughing but one glare from those black pools halted my mirth.

With bowl of milk in hand, I approached the pup.

"Hello," I whispered as I bent to stroke its head.

The baby seal opened her eyes. She barked, but so softly and so weakly that it brought tears to my eyes. Stirring the honey and milk mixture, I pressed a spoonful to her mouth.

At first, she refused. Desperate, I glanced up toward Julian and felt my heart jump to see him standing above me, watching me in a strange way. "Perhaps if you hold her head up," he suggested.

Mindful of his presence, of his gaze on me, I did as he told me. The baby now stuck out her tongue. Gingerly, she licked the refreshment I offered her. "Oh, Julian, look!" The joy flushed through me. I forgot everything but my happiness and his immediate kindness. Lifting the animal, I saw now that it had a cut on its side.

Julian, too, saw it. Bending next to me, he touched the animal gently and something in me stirred as his deep voice vibrated in the air about me. "We should move him out of the sun. Gently though. Do you think you can help or shall we get one of the men?"

"Of course I can help. Just because I am a woman . . ."

I saw the smile quirk his features again. I quickly realized that I had once more spoken out of turn and much too boldly. Tamara would not have said such. Why was I always so impulsive in my speech?

He said nothing as we each took the seal. "We must also get her out of tide's path or she will be swept away."

"Can she not swim?" I asked, thinking that I, too, seemed to be in tide's path and I, too, seemed in danger of being swept away.

He motioned for me to continue a bit further inward. "Could you walk when you were born?"

"I doubt it."

"Well, then . . ." he did not need to explain more. We had brought the seal to a sandy bed, out of the drying sun and under the shade of some overhead rocks. It barked softly — crying — and I hurried to retrieve the bowl of milk, to continue feeding it.

"She trusts you," he told me, smiling gently, giving my heart a sudden lift. "You're lucky. They're usually very suspicious at first."

"I can see why, being away from her mother." My own thoughts were on the seal. "Will she survive, do you think?"

"Perhaps." He picked up his jacket and placed the yellowed linen table cover over the pup. "If

216

she has proper care."

"Then, I shall come for her and care for her." I bent again to pet the pup. Her red tongue darted out to lick my hand. I was not sure if it was gratitude or if she wanted more food. "I'll bring you more later," I told her, softly.

Julian remained where he was, towering over me. "I do not want you coming down on your own. It can be dangerous."

I said nothing but merely continued to stroke my new pet.

Finally, after a brief silence, he asked, "Will you name her?"

"Yes, Catherine."

"How strange." I hadn't looked up, but I could feel his penetrating gaze upon my back, piercing my skin, as if he were trying to read my thoughts. My throat went dry. Something, I knew was wrong.

"Why is that strange?" I managed a whisper, forcing myself to keep my attention on the animal.

"My first wife, Jennifer, told me that as a child, she had a cat named Catherine. What made you choose that name . . . Tamara?"

My throat closed tighter, choking off my voice. It felt like the strangling rope as one is swinging. I could not speak but only shrugged. Trembling, I willed myself to talk. I had to say something . . . anything. "It's a common enough name," I said, unbelieving that the raspy sound was really my voice. "Besides . . . I like it." I stood then, feeling cold despite the sun. "I've a headache. I think I shall go lie down."

He said nothing as my weak knees wobbled to a stand. He watched as I walked unsteadily toward the rocky road, grasping the holds as I climbed. When I turned back momentarily, he was still on the beach staring up after me.

Returning to my room, I spied a note on the pillow. It was addressed to me but I did not recognize the hand.

I tore it open, puzzled, as to who might be writing to me. My skin crawled with the chills as I read and re-read the message. "I know who you are. Leave now. Leave before you suffer the same fate as Jennifer."

The paper fluttered from my hand as I stared at the parchment on the floor. Again, I forced myself to pick it up. Who had written this? I did not think it could be Julian.

I swallowed the agony in my throat. The pain in my head was staggering now. Everything seemed to be collapsing upon me at once. Did I dare ask Julian if he knew anything about a note? I wondered if that would be tipping my hand. Of course, he had engineered the whole thing. He must have. He was the only one intelligent enough to have, the only one who risked a loss if I stayed. But why did he not come out and confront me. I tried to think of how I might have given myself away but nothing came to me. Still, if I were dead, I could not pursue the question of my sister's fate. Yes, I knew that he must have an inkling at least of what I was about or he would not be so cruel to me. I wondered if he was enjoying seeing me squirm.

I closed my eyes. I should think of getting off this island now . . . but my head hurt so.

Sinking onto the feather bed, I allowed myself to be enveloped in the softness. I did not want to think about this now. I did not want to think about the note. I had lied about the headache, about the pain before, but I was not lying now.

Dinner that evening was a gloomy meal. Percy had gone somewhere and the house seemed dull without his infectious gaiety and joyous laughter. It was more frightening because I felt those dark eyes of Julian's watching my every move. What did he suspect? What did he know? How foolish I had been—calling the pet by the same name as Jennifer had once used but truly it had not even come to my mind. I wished my sister had sought to inform me that she had told him about the pet—but then who could have guessed that she would disappear as she had and that I would come searching for her as I had. It seemed, unfortunately, that there was a lot my sister had not told me.

I ate very little. I was still thinking of both the seal and the note when Julian addressed me.

"You aren't going to make a very good mother, my dear, if you do not eat well, yourself."

I saw Laura raise her head quickly. Her eyes held surprises and yes, it appeared concern. That emotion was quickly veiled as she again lowered her lids and continued to eat. Had she been the writer of the note? No, what did she know. It had to be Julian.

"I shall make a fine mother—when I choose to

be one," I responded, my voice choking with the suddeness of the response. "As a matter of fact, I *was* thinking of the seal just now." I proceeded to tell Laura about the animal we had found.

"You shouldn't have touched the seal, Tamara. It might die now," Laura cautioned me.

"Yes, I've been told that, but I was not going to leave an injured pup for the birds. It won't die, if I can help it."

Laura shrugged. How casual she was about life!

Julian said nothing further about the pet, and we adjourned to the lounge for our coffees.

After a decent interval, I excused myself and went to the bedroom. My head was truly aching now — pounding with a ferocity that I had never before experienced. I told myself that all I needed was an early night but even as I slipped on my nightdress, I could hear the cry of the birds — louder it seemed — as they circled 'round the poor pup. Was she warm enough, I wondered? Was she in pain? Then I thought about Julian and the way he had helped me care for her. Perhaps he *was* right. Perhaps I was being too concerned about the seal.

I knew Julian had seen me going up. I wondered if he would follow and "demand" his rights. I stared at the bed for a long moment. It had been several nights since he had shared the bed with me and I found I missed his presence. It was true. His touch had opened up a whole Pandora's box for me. I wished I could close the door and forget about it, but it seemed that even if I could, my body could not.

I waited for a half-hour, lying in the darkness,

unable to sleep for the pounding of my head and my fervent prayers that the seal would be all right and that Julian would come to me. I felt lonely in this big bed and wished that we could at least talk about the seal.

Tossing and turning a bit, I finally fell into a rather restless doze.

I do not think Julian ever did come up for when the shrieking gulls woke me at midnight, his side of the bed was still empty. The house was completely silent—almost as it had been the night of my attempted escape.

I could be thankful for the one fact that the pain in my head had gone but not my concern for the seal. I knew that I would not be able to sleep more until I went to check on her. Despite Julian's command that I not go there alone, I removed my nightdress and quickly donned one of my older brown gowns since I knew I would not be upset if that became soiled in the climb. Grabbing my shawl from the chest, I placed it about my shoulders knowing full well how chilly the night air could be.

If anyone woke as my feet creaked the stair boards, I did not find out about it. Only the meager light glimmered in the hall as I crept down. I assumed that all, myself excluded, were sound asleep. I glanced toward Julian's dressing room and wondered if he slept there or in one of the guest rooms. My heart pounded. I would not, could not think of him.

Once outside it took me a moment before I was sure of the direction toward the cove and then, finding the path, I hurried on. I had not thought to bring a light with me but the night was clear and starry. The half crescent moon shone its light about me as I walked on feeling the wind stir my unpinned hair as it rippled the sea and whispered in the leaves. The song of the wind upset me some for I could swear it was calling out my name — "Victoria". It was pure superstition yet I pulled my shawl closer about me, trying to rid myself of the sudden chill that had gone up my spine.

It took an effort to continue forward but I did — only to stop a few feet later. I was sure I heard steps on the path directly behind me but it was too dark there to see anyone.

The moonlight continued to shine silver on the rocks of the beach giving the scene a remote and fragile beauty.

Skirting the area of the pond, my fear seemed to vanish. No harm would come to me here. There was only a little further to go before I would reach the cove where the pup lay. I was tempted to linger here a moment and try to calm the fear that was besetting me but I decided instead to move on.

The sands on the beach reflected silver-white and empty but as I started towards the path, a twig snapped behind me. I turned swiftly but I still could see no one and could only hear the rapid beating of my heart. Yet I had been followed! I could feel someone's presence, but who? Was it the same person who had written the note? Was my life now in danger?

Had I not suddenly been paralyzed with fear, I might have run, but then I would have missed the figure that came out from the shadow of the rocks below me. It was not, I knew, the person who had followed me. They would not have had time to get down to the beach if they had been behind me and besides, I would have heard them.

I hesitated about going down now and waited a moment to see who was beneath the cove's shelter.

Only as the figure moved closer was I able to recognize the short muscular form of my husband. I gasped. What was Julian doing down there at this hour?

There was a plaintive bark from the seal and then silence. Worried, lest my pet come to some harm, I carefully edged forward, only to see him covering her wih a linen. Tears came to my eyes as I realized that he was once again feeding her. My heart warmed to the scene. I started forward. Perhaps, despite what had happened before Julian did have some redeeming qualities. I listened, heaing his deep voice vibrate: "That's a good girl."

The moonlight shone full on them now. I saw her lick his fingers with her long pink tongue and I smiled.

I am not sure if it was my own fault that I slipped, nearly tumbling headlong down those sharp rocks, or if I truly did feel the slight push which sent me forward. All I knew was that for a fraction of a second I was suspended in utter panic and grabbed out at anything.

At first, I could feel nothing but air but a second frantic grasp touched the outstretched limb of the tree. Clinging to it, I again placed my feet on solid ground as, with an effort, I struggled to right myself.

My heart pounded as for several moments, I remained motionless and fearful as I tried to recover my breath and my sanity. I was surprised that Julian did not seem to have noticed anything for his eyes were still on the seal.

Continuing to cling to the tree for support, I inched forward again. This time my foot hit a pebble which cascaded down the path. Julian did now glance up. I could feel the dark brilliance of his eyes even if I could not see him and I was glad that I had remained in the shadows.

Once more he turned his attention to the seal. I could not help wondering if he had somehow planned this. If he hadn't known something, why then did he warn me about coming here this afternoon. I thought again of the note. Had it, after all, been he. Was he just waiting for the right moment to strike? Was my death to have been an accident? My eyes darted about the path but no one revealed himself. Still, I sensed that I was not alone.

Deciding that this was not now the moment to expose myself further, I rested my rapidly beating heart a moment before standing and tiptoeing back the way I had come.

The lighthouse from Bishop Rock seemed doubly bright tonight as it shone across my path. After what I had just experienced, I was glad of that. Even so, I found myself nervously glancing over my shoulder with each petty noise.

Coming out here this night had seemed a childish adventure. Now with every stone and gaping hole outlined before the sweeping yellow light, I felt as timid as the little animals that hid among the flowers trying to get some rest. At least, I was satisfied that my seal was safe.

By degrees, I reached the ridge where I had to turn either to the town or the house. It was there, deprived of the candlepower, that I became gropping and uncertain. Something, perhaps an animal, shivered by me in the thick blanket of the night. I still had no idea of who had followed me. Obviously, it had not been Julian, himself, yet it could easily have been one of his henchmen — perhaps even the same who had conveniently placed the hole in the boat.

On the hillside, the wind seemed more like a thin, wheezing man than the soft of puffs of a fat man which I had experienced before. There was still a bit more to go before I could reach the "safety" of the house. Stopping, I stood and faced the western ocean — that vast expanse of nothingness — breathing in the sea and feeling the salt spray on my face.

It was well past one when I reached the bed chamber once more.

Promptly, I shed my clothes. They fell into a heap on the floor. Unfortunately for me, my worry for the seal could not be shed quite so easily. I found myself once again dreaming of the pond with my nightmare of Jennifer. As before, I woke screaming and breathless. My body was drenched in sweat, but his time there was no Julian to comfort me with his strong arms. How huge the bed seemed with just myself. Quickly, I changed to a clean nightdress.

Shivering, I huddled under the covers, wishing for all the world that my husband was here with me. I finally dozed off.

My eyes felt heavy and I did not want to open them. I was cold and pulled the covers up about my chin, but I knew that I could not sleep the day away — not with the poor seal needing my attention.

Finally, I did open my eyes and lifted my head toward the open window. Had I done that? I shivered again, not recalling, as I felt the chilly wind, driving the rain against the glass. It struck with a fierceness that made me shudder. The wind seemed to be moaning like a lost soul . . . like someone calling out my name. Goosepimples appeared on my skin as I forced myself deeper into the warm bed and recalled last night . . . of seeing Julian on the beach, and of almost falling. Had I been pushed? It was so hard to determine, but I was sure I had.

Bravely, I threw back the covers, determined to face them all and find out who had been my attacker — if there had been one.

Laura came up with my morning tea, and I was glad to see her. I had already dressed in the brown which I had discarded last night, but even that could not keep out the chill which I was feeling. If she noticed the unslept part of the bed, she said nothing. Only as she helped me with my hair did she comment, "Your eyes are red and you look pale. Did you not sleep well?"

"Only tolerably," I pushed the curls behind my

ears, trying not to think about last night.

"I'm sorry to hear that. Percy's back, you know."

"Is he?" I turned, feeling my spirits lift a little. Percy was at least a light touch. His smiles made me feel happier — even if he was a bit of a fop.

I sensed Laura's disapproval as she noted the change in my expression. Again, I faced the mirror and let her finish. She twisted another lock of my hair and her coarse work reddened hands made an odd contrast to the white smoothness of my neck. For a dreadful moment, I almost thought her hands had gone about my neck in a strangle hold. I glanced up into her eyes. Had she written the note?

Her concentration broke as she saw my gaze. "I do think you need a necklace there of some sort. What of the emeralds?"

Silently, wondering, I shook my head. "No. It's fine as it is." Then immediately I felt ashamed for my suspicion. Considering all she had been through it was natural, I suppose, for her to feel a little jealous of me.

The tension between us was awkward as I stood now. "Shall we go down?"

She nodded and followed me.

Outside, the thunder crashed, seemingly just outside the window and the lightning lit the still darkened sky with a ferocity that made me jump, that brought goosebumps to my skin.

In the moment of stillness which followed, I was sure I heard the seal's cry — more pleading than it had been before.

"Don't fret. It's only the storm. If you jump

like a scared rabbit each time it rains here, you'll never have any peace."

I recovered myself quickly, feeling that she was laughing at my fears. "It's not the weather, itself, that bothers me, Laura." Leaving her side, I went to the window to peer out, but all I could see were mist-covered trees and rough seas behind them. "It's the poor pup seal. I'm sure she's frightened out there . . . I should go out and find her."

"I'm afraid your seal has no hope. Not in a storm like this."

I spun about and glared at her. "Don't say that."

She seemed surprised at my sudden moodiness, but I did not care. "The seal will be fine," I said, in a calmer tone.

She laughed. Then tried to jerk me back into a good mood. "If you are going to carry on like that over every stranded animal you'll not have enough love left for your own child."

I was not in the mood to be chided. Besides, I did not like the tone of her voice. She came over to the window and again linked her arm into mine. "We had best go down."

I merely nodded and wished now that I had never suggested she sit with us—but I had and now paid the consequences. I removed my arm from hers, wanting only to forget these past few moments but Laura was still talkative.

"Julian would be pleased if you were to have a child. Do you have any idea yet . . . if you might be?"

I shook my head, blushing hotly. The idea of

my being pregnant with Julian's issue left me with confused feelings. It was an idea that I did not want to consider. It would only serve to keep me here far longer than I intended and would have undesirable complications upon my future life.

"No, I do not think there is time to know yet. Besides which, if I were, my husband would be the first to know." I managed to smile at her, trying to show that her words had not upset me — but it was difficult. Laura stared at me — as if trying to assess my situation. I could not imagine her being anxious for the child, nor could I imagine her cuddling an infant.

We passed into the hall. Even here in the very depths of the house, the rain echoed louder than it should — or was that just the pounding of my heart.

Again, I imagined I heard the wind whispering my name through the halls, mocking me. I glanced at Laura but she did not seem to notice anything.

As we passed the portrait of Lord Richard Hawley, I felt his eyes, even more forbidding than those of his son's, staring down on me. I clutched the rail for support. I was being superstitious but I was sure that HE knew and had passed the knowledge on to his son in some magical way. Still, he had not written the note — so who had?

My pallor must have shown for Laura asked, "Has something frightened you, Tamara? Tell me, what is it?"

I could only shake my head. "No, nothing has frightened me. I . . . I just did not sleep well last night."

"Well," she whispered, surprising me, "I do hope for your sake that you are not carrying. You'll be safer that way. Once he learns you are with child, he will never let you off the island."

My eyes widened, questions formed in my mind—but I did not ask them for we were now near the breakfast room and the subject was not one which I wished to discuss with Julian present.

He was there, at the head of the table, where he usually resided. I could not help but notice that his eyes were also red-rimmed. Had he spent the whole night taking care of my pet?

Immediately, I felt a strange affection for him, but it was short-lived. It was then I had to admit that he could not be all that evil. He had a gentle touch with the pup and at times with me but *he had murdered Jennifer*. The words leaped to my brain as if forced there by some preternatural knowledge. I knew that I should never feel anything except contempt and hatred for Jennifer's murderer but the two men could not seem the same.

I rethought all the possibilities of what I had learned since coming to the island. It could not have been Percy because he loved my sister. I knew that from her letters as well as from what he had told me. Anyone else who might have done the dirty work had to have been at Penporth's instigation. It had to have been. My mind stubbornly told me. It had to have been. I could not be wrong.

As I slipped into my chair, I realized that I really did not want to learn the truth for I was afraid of what that would mean for my life. I admitted that I was beginning to like being called M'Lady, being respected by the staff and the islanders in a way that I had never been back home — but for my own sanity that was all I could admit.

Breakfast went very slowly as none of us talked much. I myself merely picked at my food but managed to eat enough to avoid comment.

As soon as I could, I made my way to the hall for my wrap.

Seconds later, Julian was there at my side. "Your pet is fine, Tamara. I would not suggest going out there now. Not with the weather as it is."

Then I saw that his hair was still wet. I turned to him, feeling at a loss. I wanted to tell him how much I appreciated his kindness but I knew it would embarrass him. He was right. The rain was much too heavy. It would have been impossible for me to go walking outdoors without being soaked and becoming ill.

I lowered my gaze. In a subdued voice, I said, "I will abide by your judgment, Julian." Then, I could not restrain my tongue. "It was kind of you to go out there last night."

"And how did you know that?" He scowled.

I was not frightened for his hand touched mine. For another moment, he was the only one in the small world we inhabited. My voice stuck in my throat, making it dry.

"How did you know?" He questioned me

again.

I shrugged. "I could not sleep last night."

His eyes widened and crinkled a bit. I thought I could detect a hint of a smile in them but then he frowned once more. "I thought I forbade you going out there at night. I do not like being disobeyed, Tamara. Remember that in the future please." With that, he spun about on his heel and left me alone, standing in the hall, feeling desolate.

I told myself that I hated his arbitary attitude, hated the fact that he thought he could tell me what to do, especially since I did not consider myself his true and legal wife . . . but I knew that that hatred was slowly eroding and I would have to have a care that my emotions did not overwhelm me.

Retiring to the library, I attempted to settle down with a book, but the thunder and the lightning unnerved me so that even the crackling fire failed to soothe me. It was there that Julian found me several hours later. I had finally found a book of poetry to interest me — finally been able to subdue my worries over the poor seal and other matters — when he entered the room.

He was like a lion assessing his prey before springing, coming upon me stealthily, the thick carpet precluding unnecessary sound. Only when I had finished the poem and glanced up to turn the page did I see him standing there — staring at me. My whole body tensed.

"Did you want me for something?"

I was aware that the whole house was silent,

and that we were alone in the room.

"There's been some post, my dear. One of the fishermen brought it over with the other supplies. How he came through, I do not know." He handed me the envelope.

For a brief moment, our hands touched and I felt myself trembling. Recoiling, I left the paper. My skin was on fire. Did he notice the flush of my face?

"Well, go on. Take your letter. I have not all day."

Like the tongue of a snake, my hand darted out, grabbing at the letter and returning it to the safety of my side. I examined the envelope. Its postmark was London, but the writing was unfamiliar to me. It wasn't from Thomas—thank goodness. I did not think that Tamara would write here. Nevertheless, I could take no chances.

Casually as I could, I stuck the letter into my book and continued reading. His eyes remained upon me moments longer. My own heartbeat had increased—shaming me into awareness of my own desires for his touch. I knew that my own face had flushed but was helpless to do anything about it.

Quietly as he had come, he withdrew and shortly thereafter, I went to our room. It seemed the only place I could truly be alone but since it was cold in there I was forced to send the maid to do up the fire. Only when she had gone, when the flames were burning brightly, their orange tongues licking the logs, did I sit at the table and open the letter.

Inside was a short note of one page and a square clipping cut out from the London Times. As I started to read, I realized that it was from the landlady where Tamara and her husband had stayed.

"I am sorry to inform you, M'Lady," the letter went, "but your friends have met with an unfortunate accident. I cannot supply you details. Perhaps the enclosed will help. I will keep their luggage until you do send for it. Mrs. N.P. Nigel. P.S. They owed three pounds/tuppence for their room."

The blood drained from my hands as I glanced down at the clipping. It read: A young couple was found Tuesday morning floating in the river. Their bodies have been identified by Mrs. N.P. Nigel, of—Street, as one Miss Victoria Damien of Edinburgh and friend, Peter Franks."

I allowed both papers to flutter from my hand, staring at it. I felt the blood drain from me as fear took control. Tamara dead? But how? And her husband as well? I could not understand that. My eyes filled with tears; the same tears which choked my throat.

Slowly I bent and retrieved the notice. I read it over once more. Had Tamara, like Jennifer, been murdered? Was it Julian's doing? Of course. It had to be. There was no other answer.

I recalled now how he had asked me about "Victoria Damien" and what I knew of her whereabouts. Was he worried that "she" would come to seek him out, to seek the truth? The pain hit me like a fist in my stomach. I sank down onto the bed still in a daze. If that was the case then I was in more danger here than I first understood.

The shiver went through me as my mind spun with aimless thoughts. Someone thought that Victoria Damien should not know of her sister's whereabouts. I knew it had been a mistake to have Tamara keep my name, my trunk — but we had thought it best then if I was using her name and her trunks. We had thought it would avoid having her aunt search for her and hear of her marriage until it was well past the time when it could be annulled. Yet now I had been the cause of my friend's death. What other horrors had my masqurade caused? The tears started down my cheeks. Julian was the only one I knew with the power and the money to order Tamara's death? Had that been one of his business trips?

The tears were coming quickly now. I sniffled but could not stop them and allowed myself to collapse onto the bed. Why had I come? Why had I involved Tamara? I realized with a sob and shudder that I was now truly alone out here.

I was unaware of closing my eyes but I must have dozed for I woke to the sound of the clock chimes and a knocking at my door. My head ached more than it had before and I felt miserable.

"Who's there?" I called out, in a rather snappish tone. All I really wanted was to be left alone.

Laura did not answer me but entered the room. I saw that she carried a tray. "You did not come down to dinner. Are you ill?" She moved closer.

"You've been crying. What's wrong? Has Julian done something to upset you?"

"No. No. It's nothing," I said dully as I glanced in the mirror to see my red-rimmed eyes. No, he had done nothing but murder my sister and my only friend. I stared again at my features. My face was red streaked where I had lain against the quilt. "I shall be all right," I said, not looking at Laura but going over to the pitcher and splashing cold water on my face. "Yes, I shall be fine. You may take the tray back. I only dozed. I will come down and eat."

She put the tray down anyway. "I would not advise that. Percy and Julian are having quite a row. It seems that Julian is upsetting everyone today."

"I tell you, Julian did not upset me." I could not have Laura repeating anything to my husband about my distress for I was sure he would question me and it would be difficult to keep my upset from him.

Following her to the window seat where she had placed the tray, I sat down and stared out at the wild sea beyond as it washed white and angry over the jagged rocks.

"Shall I pour some tea?"

Numbly, I nodded. I really was not all that hungry. As I continued to stare out the window, to watch the fierce waves, I realized that nothing was turning out as I had planned. I seemed to have lost the control that I was sure would be mine to keep.

Laura handed me a cup. Feeling the warmth through the china, I touched the porcelain to my cheek. For some reason that gave me some comfort. Then, slowly, I began to sip. Laura said nothing but I was aware of her continued stare. I did not care. I cared for nothing at this moment but my own peace of mind and silence. If I could turn back the clock, I would never have allowed my father to send Jennifer. I would never have allowed Tamara to take my place in London. How odd that sounded. It was I who had taken Tamara's place here. The danger was here. It should not have been in London.

I shivered again as the steaming mist from the tea began to penetrate my befuddled brain. Laura was talking now—something about the storm and Percy, but I was only half listening.

I found that I could not concentrate—on anything. I knew that my voice sounded dull but it was not in my power to do anything about it at this moment. In fact, nothing seemed to be in my power.

"Laura, you must excuse me," I turned to look at her for the first time since she had come into the room. "My head is aching dreadfully. I simply must lie down again."

"Oh, my poor Tamara," she began to fuss over me. "How senseless of me. I should have seen you were not feeling up to par. Shall I have Julian send for the Granny?"

I shivered and shook my head, feeling the goose bumps go up my spine. On no account did I want the Granny. I had the dreadful feeling that she knew exactly who I was and was just waiting for the moment to expose me.

"I shall be fine. I have had these headaches before," I told her. "Please just take the tray and go."

She pursed her thin lips thoughtfully as if she doubted me but lifted the tray and left the room.

Unable to move for the moment, I stayed there and stared again at the waters—dark and dismal—below me. I would have loved to have indulged myself but now with Tamara dead I needed more than ever to conclude with this farce and be off the island.

Recalling the trunk I had seen up in the attic, I decided I would go up there and explore. I was sure that the attic held some clue for me.

My heart was heavy as I stood. I realized then that the clippings were still on the floor. With a horror, I wondered if Laura had noticed them. I hoped not. Tears again poured from my eyes. I sniffled them back this time and forced them to stop. I had work to do.

Picking up the papers, I placed them in the fire and watched until they had been consumed.

Chapter Eleven

Cautiously, I crept up the steps to the second floor and the attic door. I was followed — I am sure of that — but I know not by whom. All I had was the prickly sensation of piercing eyes staring at my back and the chills that ran up my spine made my hair seem to stand on end.

The gloomy weather darkened the halls and the gas light flickered menacingly, though the storm had stopped. I still could not see anyone behind me so while I could not ignore the feeling I forced myself to press on. I would not allow myself to be frightened and I repeated those words several times as I neared the attic door.

Again, it seemed to be stuck. I feared it was locked but with a few tugs, it opened. The stair had been cleaned of its cobwebs since I had last gone up. Nevertheless, it was still a dark, narrow passage—one that gave me a tight feeling in my chest when the door behind me was closed. Even the candle did little to alleviate the darkness. Taking a deep breath, I picked up my skirts and hurried up the stairs.

Almost immediately I noticed that there had been a change since I had been here. The furniture had been moved about in a haphazard way, as if someone had been impatiently searching for something and could not take the time to rearrange it all. Items had been pushed about almost as an obstacle course for anyone trying to get through to the pictures—almost as if someone did not want them to be examined. Well, I had come up, and I refused to turn back now. I was going to examine the picture again and then . . . I would have to see. Just the fact of those items blocking the way made me think that there was something up here that I ought to know of. Someone (Julian?) knew I had been here before.

Using both hands to lift my skirts so that dust would not collect on my hem, I placed the candle on the same stand as I had used before. The limited light from the greyish skies would have to suffice until I had cleared a path for myself.

Probably, if it had not been for the manipulation of the furniture and for my clumsy skirts, I would never have tripped over the book, never have noticed the chest beneath it. I saw then that it was the same one which had caught my eye the first time—only now it was on this side of the room. Chairs had been piled about it. To hide it? Curiosity took hold. I approached. There was something familiar about that chest. I stared at it a moment and then felt my heart give a jerk. Moving chairs out of the way, placing the book on the floor, I reached over and gently touched the carved initials — JD — Jennifer Damien.

My throat seemed to close up. Yes, this had been Jenny's. Even had I not seen the initials, I should have known that chest. How many times had we packed and unpacked that. Deciding what she would and would not take. The chest made me think not only of my sister but of Tamara, too, for the trunk I had left with her had my initials carved on it in the exact place.

Tears again came to my eyes and threatened to overwhelm me. Ironically, I realized now that I had always been envious of everything Jennifer had had. What my sister possessed, I had wanted as well — but seldom received. My heart was in my throat. Jenny had been Papa's favorite and it was Jenny who had received most of the presents. I reached over and brought the candle closer to me, feeling the warmth of the flame and the drippings of the hot wax on my hand. Even so, Jenny had often shared with me what she had and my life had always been linked with hers — as it was even now. Even now, I had the husband she had had; I prayed only that I would not suffer the fate that she had.

I attempted to open the lock, wondering if anything was in the chest. At first, it seemed, as if I could not budge it but then with the use of a hairpin and some jiggling, I managed to loosen it enough to release the snap.

There was no question once I had opened it. This was her chest and her clothes. I began to dig through, hoping that I would find a diary similar to my own — something that would tell me more of her life here on the island.

I had not proceeded very far when another shiver went up my spine and I paused as my hand touched the navy blue cloak with the hood. I had packed this for her. I stared at the material as I recalled Mr. O'Dea saying that this was the one she had used when she had fled — unless she had purchased a new one after becoming Lady Hawley — but considering the absence of shops on this island, I highly doubted it. Either he had been mistaken in what she had worn (and I knew that to be likely) or he had lied and my sister had never left the island. It was the latter that I still very much believed and feared.

Shaken, I continued my search of the trunk.

By the time I reached the bottom, I was sure that I would find nothing else but I was rewarded for my patience. Jennifer had kept her letters from me. Even as I put my hand on them I realized that these letters could be an additional source of danger to me. My handwriting could easily be recognized. There seemed nothing more I could do until my own morbid curiosity prompted me to undo the ribbon about the letters. Perhaps it was not just curiosity. Perhaps it was my sister reaching out to me.

In the pile I found one letter of hers which she apparently had been about to post to me — but failed. My hand trembled as I read.

"Darling Vicky, I am so afraid of Julian's temper. You can not believe what a mad man he has become. I am seriously thinking that I must leave the island for some time. I wonder—would he give me leave to return home and see you? He is desperate for a child. It's that damn will you see. He . . . ."

The note ended there . . . the ink trailing off in a line, as if she had suddenly been surprised at the writing and had stopped. Had it been Julian who had surprised her?

I tucked her letters along with my own into the pocket of my skirts. Would this be enough proof to convince the judge that Julian had murdered my sister?

Trembling, feeling it burn my pocket, I took it out and reread it. Would I, who had wanted to share whatever my sister had, now share her destiny. I would have to leave the island as soon as possible but did I dare trust Mr. O'Dea? I knew that the ferry did not stop here for yet another week. I did not know what to do.

I folded the letter again into my pocket and began to put the clothes back into the chest. Spying Jennifer's rose color ball gown I stopped. My vision blurred with the tears as I recalled how she had loved that dress and I sank down on the floor near the trunk, sobbing my heart out.

It was there, on the floor, that Percy found me nearly an hour later.

"Why Tamara, dearest cousin, whatever are you doing here? What is distressing you so?" His arms went about me as he lifted my limp form off the floor.

I shook my head as more tears ran down my pale cheeks. Even his cheerful voice could not coax me from my morbid state. I thanked the lord that I had at least put the letters back into my pocket. I knew for certain that had Percy seen them, they would surely have given me away.

Finally, through my tears, I looked up at Percy and managed to say, "I . . . I was exploring and I found . . . these . . ." I pointed to the chest of clothes, still open.

"Whatdeuced nuisance. I should have thought that . . . but why should the dresses of Julian's first wife upset you, dearest girl?"

There was a moment, when, full of fear and anxiety, I longed to confide in Percy, but I did not . . . and yet, I desperately wanted to talk to someone.

"Unless," he put his arm about me. "My darling Tamara, you really are much too sensitive. Merely because the clothes are here does not mean that the girl is dead. I have told you, Julian paid a vast amount to obtain a decree nisi from her without her signature. If we knew for a fact that she was out of harm's reach, he need not have bothered."

"But . . . how did they come to be up here? Why did she not take them with her?" Though I did not want to, my sobs started again and suddenly I found myself with Percy's arms comforting me. Before I could protest, his lips were on mine.

Aghast, I found my strength and pulled away

to stare at him.

I saw him flush as he hung his head. "Cousin, I am truly sorry. Only you seemed so sad and mournful that I wanted to do something for you. I wanted to comfort you."

I reddened. "I do not need comfort in that way, Percy." I glared at him. Had I done anything to encourage him? I could not think I had and yet . . . I felt guilt for his action.

"Please, Tamara, you must forgive me. I do promise you. The like will not happen again — unless you wish it, that is," he lowered his long lashes and took my hand. The blush of shame once more seemed to cover his face. Indeed, he did seem contrite. Nevertheless, his action had upset me.

I watched as if from another world as he lifted my hand to his mouth. "After all, what is a kiss between cousins."

I shook my head, unable to say anything, upset still by my findings. Had Jennifer actually been unfaithful to her husband? I could not believe that. She, who had duly done everything Papa had asked. It was always I who had been the rebel.

I did hope that Percy was not falling in love with me because I could only reject his suit. It was hard enough dealing with Julian — and only because I was forced to. I did not need to deal with yet another Hawley. Besides, legal or not, Julian was my husband.

Even as I withdrew my hand from Percy, I knew that I had to leave this island — very soon.

Just finding this made me realize how close I was to finding out my sister's fate. I was torn. I did not want to leave until I learned the truth and yet the fear within me was mounting.

Lost in my own thoughts, I failed to realize that Percy was still here. I was about to remove the letter from my pocket.

"I do not want you to think ill of me, Cousin."

Percy's voice startled me. Flushing with my near-fatal mistake, I tried to change the subject. "Did you come up to paint?"

"Paint?" There was an amused tone in his voice.

"Yes," I looked up into his charming blue eyes which again twinkled. Feeling uncomfortable, I glanced toward the art studio section of the attic.

"Oh, you mean the water colors. I have not dabbled in them for donkey's years. They are not very good, truly they are not."

In an effort to break way from him—and perhaps to find out a bit more—I left the clothes on the floor and ran over to the pictures. "But they are good, especially this one." I pulled back the black veil that covered Jennifer's portrait and again received a shock. My hands went to my mouth as I saw the painting of my sister had been slashed to ribbons. My throat was dry as I turned to look at Percy. "I . . . the picture . . . what . . . what did you do to it, Percy?" I knew that the hoarseness did not sound like my voice. I stepped away from the damaged portrait as I tried to avoid the other items on the floor and yet stay away from Percy.

"What the deuce are you gobbling about?"

He came forth. There seemed no surprise in his bright eyes as he examined the ruined picture. "Hmm. Not a pretty sight, is it? Poor Julian."

I stood still as the shiver ran through me. "What do you mean, poor Julian?"

Percy gave me a sad smile and stretched out his hand to bring me forward. "It's Julian's painting . . . or rather, he had it done by one of the St. Mary's artists. It's his first wife, but it couldn't be finished because she left before . . . anyway, it seems now he's gone into a temper and destroyed it."

"But why? It was so beautiful."

I felt Percy's arm on mine but I was too stunned to move. My stomach tightened and the bile was in my throat. I let the cloth cover drop down again. I could not look at the picture because I knew I would be ill.

"How . . . do you know that Julian did it. It . . ." I had been about to say that the picture looked exactly like her but then I recalled in time that I would not have seen her for a number of years and then only at school. I could only stare at the black cloth as my throat closed. "He must have been in an awful rage to do something like this?" I shuddered thinking of Julian's anger and dreading it even more now.

"I agree. He must have been," Percy pulled the black cloth back up with a morbid curiosity and then let the material fall again—like a shroud— over the painting. "Come. We had best leave here. It would not do for Julian to come up and find us." His arm was about me again. I knew I should shrug it off, I did not like the liberty he was taking, but I was too exhausted to do anything at that moment.

At the door, I turned and looked into his eyes. "Percy, tell me the truth, did your cousin murder her." I felt the hammering of my heart and wondered that I had the audacity to ask such a question. It was foolish and it had come impulsively before my brain could censor it.

Percy's eyes went wide and then narrowed. In that brief moment, all the charm went out of him. Like lead, his hand dropped from mine. "Could be. Don't know that he did, though."

"But you said . . ."

"Damnation, Tammy, I told you that his possessiveness might have driven her away. I never said that he murdered her. I do not go accusing people—especially people like Julian—unless I am damned sure. Why if he ever heard what you said . . ." His face contorted into the closest thing to fright that I had yet seen from him. Was he afraid that Julian or his spies might overhear? But who were those spies? Which servants were in favor of him and which were not? That was something I still had not determined.

"Oh," I replied in a small voice. It was true that Percy had never said anything outright, had never accused Julian, but nevertheless . . . I knew that he, like I, must think it. "Percy, I do not think we should be up here alone like this. It is not right. Please."

The smile returned to Percy's lips. "Oh, there is

no one here now who can see it. I was watching as I came up."

My heart thudded uncomfortably for that moment.

"No one will tell Julian — as long as you do not. For I certainly will not mention it. I value my hide far too greatly." Before I could stop him, he leaned over to kiss me once more.

"Percy!" I pulled back, aware of his hand on me now. "Percy, please. I *am* a married woman."

"Ah, yes," he looked at me with those changeable eyes of his. "But you are also a very attractive one, especially when you are angry. I'd be jolly stupid not to see how unhappy you are with your marriage." Like an alcoholic desperate for a drink, he grabbed my wrist and kissed my fingers. "I had not meant for this to happen, dearest girl, but I am smitten with you. Ah, if only I had the fortune. You would now be wed to me and not to Julian. What does he know of how to treat a beautiful woman such as yourself?"

I listened stunned. Me? Beautiful? Him — smitten with me? I could not believe that. No one had ever been smitten with me. With Jennifer, yes. With me, no. I tried once more to pull back but he held me close. "But what of . . . Jennifer. I mean, you said . . ." Fear rose in me.

"I said, my dearest Tamara, that myself and Julian, like many others were infatuated with her beauty, with the soft whiteness of her skin, but there is a difference between infatuation and love. You, Tamara, have the courage and the inner beauty to inspire true love. Tell me, please," his blue eyes pleaded with me, "tell me that you feel as I do."

My eyes must have widened with the shock.

"Percy, did you follow me up here?" I stared at him. Julian had warned me about his attention but I had never thought that something like this would occur.

Stunned, I saw him nod. He was like a child with his hand caught in the biscuit container. "I saw you coming up. When you did not return . . ." he lowered his eyes. "I was afraid for you."

"Afraid for me?"

"Yes." His voice was a bare whisper. "I had seen Julian come up here earlier. I did not know if he had come down or not. I feared for you . . . if he became angry with you . . . no one would ever know that you had come up."

The horror was in my own voice now. I could not help but think of the letter I had just read. "Surely, he would not be so rash as to . . . I mean . . . he is my husband."

"Just so." Percy responded. "And according to the law he may do with you as he pleases, just as he might do with Jennifer as he pleased."

"You are telling me that he did murder her then?"

Percy lowered his eyes once more. "I cannot say anything of the kind for sure. I can only warn you and watch out for you. Tamara," he reached out his hand to me. "I do love you so." Tears shimmered in his beautiful eyes. Was he just a consummate actor or was he truly in love with me?

"Oh, Percy," was all I could say. "Oh, Percy."

Further words choked in my throat. I tore my hand from his. Escape was all I could think of. I clattered down the dark stairs without my candle, nearly tripping but continuing on. My heart hammered furiously. I admitted that in many ways, I was attracted to Percy. That made it even the more difficult. He was far handsomer than Julian, more alive, more charming, easier to talk to, and yet . . . and yet I felt a strange alliance with Julian. Well, now that I had the letter, I told myself, I had the proof I would need. There was nothing to keep me on the island any longer. It remained only for me to obtain passage. I could not . . . I would not get myself involved with Percy and complicate my life even more.

Back in the room, with the door locked, I shoved my own letters to Jennifer into the fire. I did not want to take the chance of anyone finding them and discovering my handwriting to be the same as those of the letters.

As the flames shot up, crackling and devouring them with their orange tongues, I felt a sadness creep over me. Only then in my agony did I realize that I had also destroyed her last letter to me!

My proof was gone and there was only my word that it had ever existed. Was the slashed picture enough? Could I show his murderous intentions with that alone?

Blast it! I swore in a very unladylike manner. Blast it! Why had I not been more careful? Now I was doomed to another sentence on this island until something more would come to light. But I would find something. I had to. I told myself then that the letter would not have been enough. I still had to stay.

At dinner, Percy was his usual chatty self, but for once it bothered me. I could say nothing. My mind was in such a turmoil. Only Laura seemed to notice.

"Does your head still hurt, Tamara?" She pushed my platter toward me to coax me to eat. I would have ignored it if not for my worry.

"Laura, please remember your place." I snapped. "If I want to eat, I very well can." I was sorry a moment later, but as usual my tongue had gotten the best of me. It was too late for me to retract my statement.

I did not look up at him, but I could feel the cool black eyes of my husband assessing me. Did he know what I had seen this afternoon. Was he responsible for Tamara's death? I shivered and realized that as Tamara, I was supposed to be meek. An apology was on the verge of my tongue when Percy, pouring the gravy casually over his meat, blurted out, "I believe she's upset at seeing the old chest up in the attic."

Angry, I glared at him. Why did he have to say that? Perhaps he enjoyed tempting Julian's anger, but I did not. And I knew that it was I who would have to pay for it.

Laura glanced at me. "Why should old clothes upset you? I would have given them away long ago, had I known they would worry you." She smiled at me blandly. "I'll do it presently."

I shook my head, refusing to answer, feeling

the tears forming in my eyes again. Julian continued to stare steadily at me. Finally, he asked, "Why did those clothes upset you, Tamara? They were left behind by my first wife, I believe." He paused. "Are you sure it was just the clothing that worried you?"

I swallowed hard. Why had Percy brought this up? Did Julian suspect the letter? Did he know I had seen the picture?

I shook my head. "Nothing . . . is worrying me."

"Then why did you not eat? Are you ill?"

Again, I shook my head and forced myself to lift a spoonful of pudding to my mouth. I could barely taste it. I looked down at my plate.

"I am fine. The clothes just reminded me of . . . my sister." I realized that in my weak moment, I had again spoken out of turn. "She . . . she died of the fever. Several years ago."

"That is interesting." Julian tapped his finger together, watching me with those devilish eyes of his. "Why is it that I never heard of your sister before."

I glared at him. Of course he had, but I did not dare tell him.

"I don't believe that you know all there is to know about me or my family, Sir, and you do not have to." My anger surged forward as I thought again of him, of my sister, of poor Tamara. "My dear sister passed on before I was vilified by contact with you and no one thought it of importance that you know my every action past." That much at least was true. I stood now and threw down the serviette, realizing at least that I could now escape the table without having them all staring at me. "If you'll excuse me, I have had enough to eat."

Leaving the room without a reply from the others, I ran out the door. I had at first intended to go to the pond, but when I was halfway down the road, I realized that I was headed toward the beach where the seal lay. The ground here was muddy from the rain, but I hurried on. The gloom had gone from the sky and the sun was shining brightly, trying to dry up the earth's dampness. I had not seen the pup all day long and I had not thought to bring any food. All I had with me were some sugar lumps from the day before. Well, later, I would return to the house and get something. For now, I only wanted to see her and hold her. Maybe she would give me the comfort that I longed for.

I do not know why I should have been so worried about her. The water was her natural habitat and even if she did not swim, I was sure her native ability would keep her afloat. My instincts, however, and the circling of the gulls with their laughing cries made me run. I was nearly there. I should have heard her mewing cry. Why didn't I? It was the gulls only now. There were other birds—species I had reason to fear—circling the beach.

The red droplets did not startle me or attract my attention until I had gone further. Only when I was almost on top of her did I see the red pulpy mass, now covered with maggots and flies, that had once been my baby seal. She had been murdered and skinned so that only her head with those wide brown eyes remained to rebuke me for not staying with her. Beside her lay the palette knife which artists use—the very one I had seen up in the attic on my first visit; the very one (I was sure) that had destroyed my sister's portrait.

I stared at the knife. Had Julian done this? After his loving and care, it did not seem possible yet he was the only one with rage enough to have destroyed my sister's picture.

I stared again at the body and felt nausea rise in me. Did Julian hate me so that he had to take it out on this poor seal? Or maybe he had skinned my pet to pay his men for the death of Tamara?

A chill went through me. I did not want to think about it but the evidence was right here confronting me. There was no way I could draw anything but one conclusion. Tears burned me. I scarcely heard the screams which came to my throat or scarcely felt the rock as I sank to the ground.

It was Julian himself who found me on the beach. He had apparently followed me from the house and, when I had fainted briefly, had come down to gloat. I opened my eyes to find him towering over me—my vision blurred. He seemed like a lion ready to take his prey. I screamed again—and screamed and screamed.

With a quickness that I had not suspected he possessed, Julian slapped me across the face. I stared at him and felt sick. Anyone capable of hitting like that was capable of murder.

"Get up!" he commanded, when I had stopped screaming and whimpered slightly. I made no move. I could not.

"Get up!" he said again. "You're getting blood on yourself."

I still did not move and his hand shot out. I thought he would strike me again. Instinctively, I shielded my face. He only grabbed my arm and roughly pulled me to my feet. He did not — as Percy had done upon discovering my tears this morning — take me in his arms to comfort me.

I cringed, trying to draw myself away from him, unable to bear the crawling feeling of his touch as he held my wrist still in a vice grip.

"Go home!" He ordered me. "This is no sight for you."

Angrily, I shouted. "I suppose it's a sight for you, you murderer!"

He only grimaced. He did no even try to defend himself, the brute. I knew it was because he was guilty. It had to be. I began to sob afresh then, crying out all sorts of accusations — most of which I do not now remember. Again, he struck me. It was not as hard as the first time. I supposed I should have expected it.

My tears stopped almost immediately as I recalled not only what Percy had told me this afternoon but what I also knew. Should he injure me while I was his wife, I had no recourse with the law . . . no more than poor Jennifer had had. It was enough to silence me and he, too, kept his peace for the moment. I stood there, unable to remove myself from the dreadful sight and yet feeling sicker all the while.

"What are you waiting for, Tamara? I told you. Get back to the house, or wherever you want to go . . . but get away from here."

"Yes, so you can maul that poor creature more. Haven't you done enough damage, you mad . . ." I did not finish, for the look on his face was too frightening. For my own survival, I picked up my skirts. This time, of my own initiative, I fled the scene, trembling as I clutched at the rocks and climbed up, scarcely aware of my scratches and cuts. At least, I did not slip.

Once again on flat ground, I ran.

As the sun was still out, I headed toward the pond. When I reached it, I was breathless but, though the grass and stones were wet from the morning's rain, I located a dry spot and sat down. Numbly, I stared into the crystal blue water — willing answers to present themselves. Why? First Jennifer, then Tamara, then the portrait, then my seal. What was this horrid mess that I had created?

I sat there an age. My pocket watch had stopped. I did not know the time, but I did know that I was getting chilled and that I had best go. I could not risk developing pneumonia and being at his mercy. I was weak enough as it was without adding to the problem. Standing, I made ready to go.

My bones seemed heavy and ached with my burden. I was tempted to give up here and now. I glanced toward the water once more.

Lost in my thoughts, I did not hear my name

being called.

"Tammy, darling, I thought I would find you here, but I did not want to break your mood." He took me into the warmth of his arms. I should have resented his familiarity but I did not. After this afternoon's experience with Julian, I was still in a state of shock. What else could I expect from a murderer?

"I have only just now heard of your . . . pet. What can I say, dearest girl," he whispered, comforting me. "I wish I could ease your hurt, but do not say that I did not warn you. Julian can do strange and dreadful things when he is in a foul mood. Why, I doubt he even recalls half the things he has done."

I stared at him, too stunned to think properly. All I could say was "Why? Why? I don't understand."

More tears formed in my eyes. They were not only for the seal but for Tamara, for Jenny, and for myself. I realized that his actions this afternoon had hurt me all the more because I had wanted comforting that he had not been able to give me. I continued to allow Percy to hold me — I am ashamed now to say.

"Don't you see, my precious, Julian has been hurt. He thinks that you have hurt him and he wants to hurt you."

"Me — hurt him? But how?"

"He believes that you have been unfaithful to him with me."

I gasped and pulled away now. "But . . . but that is not so. You know it is not so!"

I continued to stare at Percy. "You did tell him that, did you not?"

Percy shrugged his shoulders casually, eyeing me. "Of course I did, dearest, but he does not believe me. He never does."

"But . . ."

"Don't you see, Tamara. He knew that the seal would die regardless." His soothing voice was bringing me to my senses. I continued to stare at him. He reached out for me but I would not come to his arms as he wanted. I did not want him or any man to touch me.

"Tamara, my precious, please. Will you not let me take you away from this — from him. I must admit that if you stay much longer, I shall fear for your life. He is ruthless. He is . . . mad."

My eyes widened. "It was you then. You wrote me the note."

"Note?"

"Telling me to leave the island."

He shook his head, smiling sadly. "No, Tamara, I wrote you no note. 'Twas most probably Julian himself. He does not always recall what he says and does. I have just told you that."

Unable to talk, I shook my head. "I cannot give you an answer now, Percy. Please. Do not ask me such a thing."

He came over to where I stood. His arm again went about me as if we were, in fact, lovers. "Whatever you say, my sweet Tamara. Only I must ask you at least to come to the house now. Julian is having the whole island searched for you. He is waiting supper."

"Supper? Already?" I shook my head. "I am not hungry." Percy laughed. "We already ate, but he refuses. He says that he is worried you will hurt yourself."

I grimaced. Was he worried that I would hurt myself or that I would find out something I should not?

"I admit. I, too, was worried about you."

I glanced at him. Truly, I did not know who to believe. I realized then that he was only inches from me. Fearing that he would try to kiss me again, I quickly turned away.

Like his cousin, it seemed, he was used to getting his way, only with nicer methods.

"Percy, please. I do not want Julian's words to become true. If he were to find out . . ."

"He will not . . ." Percy reached out for me but I eluded him.

"I am walking to the beach. I must see my seal again."

"Oh, Tamara." He grabbed my arm this time. "Please do not go there. It is too gruesome. Let me take you back to the house."

I could not prevent it. His lips touched the back of my neck. The hairs rose on my scalp as I felt chilled. My heart raced uncomfortably. This was not at all how I had planned things.

"Percy," I was nearly crying, "I ask you. Leave me alone."

He nodded. "Very well. I will walk with you. I cannot let you face that dreadful scene on your own. But promise me you will come back to the house immediately."

Anxious to get away from the pond now, I nodded.

In silence both of us walked toward the beach on the opposite end of the island. It really wasn't a long walk but I felt myself totally lost — listening to the twittering of the birds, the movement of the leaves and the lapping of the waves as we approached the sea. I had to go once more to see — to assure myself that it wasn't just a nightmare.

It was with Percy's help that I climbed the rocky path — the very same path which I had — in terror — run up this afternoon. The very same rocky ledge where only yesterday Julian and I had placed the pup and HE had put his coat over the seal. How could he have changed so completely? What had given him the idea that I was unfaithful with Percy. No, he could not think that. I had done nothing wrong. He must know about me. He must suspect and was therefore doing this to unnerve me, to punish me.

I glanced again at Julian's cousin, wondering if Percy had said something to Julian but then I shook my head slightly. I could think of no reason why he would make up lies.

There was nothing on the sand now. No pulpy mass, no helpless brown eyes. There was only the reddish brown stain where the stone had been soaked by blood. Where was the pup? What had happened to it? Surely, the birds had not gotten it yet? With tearful, searching eyes, I examined the immediate area.

"Obviously, Julian has had it removed," Percy

said, matter-of-factly.

I did not respond but continued to stare.

"It's better that way. Let us go. You are chilled, I believe."

Resigned, I sighed. "Yes. I guess so." I allowed Percy to guide me back up the path and we returned to the house. There was nothing more to do now.

I left Percy in the hall and silently went up to my room. I would not eat. I could not. My head again ached as did my throat. I was tired and drained. Oh, if only I could escape this miserable island. If only I could be on the packet that called here tomorrow. To think I had been here almost two full weeks now!

Reaching the top of the stairs, I saw that the door to my room—our room—was ajar. Julian stood there—standing—watching the sea from the window. Suddenly, my resolve came back. No. I would not leave until I knew exactly what had happened.

I trod cautiously but could not avoid his knowing I was there.

He turned then. "I am sorry for hitting you earlier, my dear. I did it only to calm you."

I stared at him. His hands were clasped behind his back.

"I will sleep in the guest room, as usual. Good night, Tamara."

I stared where he had stood and heard the door close behind me. Seeing that he had had a fire started I went over and tried to warm myself but even the licking flames could not warm the chill I had inside. I put on my fine lawn nightdress and shivered again. I knew that despite the apology, if he could hit me, he could kill me.

Trying not to think, I took a sleeping powder and drank it with the water from the pitcher. I think I shall always see the gruesome sight of that pup seal, its brown eyes staring at me, wide in terror. Had that been Julian's nocturnal occupation? I could have sworn last night that it was not and yet . . . he had been so insistent that I not go out there today. Why had he done it? And why had he torn the picture?

I had to admit that I did not understand either action. I found them both too unbearable to dwell on.

Thinking that I needed to write my thoughts, I crossed the room to the desk only to have another shock. The key which I had thought so well hidden was in the drawer. It took me a few trembling moments before I had the will to open the locked drawer. Who had invaded my privacy?

All was there still but it had been moved about. Thoughts of death—of Jennifer's and mine—came unbidden to me. Gently, I removed the diary. I had been a fool to place it there in the first place. Well, the only thing I could do now was rehide it and wait to see the results.

Chapter Twelve

I was ill the following morning — violently so. I do not know when I have ever felt so wretched. My whole body seemed to ache as I vomited into the porcelain washbasin which I had sense enough to bring from the other end of the room. My stomach had never cramped so badly. I was sure that I must be near death. Perhaps Julian had found out and put something in my food. Perhaps . . . but no, I had eaten very little yesterday. The deaths had grieved me so that I could not stand the sight of food.

Shivering I lay back in bed as the knock on the door came. It was not Julian. I would have known his step.

"Do you wish some tea?" Laura asked, entering without my permission and seeing my ashen features. I shook my head. Even her offer to have

Julian send for the Granny or the doctor was distasteful to me. Despite the fact that any movement made my stomach curl and cringe, I managed to shake my head. I told her that I was sure I was only slightly indisposed from my time at the pond yesterday. I would surely be better later in the morning, or perhaps tomorrow. All I needed was a day abed and hope that this illness would pass.

As she was near the door, I gathered my courage. "If you value my friendship, you'll not tell Julian I am ill. He will be furious with me."

"Yes, you are probably right." She nodded. A smile flickered across her broad face as her hand went to the knob. "If you wish anything, just ring. If you feel better, I will come up and help you dress."

Weakly, I nodded, and closed my eyes, willing the nausea to subside, willing myself to be well. I shivered and pulled the bedcovers over me. Then, I managed to return to a dazed sleep.

By my watch, it was only an hour from the time that Laura had left me to the time I opened my eyes again, yet there was a definite improvement as I got up. Granted, I still felt weak, but then that was due to my lack of nourishment. How I longed to get that sour taste out of my mouth.

There was no reason to call Laura to help me dress when I could easily do it myself. I chose a pale yellow muslin. My slippered feet made no sound as I came down the stairs. It was late, and I did not think that anyone would still be at the breakfast table. That suited me fine. I did not wish to speak to anyone.

Opening the door slowly, I stopped short. The table still had the remains of the morning repast, and Percy and Laura were in the corner, their bodies pressed hard together. Both seemed quite lost in their kisses.

Shocked, I stared a moment and then let the door slowly close. What was Percy's game, I wondered?

Neither of them saw me, for a moment later, I heard Percy's husky voice whisper, "Laura, my darling, you are so wonderful."

"I know," she responded with a laugh.

I blushed furiously. I knew I should not stay and listen but my curiosity got the better of me. It seemed that instinct would yet be the death of me.

Unable to resist, I peeked again through the crack in the door and my gasp nearly gave me away as I saw Percy's hand on Laura's breast. "You will give me the fifty pounds, won't you, Laura?"

She laughed again. "What do you need it for this time?"

"You know what I need it for. Oh, Laura. Laura." His voice was quite pathetic now. "If I do not have it this very evening, I will be thrown into prison . . . or worse."

She shrugged and glanced at the table. "I have work to do." She began to button up her tunic once more. "You should have done the work yourself, Percy. I told you." She paused and glanced back at him, unaffected. "How much did you collect for the clothes?"

"Not nearly enough." His voice was desperate. "Please," he pleaded, "Laura, my darling, my love, let me have the money. Just this once more." Taking her hand, he went down on his knees. I watched wide-eyed. She barely gave him a second glance as she pulled her hand from him. I heard the clatter of dishes as she began to clear the sideboard.

Seeing her come near me, I pulled back quickly into the shadows. Had she seen the movement of the door? I hoped not.

"Ask your cousin," she said, finally. "He's stood for your debts before."

"Laura!" Percy jumped to his feet just as I opened the door to peek once more. "Laura, this is my doom. You must help me. You know very well that Julian will not give me another farthing. He told me that the next time, he, himself, would turn me in. No! I cannot risk him knowing. You know what would happen then."

"That's your fault," she responded. "I have nothing to do with it."

"Do you not?" He grabbed her wrist so that she could not escape him. "Oh, Laura, dearest Laura, do not doom me. Julian is heartless. He will send me to debtor's prison."

"Stop making a fool of yourself," she hissed. "Get up before Julian or his wife comes in." She hissed out his wife with a vehemence that scared me and made my blood run cold.

"She is not just his wife," I heard Percy say.

"Well, we don't know her real name, do we?"

Laura's face had reddened in anger as I trembled. Only fear kept me standing there, listening, praying that they knew nothing more. My heart pounded. Yes, of course they knew I was not Tamara. I had forgotten that Percy had been at the train that day. He had made no mention of it since the wedding. If he and Laura knew, did Julian also know? Was Julian mocking me with my secret? Was all my effort at masque a farce? I wanted to move—either forward to confront them or back to my room, but I could not. It was almost as if I were frozen to the spot.

"Whoever she is, she is a lady. That much I will say for her," Percy responded.

A mild relief flooded me. So he did not know yet that I was Jennifer's sister. Did Julian then?

I forced myself to peek in once more. Laura's fists were clenched at her side now—as were mine. I wondered just how I could have misjudged the girl . . . and wondered, too, if my sister had misjudged her as well. My thoughts were in such turmoil that I scarcely heard Percy say, "Damnation, you don't think her illness is . . ." He glanced toward Laura. "You're a woman. You should know these things. It is too early to tell, isn't it?"

Laura shrugged. "She might be one who gets sickly easy. I know I would not, but then I am not soft and pampered."

My mouth dropped in astonishment. Me? Soft and pampered? I could have laughed if I were not so upset.

"Whatever," Laura continued, "He scarcely

comes near her now. Strange it is, considering his desire for the child. She has probably done something to upset him but then you know how easily Julian gets upset. I do not think we have much to worry on. Julian will soon show his hand and then she will leave, too, just as Jennifer did."

Percy shrugged. "Julian was quite irritated when she first came. You are right. I wonder why?" He paused. "But he was also taken with her."

"And you were not?"

Percy flushed. "Well, do I get the money? I do need it, Laura, my sweet love."

She gave another laugh that made me shiver. It was harsh like the birds which had flown over the seal's body. The noise seemed to echo in my ears. "That part of your brain is never exhausted, is it, Percy, my love?" She touched his cheek gently, so that I could not help wonder what their relationship was exactly. Then I watched as she planted a kiss on his brow. "Percy, if I had the money, you know I would gladly give it to you, but I've not a farthing. I gave you everything last time."

"Oh, my darling heart, you are dooming me. I truly do need it this time," he moaned. It was almost comical. If I had not been so upset I might have unwittingly laughed. I could see that Laura was not at all moved by his pleas. But then I guessed she was used to him whereas I was not.

"I am sorry, Percival. You should learn to handle your money better. Perhaps you can convince your creditors that you will pay them week after next. Surely something will come your way by then. You do have several projects in the works now — do you not? Give them what you can for now."

"Oh, Laura," he hung his head as he stood. His face, what I could see of it, had such a woebegone expression. How like my little seal he looked. "I'd be deuced if . . . well, I guess I shall have to do something. If you do not see me here this evening, you shall know what has happened to poor Percival Gregory Hawley." He sucked in his lower lip much like a child expecting punishment.

Laura shook her head. "Stop pitying yourself and leave me be. I've work to do."

He went over to the buffet and took a slice of cold ham. "I might as well eat before you take it away. Who knows when I might eat again?"

I watched as he advanced toward his chair. Shutting the doors as silently as before, I waited a few moments. Then, I tiptoed back up the stairs.

Making sufficient noise upon my descent for them to hear, I took a deep breath as I pushed hard on the door and tried to calm my features.

Putting on a smile, I greeted them both good morning. How pleasantly Percy smiled. One could almost believe nothing troubled him. What a confident actor he was.

"How do you feel, Tamara?" Laura eyed me with what now appeared to be an overly concerned look. If I had not heard her conversation before I would almost have believed her sincere.

"I am much better. Thank you." I gave her a strained smile. "You may just bring me some tea and toast," I said, trying to maintain my calm.

She stared at me a moment and then, nodding, left the room.

With her gone, the tension seemed to disperse. I had not really expected her to serve me so easily nor could I forget that they both knew I was not who I claimed to be.

As I sipped my tea, I realized that they could not have told Julian or I would certainly now be dead. I wonder what they waited for. As I reached for a biscuit, I wondered again about the note. Had it been Percy? But I did not think that it was his hand. Was it Laura's or did Julian after all know?

Ignoring my mood, Percy began to chatter on about what a lovely day it was and how glad he was that I was not ill. "It's a deuced bore when one is ill."

I stared at him. How could he be so insensitive.

I nodded only and continued to nibble my toast. On a lame excuse he left the table and I was relieved to be alone.

Having finished my lone breakfast and seeing no one about, I took a book from the library. Volume in hand, I walked to the pond.

It was not very long before I became absorbed in the pages. I was not reading after a while, however, but thinking again of Jennifer. I did not notice Percy's presence until his hands were upon my neck.

Frightened, I jumped and turned to see him laughing.

"That is not at all funny."

"Yes, your reaction was quite comical."

"You could have . . . given me a heart condition. Or I could have fallen into the pond, like last time."

His eyes were downcast. Taking my hand, he began to kiss my wrist. "Dearest Cousin, dearest Tamara, truly, I *am* sorry. Please say that you forgive me or I shall not live with myself. My life is such a bore and a misery at the moment that I needed to have the joy of seeing your face. I did not mean to harm you." Tears sparkled in his eyes.

Grimacing to myself, I thought of this morning's scene. I thought too of what he knew and forced myself to give a brief smile. How quickly Percy's affections could change. I highly suspected that the only one he ever truly loved was himself.

He bent down and whispered in my ear, "Have you thought of my suggestion, Tamara?"

I stared at him, confused.

"To leave this island with me. We could have such fun. We could be so happy. Just think of the thousand pounds my cousin has given you. It could last us a lifetime."

A sour taste came to my mouth. The way I saw Percy with money I doubted the funds would last more than a month or two. I looked up at him, studying his fine figure with the grey striped morning coat and grey silk cravat. Even if I did not love him, why could I not leave with him? Why could I not escape this dreadful island? Even as I thought it, I knew why.

"Well, have you thought?" He touched my arm briefly.

"No, Percy. I have no wish to leave the island at the moment."

"Tamara, my precious, it would be wonderful. Please I *do* love you so."

From under my lashes I glanced at him again. Maybe in his own way, he did have affection for me but it was not the affection that I sought.

I shook my head.

Puzzled, he assessed me. His baby blue eyes widened. "By jove, why not? Surely, you cannot love Julian?" He gave a laugh as if that fact was nearly impossible. He glanced sideways at me. "You don't, do you? I mean, anyone in her right mind would jump at the chance to leave this god-forsaken place in the sea."

My heart hammered quicker. "There is no love between Julian and myself," I managed to say. For even if I had to admit that I did have affection for Julian, it was obvious that he did not feel the same for me. I seldom saw him and he did not share my bed. Was he so confident of his ability to impregnate me? Was he so sure that I now carried his seed? A shudder ran through me.

"You are sure," Percy insisted. "You are sure that you do not love him . . . and that you are not carrying his child?" His eyes narrowed as he focused on my waist.

I shook my head, feeling the curls of my hastily pinned up hair tumbling down. "No, Percy, I do not carry his child. I think I should know if I did. But I believe it would be too soon to tell."

He came over and sat down on the rock next to me. His arm went about me. I wanted to shrug it off but did not think that was a wise move at this moment. Besides any sudden motion would have jarred me and sent me into the waters.

"My darling Tamara, if you are, have no fear. The baby will be yours, too, and I should love it as much as I do you. We will have a good life together."

Inside of me, I could feel myself shrinking smaller with his touch but I dared not let him know. "Percy, I tell you. There is no baby. If I can help it, there will not be one."

"Bravo!" He pulled me closer so that I could barely breathe. "I do believe it is your right not to ruin your lovely figure carrying a brat that you do not want."

"It is not a child that I do not want," I said, feeling the mixture of emotions conflicting within me, "it is his child." I looked up into Percy's sympathetic eyes. Had I not heard the conversation that morning, I would have quite believed that the man was in love with me. But he was not. He could not be. Still, he knew my secret — or part of it. I needed to tread carefully.

He continued to sit next to me, his arm about me as my heart beat uncomfortably. I was sure that, should Percy suspect I did not return his affection, he would be quite capable of telling Julian all that he knew. Most likely with Julian's knowledge of Victoria Damien — if he did not already know — he would fit the two together and then where would I be? Fear made my skin crawl.

I forced myself to stare at the water, to not think of anything.

Percy's words startled me and brought my thoughts back to him. "Tell me, Tamara," he touched my cheek and I fought to keep from cringing, "would you have my child then?" I turned to respond and met his lips as they brushed my face. Protesting, I managed to resist and, straining against him, managed to pull away.

"Oh, Tamara, Tamara. I do want you so. Tell me that you feel for me as I feel for you." His lips brushed my brow once more. Disgust gnawed at me. How could he not respect that I did not wish him to kiss me. Shame on my part for playing this game flushed me. True, he was fun to be with and had I wed him no doubt my life would have been far different than it was now, but I had not come to marry anyone. I had come to find out about my sister — and only by chance had gotten caught in Julian's trap. I would not betray myself or my sister's memories by allowing myself to be involved with this man at my side. No matter how good he had been to her, he was truly confusing the issues for me.

Once again, Percy tried to kiss me. "Please, Percy, do not." Tears choked my throat and veiled my sight. I attempted to move away but he held me tight.

"I know what I am about, Tamara." His arm was on my shoulder. "You are my life. I do not wish to confuse you or upset you. I only wish to have you leave this island and come away with me."

Again, I shook my head feeling the pain in my throat.

"Tell me the reason, then."

I glanced at him. My resolve was breaking down. In that instant, I almost did talk about my sister, about my fears for her, but I caught myself in time. "Perhaps . . . later. For now I only want to sit here."

"But you do love me."

I turned toward him, and studied him. Tears of frustration again came to my eyes. How could I love someone who was so insensitive. But what would happen if he found out that I did not feel for him. "I . . . I do not know. All I wish is that I had never set foot on this place."

He took my hands, caressing them, sending shivers up my spine. "Then, come away with me."

Once more, I resisted.

There was a dreadful silence between us before he spoke. "Can I confide in you? If you have any feelings at all for me, you will help me." His face had a troubled expression.

In spite of what I already knew, my heart went out to him. "Of course, Percy. If I can help you, I shall."

He hung his head, playing fully on my sympathy. I could not help but admire his ability to wring a tear and nearly laughed but for fear that he would suspect I had heard and then known that he could blackmail me."

"Darling, darling, Tammy," he began, "I am in miserable, horrible trouble. It is my own stupid fault, I know. I owe gads of money to some people on St. Mary's. It was purely by accident that I became involved with them, mind you, but foolishly I did. If I do not pay them tonight, I shall be . . . thrown into gaol . . . or worse." He again hung his head. I was surprised that I could see tears in his eyes.

My own voice was hoarse, affected as I was by his emotional presentation and by my own fear. "How much is it that you need?"

He took my two hands in his. I could feel the teardrops hitting my skin. He was playing the scene for all he had.

"Oh, you have saved my life!"

"I did not say I could give you the money. I only asked how much you need — and what it is for?"

Again, the tears dropped from his sapphire eyes as he shook his head. "I . . . cannot explain, my dearest. You . . . would not understand now. Perhaps . . . later." He brushed the tears with a kerchief. "How can I trust you when you do not trust me?"

My heart hammered. I stared at him — speechless. Was he asking me to tell him my true identity? I shivered. Percy was charming but I did not know how much I could trust him. He was right. My resolution remained firm, even though the moment was a difficult one.

Finally, Percy broke the spell and spoke again. "You see, you do not trust me to take care of you, to take you away? Do you not see — if you stay, you will be forced to flee anyway. He will force you away."

I swallowed hard. How could I believe that Jennifer had been forced away with her clothes here? How could I believe anything other than that she had been murdered by Julian Hawley, the man who had commissioned and then slashed her portrait.

"Why?" I asked. "Why would he force me away if he wanted me here so badly that he obtained a special license?"

Percy shrugged. "He gets into these moods. Surely you have noticed that he's not come near you in several days. Would a man in love, would a man who desperately desired a child be like that? Oh, yes, it is true that he wants a child. He needs an heir to this . . . this rock." Percy swept his hand across the pool area. "But he cannot quite deal with anyone as he should. He . . . he has this madness. Jennifer found it out and left. She left," he took my hands and stared into my eyes, "in fear for her life. Why do you think she never contacted anyone?"

My heart thudded. "Why would . . . why would she contact me?"

He gave a slight smile and shrugged. "I thought you knew her at school."

I suppose I must have nodded but I do not recall it.

"You see. She was afraid. He made her afraid. Please, Tamara, come with me. I do not want him to make you fearful as she was. Give me the money to pay off the debtors and flee this foul place with me."

278

I glanced toward the pond which my sister had so loved. What *had* happened?

The tears that were in *my* eyes were real. "I cannot Percy. Please, do not ask. If you do not want to tell me your trouble then there is nothing I can do."

"Tamara, I need fifty pounds, at least."

I glanced quickly at him and then back at the pond. "That is a fortune."

"I give you my total word that I shall never let it happen again. Please." He took my unwilling hand. "Did not Julian just give you one thousand pounds?"

My mouth dropped open slightly. "Percy, I have not even seventy-five. Twenty five is all I could possibly lend you. And you would have to return it quickly. As to the money that Julian gave me . . . I sent it to my father's banker." I pulled my hand from him and wondered then what had happened to the cheque which I had sent to Tamara. Had she put it with my trunks? Would I discover it when I returned to London?

"Just twenty-five?"

I repeated, "Just twenty-five."

He leaned over and kissed my cheek. "You are an angel, Tamara. I shall love you forever, even if you do not succumb to my charms." He continued to hold me though I tried to move away. I doubted if I would ever fall to his foppish charms but for my own safety I would pretend to accept him for the duration of my time on the island. For all I knew, I might need to accept his help in fleeing — and quite soon if my fears of this morning proved correct.

"May we go for the money now? The sooner I leave for St. Mary's the better."

I was taken back a bit by his greed but I nodded. With his help I left the rock.

As we departed the area of the pool, he stated, "you must promise never ever to mention a word of this to Julian."

"No. Of course I shan't." I promised, knowing full well that to do so would be equally dangerous for me.

Carried away with his own emotions, he took my hand and kissed my fingers. "Come, my darling Tamara, let us go!" Still laughing, he pulled me along the path with him. In that moment, I thought it was just as well that I was not as pretty as Jenny for I knew he could mean nothing of what he said.

Chapter Thirteen

Shortly after we returned from the pond, the sky became overcast and menacing. It seemed to threaten a storm worse than yesterday's. By dinner, it had grown too dark to see much beyond the immediate door. I thought of Percy rowing to St. Mary's. Then, I thought of the seal.

Well, she was beyond harm now. My heart still ached. Yesterday was still a horrible nightmare. In fact, I was beginning to wonder when I would wake from this whole nightmarish journey. If only I could be sure that I would return to London to find Tamara and her husband safe, to find that they had a position for me, to find that my sister was indeed still alive — but these were wishes which had no basis in fact.

I was in the library, staring out the window at the dangerous white waves capping the darkness as I saw the first of the lightning and heard the thunder clap. I must have jumped for Laura, who was with me, asked, "Are you nervous about something?"

I glanced back at her, calmly sewing. Did she not care if Percy returned safely?

I shivered as a chill ran up my spine and lightning once more splashed across the dull grey sky. Something evil was about to happen. I glanced again toward Laura and then towards my husband. Julian also sat calmly at his desk and made no comment about his cousin's safety or absence from dinner. It was impossible to know what it was that I feared but the same chill which I had had from the dreams seemed now upon me.

Only as I looked up did I realize that Julian's eyes were upon me — as they had often been during dinner. It was again as if he were assessing me, judging me. I shivered.

"Why are you so pale, my dear?" Julian finally asked.

"Would you not be worried if you knew someone was on the sea in this?"

He shrugged. "Who are you worried about? Surely not Percy?" His eyes narrowed with such jealousy as could have cut my throat were they knives. I wanted to tell him that yes, I was worried about Percy but instead I turned again to watch the sea.

"I suggest you read or return to your room. An early night would no doubt help you feel better. Did not Laura tell me you were feeling poorly this morning?"

I gasped and turned toward Laura, feeling my heart beating with the rhythm of the rain. "I felt only a little sluggish. It is nothing to worry about."

"No, it probably is not." His eyes again scalded me and then he returned to his work.

"Perhaps you are right," I said after a moment of silence, "Perhaps I will have an early night." Thus saying I picked up the book which I had attempted to read and went up to the bedroom. Even as I climbed the stairs, I hoped that Percy had had the sense to stay the night in Hugh Town. The choppy waters were rough enough to swamp a boat much larger than the one he rowed. I took a deep breath, warning myself that I had to be careful not to become attached to "Puckish" Percy — especially when I knew what a charming liar he was.

By half past nine, the fog outside was so dense that I could not even see the garden below my window. Earlier, after not being able to read, I had thought I might walk to the pond — despite the dark — but the fog was so thick that I knew any attempt to leave the mansion would be hopeless. I had returned to the bedroom noting that Julian and Laura were still quietly working in the library.

The idea of being lost on a night like this kept recurring to me and I knew that Percy must be having problems. Perhaps it was just the mist, creeping into the room and contributing to my feeling of loneliness but with each moan of the wind more shivers ran up my spine. Even the fire failed to warm me this night. I knew something terrible was going to happen and I was petrified of what it might be.

I believe it was about half past ten when I finally crawled between the covers. The words of the book had made no sense and fear was all I could think of. Had Jennifer become lost on a night like this? No, of course not, I told myself. I was confusing the real story with what they had been telling me.

Staring up at the ceiling, hearing the crackle of the logs in the fireplace, I felt the dull aching of my head. I did not want to sleep but I knew I had to. I knew that . . .

The thin thread snapped in my mind. There was something in Jenny's letters which would give me more of a clue. Something I told myself that I was missing and that I would learn if I re-read them. I believed that like myself, she had felt something for Percy. I fear that she must have been taken in by his sweet words were as I not. Why had he not helped her as he promised he would help me?

Outside the weather continued to ravage the house, and the thunder made me shiver. I paced a bit as I re-read the letters and then, weary, made the decision to attempt sleep once more. I could not find what I sought in Jenny's writings. I had been so sure that it was there. In fact, I saw now that she made no reference to Julian's possessive nature. Why did I think that she had?

I crawled between the cold sheets and felt the tears in my eyes. Pulling my knees up to my stomach to warm me, I told myself that I did not want Julian here in the room with me, that I was best off without him, and yet I wanted his warmth, wanted his arms about me, comforting me.

I lay there hearing the crashing of nature's fury and seeing the angry flashing of lightning. Time had passed but I was not quite sure how much. I continued to toss and turn until I finally heard the clock below strike at midnight. The bed-clothes had become crumpled with my anxiety to find a comfortable position.

I believe I had just dozed off when the sound of gunfire woke me. My heart pounded as I jerked up right in the bed. All I could think of was Jennifer. I had again dreamed of the pond and could almost have sworn that the shot was directed at me.

At that very moment, Julian opened the door and came in. I wanted to welcome him, to say something but my fright had left me speechless. All I could do was stare.

"What? Not asleep?"

"No . . . I . . . the storm has upset me." I watched as he crossed the room to a trunk which stood in the far corner. "Was that gun shot I heard?"

"No." He pulled out a heavy yellow oilcloth mackintosh from the chest and a pair of heavy boots.

"What was it and where are you going?"

"It was cannon fire and I am going out."

"But where? In this storm?"

He glanced at me a moment. I did not know if

it was concern or not but he seemed sad. "Go to sleep, Tamara."

"I cannot. Tell me what's happening?" The goosebumps on my arms rose and I shivered knowing that danger was at hand.

"Cannon fire could mean a ship's in trouble. Or again it could be those blasted Germans sounding off as they sometimes do before entering the channel. They have been warned about drawing us out but it does not seem to matter to them."

"But you can not see anything. How can you go out." I jumped from the bed in my nightdress and ran to the window. "I can barely see the garden now, let alone the sea."

He glanced at me as if to say that I knew nothing of island life. "If we can launch a boat, we will go out."

I inhaled sharply, not wanting him to go. "And if you can not?"

"Then we will wait until we are able, my dear."

I drew the curtains closed again, "feeling" the driving rain hit me like bullets even through the glass pane. He was nearly dressed now and looked ludicrous in his yellow slicker.

"What does happen . . . if there is a ship wreck?"

"What do you think?" He sneered, as if I was a stupid child. "Since you already have come to all your conclusions about life here, you should know."

I flushed hotly, wondering what he knew of my conclusions. "I . . . I don't know," I responded. I

for Jennifer's murder, the judge and jury, would, I was sure, be interested in this sideline of his.

Lost in thought, I scarcely heard him addressing me.

"You will stay here with the other women, Tamara."

"And what will you be doing?" I questioned, "while I am relaxing in this comfort."

"I, my loving wife," his tone was sarcastic, "shall be attempting to launch a boat and see if we can determine the nature of the distress call."

and how much you can get from them, I thought.

"And if you succeed?"

"If we succeed," he gave me a grim smile, "the survivors will be brought back here for the women to care for."

So they let the women do the worst part. The pictures of the mutilated, water-logged, half drowned people, crying out for help and beaten down by these beefy women (myself and I hoped Laura and Mrs. Stewart excluded) was too much to take. I blanched. The nausea rose in my stomach.

"If you were too sensitive for this work, you shouldn't have come. I shall have one of the men escort you back to the house."

"No!" I exclaimed. "I'm fine. I would rather go with you in one of the boats. I can row. I've done it once before."

"On a pleasure trip, no doubt." He gave a harsh laugh which made me cringe. "Stay here, my dear, where you are safe. If the waters becalm enough for your type of rowing, I shall call you."

He left then before I could reply and with four other men, he braved the storm. Was this, I wondered how he had gotten his wealth.

Shortly after he had gone we once more heard cannon fire. It seemed closer this time and the second blast followed in quick succession.

"Laura?" I huddled next to the fire. It was, I realized, close to one in the morning and yet surprisingly, I did not feel the least bit tired.

"What?" she snapped.

"Do you . . . do you help, too?"

I have never felt so stupid as she stared at me contemptuously. "Of course! Everyone does! That's gunfire again. I wonder if the men have launched the boat and found the ship."

I wondered, too, and I hoped for the sake of the survivors they had not.

It was nearly a half-hour later when the men returned. All of them, Julian especially, were completely soaked. They removed as much of their wet clothes as they decently could and stood before the fire.

"Too rough," Julian told us. "We will have to wait a bit until the fog clears so we can see where we are going."

They tried to launch the boats twice more before finally, at about half past three, one of the men came back. "His Lordship's gotten out." Among the other women there was elation. For me, there was only sorrow.

I, for one, was determined that I would not let this opportunity pass me by. If I could catch him in the act of attempting to murder the survivors or steal the ship's goods — all the better. If I did not actually see it, I would have no case, and my worry and my lack of sleep would be for naught. So while the others were rejoicing, I with my thick yellow coat, slipped out of the small church and made my way through the slippery mud toward the coast and the quay where the boats were now being launched in quick succession.

I did not think of my own danger, of the fact that should these people find out what I was about, more than Julian would be ready to murder me. I knew only that proof of his work would certainly help convict him of my sister's demise.

The path was dark without lights from the houses. More than once driving rain tempted me to return to the church. Within a few moments of leaving, tears were running down my cheeks from the stinging rain.

Julian was right when he said that I had rowed only on a pleasure cruise in calm waters, but I found that when one is determined, one can do almost anything. The wind was still foul as it whistled about me, and I was sure, atop the roar, that I could hear the hue and cry of the poor victims. If only I could have gotten to them sooner. Rain continued to pelt my face. I knew I was nearing the quay and began to run. I almost slipped into the sea but caught myself on a loose branch and, feeling my heart pounding, forced myself to stop a moment to calm myself.

Two boats were yet to be launched. I could see no sign of Julian among the other men who sat there, assured that he was still out to sea searching for his victims, I hurried along. For once, I blessed the wind which, because of its force prevented Mr. O'Dea and the other men from looking too closely and perhaps recognizing me.

As they began to form another party to go out, I joined them. With all my meager effort, I struggled with the heavy oars as we fought the rolling waves and were shifted, tilted, and tipped. There were three of us in the boat, and we began to row toward Bishop Lighthouse Rock from where the gunfire had first been heard.

One of the men took his turn at the oars, and as I moved carefully to change my place with him, I saw in the eerie tunnel of clarity through the dense fog the wreck of the ship ahead. The foremast was filled with people strapped to it, trying to save their lives. As I watched, the mast began to sway violently causing my own heart to lurch. The men who had fastened themselves to it fell into the cold, forbidding sea.

Feeling the frigid water upon me, forgetting my own tenuous position, I stood and cried, "Oh no!"

With my unfortunate motion, I heard the curse of my companions as our slender craft somersaulted upon the waves and we joined the harried survivors in the sea.

Shocked by the suddenness of the plunge, I could do nothing as the cold water closed about me, dragging me below the deadly waves. As I choked on the water, I was aware of a buzzing sound in my ears. My mind grew numb from lack of air and spots appeared before my eyes. I found my survival instinct then and forced myself to kick and fight back toward the surface. I gasped for air and gulped it down when my head broke the waves. All too soon I was again submerged with the force of the wind and waves as my clothing now heavy with water weighed me down. It seemed I was sinking faster than I could fight my way up. I cursed the fact that I had never been a good swimmer but at least I knew the basics.

There seemed no recourse but to discard my clothes as quickly as I could. Without air, I could barely think and yet I managed to fumble for the string that had held Julian's trousers. There was again that awful humming and the sting of the fresh wind on my face as I broke the surface once more.

Now totally nude, I was unable to do more than just keep my head above water. My vision blurred, and I closed my eyes, blinking them in quick succession as I tried to clear the water from them. All the while I moved my arms aimlessly.

It was several seconds before my sight cleared and then I saw I was only yards from the overturned boat. Where were the others? I began to swim towards it. There was no sign of them in this unforgiving depths of water. I cursed my own stupidity and prayed that it would all come out right. I had meant to save lives not to cost them but, as usual, it seems I had gone and done the wrong thing.

A wave washed over me, nearly submerging me again. I sputtered, gasped for breath, and lost my hold as I sank and surfaced once more. I was becoming numb with the cold and sleepy, too. It would have been quite easy just to let myself drift and forget everything . . . all my lonely childhood . . . all my jealousy and devotion to Jenny . . . the way I had come here and been brutally taken by . . . well . . . no I could not say it was brutal but it had been against my will . . . had it not? Yes, of course it had, I told myself. I was not his wife and yet he called himself my husband. I would die as Tamara had in a grave that was not truly my own.

Tears came to my eyes and mingled with the water. Yes, I wanted to forget it all and just let the lovely water take care of my troubles. It would be an easy way to solve my problems and then I would surely see Jenny again—but would that be of help to her? Would her murderer be brought to justice?

In that frame of apathy, I almost let go of the boat again when a rig rowed into view.

I scarcely noticed it until it had passed me by but then my inner desire for survival again surfaced. Suddenly, I no longer wanted to die.

"Help me! Help me!" I cried out.

My words were weak now but they were shouted with all the effort I could muster.

Strong hands pulled me out of the freezing hell. Only then did I realize what fickle fate had done to me. How was it that Julian's craft had been the only one to come near me? Why was it?

I had no time to think before I heard his shout over the noise of the storm. "What the devil's

shore soon."

I turned toward him, determined not to leave the boat. "No! I am not tired!" I denied, hotly.

"If you are not, then you should be. We shall shortly return to shore," he repeated again.

I pressed my lips together in frustration. I wanted to remain with the boat, to find out what would happen but he was right. I was extremely weary and wet but then, too, must be the others. I had not risked this much to be dismissed before I could learn the fate of the victims. But perhaps that was the very reason Julian wanted to put me ashore. If that were the case, I would have no choice but to try and to go out again.

Thank the Lord there was no time for argument. Two more survivors were seen as they struggled to keep afloat. Julian's orders rang out. We were to row towards them.

I saw that they were hanging onto an overturned lifeboat. Kicking to keep the blood going, they were obviously having troubles. One of the despairing I saw was a female. I was immensely glad to have another woman nearby but as we helped her aboard the gig, my eyes widened with fear when I saw that she had not had the sense to doff her rings and necklace — all of obvious value. If what I suspected were true, I feared more for her safety than my own. I stared at her, wondering what I could do to warn her but the poor woman was oblivious to my hints.

"My husband! My husband!" was all she could scream. "Please, you must save Mr. Jones, my husband."

"Madame, we have room here for only one. He will, I assure you, be picked up by another boat soon."

"Please!" she cried hysterically and threatened to stand and upset the boat. "My husband! I want to be with my husband."

Even with the wind raging about me, the slap of flesh hitting flesh was heard as Julian forced the woman down. I cringed recalling his rage. I hoped he was not taking his anger for me out on this woman. His fury, I feared, would be the end of us.

Our boat rocked violently. Stunned but quiet, Mrs. Jones sank down to our other passenger. Her face was streaked with tears. "My husband," she whispered. "My husband." My heart bled for her for I knew what it was to lose a loved one. I continued to watch Julian.

"Row for Penporth," he gave the orders.

"But what of the others?" I asked, forgetting my fears.

"They will be taken care of. The *Lady of the Isles* should be on its way now. I'm sure someone's informed the officials on St. Mary's now. Can you continue to row?"

I saw the exhaustion of the men and nodded amazed at the way my own strength was holding up. Grimly, I pulled at the wood.

The journey which should have taken twenty minutes at the most, took the better part of two hours, for we were still fighting monstrous waves. Twice more we changed positions as I admitted defeat and gave up the oars.

When we reached the eastern side of the island and beached the boat in the safe haven, Julian stood. Before I could protest, he had swung me up into his arms and lifted me out of the boat. Then, after placing me in a waiting pony cart, he brought the other two over. I can't say that I was sorry to be carried but I was sorry to leave the boat. Still, I don't think I could have moved much on my own. The whole island seemed to be waiting for us. I blushed knowing my state of nudity as Julian tucked the blanket around me.

Addressing Mr. O'Dea, he said, "You will bring these three back to the house. Help her ladyship to settle our guests in with some warm clothes and a bed."

The fisherman nodded, silently. As the cart began to draw away, I asked him, "What of you?"

"We are going out again, my dear girl, to pick up the woman's husband, if we can." His eyes met mine as if daring me to challenge him.

I did not. "Oh," I responded, and could say no more, for suddenly my heart wretched. Tears came to my eyes as I realized that in this case I was wrong. His motives, this time, were pure.

He took my hands in his. Perhaps he knew of my fears. "Tamara!" His voice was sharp but soft. "You are to stay in the house with our guests."

It was not in me to be the obedient wife and my own irksome nature made me respond, "I shall do as I please."

He glared at me as his mates called him to return to the boat.

"You will not follow, Tamara," he said, meaningfully. "Tell me that you will not."

I sighed and lowered my eyes. It would be difficult to rejoin the boats — exhausted as I was and disrobed. "Very well. You have my promise."

"Good." He turned to rejoin the boat and I watched him as they left the harbor.

Riding was quicker than walking had been. I waited outside with Mrs. Jones while Mr. O'Dea brought the unconscious man into the house. I had no idea of where he would be put but I heard Mrs. Stewart's voice inside and I knew he would be getting good care.

As I stood there in the windswept cold, I tried to understand what had happened. Exhaustion suddenly overwhelmed me like one of the many waves which I had previously experienced. I believe I must have fainted for the next thing I knew I was in the double bed with the high sun streaming in. My head ached.

I opened my eyes. What had happened?

Only as I focused my vision did I spy Julian's mackintosh which I had worn. It was hanging on a chair near the window. At that moment, tears came to my eyes as the gruesome memories of the night before returned. The shock of the wind that still pounded the waves could be heard outside. Where were the survivors? Where was Mrs. Jones?

Violently, I yanked the cord to call one of the servants. It was Mrs. Stewart who appeared. She, too, looked haggard.

"How d'ye feel, M'Lady?"

"How do you feel?" I responded, as I threw off the covers with a forced effort. Realizing that I was still naked, I hastily pulled them back. "Why was I allowed to sleep? Where is Julian?"

Her face took on a strained expression. "M'Lady, 'ee returned for a moment early this mornin' t'check on 'ee, but since then we've . . . we've not had word of him."

"What do you mean?" I jumped out of bed, this time ignoring the fact of my bareness and grabbed my dressing robe which Mrs. Stewart handed to me. "What do you mean you've not heard? Is he . . . dead?" I was scarcely aware of the hysterical level of my voice. "Is he drowned? Is that what you are trying to tell me?"

"M'Lady, I . . . we . . . don't be told."

"Help me dress," I ordered then.

"But M'Lady, his lordship did give orders before that we were to keep you abed because of your exhaustion."

"Well his lordship is not here. I am dressing."

She approached me to help, uttering a sigh of resignation.

"All you can do is relay his message," I assured her. "If he is angry, I will take the consequences not you." Even as I said that I knew it to be true and felt fear at the consequences of his anger but I would not, I could not remain idle and helpless while there was work to be done.

In the old church, only Mrs. O'Dea and another woman remained. Both were tending survivors and neither of them had heard anything about Julian. I felt sadness envelop me. After receiving their promise that any messages would be brought immediately to the house I excused myself.

A dreadful feeling told me that he was lying somewhere injured but that there was nothing I could do. Walking down towards the barren western rocks, which expressed my mood more than the populated eastern side, I let the melancholy settle in. If he were dead, then I would be free. My masque as Tamara Nilston would be done for there would be no need for me to continue it. If he were dead, then Jennifer would be avenged. Perhaps God had done what I had first longed to do . . . only now I wondered at the rightness of it.

From the top of the rocks, I could see that there were still some boats out. I put my hand to my brow to shield the rays of the sun but I could not see in any of the boats the broad back and dark hair which haunted me and plagued my waking moments. Tears came to my eyes as I began to climb down among the lower reaches of the rocks, hoping perhaps to get a better view.

Suddenly, a white arm reached out of the sea and over the ledge of rocks. Startled, I screamed until I saw that it was only Percy who emerged onto the dry shelf.

"Gracious! I thought . . ."

"What do you think?" He was free of the water now, his blonde curls plastered to his head like a Greek sculpture, and he reached for a towel that had been waiting for him.

"I thought you were one of the dead men coming to . . . back to life." How foolish that sounded, but he had indeed seemed quite eerie.

What were you doing over there?"

"Searching."

"Searching?"

"For bodies and stuff that could be returned to the company, of course." He grinned. "Gobs of stuff lost in that ship. Some of it's sure to float up and about."

I stared at him, wondering. "I see," was all that I could respond. "Have you by any chance seen Julian?" I heard my voice cracking at the sound of his name. I knew that my emotion must show.

Percy seemed to study my face for a moment before he smiled again and answered. "Well, don't worry about him, dearest. Julian can take care of himself. Only too well. 'Tis a shame almost."

He gave a quick smile as if to indicate that what he said was a joke but I did not take it that way. "You sound as if you wished him dead!" It dawned on me now the extend of petty hate that Percy must hide behind his laughter. Did he hate Julian for what he had done to Jennifer? Was that Percy's reasons for befriending me?

Percy's blonde brows shot up with my comment and his blue eyes went wide. "Darling Tammy, of course I've no such desire." His voice was properly shocked. "I am deeply devoted to dear Julian, prude that he is. As a matter of fact, now that I am finished here, I am going to join the group searching for him."

In helpless frustration I sucked in my lower lip.

"Perhaps I should attend your grandmother. She must be upset. Will you let me know if you hear anything?" I reluctantly turned feeling the pain in my heart as I did so.

Behind me, Percy gave a laugh. "You actually sound as if you, too, care for the old man. Do you?"

I stopped, not wanting to turn to face Percy because doing so meant I would have to face what I was only now struggling with. The blood rushed rapidly through me. I bit back the words that were on my tongue and told myself that Julian Hawley was a brute. He was a murderer, a seducer of young women and . . . and . . . I forced myself to turn to Percy now as full of righteous hatred I could say, "No. I am merely concerned because he is . . . is my husband."

Percy again gave one of his infamous smiles as his eyes met mine for that moment. My own heart stopped as I realized that Percy did not believe me and I wondered if I believed it myself. I thought again of how Julian's eyes had met mine as the cart drove off. No, I could not think of Julian in those ways.

I shook my head again feeling the pins loosen and my hair tumble down a bit. "I had best go to see your grandmother," I said lamely and turned again, feeling Percy's eyes on me. Within me there was a disturbing gnawing at my heart. It reminded me of the story of the Spartan boy and the fox. Like him, I could not show my pain for fear of death.

The thatched cottage had withstood the storm

remarkably well. Aunt Priscilla was, as before, upstairs watching the sea for her husband to return. I tried to tell her about what had happened, about Julian being missing but all she would talk about was her husband, Jack and the will of God.

"Without an heir, he's good as dead, anyway," she mumbled finally. I wondered if it was Jack or Julian that she referred to.

Finally, after several hours of trying to talk to her, I could tolerate it no longer. My frustration to know something reached its limit. Even watching the sea from the vantage point of the Aunt's cottage could not soothe me.

Only as I left her to return to the house did I realize that not once in the whole time that I had been there had she mentioned Jennifer or the murder. Neither had I questioned her.

Back in my room, I refused food and spent the next hours pacing back and forth. Every half hour or so, I would ring the bell. Usually Mrs. Stewart answered my summons.

"Have you heard anything yet? Have they found him?"

"No, M'Lady. They be doin' what they can, M'Lady. Ain't no knowing how long it will be. We'll inform 'ee the moment we be told. Ye should get some rest, M'Lady."

I nodded absentmindedly but rest was the last thing I wanted. "Very well," I sighed after the fourth time she mentioned it. "Very well, I will rest." Even as I said that I knew that I would not be able to sleep.

Percy came up to the room about ten at night. Naturally I questioned him as well.

"Have you heard from him?" He mocked me. "I declare, dearest, Tammy, you do sound as if you love the man."

I had continued my pacing, still dressed despite my promise to Mrs. Stewart, and until that second I had been unable to stop.

"No!" The word sprang out. "No, I do not love him!" I said vehemently, trying to deny the fact to myself.

"Me thinks the Lady doth protest too much," he quoted.

"Percy, no!" I stopped pacing but was now wringing my hands in silent agony. It was not something that I could help. "That is a monstrous thing to say." How could I possibly love the man who killed my sister, who murdered my pup?

Percy's eyes again widened mildly surprised at my vehemence. "My darling, it is quite understandable for one to fall in love, even belatedly with one's spouse. I'll not hold it against you."

No!" I stamped my foot as I continued to wring my hands. "No, I do not love him. I shall never love that monster. I tell you that for a fact."

Percy shrugged. Then after a moment, he came to me with his arms outstretched. He obviously felt that if I did not love Julian then I must love him. "Well, precious, you must not act like a frantic wife." His hands were on my shoulders. "It is a jolly good show for the servants and all, but it is not necessary for me. Come downstairs.

There's some fabulous cold beef on the table."

I shook my head as the nausea rose up in me. Even if I wanted to eat, I could not. He was right. I would have to calm down. "I am sorry, Percy. I am just tired, I believe."

"Shall I have dinner sent up for you? I am told that you have eaten precious little today." His eyes were so full of concern. "I fear you shall waste away."

I smiled at that. That was not, I believed, a problem. My appetite in general was far too hearty to allow that. Still it was wonderful to have his concern. It would be even more wonderful to love and be loved in return by the same person. The pain enveloped my heart like a dull ache. I shook my head. "No, I do not want to eat. I will be fine. Do not worry, please." I touched his cheek, thankful for his words. "Actually, I think I shall go to sleep."

He made no move to leave the room.

"Percy, I do not think it right for you to be up here with me." I began to remove the pins from my hair purposely.

He still did not leave but continued to stare.

"Please, Percy. I am in no mood for conversation now, no matter how delightful." My hair was nearly down now, flowing past my shoulders as if my burden were let down.

He cleared his throat. "Shall I send Mrs. Stewart or Laura to help you undress?"

I considered the two possibilities. "Mrs. Stewart, please. I would like to speak with her as well."

Shrugging, he turned and closed the door with a thud. He was upset with me but I could not help that just now. It seemed that I could make no one happy, not even myself."

My throat tight with emotion, I leaned against the lounge pillows and sighed. Percy was right. I was acting foolishly. I was acting as if I was in love with Julian—which of course I was not. It was, I repeated again to myself, only concern that Jennifer's murderer would have just revenge.

Mrs. Stewart came up moments later.

"Mr. Percival says . . ."

"That I want to talk with you. Yes, I do. Help me undress please? My limbs ache. I do not think I could manage the fastenings myself.

She grunted. "I thought you were asleep long before, M'Lady."

I gave her a slight smile. "How are the two we rescued? Go take care of them and get some rest, yourself."

"M'Lady, I could not rest any more than you could." She helped me to the bed and tucked the covers about me.

"Will you come up here to report every hour at the very least. I do not want to summon you."

"No?"

"No. I . . . I do not want Percy to know that I have asked this. He chides me for worrying too much," I told her.

"Of course, M'Lady," she smiled sadly at me and nodded as if she understood. "I be coming t'ee. Never fear."

"You must come to me even . . . if the news is

bad."

She pressed her lips together as if wondering what to answer and then nodded.

As she closed the door, I sank my head back onto the pillows. Alone again with my thoughts I wondered if I had misjudged Julian. It would be a shame for him to cheat the hangman for one good deed. All the evidence that I had thus gathered pointed to him yet I had already misjudged him once. But who then would have done away with my sister? Percy?

No, Percy was—as my sister had said—puckish. He was sweet and a bit tending towards foppish ways especially with his gambling and his dress. I knew, too, after what I had overheard that I could never completely trust him but he did not seem to be the murderous type. He did not go into rages as Julian obviously did. Besides, what did he have to gain by my sister's death. No, it was not Percy and unless there were other men that she had not told me about, then Julian or one of Julian's assistants, had to have done it. Even if it had been an accident, even if his rage had driven her off in a storm, it was still his fault. It only remained, if he were still alive, for me to learn the details. If he were not then I suppose that the last days of my sister would die with him for I no doubt would shortly leave this island. Where I would go I did not know. I only knew that I could not stay here.

Time crawled by slowly. I closed my eyes and tried to sleep but could not. After what seemed like three hours (my watch had stopped), I pulled the bell cord.

It was Percy who came to the door.

"What time is it?" I demanded.

"Midnight, my precious. I thought you were going to sleep."

I winced at his familiar term, realizing that I did not like it when he called me those endearments but that was part of Percy.

"I am . . . thirsty," I replied. "Have Mrs. Stewart bring me up some water."

"What about warm milk? That will help you sleep better than plain water, my love. Besides," he gave a laugh, "I should think after your experience that you've drunk enough water."

I shook my head. "No, Percy. I want water."

He touched his lips with his fingers and blew me a kiss. "Your wish is my command. I shall pass along your message," he yawned and covered it delicately, "and then I shall retire."

I knew from Mrs. Stewart's eyes that she had not yet slept. I accused her of neglecting both herself and me but then seeing her astonished look, I felt the rebuke.

"M'Lady, it has not yet been an hour."

"Oh," I flushed and reached out to rewind my pocket watch. The strain was becoming unbearable. "I am sorry. Thank you for the water."

"M'Lady, ye should sleep, His lordship . . ."

I almost screamed at her that I did not want to hear Julian's orders without having him here to give them to me. But with the greatest of efforts, I restrained myself. "Do not talk to me about Julian until you can tell me if he is alive or dead. I

312

still expect you every hour, unless you have fallen asleep. That is your only excuse."

"Yes, M'Lady," she nodded.

She left the room. I tried to get up but realized that exhaustion and worry had taken their toll. My muscles felt leaden. Searching my mind, I mumbled a prayer that I had learned in school. I hoped that God would hear; I hoped that Julian would come back alive and well.

I believe I must have dozed but I woke every hour to check my watch. Always within minutes of the twelve hand as if my inner sense knew. Mrs. Stewart would come to tell me that there was no news as yet.

At four in the morning, feeling stronger and unable to stay in bed any longer, I donned my wrap. The fire was still going strong but it was small. In the chilly room, I began to pace once more. Mrs. Stewart had just left me saying that the search had stopped for the night. Nothing could be seen since the night—even though clear—made things difficult. "I doubt we'll have much word before dawn."

In frustration, I pressed my lips together. If only I did not feel so helpless. "Please, will you continue to keep me informed. There might be someone coming in with news still. Are there not some boats out yet?"

"Aye, but precious few. Can I get 'ee anything to eat, M'Lady? Maybe that'll help 'ee sleep some."

I shook my head. "Some tea perhaps."

Nodding, she departed.

It was only a few moments later when I heard her scream. My heart went to my mouth. She had heard! He was dead! She had heard and I had to find out, too. I did not think I could stand the wait.

Unable to contain myself, not regarding my undressed state, I ran to the door, determined to hear all the details, knowing that my own life hung in balance.

I had just put my hand to the knob when the door swung open.

Julian stood before me. His clothes had been torn and they dripped with water. There were dark rims circling his reddened eyes and a shadow of a beard on his face but he was alive! It was impossible for me to contain my momentary joy and shock as I, too, screamed. "Julian!" I ran to him and despite the dampness of his clothes put my arms about him. "Oh, Julian!" I sobbed. "You're safe!" My joy startled even me.

He seemed glad of my reaction; for a moment we did not speak.

"Did you think me dead?" he asked, finally. His cold voice cut me to the quick. I looked into those same unfathomable black eyes but could not find words to answer. "Perhaps, Tamara, I should ask, 'Did you hope I was dead? You would be a rich widow then.'"

I dropped my hands to my side, confused. First I was accused of loving him too much—and could not admit to it; now I was accused of wanting his death but I could not admit to that either.

"Tell me," he continued, staring at my night

dress, "Where were you headed now, dressed as you are? To my cousin's room? To . . . celebrate my demise?"

I stared at him—even more shocked.

Surely, he could not think. . . .

He mistook my silence for guilty submission.

"I see."

There was nothing I could say and my pride would not allow me to explain his foolish notion away. Turning away from him, I started back toward the bed.

"You must be exhausted," I said, sinking down onto the feather cover, myself.

He nodded. "I am." Removing his wet clothes he came toward the bed and picked up his dressing robe. As he stood before the fire, stoking it higher, I saw his naked figure outlined with a halo.

"Are you not even curious how I survived the storm? I suppose you do not care that my boat had a leak in it?" He was still by the fire but his words chilled me. What was he trying to tell me, that someone had tried to harm him. I stared at his back as I recalled that my boat, too, had developed a sudden leak.

I shook my head just as he turned toward me. He, of course, misconstrued it. "I am hearty sorry to have spoilt your plans, Tamara." His voice was low but full of rage. I knew at that moment how scared Jennifer must have been, but more than fear I was feeling pain.

"The only plan I had had was to see you safe," I replied, trying to keep my voice an even level as I recalled what I had hoped to find out that night at sea.

I pulled the covers up about me, feeling very cold. "You can tell me about your rescue in the morning, if you so wish," I said, knowing that I desperately wanted to hear but not wanting him to know that. Suddenly, I wished that I had not gotten up that last time. I wished that I had fallen asleep and remained oblivious to all that was happening.

Realizing that I could not keep up the anger in me, I added, "Besides, you do need your rest."

His eyes met mine for a moment and then he gave an exaggerated sigh. "Perhaps you are right, my dear. Perhaps you are right." He wet his lips. "While I do not wish to offend your sensibilities this night, my dear, I do not wish to leave this room tonight."

My heart leaped as he continued. "No, in fact, I shall share your bed this night for my bones are chilled deep." His mouth had taken on a bitter hardness and for a moment, he again looked ugly. "I shall not have the audacity to touch you, since I know that you do not like my touch," he paused and I could only stare at him and know that what he said was a lie. "But I should like your warmth."

The lump in my throat was too great. I could only nod and lay back.

With the gas lights out and the fire low, he came over to me. I felt the hardness of his body as he rolled over next to me.

There was an awkward silence as I realized that

with him so close, I could not refrain from touching him. Despite my hurt, I swallowed my pride. "Are you hurt anywhere?"

My hands were on his shoulders as his back was to me.

"No," he responded gruffly. "At least not that I can tell."

"Will you . . . will you hold me then? The room is quite cold this night."

There was a moment of silence before he turned and looked at me, studying my face in the embers of the firelight. His muscular arms went about me as I cuddled next to him, my head on his chest, my hands on his sides.

I could not, however, sleep for his heart beat echoing in my ear and the sound of his blood rushing.

"Julian?" My hand touched his stomach and I felt him wince as I glanced up to him. "Julian, you hurt there?"

"Some," he grunted.

"Oh." I pulled my hand back and entwined my fingers in his matted hairs of his chest. After a moment, I again looked up to him. "I am glad that you are safe. Truly. I am." The emotion choked my voice so that I could not speak well and I felt the tears come to my eyes.

He leaned down and kissed my brow sending delicious shivers through me. "I am sorry, Tamara," he whispered. "I did not mean to jump at you so. My jealous nature does tend to get the better of me at times." He kissed me again and this time his mouth met mine. I welcomed him and his touch as I had never before welcomed him.

My hands went to his neck as we kissed and I felt my nightdress being lifted slightly. The warmth rushed through me as he touched me gently.

"Will it not hurt you?" I recalled his pain of a moment ago.

"I will be careful," he grunted, "both of myself . . . and of you, my little wife." His mouth descended to my breast delighting me so that I gasped. As his fingers began their exploration and probing I could feel my desire for him heat up like fire exploding within me.

"Oh, Julian!" I murmured. "Julian!" My own hands went to him as I held him and touched him in the way that I knew he had liked before. His return kiss told me I was doing right as we now fused in a heated passion. Joy flooded me as I lifted myself to receive him and I knew that beyond all doubt I wanted to share his life, to bear his child. Even with that thought, I knew it could never be. I would have to tell him the truth about me and whether he knew or not, his anger would be justified.

Forcing that from my mind, I allowed myself to swirl in the moment of pleasure as he held me, called out my name, penetrating and dissolving my fears and brought us to a wondrous conclusion.

When he had spent his energy, I again cuddled next to him and kissed him tenderly. Once more I felt the tears in my eyes knowing that I would miss him, knowing that if I chose not to continue seeking knowledge of my sister's fate that I would have to leave.

We fell asleep together, entwined in each other's arms. But even after this marvelous moment, I felt no closer to knowing this man than I had when I had first come.

Julian woke about ten in the morning. My head was still on his chest. I had been awake for several moments already, thinking, not wanting to move, not wanting to leave his warmth or disturb his slumber.

"Are you angry with me?" he asked, aware that I was awake.

"At what?"

"My cavalier treatment. It does seem that sometimes you irk me more than I can bear."

"But I have done nothing," I sat up, defending myself from what he suggested.

Julian lowered his eyes. "I wish I could believe that."

"Then believe it," I said, leaving his side as I quickly slipped into a simple muslin which required few fastenings.

Hurt by his mistrust, I left the room and headed for the breakfast table. He would follow when he was ready.

I was already seated when he did come in. I watched as he took his toast and buttered it slowly. I wished I could return to that moment of total joy last night but that seemed an aberration in our relationship. The silence between us was cold and forbidding. I was about to speak when Percy entered the room.

He looked from me to Julian and back again.

Unable to meet his glance, I did not look up.

"You going out again today, Cuz?"

Julian nodded. "I must see what bodies can be picked up. The funerals will be at St. Mary's tomorrow."

"But you can't. I mean, you should rest after your experience." His glance silenced me.

"Shall I come with you?" Percy asked, ignoring me, as well.

"If you want."

"Then I shall come, too," I told him.

Julian's eyes once more met mine. I blanched. I realized he assumed I was going with him because of Percy. Well, damn him, let him think that.

For a moment I thought he was going to forbid me but he did not. "If you come, you will have to do your share of the rowing. Are your hands up to it?"

I showed him my palms. The blisters were still healing. "I can do it."

"Can you?"

"Yes. I can." My lower lip jutted out in a child-like manner. I wanted to be with him and would not let him discourage me. Though I did not know why I wanted to see the corpses for I knew I should be sick. Perhaps it was that I was still not convinced that no attempt at robbery was being made . . . yes, that was it. That made more sense than my not wanting Julian out of my sight for as

Percy said, he could well take care of himself.

I hurried from the room to change to another pair of Julian's trousers which Mrs. Stewart found for me in the trunk. Even as I re-entered the room and saw the still unmade bed I found myself thinking of the darkness of the night and waiting for this night, hoping that I could again give myself up to the sinful pleasures of my body. How could I want to be with the man who I was sure had murdered my sister? How? It did not make any sense and yet just being with him gave me a sensation of delight. I had been in predicaments all my life but this seemed the worst ever.

Both Percy and Julian were waiting for me in the study. Both smiled when they saw how ludicrous I looked wearing Julian's trousers.

"Oh, I say, Tammy, you do look a sight." Percy doubled over with laughter.

"Well, it's not my fault," I cried. "I only want to help."

Julian managed to stem his mirth but Percy could not. Deliberately, I went over to my husband's side. Red flamed my face. I would do what had to be done. "I'm ready," I said firmly.

Without any unnecessary words, Julian linked his arm through mine and steered me outside. Percy followed. There was a pony cart waiting for us. I protested. "It's not that far. We can walk."

"We shall have plenty of exercise. It's best we save our strength. Get in Tamara. I do not want to argue with you."

Disliking his autocratic tone, I sighed and with

his help stepped up.

"Percy?"

"Course, I'm coming, Cuz. You know me. I would sooner ride than walk." He jumped in next to me and Julian took up the reins.

At the church there were others to greet us. All the men had the same idea—to bring in the bodies. Percy led one boat while Julian was to lead the other. One of the men had been in the boat with me the night before and balked.

" 'Tis bad luck, yer lordship," he grumbled.

"Then do not come or go with my cousin. Even better, Smiths, you can take the third boat."

"But yer lordship. . ."

"Do as I say, Smiths. I am in no mood for argument this day. Tamara will work as hard as any man. Never fear."

The man dropped his head and moved away to acquire a crew of his own for the third gig.

The water was smooth this morning. It was not long before we found the first group of bodies. My stomach reacted several times against the bloated, faceless creatures we rescued for decent Christian burials. Tears ran down my cheeks as I thought of Jennifer. If he really had sent her fleeing . . . if she had gone across on that stormy night, then she would have been lost at sea without a marker, without the comforting words of God to speed her on her way.

After awhile, my own anxiety forced me to ask Julian to put me ashore. I dreaded leaving him on his own, and yet . . . there was a limit to what I could take. My head was swimming; I felt ill with exhaustion. I could not understand it. Only once as a child had I ever been sick and then never nauseated as I had been this past week.

He did as I asked. Percy's boat had come in at the same time. "Percival, Tamara is not well. Can you see her back to the house or should I have someone else?"

Of my own accord, I stepped out of the boat. "I am not a child! I can find my own way back. Percy does not have to take me."

But Percy had already reached my side. "I've nothing of greater importance than taking care of your wife, Cuz."

"Good. You'll come back immediately afterwards then."

"Julian, I tell you. It is not necessary." Those dark eyes of his thundered.

"And I say that it is."

I trembled unexplainedly now. Percy took my hand. I saw Julian glance at both of us. Why was he doing this? I did not . . . I could not understand him.

"Percy, I expect you back in a half hour."

Percy did not respond as he steered me back away from the dock and we watched Julian's boat move off.

Only after Percy had walked me back and left me did I understand what was happening to me. It could not possible be. I could not be pregnant, not yet . . . not now. Tears rolled down from my eyes. I was legally unwed and pregnant. I had been here over a month and had missed my courses but had not thought of it until this moment.

Hand to my throbbing temples, I closed my eyes. Cruel images swam before me. The horror struck me afresh. I was carrying Julian's longed for heir! Even if I wanted to be rid of it, I did not know how it could be done. If he suspected at all, I would never be free to leave this wretched island.

I moaned softly. Frustrated, I put my hands about my stomach and pressed down hoping that if I pushed hard enough . . . but all I did was cause myself further agony and accomplished nothing. In the end, I fell asleep and did not wake, even when Julian returned.

Chapter Fourteen

The funerals were Monday. All morning I was moody and temperamental. Julian wanted to forbid my going but I refused. After an argument, he gave in and allowed me to accompany him and Percy.

It was Julian with his overpowering strength who rowed us over. How much faster a ride it was than when Percy had leisurely taken the oars.

The pier at St. Mary's was crowded. Everyone from the surrounding islands. Patiently, we waited for the *Lady of the Isles* to come from Penzance. That boat would be carrying Mr. Stevens, of Plymouth, the agent for the German boat, *Schiller,* which had sunk. Others, too, had come to look for salvage.

On landing we were conducted immediately to a spacious courtyard surrounded with stores. In the center sat Mr. Dorien-Smith, Lt. Governor of the Islands. How different he looked and how much sadder from the time of my wedding a month ago. I watched as he made preparation for all the funerals.

One had already taken place. It had been the white haired old lady which I had helped Julian with. The shock had been too great for her. Tears choked my voice and veiled my vision as I looked away from the coffin.

How desolate the little capitol looked today. All the roads were empty, all the shops were shut. It was as if the inhabitants of the island had disappeared when in fact they were all at the pier.

Julian took the chair next to his friend and sat down to give what help he could. It was difficult for me to understand how he could be so calm and unemotional about it all. Perhaps he had dealt with death — my sister's, Tamara's, and others many times before — but I had not. I found myself wandering the lonely streets until the processions were ready to start.

The funerals were ones that I had never seen before and never hoped again to see. There were few trappings of woe because there were few survivors and few family members. Only the black painted coffins, hastily built, served to remind one of the occasion. I had expected to see at least one mourning coach but the island had none. The coffins and bodies had to be content with ordinary pony traps decorated with black cotton. There were not even enough pall bearers to go around for the thirty-two coffins would soon

326

have depleted the male population of the islands.

As the long procession continued on, I felt someone come to stand beside me. Gratefully I looked up to see Julian.

"Are you all right, Tamara?" he asked as I wiped my eyes.

I nodded.

"Fine."

There was a strained silence before he moved to put his arm about me. I was glad for that small comfort.

I picked up a handful of the gorse and threw it on the boxes hearing the gentle tappings as the wood hit the wood. One flower I would hold and decided that on my way home I would throw it into the pond for Jennifer.

Suddenly, I missed my sister dreadfully. I began to cry and was sure that I would not be able to stop. I was not the only one moved by the funerals but I was the only one, I was sure, who was thinking of Jennifer. How odd it was that Julian was the one to hold and comfort me at this moment.

When I had recovered enough to walk, we trudged up the rugged road about a mile from the pier. The sea, which had taken its toll, danced on either side of us for a great part of the walk. The interment took place in the little stone church on St. Mary's, near the old town. It was then I learned that the island had once had another capitol.

With Julian at my side, I heard the solemn church service and continually dabbed at my eyes as the two large graves were filled with the coffins. It would have been nice for each to have his own space but land was so dear here and more bodies seemed to be arriving by the hour.

Our male guest came up to thank us for our help. When he took my hand, I told him that it was Mrs. Stewart he was to thank and Julian, not I. Truly, I had done nothing but hinder the operation, it seemed. If Julian had not been forced to rescue me and others from my boat chances were more people would have survived.

I thought, too, of all that had occurred in my life since that night. Another survivor was crying. Unable to watch her, I turned my attention toward the conversation of the men.

"If she had been English, we shoulda known that she be in distress. Fool Germans. Maybe now they'll not be so damn snooty and stop tootin' their horns fer the fun of it."

"Don't know if they'll stop, though," another responded. "They be doin' it since I can 'member. Germans like t'nounce themselves."

They continued on, coldly discussing the wrong use of the blasts. Unable to stay with them, I walked away from the speakers here as well. Again, I was weeping but this time the arms that went about me belonged to Percy.

Only when I heard, "So I was right!" did I look up to see Julian standing in front of me and Percy at my side.

"Oh, Coz. Don't be such a prickly prude. She was crying. I was merely comforting her."

"That is, I believe, my job, if I choose to do it,

but since you wish to take over, *you* may comfort her and escort her back to the house, too. I believe this is too much for her."

I watched horrified as he stepped into the boat headed to Tresco with the Lt.-Governor. How could he think . . .

"Julian!" I called after him—but it was too late.

"Come, Tammy, love," Percy said to me, smiling slightly. "I will escort you home." I did not move. His fingers touched my chin and I wanted to pull away but I did not. "Don't be sad, dearest," his fingers began to stroke my skin causing disgust to well up in me. He turned my head so that our eyes met. "You will always have me."

I knew then that Percy had done this on purpose, that he had flamed Julian's jealous nature. Recalling Jenny's last note I had a fleeting thought. Could Percy be trying to turn Julian against me? The idea was so despicable that I dismissed it immediately. What did he gain by putting my life in jeopardy? I could not answer that but nevertheless, I was furious.

"How can you joke at a time like this?"

"I?" His eyes went wide. "I never joke about love."

I jerked my head away from him, forgetting my need to keep Percy's friendship—or at least his silence. My heart was sick with grief as I followed Julian's cousin to the boat and I sat morosely watching the waves lap at our side while Percy rowed us home.

I told myself again and again during the trip

home that it was not that I had any affection for Julian. It was merely that he was judging me so wrongly and being so blind. If only he would listen to reason. If only my body would stop responding to him the way it did.

Chapter Fifteen

Percy and I arrived back at Penporth shortly after one. At two, the three of us — Percy, Laura and myself — sat down to a light lunch. I am sure the food was delicious but I ate very little. My thoughts were on the funeral and after, but Percy seemed to be in a good mood. With Laura, he kept up a cheerful banter. I wanted to shout at him to think of the poor souls being buried today but I said nothing.

When I could decently do so, I escaped from the dining room. As the sun was shining, I decided to walk a bit. My thoughts were still in turmoil from this morning. I wanted just to sit on my rock, to watch the calm waters — so soft and sweet, so dangerous and cunning — as they washed over the golden sands of the pond.

However, so engrossed was I, so lost in

thought, that like the first day I took a wrong turn. This time I was not panicking. I had lived on the island long enough so that I was not fooled as I had been on that first day. I could have turned back but I decided to see the old aunt. Perhaps she could now tell me exactly what she had seen. Perhaps, if I knew for sure that it had been an accident . . .

A cool breeze which should have been welcome, fluttered about me. I felt chilled, however, and my senses were taut. Evil was about me. My nerves were close to breaking. In desperation, I hurried along the path, refusing to glance back.

The house seemed welcoming and safe as the curtains flapped in the wind.

"Hello!" I called out as I entered the first floor.

"Hello, dear," the old aunt responded and came down the stairs for the first time in many days it seemed. Her eyes seemed to shine as she took in my face and the rays of the sun steaming into the tiny cottage. I decided that I would not mention the funerals to her for she obviously did not know of them.

"You look bright," she commented to me.

"Do I?" I forced myself to smile for I felt anything but bright.

"Carrying agrees with you, child. It is much better than the other. She was far too sickly."

I must have blanched for I felt the blood drain from my face. Was she telling me that Jennifer had been pregnant? That Percy had lied to Mr. O'Dea? No, that could not be. Percy was a fool and a fop but he would not purposely have lied. I decided then that Mr. O'Dea had merely been telling the story which he and Julian must have agreed upon should there be other inquiries.

"Yes, you do have the glow," she said again.

It was then I realized that she knew. I had been concentrating on her first message and not on the second. Once more, I felt the blood drain from me.

"How can you tell? I mean, it is so soon. I have only missed once."

She smiled at me as I again felt the dizzy foreboding that I had sensed in the path. I clutched at the post for just a second and then, somehow, managed to regain my composure.

She did not notice my distress, for she was grinning like a child who had just been given an unexpected present. How like her mischievous grandson, Percy, she was then. "There are ways," she said in her sing-song voice. "There are ways. I don't suppose you've told Julian yet?" She patted my hand and drew me into the room by the fireplace. "No. I can see that you've not. Doesn't matter though. He'll know soon enough, and he'll be pleased as punch." She clasped her hands in gleeful anticipation.

Before I could say another word, she went on. "Oh, yes, I am so very glad about it. Julian will be so happy. He deserves the land. He's worked at it. He deserves to have his heir and his land. Now mind you, Percy's not such a bad lad, but he's not the right type for the land. Sell it, he would. Yes, he would sell it. He doesn't have the feel for it that Jonathan and Julian did. 'Twas a shame 'bout the game, but I told him not to play."

I was confused and told her so. "What's this about the heir and the land?"

She peered at me through her specs. "Oh, dear girl, I have not even properly invited you in. What you must think of me? She bustled over to the chairs, her skirts crinkling as she walked and pulled one out for me. "You must sit down here. After all, you are my guest." I walked over to the chairs by the mantle, where she had put the picture of her and her husband.

She took the seat opposite me. "It's the will," she said, twisting her hands in a nervous gesture. "You must know about the will, surely."

I shook my head. I was surprised that today she was so lucid.

"The other knew and so should you. It is the will which says that my dear boy, Julian, must have a child within seven years after his blessed father's death. Ah, my nephew was a good man, too. My Richard treated me with the same respect like his son does. Those were happy days, before he won the place with the gambling.

"Won it in gambling? Julian's father? But I thought . . ."

". . . from Percival, girl. Don't interrupt my thoughts. My son, my Percival, took after his father. Dear Jonathan, he did so love his cards. My Percy was a wastrel just like his father. My Percy was Lord of the island. Won it in a gambling from the Duke of Cornwall, himself, but he lost it in gambling, too."

I pressed my lips together as I tried to comprehend all that I was hearing. It was beginning to make some sense. "Your son lost the estate to Julian's father, and his father's will said that Julian was to have an heir . . ."

"Within seven years or the place goes to my grandson, Percy. Dear little Percy. How he used to torment my cat and pull its tail. Haven't seen him around lately. Is he still at the house? Not married yet, is he? Though I've no doubt just like my own Percival, he's got a brat or two on the side somewhere." She gave a laugh. "Don't let it shock you. He's just like his father, he is."

I found it hard to believe that Percy might be a father, already, but then there were other things equally as difficult to comprehend. If Percy stood to inherit, that was a motive for him to get me and Jennifer, too, off the island . . . but . . . did that mean that Julian had had no part in Jennifer's disappearance? I flushed realizing that if that were so, then I did owe Julian a huge apology for ruining his life as I had. I was sure, too, that if I told him the truth and asked for his forgiveness he would be so furious that he would probably erupt in one of those rages. Yes, those rages. Had he still forced Jennifer off? Confusion forced me to put the information out of my mind as I idly picked up a picture from the mantle. Staring at it, I was amazed at the resemblance. With the frame in my hand, I asked, "Aunt, did Jennifer . . . did Julian's first wife . . . know of the clause in the will . . . about the heir?" I turned to face her with the daguerreotype in my hand but instead of facing the old woman, I faced Julian.

As I dropped the picture, the old woman broke into a laugh. Julian moved silently closer and bent to help me pick up the frame which was still unhurt.

"I'm sorry . . . I . . ." I stuttered feeling my face redden as a beet root.

With his unreadable eyes, Julian assessed me. Then he placed his hands on mine. It was like the lightning of the storm that had frightened me on Friday night. So magnetic and yet so dangerous. I would not, I could not, brush him off.

Together we stood there. Our eyes locked. Finally, he spoke. "Yes, Tamara, Jennifer knew of the clause in the will. She knew before we were married. I assumed that you also knew of it and your actions, therefore, have somewhat surprised me."

I shook my head numbly. I had not known of the will before and I tried to think if Jenny had. If so, she had not told me. Perhaps she had wished to spare me the details of her forced duty. Though as I had come to see the "duty" with Julian was not as painful as I had been prepared to find. If only my sister had confided in me. It would have answered so many questions for me. Then, I recalled that her last letter to me, the one she had never posted had had something about a will in it. Was this what she had meant?

Julian's hand was on mine, shocking me back to the present. How much had he heard? Did he know that I carried his child?

"I am sorry, your lordship," I said as coolly as I

could, as if afraid that my emotions would show through, "my aunt chose to keep me in the darkness as to the true reason for your wanting a bride here. She . . . only told me that you wanted a wife and did not wish to travel or trouble yourself in finding one."

"Or risk the rejection because I was so ugly?" His eyes narrowed.

I stepped back, shaking my head ever so slightly as I watched him . . . and his reaction. I wanted to tell him that he was no longer ugly to me but shivers convulsed along my spine as he stared at me. I waited for him to say more, wondering if he had accepted my excuse. His eyes roamed my body and for once I was able to read him. I knew that he desired me as much as I did him for his eyes were as bright as the lighthouse candles on a clear night. At that moment, I wanted to reassure him how much I did care for him . . . but I could not.

He smiled at me as if reading my response and testing me. Pursing his lips and then smiling in a mischievous way that was almost like his cousin's, he said, "I believe I shall write your aunt a reprimand. I had told her that you were to be informed of the total situation."

I blanched. "No." My voice was hoarse. "No, do not do that." My hand burned like the time I had unwittingly touched the flame with my fingers as I touched him. Did he read the fear in my eyes or see how my arm trembled. My heart beat faster. "No, please, that is not necessary. Let me write to my aunt. It is I . . . who should bring up the matter. In fact," I glanced at them both and added hastily, "I shall go now and address the letter. Excuse me, please."

With that, I picked up my skirts and fled the cottage. I did not stop running until I had reached the edge of the trees and arrived at Jennifer's pond.

There, as I had before, I sat on the rock in the shelter of the trees, calming myself.

For a few minutes, I just sat there. My hands to my temples as I listened to the songs of the birds. My eyes were closed and I savored the quiet. My head throbbed. Jennifer had known about the will. Yes, I was sure of that now. But if she were with child, I knew that she would not have done the dishonorable thing. She would have stayed until the end, at least. The only way she would not have stayed was if the child were not his. The thoughts spun in my mind but no, I could not credit my sister with being unfaithful no matter how bad Julian had been to her, but neither could I credit her running off to London for a divorce. My hands went to my head. What was the truth? What was the truth?

Behind me, a twig snapped.

Startled, I opened my eyes and turned about. My heart was beating fast. Had Julian followed me here? Did he know I was pregnant? Did he only just suspect or did his great aunt tell him?

I searched the area but there was no one about. No one came forward but I could have sworn that I had seen the leaves stir.

"Hello?" I called out again.

No one answered. For a moment, there was utter silence. Then, through the trees but in the other direction, Julian entered the grove.

"Tamara?" He nodded as he came toward me, as if he had expected to see me here. "I believe we must have a talk."

I rose, frightened as I tried to hide my trembling.

"Your aunt," he continued, "obviously left you in the darkness about a number of things, and . . ."

From the woods where I had first heard the noise, there now came a loud report. Suddenly, Julian grimaced with pain. To my horror, I saw his right side become red under the arm. The stain was spreading!

"Julian!" I rushed to him. "You've been shot."

"So it seems," he whispered. "Who is that fool?"

I looked about but could see no one and did not think it an accident after the boat incident which he had described to me. "It's all right, I told him. Just let me help you to the house." I put my arm about him. The stain was still spreading. Wet, sticky blood dripped onto my dress. His voice was a bare whisper. "Help me to the house," he said, repeating what I had told him.

Under his weight, I could only nod. I tried to walk with him but could not.

I should have searched the woods for the culprit, I thought, but my first concern was for him.

Gently, I laid him against a tree. "I cannot do it alone. Sit here, please," I said feeling the tears in my eyes. "I shall run for help."

"Yes. Yes," he said, collapsing in a heap where I had placed him. I could only stare for a moment until I realized that time was of the utmost preciousness. Running from the pond, I yelled, "Help me! Help me! Julian's been injured."

One of the men came forth from the stables. I ordered him to get assistance and hurried back to my husband. Kneeling down by the still body, I cradled his dark head in my lap. "Oh, Julian!" I cried softly feeling the wetness touch my cheeks and his.

In that moment, I knew that above all else, that despite what he had done, I did love him. The sobs came faster from me. There was no hope for my love. No hope at all.

The men came within minutes and I had to release him to their care.

"Gently," I cried, wringing my hands.

Anxiously, I supervised as he was brought to our room.

"I'll go fetch the Granny," Mrs. Stewart said.

"Do that, if you want, but I demand that the doctor see him, too. I know that there is one in St. Mary's."

"But M'lady, the Granny."

"I said that Julian is to see a doctor, even if I have to row across myself and fetch him." I glared at the woman.

"I will go, Tammy, dearest," Percy said. Only then did I notice that he was standing next to me with a pained expression on his face. "After all, we must see that my dear cousin gets better, mustn't we."

I nodded, grateful for his support, and smiled up at him.

He left immediately, and while the others went about their jobs, I stayed at my husband's side, fearful lest he should die.

The Granny did come and applied a soft herbal plaster to the wound. She wasn't happy about the doctor coming to attend, but said, "I shall be back t'change the dressin' on the morrow. 'Tis a fever he will have but 'twil not last."

I nodded, lost in thought, concentrating on Julian.

"Other things as well do not last, M'lady."

I glanced up not realizing that she was still in the room. "What are you talking about, woman?"

" 'Tis fear and hate that does not last. Not if you do not want it to. He will forgive you when you tell him, but tell him soon, you must."

I stared at her. But she made no other comment and left the room before I could gather my wits. Shivering, I knew that she also knew! Had I kept my secret from anyone? In a stunned moment, I continued to stare at the door.

It was over four hours before Percy returned with the doctor.

"Sorry, Coz," Percy came over to me and kissed my cheek as he entered. Thank goodness no one else was about to see that. I did not slap him because I was so glad he had brought the doctor. "I had the devil's own time trying to find him," Percy added.

"But he is here?"

"He is." Percy responded. I did not like the look in his eyes as he nodded to where the doctor stood. I wanted to stay in the room while Julian was examined but the doctor refused. He feared that I would faint. I tried to tell him that I had stayed there all this time, but he insisted that as a woman I was not strong enough. I was furious but there was nothing I could do if I wanted his help.

Returning to the ground level, I began to pace again.

Laura and Percy were talking in the library and not wanting to be a part of it, not even caring to eavesdrop, I entered Julian's study. The room was chilly as no fire had been lit. I crossed over to the window and drew the curtains against the night, pausing a moment to watch the sea. How calm it seemed now. How deceptive. Where else was I deceiving myself?

Taking a deep breath of the cooler evening air, I realized that except for the first day, I had not been in this room. Indeed, except for my experiences in the attic, I had scarcely examined the house.

It now seemed sacrilege for me to be perusing Julian's private papers while he lay injured, but as the desk chair was the only possible place I could sit—the others being filled with letters and books—I took my place.

I wanted to do something other than pace for I was becoming exhausted and my hands fell quite naturally to the group of papers in front of me.

To my shock, I saw that they were dress bills with Jennifer's name on them! I nearly choked at that moment. Two hundred and thirty pounds for gowns! My eyes widened with horror. The papers were like spikes driven through my heart. It was inconceivable that she could have spent like that. Father had always raised us to be frugal and make do with what we had. But for that, I would never have been able to make over Tamara's gowns to fit me.

The date on the bills drove the sharp spikes deeper. The purchases were listed as being made in London on the 15th of October, 1871. That was over a month from the date of her last letter to me — from the date of her supposed disappearance!

My hands shook as I examined the other bills. More of the same — accessories, shoes, and even a hotel bill! Had I been wrong all the while? Had my sister totally changed from the sweet innocent that I had known? Had she truly gone off as these papers seemed to indicate? Was Julian then innocent of all I had secretly accused him of? But then what had actually happened to my sister? And what had happened with the picture? With my seal pup?

Lost in my thoughts, I scarcely heard the door open.

"Oh, there you are, darling girl."

Startled, I swirled in the chair and saw Percy. Dropping the papers, I stood. "I was only sitting for a bit."

He looked at me quite strangely but said nothing.

"Is the doctor finished? May I up now?"

Percy was unusually quiet as he nodded and held the door open for me. Without a backward glance at the desk, I left the papers and hurried up the stairs. The doctor had pulled a chair up to the bedside and was sitting there, watching me with an intensity that frightened me.

Silently, I closed the door behind me and came forward. Julian looked ghostly white and so near death. I wanted to cry, to at least ask his forgiveness . . . but there was nothing I could do.

"Will he . . ." tears choked my voice ". . . will he be all right, Doctor?"

Glancing briefly at me, he said, "Yes, M'Lady, he will. Probably he will have a fever but I think in a few days he should be up and about. In fact, knowing his lordship as I do, I should think he will make quite a quick recovery. He's mainly shocky now—loss of blood and all that, but the bullet only just grazed him." He held something up to the light. It was a heart shaped object, gold in color. "This saved him, I think. But for his wearing it, the bullet would have pierced his heart."

I gasped. I did not have to advance further to see that object. "Jennifer's medallion!"

Behind me, I was aware that Percy was standing. "How did you know that Tammy?"

"I . . . I merely guessed. I mean, I have something similar from school." Lowering my eyes, I went to the window. "We had been discussing his first wife before Julian was hit."

"Really?" Percy's voice and eyes held disbelief. "What an amazing coincidence? Well, I for one," he moved forward to the bedside, "am glad of it. At least she accomplished something while she was here."

I wanted to deny Percy's statement but in the light of what I had just learned, I did not dare. "Yes, at least she did that."

The doctor looked from the unconscious Julian, to Percy, and back to me. "Well, the bullet is out. He shall probably sleep these next few hours. I shall visit again tomorrow, to check on him."

"Yes," I replied, unable to take my eyes off the pale form on the bed. "That would be appreciated, doctor."

"Actually, doctor, I do not believe it necessary for you to trouble yourself. My cousin has a strong constitution. Besides which, our Granny is quite capable," Percy said.

The doctor grunted as I glared at Percy.

"Doctor, I want you to come," I told him. "Meanwhile, please tell me what is to be done. I shall nurse my husband, myself." I could feel Percy watching me but it no longer mattered. I would not, however, meet his eyes.

"That would be commendable, Lady Penporth, but I can bring a nurse over from the main island."

I shook my head and then motioned him to follow me into the hall. There I received the needed instructions. It seemed there was precious little I could do but bathe his brow and be on hand to give him water—or other nourishment—should he require it. At least, it would keep me occupied.

After I had thanked the doctor and seen him to the door, Percy stepped into the hall. I knew he had been observing the whole interaction but it did not matter.

"Tammy, my love, I'm sure Julian would appreciate your concern, but do you think it wise."

"Of course it's wise. He's my husband . . ."

". . . and already he is jealous of you—suspecting an affair with me. Yes, I know well what you mean. On all accounts, it would not do for you, my dearest cousin, to be scared off as was Jennifer. Nevertheless, darling, considering your condition . . ." He paused, and I was sure I reddened, but I said nothing. ". . . I do feel it is unwise for you to expose yourself to any problems. My cousin, as you well know, is prone to violence. He might strike out at you in his delirium. Mrs. Stewart, Laura, and myself can all take care of him in turns."

Did he really know about my pregnancy or should I deny it, I wondered as I stared at him. How could he know when I only just suspected.

My fear and my blush must have betrayed my thoughts. "Percy, please. I am not at all certain . . . of my delicate condition . . ." I took his hand. "Please don't tell Julian what you suspect."

He looked puzzled. "In heaven's name why not? My cousin would be damned please to know . . . unless . . ." the wrinkles of amusement seemed to increase about his eyes. "My dearest

Tammy, surely you are not so naive as to think . . ." he took my hands in his and I felt a cold chill from the open window behind us. "After all, I did only kiss you briefly."

I pulled away sharply. "And considering my status here, it is to my shame that I allowed it. No, Percival, I am not such a dolt as to think that breeding comes from a mere kiss."

"Well then, I can think of no reason for Julian not to know that you are expecting a child, unless you fear that the child is not his."

I shivered now and feared that my fright was visible.

"Oh, Percy!" He was right. Without confiding in him, there was no reason why I could not let Julian know. "Just please. I must tell him this in my own way. Please ask Laura and Mrs. Stewart to be silent as well."

He was thoughtful a moment and I watched him, waiting for his pledge. Did I detect a smile on his lips? My heart hammered . . . almost too loudly. I longed to leave the drafty hall . . . to be back in the warm room with Julian. He shouldn't be alone for so long, I thought.

"Very well," Percy said, "I will keep your secret . . . just as you've kept mine." He took my hand and it reminded me of that other secret I knew he was keeping. Not wanting to linger, I nodded my thanks and releasing myself I ran up the stairs to where Julian lay.

In the warm room I approached the bed. My "husband" was peacefully asleep; his breathing rhythmic. Thankful, I adjusted his covers and paced a moment in the dim light to ponder my discordant emotions.

Finally, I moved over to the desk, and with the glimmer of the single candle wrote some of my thoughts.

My heart was wretched. I couldn't call him "husband," because he wasn't mine, and I was not his wife. When he was well . . . or at least when he was safe from harm I would then leave this miserable place and forget that there ever existed a Julian Hawley or an island called Penporth. I would even forget that my sister had come here. He would despise me if he knew. It would be better if he had a second runaway wife than one whose very name would provoke curses. Besides which, those bills made me hopeful that indeed I had been wrong. Perhaps Jennifer really was still alive in London somewhere. But even with the divorce she was still a part of him. Had she not saved his life just now? It had been she that he thought of, not me.

Miserable, I placed a cool cloth on his brow. He groaned softly—crying out Jennifer's name. In love? In guilt? I did not know but tears came to my eyes. He had loved Jennifer in his own way. That much was obvious and if he loved her, he would never love me. How terrible it was to love and not be loved in return.

Chapter Sixteen

After a restless night, Julian settled into a more natural sleep. As predicted, he had a fever on Monday night but by the time the doctor returned on Tuesday afternoon, the infection had subsided. Julian had not woken at all since the accident though for a time during the fever I was sure that he would. He mentioned Jennifer's name several times as if calling out to her. I could not help feeling a little jealous of my sister and I still did not know what had happened to her.

Our doctor complimented me on my excellent nursing. I accepted the praise silently, feeling that it was little enough I could do.

"You should rest, yourself, M'Lady."

"No. No," I pushed away his concern. "I am quite all right," I began to cry then. After all I had been through I did not want Julian to die — at least not this way. "Doctor, you said he would only sleep a few hours. He has not yet opened his eyes."

"Tut. Tut, my dear." The doctor patted my shoulder. "He's merely having a natural sleep — albiet a longer one than usual, but the body has great healing powers. I should say that he is out of danger, and within a day or so, he will be up and about. Of course, it will be a while yet before he is back to normal."

The relief I felt must have been evident.

"Shall I come again tomorrow, M'Lady? There really is no more I can do, but . . . "

I nodded, "If you would, I would be grateful."

"Your affection for your husband is touching. Of course. I shall call again."

He left then, and I, disturbed at what he said, failed to show him out. His words echoed in my mind. "My affection for my husband." If only he really were my husband. Undoubtedly, he took it that I did not wish to leave Julian's side — which was true. Every minute I had left with him was precious to me. It would be a memory that I would cherish.

Mrs. Stewart came in shortly after. "M'Lady, 'ee'll be sick like if ye don't take a care. Let me stay a bit."

I shook my head. "Not now, Mrs. Stewart. Later perhaps. I will call if I wish you."

She seemed hurt at my refusal to accept her help, but then I had more pressing worries.

Mrs. Stewart reached the door just as I called her back. "Would you come talk with me awhile

. . . I get lonely by myself." Gratified that I did need her, she quickly brought over a stool from the corner of the room and moved it close to where I sat.

We were both silent for a few minutes — watching Julian's deep breathing. Finally, she asked, "Was there something special ye wanted t'talk on, M'Lady?"

There was so much I wanted to talk on, but so little that she could tell me.

"Yes, his scar." I regarded that long white slash that stretched across his cheek and mouth. "How . . . how did he get it?" In his sleep, it relaxed but nevertheless it marred what might have been a handsome, if irregular face.

"Oh, that! That be when he were a boy. 'e and young Mr. Percy, they be off swimmin' the coast and well," she shrugged, "Mr. Percy was always the adventurous lad. Not like his lordship who stayed in a safe place."

"Well, what happened?" I urged her on, not taking my eyes from the white line.

She shrugged again. "Master Percy, 'e be in the water too dangerous fer 'im. It began t'pull and tug at 'im and 'e be screamin' louder than the devil. Course, 'is lordship be right near but everyone says 'Don't go in there. Ye both be killed.' But 'is lordship says "I must" and so he swims in . . . quick as 'ee be . . . but 'twas a powerful struggle. There be them — Master Percy and 'is lordship and the current."

"But how . . ?" I glanced at her and then at Julian as he moaned. My attention was immediately to him as I placed the cloth on his brow. My heart beat quickened. Was he coming awake? I could have sworn that his eye lids flickered but they remained closed.

"Yes, go on." I turned to Mrs. Stewart again.

"There not be much more. Master Percy was hauled out safely, but afore they could get to 'is lordship, the current be so rough that it drove 'em against the rocks. 'Twas a terrible sight to see. We all fer sure thought 'em dead like, but 'e be a strong lad and . . ."

"And the scar is all that remains," I said softly. My fingers tingled and I ached to touch it, to stroke that craggy face, anything that would give me contact with him. How wrong I had been! I assumed that he had gotten his scar in some fight or perhaps when he was wrecking.

"Mrs. Stewart, I am thirsty. Will you bring me some tea?"

"Why, surely," she beamed, pleased with her recitation. She bustled up along to the door and closed it behind her with a dull thud.

After she had gone, I found myself re-arranging his bedcovers and placing another cool cloth on his forehead. Oh, how my hands trembled as I touched him. Tears flecked my eyes and spotted the sheet. I had to turn away and blow my nose. I knew that I was being foolish. I had created this whole situation myself. It was my own fault for getting into such a mess and I would have to see my way clear.

He moved again and groaned once more. My heart lurched. Surely, he must be awake now. I started to move, thinking that I did not want him to see me in the room with him but in his delirium he called out the name of my sister again. Jealousy struck me more than it ever had before. It wasn't fair that I should love him so and he not love me. Nothing seemed very fair at all.

Mrs. Stewart returned with my tea and I allowed her to take over the nursing while I had some much needed sleep in his dressing room . . . the same room where he had gone to get away from me.

I came back to my duties several hours later, feeling more refreshed and determined to hold up until he should wake.

Time went very slow. On Thursday morning, the thirteenth day of May, he was still unconscious. I left the room only for a few moments. There seemed so little I could do. At one point, I took his hand — just for a second and willed him to wake. Then I dropped his hand, more gently, of course, knowing that when he did come to my hopes of happiness would be destroyed.

Towards late day, five minutes after the grandfather clock in the hall banged four, he opened his eyes. It was quite miraculous. They were as bright and as alert as the day he had been shot.

"Water?" he asked hoarsely.

I handed him the glass and lifted it to his lips, intending that he should remain quiet, but he moved in the bed and quickly took the glass from me. "I can manage myself," he grimaced slightly. I knew that he was still in some pain.

"No doubt you can," I responded, unable to hold my tongue and cursing myself for it. "It's about time you woke." I rang the bell violently.

"Why are you here? Hasn't Mrs. Stewart been caring for me?"

I glared at him. "Of course she has. Do you think I could stand a moment more than necessary with you?" It was spiteful but I had already decided that it was best if he not care about me (not that he did), but I hoped then he would not be concerned when I left. Also, I had to admit that I was upset he did not think that I could assist him. Of course, I probably had not given him much reason to trust me.

"I've only been here on the odd moment when Mrs. Stewart has had other items to care for." I went to the door and called out, "Mrs. Stewart!"

She appeared on the stairs, huffing and puffing. "I don't yet have yer tea, M'Lady."

"Never mind that, Mrs. Stewart, your patient is awake. Kindly attend to him. I am going out for some air."

She gazed at me, astonished. I prayed she would not give me away. I could not let him know of my feelings, could not allow him to stop me from leaving the island. Without a further word, I left the room with the shawl in my hands.

Leaving the house, I stood a moment on the steps and stared at the sea. I knew my emotions were just like that—raging and angry. I could not go to Jennifer's peaceful pond. No, the rocks of the western shore with their craggy face that stretched into the void of the ocean depths was where my restless spirit took me.

The sun was out today and shining in full force but there was a wind that tugged at the tendrils of my hair, releasing them as Julian had released the lock on my heart.

How strange that this beautiful, cloudless day should be following such a terrible storm. I watched as the sea gently caressed the jagged shore and washed up some left over fragments of wood from the German boat, *Shiller*.

As I sat on the warm rocks allowing the rolling tide to absorb my thoughts, I realized that even at Jennifer's pond, I had never experienced such a peace. There was not a sound save the faint whisper of the wings as a large gull invaded the land on the hill behind me. The bustle and rush that I remembered from London and from Edinburgh were now so remote as to be non-existent, yet it was to those cities that I would return.

Silently, sitting there, I was overwhelmed by a great sense of timelessness. These huge cairns, these rocks and hills, had survived thousands of storms and would continue to do so long after I was gone and forgotten. All my elations, depressions, and worries I had dealt with in my life were but a small drop here. There was a whirling of wings as the gulls moved about. How many people had surveyed this same scene before me and how many would do it when I had gone.

I breathed deeply of the salty air and saw the tide had ebbed, revealing more weed covered rocks. It heightened my desperate feeling of loneliness. Tears pricked my eyes. What a melancholy place this was, and yet, I had grown to love it . . . as I guess I had grown to love Julian but both would have to leave my life.

I turned to go when I felt a hand on my shoulder and my heart leaped with fear. For some unexplained reason I was sure that death was near. I recalled now that night when I had been pushed and I wondered in that flash if the bullet had been meant for me. But who would want to kill me — unless it had been Julian? Unless Julian had discovered my secret and wanted to be rid of me.

Relief flooded me as I realized it was only Percy standing near me. I breathed easier. Percy was a fop but he was harmless.

"You startled me, Percy. Why did you not say something? Is Julian . . is something wrong at the house?"

He shook his head. All his usual gaiety was gone. His voice was dull. "I am sorry, Tamara. I meant only to prevent you from falling. You are deuced close to that edge, you know."

He was right, but I had only just then noticed it.

"These rocks are a danger. You had best be more careful."

I glanced down at my feet and realized then that he was right.

"The sea can fool you," he continued. "Do you see down there?" he pointed to the small peninsula with a cluster of "children" about it. Soft waves licked her like a gentle mother.

I nodded.

"It's a good place to fish, if you are careful. But

I know two who misjudged the water. They went out there just as the tide was turning, never thinking that the sea would attack them."

The saliva stuck in my throat. "And what happened?" I asked, not taking my eyes off the shore.

"A wave came up upon them and knocked them over. Then she sucked them into her depths and their bodies were never found." His voice was cold and very matter of fact. I shivered. This was not the Percy I had come to know.

"Thank you . . . for the warning. I shall be careful."

He stared at me as if he did not see me. "You are quite welcome," he said softly.

There was an awkward silence between us before I asked, "Percy, who shot Julian?"

His vague gaze turned upon me. "Why do you ask? Do you think that I am guilty, too?" His voice had now risen to a shout. I had never seen him quite so upset. "Mrs. Stewart thinks so."

"Oh, no. Surely not." I flushed for I had to admit that the thought had occurred to me but I had dismissed it.

"Well, she has not accused me outright but I can tell." His notrils flared with his anger. "I can tell the way she looks at me . . . "

"But Percy," I took his hand, wanting to tell him that everything was all right.

"Every single person on this island — including Grandmother — knows how to use a gun. Perhaps it wasn't Julian the person intended."

I felt the fear go through me. I wanted to ask Percy to explain but he would not. Without another word, he pulled his hand from mine and strode briskly toward the house.

I sat, watching him; his grey satin frock coat seemed to shimmer in the sunlight. His words echoed past him. Who would want to harm me . . and why? I realized that it could not have been Julian that day since he was with me. I looked again to the spot where Percy had told me about his friends who had perished. Obviously something was upsetting him, or he wouldn't have acted that way. I was too deep into my own problems to worry about what problems Percy might be having.

I remained by the rocks for another several hours and then, feeling very tired, I went slowly back to the house. I was careful to avoid Mrs. Stewart and would not go near the room where Julian lay—though my heart wretched as I passed it. My appetite seemed to have left me, and sleep was the only thing I wanted. I went into Julian's dressing room down the hall. It was the room I had used for the past few days. How close I was to him and yet how far. It hurt terribly as I lay down on the very same pillow he had used, the very same cover he had used, and I cried myself to sleep.

I could barely leave the bed. Certainly I could eat nothing but tea and toast. I hated being a further burden on Mrs. Stewart and Laura. I begged them both to ignore me and just take care of Julian but they would not hear of it. I then commanded them that Julian not know of my illness. (If it were only an illness. I wished my monthly course would come and deny my fears but it was far later than it should have been.)

I was told that he was better which relieved me some and I began to think about my life away from here. The 1,000 pounds he had given me, if I could find it among Tamara's things, would help to set me up at least until the baby was born. After that, I did not know.

Despite my pain sleep claimed me. I woke once during the night, having dreamed of Jennifer again and wishing for the comfort of Julian's arms but there was nothing there to comfort me. Holding my stomach, I curled up and again I cried.

Towards afternoon of the next day I was feeling better and went downstairs for a cup of tea and some porridge. Mrs. Stewart told me that Julian was out of bed and that he would be down for dinner. She also told me that he had been asking for me. I hoped she did not tell him that I had stayed with him all the time that I had.

The toast in my hands crumbled as she asked if I would wait for his lordship to come down.

"No!" I caught my breath and tried to calm the quickening of my heart. "No, I mean, I do not think it would be wise. I've got a headache still. I want some air."

"But he does want t'see ye, M'Lady."

"I know that . . . " My hand trembled as I drained the last of the tea, "I know that Mrs. Stewart." I sighed. "You may tell Julian that I will

359

see him later. He should . . . he should still be resting as much as possible. If we talk here, he will be up too long. I will come to his room."

"As 'ee wish, M'Lady," she said, shrugging. "More tea?"

I recognized that as a ploy for keeping me here. I shook my head. "Later, perhaps. My stomach is still upset.

She nodded as if she knew the reason and left the room.

It was then that I took the opportunity to escape the house. The longer I stayed here, the more chance there was that I would see Julian. Yes, I did want to see him, to touch him, to have him touch me, but I was afraid that I would break down that I would cry and tell him everything and then he would hate me. It was best to wait until I was ready to leave the island. Then, whatever would happen, would happen.

As I left the house, I decided to pay another visit to the old aunt. Certainly, I would not see him there today.

She was sitting on the ground floor rather than in her room by the window. Sitting by the fireplace she was holding a picture of her husband.

"He's gone," she said, simply as I walked in the house. "Gone like the rest of them."

I said nothing but took the seat opposite her. I watched as her sad mouth turned to a smile. "But there is a future, you know. Have you told him/ Was he pleased?"

"No, Aunt. I've not said anything yet. I . . . I do not want to raise his hopes until I am certain,"

I lied. "Besides, I thought you told him."

"Gracious, no!" She shook her white head and gave me a secret smile. "It is the wife's privilege. He does not know yet." She giggled, like a child. "He thinks we were talking about the other one."

I was relieved and felt my face flush. But I had not come to talk about the baby. "Aunt, the first day I met you, you mentioned something about Jennifer's being murdered by the tree. Did you see something? Will you tell me about it?"

Her blue eyes were bright as they stared at me. She pursed her lips. "It was him."

My eyes were wide as the lump and saliva stuck in my throat chilling me. I did not believe that I could actually be right. A dizziness came to me.

"Aunt," my voice quivered. "Are you quite sure?"

She pulled away from me and stood. Twirling about so that her skirts widened with the breeze, she gave her secret smile and walked over to the staircase. "I will show you." She gave a laugh—a child's laugh as one about to show a secret toy.

Worried, I followed her and then, as if time had been suspended, she stood absolutely motionless. We both heard the sound then. It was the explosion of a gun—just outside. The muscles of her face went rigid. She had stopped before the shot was fired . . . almost as if, like me, she had had a premonition of the evil to follow.

The memory of Monday still etched in my brain, forced me into action. "I must go see what has happened," I said, after first checking that the old woman was unhurt.

Then, frightened, I flung open the door and ran down the path. I was out of breath when I reached the western rocks where the noise had come from.

Laura was there, wearing one of her prim maid uniforms. Her white apron was spotted with mud. The gun in her hand was still smoking.

"Laura!"

She glared at me. "Be quiet! Don't you see I'm trying to aim." She lowered the gun ominously but casually pointing it at me.

I backed away. "Was that shot you then?"

"Of course it was me. Mum wants some pigeon for a pie. It's Julian's favorite. Why? Did you think it was something mysterious?" Her smile made me feel like a fool.

"I am sorry. I heard the shot and I came out running."

Laura gave another smile and waved the gun back toward the town path. "Well, you can return to wherever you came from. I am not about to shoot myself or anyone else . . . unless they interfere with me and my bird collection."

I had no desire to question her further at this point nor any wish to get in her way, and within the moment, I was running back toward the aunt's house. She had been about to show me her proof that Julian had murdered Jennifer. While I admitted that I was now hopelessly in love with Julian, I did not want to think that he was innocent when he was not. For my own peace of mind, I had to know the truth.

Running up the path, I called out, "Aunt!"

The door swung open with the same creaking that had startled me on my first visit. The ground floor seemed empty. The picture was in the chair as she had left it when she had gone to get the proof for me.

"Aunt?" I called.

Puzzled, I ascended the stair. She had seemed quite lucid before, but I knew that old as she was, she was liable to move back into her senility at any moment. Perhaps, she had gone back up the stairs to wait for her husband's ship once more.

"Aunt?" I called out again.

The upstairs was empty. Her room held no trace of her recent presence. Where could she have gone?

"Aunt Priscilla, where are you?" I called out worried once more.

There was no answer.

My stomach queasy, I again trod the stairs. She was not the type to wander about the island—especially after the shot had startled her. Poor Aunt Priscilla was in no shape to be wary of the dangerous rocks that Percy had warned me of.

Without luck, I walked about this cottage several times and then, feeling chilly, decided to go back in and claim my shawl. Perhaps I had had too much sun. My head ached and I knew that I should go back to the Hall and get some sleep before I fainted for the past week had taken its toll on me but I could not do that until I found her.

The clothes chest was in the corner near the stairs. She must have put my shawl away for it was not on the chair. As my sight again became accustomed to the dimmer room, I was aware now that things were out of place. Then, I saw her!

Her body was slumped on the floor, against the door of the stairway closet. She leaned over in an awkward position.

"Aunt?" I whispered, almost afraid. "Aunt?" I kneeled over to touch her wrist and then dropped it as the horror pervaded me. She was dead. In the few moments I had left her, she had died. In anguish, I pursed my lips as I tried to understand what had happened. It was then I saw the bullet in her neck.

Gasping, I moved away. She had been murdered as Tamara had, as Jennifer had. Even as I stood, I saw that in the dirt and dust next to her she had managed to draw a crude "J".

"No," I shook my head, not believing it. "No, Julian could not have killed her. He was so devoted to her — unless the devotion had only been recent, with the knowledge that she might have proof against him. Chills and goosebumps covered my body as the nausea rose up. I could not believe that he would do something so cold blooded as this — yet here was his initial.

Tears blinded me as I closed the cottage door. For once it did not creak. Now, it seemed that I would never have the proof that she had wanted to show me.

Weakly, I leaned against the tree. Julian had done it it seemed. From his sick bed, he had followed me and waited for the right moment. It had been just luck that Laura's shot had called me away just as the aunt had been about to talk to me. Or was it luck?

My mouth was dry as I knew that I would have to get the constable out from St. Mary's. My premonition of evil had come to pass but was that all?

Frightened of my own emotions, I ran all the way back to the house.

Julian was not, thank goodness, in the hall. I had not expected him to be but anything was possible. Mrs. Stewart entered the room just as I was about to go up and search for Percy. I did not want to tell Julian for I feared that he would go and hide whatever evidence might be found.

"Where is Percy?" I asked. "There's been an accident."

"Oh heavens be. Tain't his lordship again, is it? I told 'im as he shouldna go out but he was insistent. Said as he had things t' attend."

"He is out? What time did he leave?"

She shook her head and shrugged.

"Well, it is not him. It's his great aunt. I think she is dead. Someone should find Percy and Julian and tell them. Someone will also have to cross to St. Mary's for the constable.

"Poor soul was old. Why should the constable be told?"

I stared at Mrs. Stewart wondering just now what her real role here was. "She was murdered."

The housekeeper gasped.

"Please. Go find Percy or Julian. Something needs to be done."

Nodding, she disappeared. I collapsed into a

chair as I tried to recall the exact sequence of events. Julian was out. That meant he could have done it. "No," I shook my head, and spoke out loud hoarsely. "No, it's not possible."

"What is not possible, Tamara?"

"Oh, Percy!" I cried as I stood up. It was horrible to be the bearer of such news. As soon as I had related the story, Percy and several men went to the house. Laura, who had just come in as I was explaining things, stayed with me. She put her arm about me as she tried to calm me.

"Poor Tamara, how dreadful for you? I feel so guilty that it was my hunting which kept you from her side at that crucial moment. Do you really think Julian did it?"

A pain shot through me. I did not know what to think and so I merely shrugged. She gave me a Cheshire smile which disappeared almost as quickly as it had come.

I drained the cup of tea and now felt oddly numb. Laura repoured it but I did not even notice until she handed it to me. I had only one concern. "What of Julian? Where is he now?"

Laura's face was so sympathetic . . . and yet so stricken that momentarily I forgave her for whatever minor misdeeds she had done.

"Laura, I cannot face him. I cannot be the one to tell him. He . . . he was . . . "

"Yes, I know," she said softly, "he was devoted to her. Even in his moments of madness, he probably does not even realize what he's done. I shall tell him that she has died."

That was not my meaning but nevertheless I

was grateful to have that burden removed.

Quite suddenly, she touched my brow. "Why not go and have a rest now. This has been too much for you. Mum will bring you something later."

She poured me yet another cup which I obediently drank. It seemed an excellent suggestion and so, wearily, I headed for the stairs and Julian's dressing room.

Chapter Seventeen

Despite the thoughts that poured into me like the waves of the Atlantic crashing upon the western rocks, I went to sleep. The speculations were almost too much for me to bear. Again, I remembered that Aunt Priscilla had been murdered just before she could tell me what she had seen. I allowed myself the luxury of crying. If only Laura's shot had not drawn me out of the cottage at that very moment. I still did not understand — madness or not — how he could have done it.

I don't know how long I slept but when I opened my eyes again, I found I had been covered. My mouth was thick and dry like cotton wool, and my head ached. The light which I had left burning had been extinguished. The room was totally dark. Still exhausted, my brain called out for more sleep. What had woken me then?

The sound came once more . . . the creak of the floor boards near the bed.

"Who's there?" I tried to whisper without success.

There was no answer, only a soft stepping coming insidiously forward. My heart hammered as I struggled to sit up, but could not. "Who is it?" I asked again, my voice hoarse. My limbs were like lead.

I realized then that to calm me, Laura had obviously put something in the tea . . something that would now mean my death. Even my voice seemed paralyzed as I tried to scream.

There was a swish of a cloak before the pillow came down over my head, and I was forced backwards into oblivion. I think I kicked; I could hear some muffled cries but in the end the pressure was too much for me to fight. Whoever held the pillow had the advantage of alert strength.

My mind seemed to soar like the wings of the sea gulls and lights flashed in my head. My lungs hurt as they had when I was in the sea. For several moments, I lost the desire to live. Death seemed so peaceful, so beautiful. I ceased my struggles as a warm, relaxed glow from several glasses of wine spread through my limbs. I saw Jennifer standing by the pond, smiling at me, her arms were outstretched.

"Death is nothing to fear, dearest little sister, but do not join me yet."

She faded from view and with her disappearance came a horrible pain in my chest and a buzzing in my ears. I realized then that I was still alive and frantically gasping for air. I was alone.

Numbly, I lay in the darkness for several moments. I was cold, shivering with sweat, and feeling my pounding heart as it rushed the oxygen to my deprived brain.

It had not been a dream. The pressure of the pillow about my face had been far too real as had the struggle for air and the slow suffocation.

Even as I lit the candle by the bed, I could see the pillow on the floor and the muddy prints as well. Tears rolled down my cheeks. I lay there for quite some time, unable to move, watching the flickering of the candle.

Finally, with some pain, I left the bed and donned a dressing gown. I went into the hall, determined to find out for myself if Julian was asleep . . . if he . . .

I reached the door to our room and cautiously opened it. Would he be standing there now? Waiting for me? Waiting to continue what he had now started?

How deathly silent the hall was. I shivered. The candle before me cast gloomy shadows on the walls and in my frightening mood, I could not ignore them. Trembling, I advanced across the hall. Quietly as possible, I opened the door to the room to which I had my pleasant memories of Julian. I wanted and prayed that I would find him there, asleep, and even that could mean nothing. Enough time had passed, I was sure, since my attack that he could easily have returned to bed now and feigned sleep.

I remembered when he had been hit there had

been such a look of shock. Had he planned for me to be the target? Perhaps he had had second thoughts and that was why he got in the way. I did not know. I only knew that this room was now empty. The bed was smoothly covered by the heavy quilt and looked as if it had not been slept in for some time.

Strangely enough, my first concern was for Julian. Where had he gone? Ill as he was, he should not be up. Then realization forced me back to terms with myself. Surely, if he was well enough to apply such force and to be out this afternoon he could be anywhere. My head ached with the dizzy sensation of the past few minutes and the tears were still wet on my cheeks.

It was then I saw the navy blue cloak folded over the chair. Jennifer's! How could he have used this! I could taste the sickness in my mouth. He had used my own sister's cloak to secret himself and fearful that he might still try something, I ran from the bedroom.

"Percy would help me," I told myself. Hadn't he been constantly coaxing me to leave the island, to run away with him. I did not plan to run anywhere with him but at least I would allow him to take me off this wretched rock. I did not trust his vows of love but we were, it seems, partners, in a crime of silence. I had vowed not to tell Julian of his trip to London and in return, he had kept quiet about me—or so he said. Though it seemed somehow Julian had found out. His actions proved he knew about me. I had to leave!

Regardless of the fact that I wore only a simple

nightdress under my robe, and of the ungodly hour, I knocked on Percy's door. Had circumstances been different, had I not been so desperate, I would never even have considered this.

"My darling Tammy! Why, whatever is the matter, Sweet? You look a fright!" He took me into his arms and drew me into the darkened room.

I sobbed out the whole story of this evening and buried my head in the velvet pile of his soft robe.

"Now you know why his first wife left, my dearest heart. Julian was as demented as Gran was. More so."

Those were exactly the words that my sister had used in her letters. I had not wanted to believe it. I had allowed my emotions to lull me but now I had no choice but to leave.

He stroked my hair, murmuring calm words. I scarcely noticed that his lips were on my brow. Not until his mouth bent to mine did I realize what he was about. "No, Percy. Please, do not."

"But you have come to me, finally. You are in your dressing gown and I am in mine. Tis something that Julian will surely find out about and . . . draw his own conclusions," he shrugged. "So we might as well enjoy this moment."

"No," I said softly as I drew back toward the door!" There will be time later," I added. "I would have us wait until we leave the island."

"But what's the harm, my love. One day more or less."

It was difficult to hide my disgust. "I will talk about this with you only after we have left the island."

"Oh." The light of truth seemed to gleam in his eyes. "Of course, Angel, we would not want to get involved until after your divorce is granted. Or it will make it harder for us." Once again, his mouth was on mine. He looked frail but he was strong. This time I did not struggle but neither did I respond. I disengaged myself as quickly as possible. Footsteps in the hall reminded me of my position. "Percy, I wish to leave the island tonight. Can we do it?"

With gentle fingers, he stroked my cheek. "Not tonight, precious. These rocks are hazardous even for the most experienced seamen. By night, they would be treacherous. Besides, there is another storm brewing. Tomorrow, we can go. Laura will see that Julian is occupied, if I ask her. Then, we can make our escape.

"You won't tell her, though, unless you have to, unless it's necessary?"

"Of course not." He kissed my hand. "Darling, don't you trust Laura. You should. She is the best friend I have ever had."

I did not answer. I was doing the right thing, I told myself. I was. Yet my whole being felt uncomfortable. Being with Percy was not natural for me. Being with Julian was—but I could not stay.

I scarcely heard Percy talking. Only as he opened the door to pull me out did I stop him. "Hush, it's all right. If Julian is in one of his moods, he will have gone to the western rocks directly from his attack on you."

I shivered. The western rocks was where I had found my seal—and her remains.

"You are doing the right thing, Tamara," Percy said, sensing my fear.

Dully, I nodded.

I disliked lying to Percy but he was the only one who could help me to the mainland. I knew that Mr. O'Dea had promised that one time but he was surely in Julian's pay. To remain here would be to risk death anyway for if Julian did not murder me now he would do so when he learned who I was and that I carried his child—if he already did not know. Even so, I loved him.

Together, we opened the door. I stepped out first into the lighter part of the hall. I had advanced along nearly to the dressing room when I saw Julian entering our room along the corridor.

I stopped but the astonishment made me gasp. It was too late for me to close the door and slip in. He had seen me and there was nothing I could do but speak out.

Strange how my concern for him took precedence. "You are well enough to be out walking?"

He frowned but came toward me.

"I was restless. I needed to walk and think about things, Tamara."

At that moment, Percy chose to emerge from his room. I will never forget the look on Julian's face—the utter disgust it showed. I wanted to cry out, to explain, but as I started to speak, my words died on my tongue. It was *he* who caused this. *He* whose attack upon me turned me and forced me to seek his cousin for safety.

There was no time for me to explain. He had reached me. Disregarding Percy, he yanked me towards him. His hands gripped my wrists painfully.

"You little bitch!" His slap stung me, bringing tears to my eyes. "Even when I am ill, you cannot pretend to be a true wife. Well, then go to him." He pushed me backwards. "Stay with him."

Stunned, I could only stare at Julian. Why did Percy remain so silent? If he wanted to, he could have cleared me. I glanced at my "dear cousin" and thought I could see a smile on his lips. It was so slight that had I not been sensitive I might not have noticed.

As we stood, like statues, it dawned on me that, like the incident of the funerals, Percy had wanted this. He was pleased with himself! What Papa had always called my rebellious leanings now surfaced.

I decided that neither men should have the pleasure of my discomfort. Using language I had learned from below the stairs, I stated, "If I am the devil's bitch, then you, your lordship, are the Devil, himself. Worse, you are a murderer, a bastard, and," I lied foolishly, "I have proof to that effect. Not only did Jennifer suffer at your hands but your aunt . . . "

His eyes narrowed in astonishment. In two steps he had reached me again.

Fear made me speechless as I saw that I had caught his attention. He, again, turned the full force of his fury upon me. The shock in his eyes told me that he was either an excellent actor or that, he had in fact no knowledge of his aunt's demise. Could he have forgotten his own actions?

Hands were clamped on my shoulders, gripping them with such a strength that I wanted to scream out but I would not give him the satisfaction. He began to shake me. "What did you say of my aunt?"

It was impossible for me to speak. Finally Percy said, "Tammy found her, Julian. It was a weak heart. The old girl died quickly. Brought the doctor over myself I did. Didn't want to bother you,"

I glanced at Percy. His grandmother had not died of a weak heart. I knew that and so did Percy. Why was he lying to Julian? I saw Percy's glance indicating that I was to keep silent.

Julian's hands were like claws tearing away at my flesh, the lion devouring his prey, alive.

"Why wasn't I informed sooner?"

Percy glanced at him, then again at me. I knew he was trying to tell me that Julian had known and had obviously forgotten. "No one wished to wake you and then . . . well, everything was done that could be done."

"I see," he said, stiffly. Recalling that he still held me, he dropped his hands.

I felt the blood rush to my injured shoulders and to my face. I was positive from his reaction that despite what Percy said, Julian had not known. Perhaps it was an instinct but I suddenly did not think him guilty of his aunt's death. I did think him still responsible for the attack on me, however. How I wished I could have told him about his aunt in a more careful fashion.

"Julian?" I stepped into the light, hesitatingly. Despite my fear, I wanted to put my arms about him, to comfort him as I would have wanted comforting myself. But he continued to glare at me and I backed down.

Silently, I stood there as he walked back down the hall. I said nothing to Percy until I heard Julian slam the door to our room.

"I am going to my own room."

"What?" Percy's eyes widened. "With him?" Percy's whole face was a study then. I would have laughed if I were not so upset.

I shook my head. Sleep was dragging my lids closed again. "No, I mean the dressing room."

"To pack?" He smiled and suddenly I hated him. He had no considerate feelings at all toward his cousin. How could I ever have the slightest affection for him?

"No, I shall pack in the morning."

He nodded. "Good night then, Angel."

Thank goodness he did not see me cringe. "Yes, Percy. Good night."

Chapter Eighteen

Despite what had happened, the fact that all the evidence I had showed against him, I was now sure that if Julian had had any hand in the matters, it was accidental — or perhaps part of a sickness. The look on his face had shown me plainly that he had no part in his aunt's death — bother the letter. She had to have meant something else. Now I began to wonder if Jennifer, too, had not met with some accident, perhaps after she had gotten to London. Perhaps, she had changed her mind and was coming back here. Perhaps she had gotten too close to the rocks. All these possibilities now came to my mind.

I lay down on the couch and was drawn into a whirlpool of recriminations. Alas, I was sure that it was too late for me to mend things. If Julian was disgusted with me now, wrongly so, he would be even more disgusted when he learned that I was Jennifer's sister, Victoria. The same Victoria whom he had spoken so poorly of that day. I was at wit's end trying to keep up the pretense. There were times when I even forgot to respond to my name "Tamara." And for once, even in anger, I wanted to hear Julian call me by my rightful name.

I still did not know who had read the diary or who had left the note but as long as I left the island safely, I would not care.

My hands went to my stomach. I wondered if Julian thought me barren as he had thought Jennifer. Whatever, my marriage was a hoax. I knew that my love could never be returned so it was silly to subject myself to the torment.

It was past eight when I woke. Laura brought me my tea. I wondered if Percy had told her of the night's events. I wondered too just how she would keep Julian occupied. Yes, I was jealous but I could do nothing about it now. Soon I would be off this miserable island and be on my own.

"Shall I bring you up your breakfast?" She picked up the pot and poured me some tea. It seemed that she was unusually cheerful this morning — perhaps because she was the only one in the house who had slept the whole night.

I inhaled the delicious milky steam. Somehow, it revived my spirits. "No. I will be down shortly."

"Well then," she smiled and laid out Tamara's blue linen morning dress. It would be perfect for travel. Did she know? I dared not ask for fear that if she did not, she would betray me to Julian. Percy would acquaint her with the matter, in due course, when he thought it was time.

Sadly, my thoughts turned again to Julian. After last night, one would think that he did want me to leave. Would he petition the House of Lords for another divorce and pick a new bride? Would he start afresh with another unsuspecting girl? The idea of him in another's arms gave me a sadder feeling than even the grief I had experienced at Tamara's death.

"Shall I send up someone to help with your dressing?"

"There's no need. I can do it myself."

She shrugged and turned to the door. Then, as an afterthought, she added, "Oh, Julian has just told me that he is going to St. Mary's today. He asks if you would like to accompany him?"

I stared at her. I could not believe what I had heard. He wanted me to go with him? Did he suspect my plans? Did he perhaps forget what had passed between us last night? I hoped that my trembling hand did not betray my nervousness too much.

"No . . . I do not think so. I want to visit Mrs. O'Dea. I hear that she is ill again." That much, at least, was true. It did not matter if she believed me or not — as long as Julian did.

"Well, I will see you downstairs," she responded, smiling.

I nodded as a shiver went through me. Not even the burning tea had warmed me. I placed the cup on the stand.

I was correct in leaving, I told myself. Maybe Julian was telling me by his offer to go to St. Mary's that he did not mind my going, that he would help me. It almost made me angry.

No, going with him was something that I could not do. Saying goodbye to Julian, holding his hand that one last time, knowing that I would never see him again, would be too much to bear. Besides, he might even at this late date guess my situation and force me to remain.

It was far better that Percy row me across after Julian had gone. From St. Mary's I would hire a boat with my few funds. I had just enough to get me to London and from there . . well, I hoped again that I would find the money that I had sent to Tamara.

With a sad heart, I dressed in the simple costume and plaited my hair. It was not a style which was flattering but I was in no mood to play and tease my curls as I usually did.

Downstairs, the house was silent. I knew from the mirror that my eyes were red-rimmed and puffy from crying and lack of sleep but it could not be helped.

Julian sat at the head of the table and nodded curtly as I entered. He seemed the same cold man I had first known. I was still confused by his motives for asking me to accompany him. If he knew something, why did he not speak?

Unable to eat much, I took a piece of toast and nibbled the edge while the maid poured me more tea. Laura ate quickly and excused herself. I, then, found myself alone with him. Something that I had wanted to avoid. I wished Percy would come down.

"You don't wish an outing to St. Mary's, my dear?" Julian raised his eyebrows. "I would have thought you would have loved it. Perhaps you have more letters to post . . or perhaps you are waiting for my cousin to accompany you."

"I . . ." I sucked in my lower lip and tried to keep calm. I longed to tell him in that same mocking tone that I was going not only to St. Mary's but out of his life as well but I kept my silence. For once I would play the passive wife. "Surely, after your ordeal, you're not well enough to row there and resume your affairs."

The grim half smile he gave me, shocked me and tore further the hole at my heart. His eyes, I saw now, had laugh lines like Percy's. In his own way he was very handsome. My heart thudded, beating against my ribs like a trapped bird. I wished I could tell him now but I had already decided that I would write the note to him and explain it all.

His voice brought me back to the present. "It is a special trip that I am making today and yes, I am quite well. Besides, Mr. O'Dea will be rowing me over. Though it is good of you to concern yourself about me, as you did the other day." He looked up at me and his eyes met mine.

My face turned the same crimson as the velvet covering of the chairs. I wanted to look away but I could not. It seemed that he knew I had been in the room with him the majority of the time. Mrs.

Stewart came into the room then to replace the tea pot. His smile at her told me that she had been the one to betray me. Thank goodness she did not know of today's plans for she would surely have betrayed those, too.

"Thank you for your offer, Julian, but I . . . wish to stay on the island today."

Quickly, I glanced up. His eyes were on me again. He shrugged. "If you wish . . . " I could see that he really did not believe me. I could not give him the excuse I had given Laura because that was false. Instead I pleaded exhaustion. Considering how I felt, that was not a hard task.

"Yes, that is what I wish," I said, pouring more tea and taking some eggs from the huge platter. "I shall stay in today. I slept rather poorly last night."

"Perhaps you wish to return to our room now that I am again well."

I swallowed the pain in my throat. "Perhaps."

Had my mind not been so set, he would have probably swayed me but like Pharoah, I had hardened my heart.

Now, he pushed away his plate and came across the room towards me. I remained motionless—not knowing what to expect and too afraid to run.

I must have cringed for he said, "I shan't hurt you, my dear. I am sorry if I did so last night."

So, he remembered last night.

I was about to say something when he bent and kissed my brow. "Is there anything you need from the mainland?"

I shook my head. All I needed right now was for him to hold me and touch me, but I could not ask that, especially not since I was leaving.

"Well, if there is anything that you want, I will be leaving at quarter past the hour."

I nodded but did not watch him as he left the room. A sadness enveloped me. I realized that this was the last I would see of him and allowed myself a moment of sorrow.

The quiet was interrupted by Percy's jovial banter. *"Are you well this morning, Tamara?"* he fairly shouted.

I glared at him. Did he wish to bring Julian back in here?

As I stared at him I wondered how long it would be before Percy returned the 25 pounds that he had borrowed from me. Now that I was on my own again, every penny would count.

He sat down next to me. "Do not worry. I shall take good care of you. Can you be ready for the boat at half past nine?"

"But Julian is not leaving until quarter past. What if we run into him? Can't we do it a little later?"

"Well . . . " he shrugged and helped himself to a generous steak. "I guess we can but not too much later. Don't want to miss the tides, you know."

"Quarter to eleven? I still need to pack . . . and I wish to write a goodbye note to Julian."

Percy frowned. "You needn't do that."

"I do." I remained firm.

"Very well," he frowned again, but not a moment past quarter of. Would not do for Julian to be rowing back just as we are leaving."

I nodded. No. That would not do.

Back in my own bedroom, I looked at the clothes in the trunk. Tamara's portmanteau would be difficult to take with me. Besides, I did have the clothes I had left with her back in London. Remembering that my friend was dead brought more sadness to my heart. Still, I would only take one change of clothes—enough for the train trip and a day in London.

On second thought I included the emerald necklace. Not for my sake, mind you, but the baby's. I had such mixed feelings about this child. I wanted Julian's child and some remembrance of him but I could not fathom how I was going to manage. Well, I supposed I would survive as I had survived it all from the time of Papa's death.

Tears came to my eyes. I knew that I could not leave without some note of goodbye to Julian. That was going to be the hardest thing.

Sitting down at the desk, I took out a quill but the words which I had planned to write suddenly seemed to have fled. Then there was no ink, and finally no proper paper.

When I was ready to write I could not think. "Julian, dearest . . . " I began. No, that was not good. I scratched out the dearest. "Julian," I re-wrote on a fresh page, "Despite your desire to ful-fill your father's will, I wonder if you truly wish me here. After all that has happened, I now must tell you . . . " I paused and wondered. Should I tell him who I was or only say that I was leaving?

There was a knock at the door. Only then did I realize that it was nearly quarter of.

"I am coming, Percy."

I folded the paper and moved toward the door.

Percy looked quite upset standing there. It was almost as if he carried bad news.

"What's wrong? Has something happened to the boat?"

He shook his head. "No there is nothing wrong with the boat, my love, but . . ." he paused. "We must leave now."

I glanced back toward the desk. "I'm not finished yet."

"I do not care." He pulled at my hand. "We must leave, *now*."

The insistence in his voice and manner gave me a moment's worry. I glanced again at the note and decided that I had best write it once I was safely in London. "Very well, Percy." I picked up my reticule and my cape as he smiled sadly.

"Well, come then." He grabbed my hand. "We've no time to waste."

"Is it the tides? Is Julian coming back?"

He did not answer but began pulling me along the stairs so that my feet barely touched the steps.

I don't think the walk to the eastern shore had ever been accomplished as quickly as we did it then.

Percy reached the quay before I did and just stood there staring out to sea.

"Percy, where is the boat?" I asked him, seeing the empty sea.

He turned to me. His face sad like a forlorn puppy. "I . . . "

"Percy," my worry was rising now," where is the boat?"

"Yes, Percy," Laura said coming up from behind us. "Where is the boat?" She mocked him. "Oh, Percy, Percy, my love," she pointed her gun at us both, "you sadly disappoint me. Did you really think I would let you both leave like this. Percy, don't you realize you are my ticket to success. Don't you see how I have planned and worked for you?"

I stared at Laura and then at Percy. "What is she talking about?"

"What am I talking about?" Laura mocked again. "You should know, Victoria Damien . . . or perhaps you would still prefer being known as Tamara Nilston Hawley. Do you think you fooled any of us? Do you think you fooled Julian? He was the one who told me what to do."

"No." I shook my head. "No, I don't believe it." My heart pounded. "Julian did not . . . does not want me killed."

"No? What makes you think not? He had your sister killed."

"No," I said weakly, staring at the gun she held, staring at her wild eyes.

"Yes," she smiled and waved the firearm to indicate I was to walk. "We are going to the western rocks not the eastern ones Percy. I am surprised you made such a mistake, Percy," she said, looking at me while pointing the gun at us both. "After all, Percy, you knew that this was

Julian's plan."

"No," he replied, hoarsely, "I did not know, Laura. I did know that it was yours."

She smiled. "Walk."

I took a deep breath and felt my heart pounding, felt her eyes on me as I bravely turned. I did not think she would shoot me now for too many town people would be sure to hear. I knew I could scream but that would not help either Percy or myself.

"I am sorry, my love," Percy said, walking beside me. "I did not think Laura would mind. All I knew was that she wanted you off the island."

I glanced at him as everything now came together. It was the will. It was the will, Percy and Laura all along.

"You had no intention of marrying me, did you Percy?" Not that I cared but I needed to confirm it.

Like a sad puppy, he shook his head. "Laura and I have been secretly wed for nearly a month now. We did so when we were in London."

Again, my mouth opened in surprise. "Those bills then, they were Laura's—under my sister's name?"

He nodded. "Laura had Mr. O'Dea row her across wearing your sister's cloak. I was waiting for her already and we fled to London."

We were nearly at the rocks now.

"How did you know who I was?"

"We didn't," Laura responded, "not until recently. It was your friend, Thomas."

I blanched.

"Do you recall when we rowed over?" Percy said, "I never mailed your letter. I gave you an empty envelope which you did not even notice. In fact, I have a half penny for you with the post mistress's note." He reached into his pocket to get it when Laura yelled at him.

"Don't be a fool, Percy. Victoria doesn't need the money. You were brilliant that day, Percy. Don't foul it up now?"

We had passed the point where my seal was. I paused a moment. "Was it you then Percy who killed the seal?"

He shook his head. "Laura did it. She wanted a new coat for when we go to London, again."

"I see." Once again the hurt took hold. "And Tamara?"

"We could not take the chance of her coming to you here, of exposing you, and telling Julian the truth and of . . . having Julian find out our part in Jennifer's death."

"Where . . . where did you kill my sister? Was it by the pond?"

He stared at me, startled. "How did you know?"

I shrugged. "You know you won't get away with this. My friend Thomas will come searching for me."

"No, he won't," Laura laughed. "Percy met him in London a few days ago. Told him that you had left just like your sister." She smiled evilly. "Because you will."

I cursed under my breath. Thomas always had been gullible.

I was at the end of the road now. "Julian knows nothing at all of this, does he? He doesn't know about the baby, either?"

Laura only smiled but Percy managed to shake his head.

"That was your decision, Victoria, not mine, but it fit in nicely with our plans. You will jump off the end of the rocks there. The tide and currents are just right. They will grab you and sink you, and your body will never be found again — just like your sister's."

I glanced at Percy again, pleading. I did not want to die. "How could you murder your own grandmother?"

"I couldn't help it," he pleaded for my forgiveness with tears in his eyes. "Laura was going to do something awful if I did not do as she wished."

I stared coolly at him. "What could be more awful than murder?"

He shrugged. "Debtor's prison."

"Poor, poor Julian." Laura sympathized, tisking. "He will think both wives have run away from him and he does not know why."

"Percy, please, do not do this. I will give you the 1,000 pounds I have and you will not go to jail. I will help you get cleared."

"Don't listen to her, Percy. She's lying. She doesn't have the money. I searched her things."

"I have it in London."

I stared at Percy but Laura's power was more than mine. I was a few feet from the edge now and I feared that he was going to push me. He came forward.

"No, I only want to kiss you one last time. You are so good, and so brave. I wish I could be like you sometimes. No matter what Laura tried to do, she could not frighten you off. I was sure that she would succeed. I did not want it to come to this. I . . . " He took me into his arms. I closed my eyes, thinking of Julian, praying for Julian, wishing that I had told Julian this morning how much I loved him. He was innocent of all my accusations and only my stubbornness had caused this misery. If only I had listened to my heart I should have known the truth.

"Come, my love," Percy coaxed. "We are almost at the edge and . . . " I saw that his blue eyes were wet with tears. Like a naughty little boy, he was begging forgiveness as Laura held the gun on us. I could not believe this was actually happening to me. I grabbed a rock for support. If only I had confessed to Julian this would all be a bad dream. I would have withstood his anger but at least he would have saved me.

"Go on, Tamara or Victoria, whatever you wish to be called. Go on. Now!"

Laura had the gun directly on me. I knew she was going to fire in a moment and I knew, too, that I could not die without a struggle. Throwing the stone which had come loose, I hit her. The gun fired as she fell backward but the noise sent more rocks sliding down.

Grabbing another stone, I hung on for a moment as I cried out, "Help me! Help me!" I found my footing and tried to climb back onto the solid ground but Laura, who had already regained her stance, now pointed the gun at me. No longer worried about anything, I rushed her and struggled with her. Her gun was now useless. A flash of metal came through the air. I deflected it, feeling the cut on my hand as I kicked and bit for all I was worth.

Suddenly the welcome sound of Julian's voice came to me. "Tamara! Tamara where are you?"

I could not answer for Laura's hand was on my mouth. I bit her palm. She released me. "Julian!" I shouted. "Julian!"

There was a tremendous force at my back and with a cry of terror, I found myself flying over the edge of the world into the icy waters. As the shock of the water hit me, I screamed again and found myself sinking into the depths. Light headed and dizzy, I fought my way to the surface. I could not have imagined a more difficult task, for the current about me was swifter than I remembered, swifter even than the storm waters of the previous week.

The number of times I surfaced for air and then again sank below the waves were too numerous to count. Finally, I managed to swim back and grab hold of one of the rocks, but I knew that my grip was weak and would not hold. It seemed as if I had been in the water for ages, and yet as my head broke the surface this once more, I saw Julian's form towering above the path.

Shouting, my cry mingled with that of Laura's as she broke away from her captors and ran the only way she could — toward me and the water. I do not know if she saw me, but she jumped over the side only inches from my head. The fright nearly made me lose my hold. Her dress ballooned about her even as she descended into the depths.

My first thoughts were to release myself and save her but that would have meant sure death for me. I could not have grabbed hold of the rock a second time. Already, in the rising water, my grasp was slipping. I turned and tried to find her but I could not see below me for the froth. Then, mercifully, I felt Julian's strong arms lifting me from the water.

Dripping wet, I clung to him and let the tears fall freely as I babbled about the murder, about Jennifer, about everything that came to my mind. He held me, comforting me as I had hoped he would. The others were at the edge, too, now. I presumed they were trying to find Laura. Percy sat against a rock with a dazed expression on his face.

Everyone, I believe, was startled when Laura's call for help came over the waves several hundred yards out. Percy rose like a zombie and cried out. "I love you, Laura!" He, too, ran to the edge of the rocks and jumped in before anyone bothered to stop him.

I continued to cling to Julian and then I looked up into his deep, dark eyes. I was trembling now with well deserved fear but the whole story would have to be told.

"Julian?" My voice was small.

"Be quiet for once, *Victoria*. Percival and Laura deserve their fates. If they survive, well so be it." With his masterful movements, he turned me away from the raging sea and directed my shivering steps toward the house. It was only as we reached the safety of firm land that I saw Thomas!

I blanched as he gave me a weak smile.

"Hello, Victoria."

More tears came to my eyes as memories flooded forth. Once more, I sobbed into Julian's strong shoulders thinking of Jennifer, and of myself. I feared that this would be the last time that he would hold me.

From then on I remembered nothing until I was put down upon the bed which I had once shared as Lady Tamara Hawley.

I lay listless in the bed for a good half hour trying to recall the events of the day and of the past month since I had come to Penporth island.

With hot shame I flushed for I saw now how miserably I had misjudged Julian and how well I had been fooled by Percy and Laura. How wrong both Jennifer and I had been. I wondered if my sister had known before her death just what she had come to mean to Julian. I doubt it for her last indication was that she still feared him. Even I feared him now and I no longer had Percy here to poison my mind. I had seen enough of Julian's temper to know that I had to leave, to know that he would never forgive my deceit.

My heart ached. If only I had understood before. So many little things about Percy should have warned me. But I had been too stubborn to alter my first assumption.

The sorrow was like a sword thrust into my throat. I could not swallow. I could only cry and think of the ache, the deaths and of Julian. Slowly, painfully, I sat up and left the bed. Other than a few bruises, I was remarkably unscarred — physically by the ordeal I had suffered. I could not help but think of Percy and Laura. I wondered if they survived.

Well, I would survive. I would be sad but I would survive.

Carefully, I dressed in my mint green travelling gown. It was, despite Tamara's many clothes, my favorite, and it was fitting that I should wear it now since I had worn it over.

With heavy limbs and great effort, I buttoned my boots. No one I knew would row me across — not against his orders. I would have to get a boat, myself, or die trying. Anything was preferable to Julian's justifiable wrath.

My steps were leaden as I walked toward the door. The letters from my sister were in my hands and I stuffed them into my pocket. I would find the closest boat and borrow it.

The hall was empty and quiet. I closed the door behind me feeling a hush. Only after I had started down the corridor did I hear Julian's footsteps. There was no mistaking those firm steps. Without thinking, I opened the first door and stepped into a linen closet.

I hated the darkness, the close smell, and the fear as my heart beat warned me of his approach. I had no choice but to wait. His steps passed. I held my breath until I heard a door open down the hall. It was now . . . now that I had to make my escape.

Taking advantage of the moment, I opened the closet door cautiously. The corridor was empty and I picked up my skirts and sped down the stairs and out the door to the path. The sun was fading, and it was growing chilly. Only then did I realize I had forgotten my cape. I would need one, especially in London but I was reluctant to return.

It seemed that I knew the route by heart now. I detoured briefly toward Jennifer's pond. I had to say one last goodbye to her.

It was all stillness when I reached the pond, and the water was calm. The leaves swayed only gently, and the twilight deepened the shadows around me. I stood, for a moment, on the spot where I had cuddled Julian's unconscious form, where I had finally admitted my love for him. As a bird gave a chirp, tears started in my eyes. The letters were now in my hands. I threw them into the water and watched the ink fade.

The sun was now a rosy pink with deep purple streaks — like claw marks. There was no movement on the land or the sea. No human form desecrated my final thoughts on this rocky road as I ran down toward the peninsula where earlier this morning I had so narrowly escaped death.

There was white foam on the water but the tide was receding. It look cold and uninviting. But I felt that I had to go down there and say goodbye, too, considering all the moments I had spent there.

I stood very near the edge now. Hesitantly, I stepped forward meaning only to peer down.

There was a rush of movement from the rocks behind me and at that instant a hand gripped my wrist. I tumbled backwards with a cry. Only then did I see who it was.

"Foolish girl! Do you think I would let you kill yourself? I wondered how long it would take you to get here. As soon as I found the room empty, I knew you would come."

I tried to deny that I had considered suicide but it had been on my mind because without his love I really did not want to live. His fingers still had me in their vise hold. "Now perhaps you will explain some things — back at the house." He was above me and I looked up helplessly into his eyes.

Choking back my tears, I shook my head. "I am sure you know everything there is to know," I turned my head away and felt the rock against my cheek. Tears streamed down my face.

He let me go and I was free to sit up.

"I am sorry if I have hurt you," he said and sat down next to me, not touching me. "Yes, Victoria, I know a lot but I am sure I do not know everything. Your friend, Thomas told me what he could but . . . " he stopped and I gave him a swift look. I saw sadness in his eyes. I turned away again.

"I even know about your accusations against me . . . but I knew about those before Thomas had even come. I have known who you were for some time now. Why do you think it was that I was so distant for so many days?"

I stared at him, my mouth dropped. "But how?"

His eyes were on mine for a moment. "I suspected that you were not the meek Tamara on the day that you arrived. Her aunt had given me a detailed description of her and somehow you did not fit my pictures. I wanted to give you a chance to confess and to get out before the marriage but I needed an heir desperately and did not want to wait to find the real Tamara or another.

"Besides, I rather liked your spirit. It was only when you left your diary in the drawer not knowing, I am sure, that I also had a key, that I learned of your story. It was most interesting.

So that had been him.

"But why did you not confront me then?"

He picked up a handful of pebbles and threw them into the water. "Because," his face colored slightly, "I did not want you to leave. Confound it, I knew I was innocent and I was beginning to like having you about." He paused and took my hand. "I am sorry about your sister, Victoria. Truly. I am. I had asked Percy to write to Jennifer's family, to see if she got home safely and I assumed that he had, but obviously not. When I received those dress bills, which I now understand were Laura's, I hated her very being and wanted nothing to do with her or her family.

"I suspected that Percy might be involved with her but when she left and he did not, I could not place any blame on him. Even so, I was sensitive to every time he touched you."

"So was I." My voice was tight. "He had me convinced that you would kill me, too. Even so, I could not bear Percy's touch, not after you." I looked up at him.

He leaned over and kissed me.

"Oh, Julian," I cried as my hands went about his thick neck. "Julian," my fingers traced his scar.

"Am I so hideously ugly? Could you possibly come to love me?"

I kissed him again. "I do not find you ugly. I find . . that I love you." There, I had said it. "I know that . . you must hate me for all that has happened . . . " I broke into sobs and he held me, rocking me with more tenderness than I had ever before felt from him.

His lips grazed my brow and then my face. Despite my sorrow, my longing for him returned. When his lips touched mine, I showed him the passion I felt.

Moments later, breathless, I lay my head against his chest. Silently, I listened to the beat of his heart . . . and to the lap of the waves. "You were furious, though, when you found out. You must have been."

"I was." His hands were on my hair, undoing the braids, stroking it. I was in a rage that Jennifer had come back, that she had sent you to haunt me. I felt I had not been good enough to her. Then, I realized that I never loved her. Not as I loved you, my Victoria." His kiss again stirred me.

"What will happen now?"

He held me apart and looked into my eyes. "What do you want to happen?"

I took a deep breath. "I want . . . to stay with you but . . . but the marriage . . . our marriage . . . "

"Can be made perfectly legal as soon as I write to the Archbishop. He can alter the certificate . . . if we want that done. If you don't object."

"I hope he will do that before your son is born."

Julian looked at me with a shock on his face. I knew that he had not suspected that. "Oh my darling. My sweet sea nymph."

We kissed again—a long and lovely kiss. When I looked again toward the sea, there were two trawlers on the horizon. Travelling side by side on the ocean, they made me think of us. I slipped my hand into his and together we stood watching the ocean surging about us, watching the distant boats in the dying sun.

We, too, would be together for eternity.